Praise for the first Morris Brick thriller
Deranged
by Jacob Stone

"*Deranged* is a dark and different serial killer novel that will haunt the reader long after the book is closed and back on the shelf. Author Jacob Stone transfixes us with dread, and something more. He has the rare capacity to startle. Read if you dare."
—John Lutz

"*Deranged* is a fascinating and exciting blend of misdirection, topsy-turvy, and violence."
—Reed Farrel Coleman

"Gutsy and written with such casual grace, as if the author were sitting across the bar from me, telling me the story, *Deranged* just might be one of the most compelling, thrilling and truth be told, at times look-away-from-the-page-frightening serial killer novels I've read in a long, long time."
—Vincent Zandri

"Los Angeles has seldom seen such grisly fun. It's James Ellroy meets Alfred Hitchcock in a bloody, yet bizarrely humorous romp on the psychotic side of the street."
—Paul Levine

Also by Jacob Stone

Deranged

Crazed

A Morris Brick Thriller

Jacob Stone

LYRICAL UNDERGROUND
Kensington Publishing Corp.
www.kensingtonbooks.com

LYRICAL UNDERGROUND BOOKS are published by

Kensington Publishing Corp.
119 West 40th Street
New York, NY 10018

All Kensington titles, imprints, and distributed lines are available at special quantity discounts for bulk purchases for sales promotion, premiums, fundraising, educational, or institutional use.

Special book excerpts or customized printings can also be created to fit specific needs. For details, write or phone the office of the Kensington Sales Manager: Kensington Publishing Corp., 119 West 40th Street, New York, NY 10018. Attn. Sales Department. Phone: 1-800-221-2647.

Lyrical Underground and Lyrical Underground logo Reg. US Pat. & TM Off.

First Electronic Edition: September 2017
eISBN-13: 978-1-5161-0181-8
eISBN-10: 1-5161-0181-2

First Print Edition: September 2017
ISBN-13: 978-1-5161-0184-9
ISBN-10: 1-5161-0184-7

Printed in the United States of America

Acknowledgments

I would first of all like to thank my editor, Michaela Hamilton, as this book, and the entire Morris Brick thriller series, wouldn't exist without her.

In advance I'd like to thank the Kensington team who'll be supporting this book and doing their magic to make it shine: Lauren Jernigan, Michelle Forde, and Alexandra Nicolajsen.

A big thanks also to my college buddy, Alan Luedeking, who, as with all my books, muddled through my initial draft and helped smooth out the language. Also my longtime friend (since second grade) Jeff Michaels for also providing feedback.

I'd also like to give a special acknowledgement to Bill Crider, to whom I am dedicating *Crazed*. For those unfamiliar with Bill's writing, Bill has written several excellent mystery series and is also a top-notch Western writer (Ed Gorman and I had the honor of publishing one of Bill's stories in our Western noir anthology, *On Dangerous Ground*), and even occasionally writes horror. When I was first starting off, Bill was kind enough to read and blurb my first book, *Fast Lane*, and has reviewed on his blog all my books since. I am far from the only author Bill has mentored and helped over the years—there's a long parade of writers like myself. There are few writers out there with Bill's generosity of spirit.

As always, I'd like to thank Judy, my wife and best friend, for her encouragement and support, and for also helping to make my manuscript more readable.

For Bill Crider

Chapter 1

Seattle, the present

G riffin Bolling broke out laughing, partly from outrage, but mostly from the lunacy of what he was reading.

"What's so funny?"

Griffin looked up to see that the soft, feminine voice asking this question came from the slight redhead who had taken his latte order fifteen minutes earlier. At the time she had blushed a nice pink as she flirted with him, making sure he knew she was interested. In her petite, tiny way, she was cute, and with the way her hair was pulled back into a ponytail, she looked like a fresh-faced teenager even though she had to be in her early twenties. She must've left the cash register to bus tables so she could continue flirting with him. Now she stood off to his right with this funny, lopsided smile, hopeful that he would show the same interest in her that she obviously had in him.

"The latest insanity concerning Sheila Proops," Griffin said.

She stared at him blankly, not making a connection with that name. He smiled inwardly at her reaction. That was the thing with these Seattle slackers and hipsters. They were so insular. If it didn't have anything to do with their local scene, they had little interest.

"I'm reading about how they're not going to prosecute her for any of the Skull Cracker killings."

Her eyes scrunched up as she gave him more of a confused look. "That happened in Los Angeles?" she asked.

"And in New York five years before."

"But I thought they caught the psycho who did those murders?"

Griffin could've explained that the guy they arrested was Sheila Proops's husband, and while they had him dead to rights for the Los

Angeles killings, anyone who'd been following the story carefully knew that Sheila had to be the one who killed the twelve people in New York. The problem the authorities had was the dumb slob husband took the blame for all the killings, and that they couldn't find enough evidence to charge Sheila. So she was going to skate on twelve murders that anyone with half a brain knew she had done. But Griffin didn't bother saying any of that to the girl. Instead, he smiled wickedly at her and told her that he thought she was cute as hell. "What time do you get off work?" he asked.

That caused her to blush even deeper than before, leaving her cheeks almost the same red as her hair. "Three o'clock." It was only 9:30 and a hint of impatience and disappointment showed in her eyes. She moved closer so she could tell him slyly, "But if I put on a good enough act that I'm coming down with something, maybe I'll be able to cut out earlier."

She winked at him as she faked a faint cough.

Griffin held out his hand to her. "Trent," he said. He'd been using the name Trent Regan since coming to Seattle nine months earlier.

"Zoe," the redhead said. Her small, slender right hand disappeared quickly into Griffin's. He couldn't help noticing how warm her flesh felt. A thought struck him. A thought so deep and profound that it startled him and had him almost laughing out loud.

"Is something wrong?" Zoe asked, concerned.

Griffin recovered quickly and flashed her a wolfish grin. "The feel of your skin took my breath away," he said.

That caused her to blush even deeper, her cheeks now blood red.

The manager of the coffeehouse, a heavyset thirtysomething dude with a buzz cut, neck tattoos, and a dozen face piercings, must've had the hots for this redhead given the way his voice sounded as he called out from behind the counter that he needed her to take over at the cash register. Zoe rolled her eyes to show her annoyance at the way her boss had intruded on their moment. Griffin shrugged in a *what-are-you-gonna-do* kind of gesture, and he watched as she reluctantly left him. Then he settled back in his chair and took a sip of his latte and thought more about the delicious idea he'd had. That he was going to kill Sheila Proops.

Ever since arriving in Seattle, he'd been drifting aimlessly, wallowing in a low-grade depression, his mood more often than not matching the weather of this dreary city. He worked day jobs here and there, and supplemented his income by ripping off the women he slept with, almost always tourists. There was no shortage of women coming to Seattle on vacation or for business who'd spot him in a coffeehouse, bar, or nightclub, and let him know that they wanted to hook up with him for the night. But he'd never really gotten much satisfaction from the sex part of it, and had badly fallen into a rut since coming here, not killing a single person. There just no longer seemed any point to it. But as he thought about snuffing out Sheila Proops's life, he felt inspired. Truly, the desire that had been absent for so many months once again burning deep inside him. He could feel his true self that had been missing for almost a year coming to the fore. The phoenix reborn.

As Griffin imagined all the things he was going to do to Sheila Proops, he found himself growing rock-hard between his legs. He was going to take his time with her, that he knew for certain. And she was going to deserve every single torment that he inflicted on her. While he was able to kill thirty-nine people in the shadows without anyone suspecting it (well, really thirty-eight, since he wasn't even a teenager when he killed his first victim, and there were certainly some who suspected him for that one—but he was so young at the time, and he more than learned his lesson since then!), this twisted broad only murdered twelve people, but she had to do so in a way that screamed out for attention! Why? For the notoriety? Griffin's jaw clenched and his lips hardened to thin, bloodless lines as he thought about it. It was infuriating, it really was. Yeah, she deserved everything that he was going to do to her.

He was so caught up in his thoughts that he only half noticed the blond woman who placed a business card on his table before sashaying past him on her way out of the coffeehouse. He looked up to see the door closing behind her. A few seconds later he caught a glimpse of her through the front window. She turned briefly to look his way and give him an impish smile, and then she was gone. He remembered her from when he had first come into the place. Professionally attired in a gray skirt that fell past her knees, a white blouse, and high heels. She'd been sitting alone at a table diagonally across from him. While he hadn't taken the time to study her, he had the impression that she was roughly his age (thirty-two), very attractive, and had long, slender legs. She had been so tunnel-focused on her laptop that he didn't think she had noticed him.

He picked up her business card and read what she had scribbled on the back of it: *My meeting lets up at 1. You don't have to wait until three—Claire*

He smiled as he sniffed the card and picked up the lilac scent of her perfume. After so many months lost in the wilderness, he deserved a treat: A going-away present. But which was it going to be? The willowy blonde with the long, slender legs or the petite, fresh-faced redhead? Decisions, decisions. He would have to flip a coin.

Chapter 2

Los Angeles, the present

Parker, an all-white bull terrier with the exception of a small black smudge on his left ear and a slightly larger smudge on his tail, lay on his side on the kitchen floor by Morris Brick's feet, one eye open, his ears perked up. Morris noted, between bites of oatmeal, that the dog did not look happy. He couldn't blame him. Three weeks ago Morris had switched to eating a healthier breakfast, which meant no bacon, sausage, or scrambled eggs to mooch. Morris used the big toe on his right foot to rub the dog's chest. Parker consented to halfheartedly thumping his tail once.

"You're going to hold a grudge, huh?" Morris said.

Parker's open eye shifted to peek at him, but otherwise no reaction. All at once he lifted his bullet-shaped head and his tail began thumping more enthusiastically.

"*Buongiorno,*" Natalie announced cheerfully as she entered the kitchen. Parker's tail thumped against the floor more rapidly and he let out one of his pig-like grunts. Natalie gave Morris a quick kiss, then dropped to a knee so she could hug the dog around his thick neck.

"You'd never guess by the way he's acting now, but he's been sulking ever since we got back from his walk. B-a-c-o-n withdrawals."

"You gave him a can of his f-o-o-d?"

"Of course."

"That should be enough for him."

"You can be a cruel woman, Nat."

She smiled at that. "But just."

"No question. I've got more oatmeal warming on the stove. Would you like some? With a sliced banana and cinnamon?"

"That would be lovely."

Natalie kissed Parker on the snout and took a seat at the table while Morris got her breakfast.

"*Grazie.*" Natalie flashed him a dazzling smile. After twenty-four years of marriage she could still bring a lump to his throat and make him weak in the knees. He was a lucky man, no question about it. His wife was still the same slender, dark-haired beauty he'd fallen in love with all those years ago, while he had always been a funny-looking guy with big ears, thick, long nose, spindly legs, and a short, compact body. The type of guy who should own a bull terrier. People had to wonder how they ever ended up together, but the answer was simple: He got lucky when she somehow also fell in love with him.

Morris finished his breakfast, his spoon scraping the bowl. He wondered briefly how the oatmeal would taste with crumbled-up bacon mixed in, but he forced the thought out of his mind. He smiled thinly, thinking how Parker must be sending him psychic messages.

"I'll get coffee started," he offered as he took his bowl and spoon to the sink.

"It's nice getting a later start today," Natalie said.

Morris nodded. It was almost ten and usually they were both out of the house by seven; Natalie, so she could see clients at her private office where she worked as a therapist, and Morris so he could run Morris Brick Investigations, more commonly known as MBI. But since Natalie had her eight o'clock and nine thirty appointments cancel on her, and since operations at MBI were running smoothly and Morris didn't have anything scheduled until one, they'd decided to take it easy this morning, which was a luxury for both of them.

Natalie waited until Morris brought the coffee to the table before commenting on how in nine days they would be jetting off to Rome. While it was ostensibly a statement, it was really a probing question: Was he as excited about their upcoming vacation as she was? Morris hesitated just enough before nodding to give away that he had concerns.

"This will be our first real vacation in years," Natalie said. "Two weeks in Italy. Rome, Sorrento, Florence, Venice, and Milan. This will be a dream for us, Morris. You'll love it as much as I will. I promise."

Morris forced a smile and nodded. Nat was right, of course. Outside of a four-day trip upstate to wine country, they hadn't been on a vacation since they took Rachel to Yosemite National Park for a week when she was twelve. Nat was also being kind in not mentioning that this would make up for the honeymoon they'd never had. Back when they had married, he was a rookie on the force, busting his ass to make something of himself. A year later they had Rachel, and money became too scarce to go on any sort of extended vacation. After Morris was promoted to detective they started saving some money, but whenever they'd plan a big vacation he would get caught up in a case and they'd have to cancel their trip. In fact, they had this very same trip planned three years ago when the Hillside Cannibal case broke, and by the time Morris caught up to the twisted monster, Vincent Robusto, who murdered and ate the internal organs of his eleven victims, they were in no shape to go anywhere. Then, eighteen months ago, Morris retired from the force and started MBI, and with all the hours he was putting in to get his fledging firm off the ground, any sort of vacation seemed impossible. But now things were humming along nicely at MBI, and Natalie convinced him the place wouldn't collapse if he was gone for two weeks. That they could finally go on the trip that they'd been waiting twenty-four years to take.

"MBI will still be standing when we get back," Natalie said. "You'll be leaving it in good hands with Charlie Bogle. Now maybe if you'd picked Polk to run the place while you were gone, you'd have something to worry about!"

"I'm not really worried about MBI," Morris conceded. "More about leaving this little guy for two weeks. He's mad enough at me as it is for the current b-a-c-o-n situation."

"Parker will be fine. More than fine. Rachel will be spoiling him rotten. Like daughter, like dad."

"What are you talking about? I've been tough as nails with the little guy. I barely let him mooch anything from me these days."

"Ha! I bet you've been thinking of frying up b-a-c-o-n and crumbling it into your oatmeal just so you'd have an excuse to give him some each morning."

Morris made a harrumphing noise. "The thought never crossed my mind," he insisted. His expression softened. "And Nat, I really am looking forward to Italy."

"Good." She hesitated before adding, "And you'll be careful with the cases you take?"

"I promise. Nothing that will make me cancel this trip."

Chapter 3

Allen Perlmutter had slipped the hostess twenty dollars to seat him at the table directly in front of Lawrence Getzler's. He waited until the waitress brought over Getzler's breakfast order before jumping up and taking the seat across from Getzler. The studio executive at first looked startled by the intrusion, then his eyes narrowed and he told Perlmutter to leave immediately or he would ask his waitress to call the police.

"A two-minute pitch, that's all I'm asking for," Perlmutter said, his words tumbling fast out of his mouth.

Getzler's expression had become as hard as stone. He signaled for his waitress.

"Come on, it will be worth your while, I promise." Perlmutter tried to smile and exude confidence, but that was a tough thing to do when you were covered in flop sweat and your shirt was soaked through. Jesus, he hoped he didn't smell as bad as he imagined he did. "You've got to admit, it takes chutzpah to do what I just did."

Getzler lowered his hand. "Sixty seconds," he said. He then looked away from Perlmutter so he could time him with a ridiculously expensive-looking watch.

"Thank you. I really appreciate it," Perlmutter blabbered out. All at once his mouth felt as dry as if he'd swallowed a handful of sawdust. Even though every second was precious, he reached back for the glass of water that he had left on his table, but a waitress had already cleared it away. Damn it! He eyed Getzler's water, but he knew it would be a fatal mistake if he asked if he could take a sip of it.

"Forty-five seconds," Getzler said.

"A *Planet of the Apes* reboot, but instead of apes, androids," Perlmutter croaked out, his voice now barely a rasp. From the way the film executive's eyes glazed, Perlmutter knew that idea wasn't going to fly. That was okay; he had treatments worked up for over a dozen ideas, all of them killers. Except now his mind was a blank. Nothing! The most important minute of his life and he couldn't think!

"A movie about being married to the Skull Cracker Killer," Perlmutter stumbled out.

That got Getzler's attention. He looked up from his watch to ask whether Perlmutter had the wife's permission for her story. "What's her name again?"

"Sheila Proops. Not yet, but I'm negotiating with her," Perlmutter lied. "I'll be wrapping things up with her soon."

From the way Getzler's eyes glazed completely there was no mistaking that the film executive thought Perlmutter was full of it, which he was. But Perlmutter had definitely seen a glint in Getzler's eyes. If he could make this deal happen, Getzler would be interested. Perlmutter was also aware enough to know that his time with Getzler was over. That it was time for him to get moving.

"Once I have her story rights under contract and a treatment written, I'll contact you again." Perlmutter winked at him. "I know where to find you."

Without saying another word, he placed one of his business cards on Getzler's table—a ritzy affair with raised gold lettering and calligraphy that he had spent big bucks on—and moved back to his table, somehow doing so without collapsing.

Perlmutter's heart raced wildly in his chest as he sat and made sense of what had just happened. This had been the biggest moment of his life, and while he might not have hit it out of the park, he definitely stroked a solid single. That glint in Getzler's eyes was real. No question about it. He wondered where he had pulled the idea from, because it wasn't one of the film treatments he'd been working on. As far as he knew, it wasn't even something he had thought about until that moment. Even the fact he had remembered that woman's name was remarkable. But the subconscious was a funny thing. Somehow he came up with the perfect pitch when he absolutely needed to. Kismet, pure and simple.

He bit his tongue to keep from bursting out giggling. He was that giddy. This was bigger than big. Absolutely huge. The break he'd been dreaming of for years. A wide smile broke out as he thought about how he was going to rub this into Sammy Bloom's face. Bloom had traded him Getzler's Tuesday-morning breakfast routine for the name of the fitness studio where Faye Riverstone took private Pilates classes, a piece of knowledge Perlmutter had stumbled on a week ago. Bloom, the delusional putz, had it in his head that if he could get Riverstone to read his latest script she would not only want to star in it, but she'd help him arrange for the film's financing. Fat chance! Bloom had showed Perlmutter the script, and it was a joke. Not only was it cliché-ridden, but there were no parallel narrative streams, no sudden reversals or surprises, no misdirection. Bloom was a hack who was wasting his time trying to make it in Hollywood, but he was too dumb to realize it. Of course, Bloom wouldn't have traded his information if he had known Perlmutter would have the success he did with Getzler. Yeah, Bloom wasn't going to be happy!

Perlmutter absently ran his hand through his hair, and as he felt the dampness of his hair as if he'd just come out of a sauna, he realized it would be a good idea to leave before Getzler had any more time to notice how sweaty he'd gotten. His legs felt rubbery as he got to his feet, but he forced himself to nod with all the confidence in the world as he passed Getzler, even though the film executive didn't bother to look his way. It didn't matter. He had seen the glint in Getzler's eyes. As far as he was concerned that was as good as a handshake. All he needed was to arrange a deal with Sheila Proops for her life story, and this would happen.

As he walked out of the restaurant a stony resolve hardened Perlmutter's round, doughy face. No matter what it took, he was going to make a deal with Sheila Proops.

Chapter 4

Brett Dickerson was one of the city's preeminent real-estate developers. At fifty-four, he still had the long, lean body of a marathon runner. With his square jaw, full head of carefully groomed hair (dyed chestnut brown), and tanned skin, he should've looked like a Hollywood leading man, but there was something slightly off about his features that instead gave him the look of a sitcom actor. Morris had seen him several times over the years at charity events and thought of him then as stylish, but as Dickerson now sat across from Morris, he appeared more rumpled, even in his custom-tailored suit.

"I'm here about my daughter, Mia," Dickerson said, looking miserable.

The real-estate developer had clamped his mouth shut, his jaw clenched tightly. He seemed like he needed some prodding, so Morris prodded him by asking what was wrong.

"She just got engaged," Dickerson forced out through clenched teeth.

"I take it *mazel tov* isn't in order?"

"No, I'd say not." More jaw-clenching as well as some teeth-grinding, then, "She's known this guy for only three months."

"That was fast."

Dickerson nodded. He took a deep breath and his jaw slowly unclenched. "Mia's always been impulsive," he said after a pained sigh leaked out of him. "She's only twenty-two and just graduated this May with a theater-arts degree from UCLA and, of course, thinks she knows everything."

"My Rachel is at UCLA now. Second-year law student."

"You've got a serious-minded daughter," Dickerson said.

"Bound to have happened with me being a homicide detective all those years."

"Sins of the father," Dickerson said with a tired smile. "In my case, I spoiled Mia and indulged her with whatever she wanted. There wasn't much chance she would've ended up in business or law. But even if I hadn't, she would've wanted to be an actress. Mia's always been very theatrical. And stubborn like you wouldn't believe."

Dickerson pulled out his cell phone and fiddled with it for a moment before handing it to Morris. The screen showed a photo of a very pretty girl smiling brightly, her light brown hair falling well past her thin shoulders.

"Your daughter's very pretty," Morris said.

"She is."

"What's wrong with her fiancée?"

Dickerson made a face as if he had just tasted something vile. "Where to begin? How about that I'm sure he's a psychopath. Or at the very least, a con man."

"Why do you think that?"

"A strong gut feeling from the way he tries so damn hard to ingratiate himself with me."

Morris shrugged. "It's not uncommon for a boyfriend to try to make his girlfriend's father like him. Several of Rachel's boyfriends have done the same with me, and none of them have been psychopaths."

"Yeah, I know, but there's something unnatural about the way he does it. Like he's trying way too hard, if you understand what I'm saying."

Morris understood. He had dealt with enough sociopathic personalities not to understand. "Is he an ex-con?"

"If he is, he hasn't said anything to Mia about it. But if I had to bet on it, yeah, I would think so. I've been around plenty of ex-cons in the construction game, and I get the same vibes from him."

"Any tattoos?"

Dickerson raised an eyebrow at that. "Don't all millennials get ink these days?"

"I'm thinking more about prison tats."

Dickerson thought about it and shook his head. "None that I've noticed, but I don't think I've ever seen him with his shirt off."

"We'll need to rectify that. What does your wife think about him?"

"I wouldn't know. We're divorced."

"I'm sorry."

"Don't be. The best thing that ever happened to me. Other than Mia."

"It might be worth giving your ex a call and getting her sense of the guy. Also, it wouldn't hurt to have a united front on this."

Dickerson laughed at that, some bitterness showing. "Not a chance that will happen. If Diana knew I didn't like him, she'd be grabbing a set of pom-poms and becoming his personal cheerleader. Besides, she hasn't met Kyle yet. That's what he calls himself. Kyle Lindsey. The last I heard, my ex is jetting around the French Riviera with her latest twenty-five-year-old boy toy."

"You don't think Kyle's his name?"

Dickerson gave Morris a hard, unflinching look. "I don't trust a damn thing he says."

"Okay, tell me everything else you know about him."

There wasn't much more for Dickerson to say. Lindsey claimed to be from Phoenix, Arizona, his story being that he moved to Los Angeles three months ago to start a software app business, something to help fantasy sports players. He was now living with Mia in a West Hollywood condo that Dickerson owned. What Lindsey actually did during the day, Dickerson had no clue and neither did Mia. Since she was going back to UCLA in the fall to continue her acting studies, he had pulled some strings and gotten his daughter a summer job at one of the studios. Dickerson brought up another photo on his cell phone. This one showed Lindsey dressed in a white button-down shirt, jeans, and cowboy boots with his arm around Mia's shoulder.

"You should be able to tell from that he's bad news."

Morris grunted noncommittally. The photo showed Lindsey smiling boyishly while Mia beamed the way a young woman madly in love would. Lindsey was good-looking with well-chiseled features, sandy brown hair, and an athletic build. It was impossible to tell anything about his psychological makeup from the photo.

"How old did you say he is?" Morris asked.

"He claims he's twenty-six."

"Hmm," Morris murmured, because he thought Lindsey looked older, but it could sometimes be hard to judge someone's age from a photo. "Have you tried talking to Mia about your concerns?"

Dickerson made a face. "No, certainly not. If I did, she'd run off and elope with him. I know Mia well enough to know that." He hesitated before adding, "She can't find out that I'm having him investigated."

"We'll make sure she doesn't. I'd like to have one of my investigators get up close and personal with him. I'd do it myself, but I've had too much media exposure the last few years, and I don't want him recognizing me. Or your daughter. Do you have a pool you can use?"

"Yes, of course. At my Brentwood home."

"Okay, I'd like you to throw a pool party to celebrate the newly engaged couple."

Dickerson smiled thinly at that idea. "Interesting. So you can see Lindsey without his shirt and whether he has any prison tats?"

"One of the reasons."

"Sure, I'll get an impromptu party put together. As soon as possible." Another thin smile. "I'll also be scoring brownie points with Mia for embracing their engagement."

"Either that or she'll decide she no longer wants to be with the guy."

Dickerson shook his head. "No, it's not like that. Mia's not rebelling against me. That's not why she's with him. It's only because she's too young and naïve to see through his act."

Morris wasn't so sure of that, but he didn't argue the fact. Instead he spent the next fifteen minutes wrapping things up with Dickerson, and afterwards he asked MBI's computer and hacking specialist, Adam Felger, to find out what he could about Kyle Lindsey from Phoenix, Arizona. Felger, a twenty-eight-year-old millennial who had plenty of ink of his own showing on his arms whenever he wore short sleeves, promised Morris he'd get right on it.

While Felger was a quiet and, at times, odd sort and the only introvert on the MBI team, he was good at what he did, and Morris knew if there was anything to find about Kyle Lindsey, Felger would uncover it no matter how deep he had to dig.

Chapter 5

Claire answered the door barefoot and wearing one of the hotel's plush Egyptian cotton robes, her long, slender legs on full display.

"You look out of breath," she told Griffin.

"I should be," he said as he slid past her into the room. He waited until she closed the door behind her before adding, "I jogged up the fire stairs to get here."

She seemed surprised by that. "All seventeen floors?"

"That's right."

"Why? Are the elevators broken?"

"Nope, just wanted to get the juices flowing. You know, have a warm-up for the marathon session we're going to be having."

Griffin was lying about his reason. He took the stairs because he didn't want to be caught on an elevator security camera. Possibly there'd be hotel employees who spotted him in the lobby, but their recollections would be far more vague than what a video could provide.

She smiled wickedly. "I certainly would prefer a marathon over a sprint."

"I promise I'll be using a slow hand and will be taking my time with you."

"In that case, I believe you're overdressed."

Claire loosened the sash holding her robe closed and let the robe slip to the floor, revealing that she didn't have anything on under it.

Griffin's wolfish leer was so intense that Claire began to blush. "Very nice," he remarked.

"How about taking off your own clothes?" she said in a voice not as confident as it was a moment earlier.

"In a little while." Griffin looked away from her so he could take in the room. He nodded admiringly at what he saw, especially the four-post queen-sized bed, and knelt so he could feel the richness of the burgundy carpeting. "This is quite a place. You must be a big shot where you work?"

She gave him an uneasy smile. "I do okay, but let's not talk about that now." She began to fidget self-consciously as she stood naked in front of him, and with one arm covering her smallish breasts, she reached down for her robe.

"I prefer that you stay naked," Griffin said, his wolfish leer intensifying. "It will make things more exciting. I promise."

She hesitated for a moment, and then straightened up, her eyes challenging and defiant. "So what next?" she asked.

"I'm going to call room service and order us food so that we have some nourishment on hand after what's going to be a very exhaustive session. While we're waiting for room service, you're going to sit naked on my lap and whisper in my ear every single naughty thing you want me to do to you, and after the food arrives we'll begin."

A transformation occurred as her earlier hunger once more showed in her eyes and her lips twisted up slightly to show a mischievous smile. She understood this was all fun and games, and that the perceived dangerousness she had sensed minutes earlier was only her overactive imagination at play. The two of them perused the room-service menu together, and she ordered a sirloin steak rare for Griffin and a crabmeat and shrimp salad for herself, as well as a bottle of champagne for the two of them. After she did this, Griffin counted out $150 from his wallet and placed the money on the table.

"That's not necessary," she said. "I'll expense this."

"Uh-uh," Griffin said. "It wouldn't be gentlemanly for me to let you do that. Now, how about sitting on my lap?"

She looked like she wanted to argue about the money. After all, given the grungy clothes Griffin wore and the beat-up backpack he had brought along, he certainly didn't look like someone who could blow $150 on a room-service charge. But she accepted that he was going to be insistent on paying, and she found herself even more turned on by that, and so she sat on his lap and whispered her darkest sexual desires into his ear, her breath growing hot as she did so.

"You look so much like Ryan Gosling," she breathed in a soft whisper as her index finger traced the outline of his jaw. "Women must tell you that all the time."

"Most of them used to tell me I looked like the actor Philip Stonehedge, but then he got that nasty scar," he said.

"I can see that also," she said, her tongue lightly licking the inside of his ear.

There was a knock on the door. Griffin told her not to put her robe back on when she let the room-service attendant in. She got up from his lap to attend to the food while he hid in the bathroom, keeping the door open a crack so he could watch. She had kept the robe off as Griffin had asked, and the thirtysomething man who had brought up room service looked increasingly uncomfortable as he set up a table with the food and tried to pretend that he wasn't noticing anything unusual. After he left, Claire broke out laughing and Griffin came out of the bathroom, stripping off his clothes. She waited until he was naked also before rushing into his arms, her skin hot against his cool flesh.

"I am so turned on right now," she said, her mouth seeking out his.

"I've got a surprise," Griffin said after he was able to pull his mouth away from hers.

She gave him a quizzical look as he untangled himself from her and retrieved four silk ropes from his backpack.

"I don't know about this," she said, uncertainty weakening her eyes and mouth.

"It will make things so much more exciting when I do all those things you whispered into my ear."

She didn't seem too crazy about the idea, but she lay spread eagle on the bed and allowed Griffin to tie her wrists and ankles to the bedposts. Griffin had become proficient in tying knots long ago when he was in military school, and he used a type of slipknot that would feel loose until she struggled against it, and then the knot would tighten up. Her being five feet eight and having such long arms and legs helped, but if her arms and legs were shorter or the bed didn't have posts, he would've found a way to make do. When he had her secured, he told her he'd be right back. Less than a half minute later when she saw him coming back to the bed with a pair of her panties that she had left discarded on the floor and the bathrobe sash, she stared at him, confused for a moment, and realized too late what he was going to do with them.

She tried screaming, but before she could get much more than a squeak out, Griffin pushed her panties into her mouth and gagged her with the bathrobe sash. As she struggled to free herself, all she accomplished was making the knots painfully tight around her wrists and ankles. Griffin ignored her so he could sit at the table the room-service attendant had prepared, and methodically cut his steak into tiny pieces. Slowly, thoughtfully, he ate his meal, savoring each bite, while Claire continued to struggle to free herself. By the time he was done eating, she had done little more than exhaust herself. He decided to save the champagne for later.

They make things so damn easy, he thought as he retrieved a pair of latex gloves from his backpack. That was okay, though. He never much cared for the hunt or the chase. It was the killing that mattered to him. Even more, the pain he inflicted. That was what excited him and the thought of what was coming made him rock-hard. He fished a condom out of his backpack. Not that he had any intention of raping her, but he didn't want any leakage left behind that the police could use to get his DNA.

He brought the steak knife and fork he had used to the bathroom so he could wash them—again, he didn't want to leave any DNA or fingerprints behind. When he was done he brought them over to Claire and sat down on the bed next to her. Her face had become wet with tears and she pleaded with him with her eyes. He knew what she'd be begging him to do if he hadn't gagged her. *Take my money, but please don't hurt me.* Pathetic in a way, because of course he was also going to be taking her money afterwards.

"The coin came up heads," he explained to her. "If it had been tails, you'd be alive tomorrow."

She tried once more to scream, but only a low, muffled noise escaped her gag, certainly nothing anyone in the hallway or a neighboring room would've been able to hear. As he watched her, he could see the terror within her becoming something palpable. It wasn't just because she was afraid of what he was going to do to her, but because she could see that the beast that had been dormant for so many months had finally arisen within him.

For a long moment Griffin sat still and admired the long, willowy canvas that he had to work with. When her terror made her try screaming again, he didn't bother to hush her, and instead went to work, using the fork and steak knife on her. The beast could be patient and meticulous, though, and as he had promised, he took his time. After all, even though the beast had been let loose, keeping his promise was still the gentlemanly thing to do.

Chapter 6

Jane Wickford's shift at the Star-Crossed Diner started at two, and as much as Perlmutter was dying to fill her in about his latest news, he didn't want to appear too eager, so he waited until two thirty before heading over to the diner. Since ambushing Getzler at the Beverly Hills restaurant, he had returned to his small studio apartment above a Korean barbecue joint in K-town so he could shower and change into mostly clean clothes. As he drove to the famous downtown Los Angeles diner where Jane worked, he detected a faint mustiness from his shirt and considered stopping someplace to buy a new one. After a few moments of internal debate, he decided not to bother. The shirt was one of his favorites: A light blue crew-neck T-shirt that made him look ten pounds lighter.

It was almost three by the time he entered the diner, and his stomach had begun rumbling during the drive. He didn't order any breakfast earlier while he was waiting for the right moment to grab a seat at Getzler's table—both because he was too anxious to eat, and he didn't want to risk pitching his ideas to the studio executive with egg yolk or some other sticky food substance smeared on his face. Afterwards he was too excited to think about eating. Now, though, he realized how completely empty inside he was feeling. Like his stomach was a bottomless pit that would never fill up. He smiled inwardly. At least this time Jane wouldn't be able to accuse him of coming there simply to annoy her.

Trudy, the diner's longtime hostess, sighed noticeably when she spotted him, and gave him what could only be described as a look of pity when he asked to be seated at one of Jane's booths, but this time she didn't tell him that he was only wasting his time. That was too bad. Perlmutter had been looking forward to seeing the expression on her face when he explained to her why this time would be different. But since she didn't say anything to him, he decided he'd keep his news to himself for now. After Trudy left him at his booth, he sat back and imagined how Jane was going to react when he told her what had happened, and soon he was giggling to himself. He couldn't help it. It had been such a long, hard struggle with so many sacrifices, and he'd finally gotten the break he'd been hoping for. Forget that. The break he'd been working his ass off for! Jane was going to see him in a whole new light after today.

Perlmutter's face flushed as he pictured her. What a beauty! Blond, dimples, and a gorgeous, voluptuous figure. He'd been smitten since the first moment he laid eyes on her. That was eighteen months ago, when they were both taking the same acting class. Back then Perlmutter was still thinking he could be a triple threat—acting, writing, and directing, but he had since realized he was spreading himself too thin and it would be better for him to focus on writing and directing. Of course, he would still make cameo appearances in his movies, but that would be for later.

"Oh Jesus, you again?"

Perlmutter had been so absorbed in his daydream that he missed Jane coming over to his booth. He looked up to see her standing with her hands on her hips, smirking scornfully at him.

"That's right, darling, me again."

"I told you not to call me that," she snapped.

"Sure thing, Miss Wickford. Or can I still call you Jane?"

"I don't care. Just don't call me *darling*." She shook her head, her eyes momentarily rolling upward. "What is wrong with you?"

"Absolutely nothing."

"No? Then why do you keep pestering me?"

"Because I'm going to win your heart."

She gave him a pitiful look. "That's never going to happen."

"Why not?"

"Because I'm well out of your league."

Perlmutter flinched. She had implied as much in the past, but this was the first time she had been cruel enough to say the words. For a brief moment he felt his confidence ebbing, but then reminded himself about what had happened earlier.

"Yeah, you think so? What if I give you a role in my movie? You'd still think I'm out of your league?"

"Ha! What a laugh."

"Laugh all you want. I had a meeting this morning with Larry Getzler. Do you know who he is?"

Jane's eyes narrowed as she tried to decide whether Perlmutter was full of it. "Of course I know who he is. There's no way Getzler would meet with you."

"Okay, so it wasn't an official meeting. I crashed the restaurant where he eats breakfast. But he let me pitch him, and he loved one of my pitches enough to give me the go-ahead to develop a treatment and script."

Her eyes narrowed to slits as she tried to decide whether he was lying.

"You're lying," she said at last.

"Uh-uh, this is real. The break I've been waiting for. And it can be a break for you too."

"Tell me the pitch."

Perlmutter shook his head. "You'll know it after I have the deal wrapped up with Getzler. But I promise you there will be a nice, juicy role for you. One that will make you the star you deserve to be."

Jane stood silently for a long moment, considering him. Then her features relaxed and she showed him a sad smile.

"Allen, even if you're telling me the truth, it doesn't matter."

"What do you mean, it doesn't matter? Getzler gave me the go-ahead. This is real!"

She gave him a look as if he were a lost child she was trying to comfort. "How much money do you have left from what your mom left you?"

Perlmutter was confused by the question. When his mom died ten months ago, she had left him $40,000, and he immediately quit his job at a copy store so he could pursue his dream full-time. He had exaggerated the amount when he had told her about his inheritance, hinting he'd been left over a hundred grand. But what did that have to do with anything?

"Plenty," he lied, because the money was almost all gone.

"You should save what's left, get your old job back, and forget about this movie business, because it's not going to work out for you."

"I'm sure plenty of people were telling M. Night Shyamalan the same when he was trying to make *The Sixth Sense*, and also Billy Bob Thornton when he was pitching *Sling Blade*."

"You do realize that *The Sixth Sense* wasn't Shyamalan's first movie, and that Thornton had been acting and writing long before he made *Sling Blade*? I hope you also realize that you're no Shyamalan, and you're certainly no Billy Bob Thornton."

She had him so rattled he could barely think straight. Didn't she understand that Getzler had given him his blessing?

"What am I then?" he demanded.

She sighed and gave him a pitying look. "Allen, I'm telling you this straight because you need to hear it. You're a loser like all those other losers you hang out with. The ones you're always calling no-talent hacks. Even if you're not grossly exaggerating Getzler's interest in your pitch, you'll find a way to mess this up. There's not going to be any movie."

Tears welled in his eyes as stared at her. For a long moment he was consumed with the thought of taking the knife that had been set on the table and shoving it deep into Jane's throat. He trembled in his rage and hurt as he hurried out of the booth so he could get away from her.

"You just blew it big-time," he called out over his shoulder to her, his voice ragged as he fought to keep from sobbing. "This movie's getting made and you no longer get to be a part of it. Oh yeah, go to hell. You can suffer the rest of your life in obscurity for all I care!"

Tears began spilling out of Perlmutter's eyes. He lowered his head and ran past the hostess station and out of the diner.

Chapter 7

Although it was early—not even five o'clock—Morris normally wouldn't have been able to get into Trepanos on Hollywood Boulevard, but when he told the maître d' that he was meeting Philip Stonehedge for drinks, the maître d' consulted a notepad, asked for his name, and then promptly brought him to Stonehedge's booth. Thanks to the vivid scar that ran almost the full length of Stonehedge's right cheek, the grin the actor showed Morris had an especially sardonic look to it. Stonehedge got the scar when six months earlier he had tried playing the hero during a jewelry-store robbery. The same criminal who viciously slashed him across the cheek with a gun barrel also shot him in the leg. The actor would've bled to death if Morris hadn't saved his life.

Stonehedge got to his feet and showed only a slight limp as he hustled over to meet Morris for a handshake and embrace.

"I thought you were going to bring the little guy?" Stonehedge asked.

The actor was referring to Morris's bull terrier, Parker, who had also helped, in his way, in saving Stonehedge's life. As far as Morris was concerned, there was no dog in the world better than Parker, but bull terriers weren't the kind of dog you could leave alone all day, so either Morris took him when he left for work, or Natalie did.

"I was planning to, but Nat grabbed him. I wasn't going to fight her on it since she was seeing a couple of clients today who respond well to Parker."

"That's too bad. Among other appetizers, I've got two orders of wood-grilled lobster wrapped in bacon waiting at the booth."

Morris exaggerated a grimace as he shook his head. "If Parker knew he would be inconsolable."

Stonehedge shrugged. "You better not tell him. I don't want to be responsible for any hard feelings between Parker and Nat." The actor hopped back into the booth, which had, in addition to the aforementioned orders of wood-grilled lobster wrapped in bacon, four other plates of appetizers. Once Morris was seated across from him, the actor snared what looked like a mix of caviar, egg, and crème fraîche artistically layered on a fancy cracker, and waved the waitress over.

"No beers tonight," Stonehedge warned Morris. "Live a little, okay? I'm drinking margaritas, and they're very good here. Topnotch tequila."

Morris had been planning to order a beer, but he relented and told the waitress he'd have what Stonehedge was drinking. He had to repeat his order because she didn't hear him as she stared, starstruck, at the actor, looking like she might pass out if Stonehedge as much as winked at her. After she left, the actor asked how Natalie was doing.

"Good. She's excited about our trip to Italy. We leave in nine days." He hesitated and added, "She's afraid I'm going to get sucked into a case that will make us cancel the trip."

"Is that going to happen?"

"Not a chance."

"That's good." The actor shook his head. "I still can't believe you're going to Italy and you're not taking me up on my offer to stay in my friend's villa in Tuscany. The place is spectacular."

"Nat has her heart set on the tour," Morris mumbled awkwardly. He hadn't mentioned Stonehedge's offer to Natalie for the simple reason that he would've felt uncomfortable accepting that type of favor from someone he didn't know. Partly to change the subject, he asked, "How about you? Seeing anyone these days?"

The actor grinned at him. "You think the scar might be keeping the leading ladies away?"

"I wouldn't think so."

"Correct. I think it's actually having the opposite effect." Stonehedge ran a thumb along his scar, his grin tightening. "I guess it gives me a more dangerous look. In any case, I'm doing better than ever. Same with movie roles. Offers have been flooding in the last few months. Mostly villains, which I'm happy about. Those are more fun to play. But to answer your question, I have been seeing someone in particular the last few weeks. Brie Evans."

Morris shook his head, not recognizing the name.

"Come on, Morris. Brie's one of the hottest stars in the business right now. *The Drasti Conspiracy. The Last Love Letter.* The kids' flick, *It's Snowing Strawberry Ice Cream.*"

"I don't go to the movies much," Morris explained.

"I guess not," Stonehedge grumbled. He pulled out his cell phone and played with it for a moment before handing it to Morris. The screen showed a photo of a slender and very beautiful blonde with a dazzling smile. The woman in the photo wore a skimpy bikini as she stood by what Morris guessed was the pool at Stonehedge's Malibu home.

"A beautiful woman," Morris said. He handed the phone back to Stonehedge. "Things getting serious?"

"Too early to tell. Ask me again in six months."

The waitress returned with Morris's drink. Stonehedge waited until she left, before leaning forward and telling Morris that he was jonesing to do some more investigative work.

"Don't get me wrong, being a movie star certainly has its perks," the actor said, lowering his voice. "And it pays damn well, but acting can be boring as hell. Or maybe it only seems more boring now after the days we spent together chasing after the Skull Cracker Killer, but those were fun days. And you have to admit, we made a damn good team."

"Surprisingly, we did. But you also ended up with that scar and almost dead."

"Yeah, but that didn't happen as part of the investigation."

Morris took a sip of his margarita as he studied Stonehedge more closely. "Are you saying you want to quit being an actor and work for me full-time as an investigator? Because the pay's not that good."

The actor waved off the last part of what Morris had said. "I've got plenty of money. And as I have already mentioned, the perks of being a movie star are too good to give up. I'm thinking more along the lines of letting me tag along for a week or two when you've got something where I can be of help. Like before."

"I'm sorry to have to tell you this, but these days most of the jobs we're taking on are little more than grunt work. It would bore you silly."

"Well, maybe when you get something interesting, you can think of me. Who knows, maybe when you get your next serial-killer case."

Morris's eyes dulled as he stared at the lime-colored liquid sloshing around in his margarita glass. "I'm done with serial killers," he said.

Chapter 8

Griffin stood at the corner of Pike and Second Avenue with his duffel bag at his feet. Before too long a newer-model BMW pulled up alongside him. The passenger window lowered, and the driver squinted at him through a pair of hipster glasses and asked if he was Trent Regan.

"Yep, and you must be Bryan Tasker?"

The driver nodded. A car behind him honked, annoyed that Tasker was blocking traffic. Tasker quickly looked back, and then again at Griffin, his expression showing his uneasiness at stopping where he had. This was the reason Griffin had picked this meeting spot. There was no place nearby to park, so Tasker wasn't about to get out of his car for the two of them to talk first and for anyone to see them together. Just as importantly, Tasker would feel obliged to speed things up, which he did when he asked Griffin to toss his duffel bag onto the backseat. Griffin did this, and also his backpack, then climbed into the passenger seat, and Tasker drove off in a hurry. It wasn't until he reached Virginia Street and was able to pull into an empty parking spot that he turned to Griffin and offered his hand, a big, goofy smile on his lips.

"Sorry for not being friendlier before, but I felt a little rushed back there," he explained.

Griffin took his hand. Bryan Tasker was a heavyset, soft-looking man in his early thirties, and shaking hands with him was like squeezing a lump of mozzarella cheese. Along with the hipster eyeglasses, he also wore a long ponytail, and to further prove his hipster credentials, had let scraggly whiskers grow out from his chin while keeping the rest of his face as smooth as a baby's bottom. Griffin had the impression that he could crush every bone in this hipster's hand, but he behaved himself.

"I'm glad you saw my ad about sharing this ride," Tasker said. "Seattle to San Francisco is a long fourteen hours by yourself. It will be good to have someone along to help with the driving." The hipster hesitated for a moment, then with his goofy smile turning apologetic, he asked if he could see Griffin's driver's license. "My dad's a lawyer. He'd kill me if I didn't check that you had a valid license since you're going to be spending time behind the wheel," he said.

"Of course." Griffin didn't have an actual license for himself, but he had half a dozen fake ones in his wallet, and he deftly removed the one for Trent Regan. Whenever he had fake licenses made up, he'd pick rural, little-known towns. It made it less likely anyone looking at the license would know the area.

"Rathdrum, Idaho," the hipster said as he read the address on the fake Idaho license. "I've never been there."

Neither had Griffin, although several years back he did drive through Idaho and ended up killing a college student in Boise. The fact that he could pass as someone from the Idaho panhandle was remarkable in a way. He had been born and raised in a Boston suburb, and had spent years working hard to remove all traces of his Boston accent. The way he sounded now he could've been from anywhere: Hicksville, USA.

"Few have," he said. "I think we have more bears than people."

Tasker nodded, accepting that Griffin was legit. "I hope you like Mumford and Sons," he said. "The Decemberists, Death Cab for Cutie, and The Shins also. I've got a lot of their music queued up for the trip."

Griffin might've heard the names of a couple of those bands in passing, but he didn't know any of their music, which was pretty much par for the course. The only music he listened to by choice was heavy metal: Metallica, Iron Maiden, Megadeth, Slayer. Anything softer than those bands he considered bubblegum music.

"Whatever you want to play," he said. "I'm easy."

For a half hour Tasker played his music, but then he abruptly turned off the car stereo and got chatty as he volunteered to Griffin his life story, telling him, among other things, about how his girlfriend of seven years broke up with him recently and that he worked as a software engineer in San Francisco.

"My company needed me to be in Seattle the last three weeks. I thought it would be an adventure driving instead of flying. On the drive over I took two extra days, and it was fun. But now I just want to get home as fast as possible."

"I figured you were a computer programmer," Griffin said.

"Software engineer," Tasker corrected.

Griffin didn't bother asking him what the difference was. The hipster could call himself whatever he wanted as far as he was concerned.

"Okay, so you know about me. What are you going to be doing in San Fran?" Tasker asked.

"Nothing. I'll be traveling on to LA."

"Do you have a ride already arranged?"

"Not yet, but I'll figure something out."

Tasker nodded, as if he accepted that was likely. "Let me guess: You want to be an actor?"

Griffin smiled thinly because Tasker couldn't have been more wrong. Actors wanted the spotlight. He wanted only the shadows.

"Is it that obvious?" he asked.

"Not because of anything other than your looks."

An awkward silence followed, and Tasker turned the stereo back on, and kept it on for the next three hours until he pulled off the highway so he could stop at a roadside diner.

"I did some research before leaving. This place has a four-star rating from Yelp," he confided. He got out of the car and looked surprised to see that Griffin had remained seated where he was. He walked back to the car, tapped on the passenger-side window, and waited for Griffin to open the door.

"Aren't you coming in?"

"I thought I'd take a nap since I'll be taking over the driving soon."

Tasker nodded as he mulled this over, then took several steps toward the diner before returning back to the car. He again knocked on the passenger-side window and waited for Griffin to open the door so they could talk some more.

"I hate eating alone," he said. "It's one of the things I hate most about my girlfriend dumping me. Look, if it's a matter of money, I'd be happy to treat for dinner."

"You're right, I can't afford to eat here," Griffin said. "I have this trip budgeted out so I can pay for my share of the gas, as promised, but not for anything else. It's awfully generous of you to offer what you did, but I was raised not to accept handouts. And besides, I really should take a nap if I'm going to take over driving duties."

Griffin said all this as if he actually meant it, and Tasker stood for a moment looking like he wanted to convince Griffin to change his mind, but quickly accepted that he was telling the truth and was going to stick to his guns. He gave Griffin a nod before turning away, his shoulders slouched as he trudged to the diner. Griffin, of course, had lied through his teeth. Before leaving Claire's hotel room, he took over eight hundred dollars from his latest victim, and he had another $2,249 squirreled away in his duffel bag. He certainly didn't want to be seen in public with Tasker, and he had planned ahead with his steak dinner. He'd be fine without eating anything else for hours. He also wasn't going to be napping during this stopover—the anticipation of what was going to be happening soon had him too hyped up for sleeping—but he nonetheless closed his eyes and pretended to nap for Tasker's benefit in case the hipster looked out the diner's window. The parking lot was poorly lit, but at least Tasker would see in the darkness what looked like a person napping. Nobody else in the diner would be able to see Griffin well enough to provide the police a useful description.

When the hipster later emerged from the diner, he brought with him a paper bag, which he handed to Griffin.

"I know what you told me," the hipster said. "But I couldn't in good conscience let you go hungry, so I picked you up a burger and fries. No big deal."

Griffin grudgingly accepted the food. "This is awfully nice of you. Thanks."

They switched places, with Griffin behind the wheel. Less than two hours later Tasker drifted off to sleep. Griffin waited another ten minutes until they were on an especially dark and remote stretch of highway before unlatching the hipster's seat belt and flinging the passenger door open, all the while keeping the BMW speeding along at over ninety miles an hour. There were far easier ways to kill Tasker, and Griffin almost lost control of the car as he swerved violently to the right, while at the same time maneuvering his body so he could kick the hipster out the open door, but he had settled on this plan hours earlier, and the idea of it excited him. Tasker woke up just as he was about to tumble out of the car, and then he was gone.

Griffin had to fight with the wheel to keep the car from flipping over. Once he had control of it, he brought the car to a stop, and then backed up on this pitch-black stretch of highway until he was able to spot Tasker's body on the side of the road. The damage done to the hipster was dramatic, as he was reduced to little more than roadkill, most of the skin torn off from his face and a good part of his body. Griffin dragged him off the road and into a woodsy area. He used a cigarette lighter so he could look into the face of his latest victim, and was amazed to see that the hipster was not only still alive but conscious, his lips trembling as if he were trying to say something.

For Griffin, the thrill of killing was not only the pain he inflicted, but looking into the eyes of his victims at the very moment when life left them. He badly wanted to do the same with this one, but at this point killing him would be an act of mercy, and Griffin was anything but merciful. So instead he took Tasker's wallet. There wasn't much cash in it; only sixty-three dollars, and Griffin certainly wasn't going to use any of Tasker's credit cards, but he wanted to make it harder for the authorities to identify the corpse. The right side of the hipster's body had been ripped apart, and Griffin had to spend several minutes searching the area before he found Tasker's smartphone. It had been smashed up pretty good, but Griffin picked it up anyway just in case the police could still get something from it.

The hipster was as good as dead. If the police somehow found him while he was still breathing, they weren't going to get anything from him, nor were they going to be able to keep him alive for very long. They would identify him eventually, but it wasn't going to be easy given the shape he was in. In any case, there was nothing that would connect Tasker to Griffin, or even to the alias he used, Trent Regan. Still, to be on the safe side, he would be retiring that alias immediately.

All in all, Griffin felt very pleased with himself as he walked back to where he had left the BMW.

Chapter 9

Adam Felger didn't look particularly happy as he reported to Morris and the other MBI investigators the scant little that he'd been able to discover about Kyle Lindsey.

"Birth certificate puts him at twenty-six, like he's claiming. Graduated South Central High in Phoenix, Arizona. Five years ago both parents died when their car was broadsided by a drunk driver. No siblings. Nothing interesting on his credit reports. I can't find anything suggesting he has a criminal record. One thing that does seem odd is that he has no social-media presence, at least none that I've been able to find. I'll keep digging, but so far no Twitter account, no Facebook, no LinkedIn, no Instagram, nothing."

Fred Lemmon, one of the investigators, smirked at that, and said, "I thought you millennials are required by a secret oath to do all that stuff?"

"And I thought it was Polk's job to make smart-ass comments," Felger responded with a straight face.

"Touché," Charlie Bogle said.

Lemmon shrugged. "Someone has to pick up the slack with Polk not here."

The aforementioned Dennis Polk was on assignment that morning to tail Kyle Lindsey. Morris asked Felger to get Polk on the conference room's speakerphone.

"That's a shame," Bogle said. "It's been such a peaceful morning so far."

"Can't be helped," Morris said without cracking a smile.

Polk surprised all of them by reporting the facts straight when he came on without making any of his usual bad puns.

"I'm camped out across the street. The daughter, Mia Dickerson, left two hours ago. Lindsey's still in the condo. I've got a spy cam covering the front door of their condo, which is the only way in or out of their penthouse unit, so I'll know if he leaves or he has any company. I also have a GPS tracking device attached to the undercarriage of his car. I've got him well covered."

"What did you take this morning?" Lemmon asked. "Thorazine?"

"No idea what you're talking about."

"Only that I'm finding this sudden bout of professionalism of yours disorienting. Like I've been dropped into some sort of bizarro universe."

"That's enough," Morris said.

"That's okay, let Fred flap his gums," Polk said. Somewhat sheepishly, he added, "I got a good look at Mia this morning when she left. A sweet-looking kid. If this Lindsey character is bad news, I want to know it."

Morris could appreciate Polk feeling that way, since his investigator had a twenty-four year-old single daughter, just as Morris had Rachel.

Morris asked, "What if he exits the building from the back fire door? Do you need another set of eyes out there?"

"Not necessary. If he does that he'll still have to come around to the front of the building. He's not slipping past me."

"Okay, stick with him. Our client has arranged a pool party at his Brentwood home for seven tonight. Charlie will make contact there, so once you follow Lindsey to Dickerson's Brentwood address, you can call it a day. If you need a break before then, give me a call and I'll take over."

"Won't be necessary. I've got a full gallon of Pepsi, a thermos of coffee, a bag of doughnuts, a roast-beef sandwich and chips, tunes to listen to, and a mostly empty gallon jug to fill up. In other words, paradise."

"What's the plan tonight?" Bogle asked Morris.

"Dickerson is going to introduce you as an interested investor in Lindsey's supposed fantasy-sports betting app. Find out what you can about it, whether it's real or a smokescreen. Make it sound like you're dying to dump a lot of money on him, and use it as an opportunity to dig into his background. Ask for references."

Bogle nodded as he thought it over. "Sounds like a plan," he said. "If I'm going to fit in as one of Dickerson's well-heeled associates, I'm going to need some fancier duds than what I own, maybe an expensive watch. Some other jewelry."

"Philip Stonehedge already told me he'll help out with that. He's expecting your call."

Bogle looked disappointed, probably thinking he'd be able to pick up some expensive designer casual wear on the client's dime. "Any shirt from Mr. Hollywood is going to be tight on me," he complained.

"So leave it unbuttoned. It's going to be a pool party, after all."

"Anything you need me for?" Lemmon asked.

"Are you still meeting that fence you suspect was involved in the Roget burglary?"

"Not until three."

"Stay available. If something comes up, I'll let you know."

"Sure thing, but if I'm able to wrap up the Roget case, I could fly down to Phoenix and kick around some. Maybe talk to Lindsey's old neighbors, also find some of his classmates from South Central High."

"Not a bad idea, but let's wait and see what shakes out from this pool party."

The office manager, Greta Lindstrom, opened the door enough to give Morris an apologetic smile. "I'm sorry for the interruption, but there's a Mr. Perlmutter out here who wants to see you. He claims it's about Sheila Proops. I tried asking him for more specifics, but he's being stubborn about it, insisting he'll only talk to you."

Morris winced as if he'd been struck with a fast-hitting migraine. He had hoped to go through the rest of his life without ever hearing that name again, and his initial reaction was to have Greta tell this man to hit the bricks, but after a moment of reflection he instead told her he'd be right out. Once the door to the soundproofed conference room closed behind her, he asked whether anyone had other ideas about how they could be handling the Kyle Lindsey investigation. Nobody did. Proops's name had taken some of the air out of the room.

Greta had kept Perlmutter seated in the waiting area so she could keep an eye on him. A balding, square-shaped man in his early for-

ties, dressed in a cheap T-shirt, worn khaki chinos, and a pair of tennis sneakers that had seen far better days. He wasn't sweating right
then, but he looked like the type who would sweat profusely. Morris
walked up to him, introduced himself, and offered his hand. Perlmutter seemed surprised that Morris had done this, and he looked nervous when he stood and took Morris's hand. Morris noted how thick
his arms were. They weren't muscular, but they were thick and heavy
arms matted with black hair. A quick look showed he also had simi-
larly thick, heavy legs.

"What do you want to tell me about Sheila Proops?" Morris asked.

"Can we talk in your office? It's confidential."

"Here is just fine."

A hitch showed alongside Perlmutter's mouth, as if he were about
to argue further with Morris, but forced himself not to. He took a
business card from his pocket and handed it over. The card looked
expensive and was done up in a fancy calligraphy with raised gold
lettering. It read: *Allen Perlmutter, screenwriter & film director.*
Morris gave the card a quick glance and gave it back to Perlmutter,
telling him he wasn't interested.

Perlmutter reacted as if he'd been slapped. Dumbfounded, he
said, "What do you mean, you're not interested? I haven't even told
you my offer!"

"Whatever it is, it doesn't matter."

Morris took a step away, and the chunky, self-professed screen-
writer/director reached forward and grabbed Morris by the wrist. He
peered down at Perlmutter's hand, then into Perlmutter's eyes.

"You've got three seconds to let go of me before I snap your
wrist," Morris said.

Perlmutter let go of Morris. Flustered, his cheeks quickly mot-
tling white and red, he sputtered out, "Starlight Pictures has given me
the go-ahead to make a movie about Sheila Proops, and I'm offering
you two points on gross for your help. That could be a million dollars
for a few hours of your time!"

"Your card has you as a screenwriter and a director. You're an executive producer now also?"

"What do you mean?"

"You're offering me points on the film. That's something an executive producer does."

Perlmutter looked more flustered as he rubbed a hand across his mouth. "Larry Getzler himself gave me the okay to make this movie. I'm sure two points can be arranged!"

Charlie Bogle had joined Morris, and he asked his boss what the problem was.

"This aspiring filmmaker seems to be having a tough time taking *no* for an answer. Would you mind escorting Mr. Perlmutter out of the building?"

"Sure thing."

Perlmutter looked bewildered as he turned from Morris to Bogle. When Bogle grabbed ahold of his arm, Perlmutter tried to pull free but was unable to break Bogle's viselike grip. With seemingly little effort, Bogle turned Perlmutter toward the door and had him moving several awkward steps toward it.

"Okay, forget it," Perlmutter spat out. "You don't want to make an easy million dollars—fine, your loss. Have your goon let go of me! I'll leave on my own."

Bogle let go of Perlmutter's arm, and the chunky wannabe screenwriter/director moved quickly as he continued on out of the office suite. He made sure to slam the door behind him.

"You can't please everyone," Morris said with a sigh.

"No, you can't," Bogle agreed. "Goon, huh? I'm not sure whether that's a promotion over my current job duties or not."

"Let's just be glad Polk wasn't around to hear it," Morris said.

Bogle cringed over the prospect of that.

The two men walked back to Morris's office so they could brainstorm more over how Bogle should handle Kyle Lindsey later that evening.

Chapter 10

San Luis Obispo, the present

Griffin had never felt more alive than he did right after pushing Bryan Tasker out of the speeding BMW. This was the first time he had killed two people in the same day—in fact, he had always waited months after snuffing out a life before choosing another victim—and the thought of what he did to that willowy blonde in her luxury Seattle hotel room and that flabby hipster out on that darkened highway left him giddy. In his mind's eye he imagined the beast towering over his latest victims as it bristled in its ferociousness. The funk he had slipped into over the past year or so had become little more than a bad dream, as if it had never happened.

Still, given his overwhelming sense of elation, he knew he'd better concentrate to make sure that he drove no faster than five miles over the speed limit. He didn't want any state troopers pulling him over—although given the way he felt, he was sure he'd be able to tear apart any who tried with his bare hands. The euphoria surging through him was so intense that the miles disappeared in a blink of an eye, and it hardly seemed possible that he'd driven ten hours straight when he pulled into the San Jose International Airport. He didn't spend much time there, only long enough to replace the license plates on the BMW with ones taken from a car in long-term parking. After he left the airport, he found a used record store in downtown San Jose and bought a compact disc of Iron Maiden's *The Number of the Beast*.

Once he was back on US-101, Griffin cranked the volume of the stereo to an ear-splitting level and let the heavy-metal music and Iron Maiden's nightmarish satanic lyrics pulsate through him. After three more hours of driving he realized how famished he was feeling; as if no amount of food would be enough. He was right outside of San Luis Obispo then, and he pulled off the highway. Before too long he came across an extraordinarily gaudy sign for a resort that advertised rooms, three restaurants, golfing, and the area's largest outdoor pool. Something about the sign appealed to him, and he followed additional signs to an even more gaudy-looking collection of buildings and an immense parking lot overflowing with cars. He found a spot for the BMW and followed a pathway to the main building, where he found one of the restaurants that was set up as a fifties diner.

The hostess sat him near a young couple, which after a few minutes of eavesdropping, he discovered were on their honeymoon. The diner served breakfast all day long, and as he ate a hearty meal of pancakes, ham steak, fried eggs, and hash browns, he listened to the couple fight. The husband was determined to play eighteen holes of golf, while his new bride wanted them to go horseback riding. The husband patiently tried explaining that he had already reserved his tee time, and that they could go horseback riding in the early evening. That it would be better then anyway, since they'd be able to look out over a spectacular sunset from the top of the trail.

"It really stinks that you want to go golfing! On our honeymoon!"

"Come on, love muffin, I mentioned how they had a golf course when we picked the place, didn't I?"

"So? I was supposed to guess from that that you were planning to abandon me for an afternoon?"

"Ah, for fudge sakes, I'll only be gone for a few hours. Why do you have to be so dramatic?" He hesitated before adding in a voice low enough that Griffin had to strain to hear him, "We'll go riding when I get back. Just don't be a bitch about this, okay?"

Griffin couldn't help smiling, seeing the frigid look she gave her new husband, and she caught him doing it. For a brief moment she appeared absolutely apoplectic and Griffin expected her to say something to her husband about how she had caught him eavesdropping on their quarrel, but then something unmistakable flashed in her eyes, and she looked away from him.

"I'll have to go to the pool by myself then," she said loudly enough so that Griffin would have no trouble hearing her.

"That's a fine idea," her husband said, relieved.

"And I'll wear my new bikini. The really tiny one. The one you told me you don't want other men seeing me in."

"Wear whatever you want."

That was that. Their quarrel ended, they finished their lunch, and when they left their booth, the wife flashed Griffin a sly look. He hung around a while longer as he ordered apple pie à la mode, and drank several more cups of coffee. After paying his bill, instead of getting in the BMW and continuing on to Los Angeles, he wandered over to the pool area. The young wife was there, and as promised was wearing an exceptionally skimpy bikini. When she saw Griffin, she flashed him another look that was a mix of lust and anger, and then dove into the pool. After she climbed out, she stood in front of him so he could see the water dripping off of her somewhat plump, but still attractive and very young body. She flashed him a smile that showed a hint of nervousness in it. She wanted to punish her husband for abandoning her to play golf, but she still had no intention of having sex with Griffin. In her mind she must've worked out a scenario where they would share a passionate kiss in her hotel room, and then she would demand that Griffin leave. That would teach her new husband for treating her as shabbily as he did.

As she walked past Griffin on her way back to her room, she exaggerated the wiggle of her rear end, and she looked back to catch his eye to make sure he knew he was supposed to follow her.

This was all a nice stroke of luck on his part. Ever since he had left San Jose, he'd been thinking about Sheila Proops and how he wanted a trial run so he could test all of the devious little tortures he wanted to inflict on her, and make sure that none of them would kill her until he was ready for her to die.

He kept his distance as he followed the bikini-clad new bride to her room. When he got to her door, he knocked softly and she let him in.

Chapter 11

Dennis Polk was munching away on a roast-beef sandwich while also keeping an eye on his cell phone screen that showed the video feed from the spy cam he had set up, when a hard rap sounded on the driver's-side window. He looked up to see a patrolman glaring at him. He rolled down the window.

"Chip Harrison?" Polk asked. "Is that you? Almost didn't recognize you with that spare tire missing."

The patrolman's expression softened as he recognized Polk, who had spent eighteen years on the force before joining MBI. All of MBI's investigators were former homicide detectives who had worked with Morris Brick.

"Polk," Harrison said, nodding. "Yep, my wife's got me on some sort of caveman diet, and the damn thing actually works. I've lost fourteen pounds." He scratched his jaw and gave Polk a hard grin. "We had a call about a suspicious-looking individual parked out here. And what do you know, the caller was right."

"Yeah, let me guess: It came from a sour-faced old biddy with one of those little yappy dogs. Her mutt took a dump on the sidewalk over there, and when I told her she needed to pick up after her pet, she gave me one of those indignant *how-dare-you* looks. I bet she couldn't wait to call the police on me."

"That sounds about right. Are you here on a job?"

"Yep." While talking with Harrison, Polk continued to keep one eye on the video feed, and he caught Lindsey leaving the condo. "Speaking of which, my target's on the move."

Harrison nodded okay. "Say hi to the wife and kids for me."

"You too."

Harrison moved on so as not to draw any added attention, and Polk picked up the newspaper he had brought along so he could hide behind it. After Lindsey pulled out of the building's underground garage, he waited until Lindsey had driven two blocks before following. He was tracking the car's GPS coordinates, so he wasn't going to lose it, and that allowed him to give it that much distance.

He followed Lindsey to Inglewood, and once he realized that Lindsey was heading to the Hollywood Hills Casino, he sped up and cut down the distance between them to half a block. The casino was massive and would be an easy place to lose someone. He was right behind Lindsey in handing his car over to valet parking, and followed his target on foot to one of the poker rooms. Once he saw Lindsey seated at a table, he called Morris.

"Our boy's not working all that hard today," Polk said.

"Is that so?"

"Sure is. He just arrived at the Hollywood Hills Casino, and is sitting at a fifty-dollar minimum-bet table. I think seven-card stud. It looked like there was a twenty-five-dollar table in the same room. I might have to lose some of our client's money if I'm going to keep an eye on him."

"Try not to lose too much."

"Sure thing."

Polk took a seat at the twenty-five-dollar table that would allow him to keep Lindsey in his peripheral vision. His first twelve hands, he was dealt nothing but dreck and had to fold early, leaving him $550 in the hole. The next hand he was dealt a full house, aces and eights, and unless the woman next to him had four nines, he had a sure winner. Better still, everyone at the table was either bluffing or had what they thought were winning cards with the way they were betting. He was going to walk away from this with a nice, tidy sum in his pocket, and was so caught up in the betting that he almost missed Lindsey leaving the room. When the bet came to him, he swore fervently under his breath, calling Lindsey every dirty name in the book before folding and hurrying out of there to catch up to his target.

For a couple of minutes he was sure he had lost Lindsey, but then he caught sight of him heading to the men's room.

"If I threw away five grand because this joker had to take a leak, I'll kill him myself," Polk whispered under his breath. But these thoughts disappeared a few minutes later when another man tried walking into the same men's room, and a couple of hired tough guys in cheap suits appeared out of nowhere to tell him the facility was closed. The man at first seemed surprised, then looked at them suspiciously as if he didn't believe they were casino employees, but he had the good sense to walk away without arguing with them. Polk surreptitiously took several photos of the hired muscle. It didn't surprise him when ten minutes later a hard-looking man with a thick, bull-like body came out of the men's room. This one was wearing a much more expensive-looking suit than his two hired hands, who both fell in behind him as their boss continued on past Polk. As with the hired muscle, Polk had taken several photos of their boss. It didn't take long after this for Lindsey to walk out of the men's room. As far as Polk could tell, Lindsey looked unscathed, and he certainly didn't look as if he'd been rattled in there, so the meeting had most likely been cordial.

Polk followed Lindsey out of the casino, and he waited until he was back in his car before calling Morris.

"Lindsey's on the move again. Something of interest happened in the casino. He didn't go there just to play poker."

"No?"

"No. At four forty-five he left his table, screwing up the first winning hand I was dealt. Full house, aces and eights. I could've made a bundle on it, but I had to throw in my cards so I could follow my target."

"What a shame."

"Yeah, you're telling me. But there was a nice payoff at the end. Lindsey had a private meeting scheduled in one of the casino's men's rooms. There were a couple of knuckle draggers making sure the meeting was kept private. I took pictures of both of them. Their boss also, who came out of the men's room ten minutes after Lindsey headed in there. The guy's got *gangster* written all over him. I'll send the photos over first chance I get."

"Okay, where's Lindsey now?"

"On the move. He got a five-minute head start on me, as I had to wait for valet parking to bring me my car. But I'm tracking him through his GPS coordinates, and I'm guessing he's heading back to the condo, probably to pretty himself up for the pool party."

"I'll fill Charlie in on what you found. Maybe he'll be able to make use of it."

Polk had to speed through a red light to keep the distance between himself and Lindsey from growing any greater than it already was.

"If this guy is legitimately building some sort of betting software for fantasy-sports geeks, then it might make sense for him to look for financing from some unsavory characters connected to gambling," he said after a moment of reflection. "But Mr. Big, who emerged from the men's room, looked like he was far more than a bookmaker, and his two hired hands looked like professional arm breakers. This Lindsey character is beginning to smell bad."

"I can't disagree with you."

Chapter 12

One of the kitchen workers Perlmutter knew from the Korean-barbecue restaurant sat on the back stoop near the dumpsters while he smoked a cigarette. Perlmutter waved hello and the kitchen worker gave him a disinterested nod in return.

It was still early, only six thirty in the evening, but Perlmutter asked anyway, "Any takeout orders tonight that weren't picked up?"

"Three." The worker let a stream of smoke escape out the side of his mouth. "I'll let you have them for ten bucks."

"You should give them to me for free," Perlmutter complained. "Because of this restaurant, my apartment's noisy all night, and it always smells like fried pork and kimchi."

The worker shrugged as if to say *it's not my fault you chose to live over a restaurant*. Perlmutter made a face as he handed over ten dollars.

"What am I getting?"

The worker deadpanned, "An assortment." He took several more drags on his cigarette before flicking it away and disappearing inside the restaurant. A short time later, he came out and handed Perlmutter a bag with three takeout cardboard boxes in it.

"Bon appétit," he said with a thin smile before heading back into the restaurant.

To get to his studio apartment, Perlmutter needed to use a different entrance, and then had to climb a set of narrow, rickety steps that creaked badly under his weight. When he opened the door to his place, Orson, a big, fat orange tabby padded over to him and meowed.

"You want dinner, huh? What else is new."

The cat meowed again.

Perlmutter only had to take a few steps to enter the meager kitchen area in his apartment. He placed the bag on top of the small patch of open counter space next to the sink, and then held his breath as he opened a can of discounted cat food and dumped it into Orson's bowl. The stuff was supposed to be a mix of chicken and tuna, but it smelled awful, and God only knew what was actually in it. Orson meowed angrily as he watched Perlmutter do this—he didn't want the canned food, but the Korean-barbecue takeout. If he wasn't so fat, he would've jumped onto the counter and tried nosing his way into the takeout containers.

"Sorry, guy," Perlmutter said. "Things will be changing soon and you'll eat better then."

He placed the bowl on the floor. Orson sniffed it and then followed Perlmutter to his computer desk where he ate his meals. Perlmutter looked inside one of the cardboard boxes, and Seung-hwan hadn't been kidding about it being an assortment. Mixed inside were dumplings, short ribs, and spicy pork with cabbage. Table scraps. Seung-hwan wasn't even pretending any more that he was selling him takeout food that hadn't been picked up, but was now rubbing it in Perlmutter's nose that he was scraping leftover food off of plates. Perlmutter decided it didn't matter. He had suspected that for a while, and so what? The food was still good.

Orson jumped up on him and sunk his claws into Perlmutter's belly as he tried to nose his way toward the open container. Perlmutter grimaced as he pulled the cat off of him and placed him on the floor.

"Okay, okay, I'll give you some."

He brought the container over to Orson's bowl, added one of the dumplings and some of the spicy pork, and mixed it in with the foul-smelling cat food. Satisfied, Orson nibbled at what was in his bowl.

Perlmutter returned to the computer desk and wiped the back of his hand across his brow. The worst part of living above the restaurant was how hot it got thanks to the grill and stoves they had working down there all night. He needed a new window air conditioner; the one he had barely did anything other than make a lot of noise. Soon things were going to change, but for the time being he would have to continue to make do. The price of being a budding filmmaker. Not that the studio apartment was all bad. It might've been cramped, and made even more cramped by the piles of film scripts, old videos, and DVDs that Perlmutter had stacked on the floor, and it might've smelled, and was noisy a lot of evenings, but he loved the K-town location, which made him feel as if he were part of the Hollywood scene. The studio was also cheap, which was important since the money he had inherited from his mom was almost gone. He still had enough to cover this month's rent and to pay the minimum that he needed to on his maxed-out credit cards. He was going to have to get a couple of more cards so he could max those out also. But none of that mattered. Things were going to be changing soon. He had no doubt about that anymore, although he did have a moment of crisis yesterday when Jane told him that he was no different than the losers he hung out with.

That stung badly, no question about it, and it left him doing some serious soul-searching for the rest of the day, at least until he remembered the glint he had seen in Getzler's eyes. That glint was real, and it guaranteed Perlmutter would be able to make this movie as long as he could come up with a killer treatment and an equally killer script, and he knew he could do both. Jane had no clue what she was talking about, and was simply flapping her gums. Perlmutter might've fallen in with a crowd of loser wannabes like Sammy Bloom, but that didn't mean he was one of them. He'd seen their attempts at screenwriting and knew they were hacks, just as he knew he not only had what it took, but that he was on the verge of making it big. He all but had Getzler's go-ahead, which was something none of those losers had, or would ever have.

Orson finished his dinner and padded over to Perlmutter so that he could jump onto his stomach. Perlmutter gritted his teeth as the cat once again dug his claws into his flesh. After Orson had settled down, Perlmutter stroked the cat's fur while he finished off the assortment of table scraps that had been dumped into two of the take-out containers; the second one consisting of seaweed salad, garlic fried chicken, and barbecued beef tongue. A bite had been taken out of one of the pieces of fried chicken, but he didn't let that bother him. He picked up the third cardboard container, thought about opening it, but instead decided to store it away for another night.

"Things are going to be changing real soon," he promised Orson as he absently stroked the cat from the top of his head to the end of his tail. The cat purred contentedly in response.

"Jane can go to hell," he said, and Orson again purred. "She thinks she's something special, huh? Well, there are plenty of women in Hollywood hotter than her, and I'll hook up with one of them. Someone smart enough to recognize my talent and know that I'm going places. Once I get Getzler's blessing, I'll give my new squeeze the juicy role I was going to give Jane, and that rotten bitch can spend the rest of her miserable life waiting tables for all I care."

Orson purred again as he stretched his legs.

"As far as Morris Brick goes, let's see if he's still so damn smug once he realizes he lost out on an easy million bucks."

Orson closed his eyes and went to sleep.

Chapter 13

The client brought Charlie Bogle over to his prospective son-in-law and introduced the MBI investigator as Bill Hodges, as had earlier been arranged.

"This is someone you want to meet," Dickerson told Kyle Lindsey with a wink. "Trust me, Bill's got enough money to buy and sell me ten times over."

Dickerson slapped Bogle on the back and gave Lindsey a second wink before walking off to talk to another guest at what had turned out to be a well-attended and rather elaborate pool party, even though it had been thrown together at the last minute, complete with tuxedoed waiters and waitresses serving up five-star quality gourmet food and interesting-looking drinks. Bogle grabbed a pinkish-colored cocktail from a passing waitress's tray, and smiled good-naturedly at Lindsey.

"Brett's always exaggerating," Bogle said. "The last I checked I could only buy and sell him seven times over." Playing the part of a wealthy businessman, he chuckled over his own lame joke, took a sip of the cocktail that he had snared—which turned out to be something very tasty with vodka and muddled strawberries—and added, "I understand you're starting up a venture involving fantasy-sports betting software? I'm always looking for a good investment. Do you want to tell me about it?"

Lindsey showed a blasé smile. He wore a long-sleeved white cotton shirt, swimming trunks, and a pair of tennis sneakers without socks. He looked too pale to Bogle for someone who'd been spending the last few months in Los Angeles without an office to go to each day, which could've meant that he was spending most of his time inside his girlfriend's condo working on his software venture, or alternatively, holed up inside of casinos playing poker like he did today.

"We're in stealth mode right now," Lindsey said in a casual, friendly manner. "I'd like to be able to tell you more, but I can't at this time."

"I understand, but this isn't just polite cocktail talk as far as I'm concerned," Bogle said. "I'm serious about wanting to invest. Everything I hear, fantasy sports is the future of gambling."

Lindsey nodded in agreement. "No doubt about that." He manufactured a pained look before adding, "As much as I'd like to tell you what we're doing, it's just not the right time now. In a couple of months we should be looking for investors, and you can bet I'll be looking you up then."

"How about a hint so I'm not wasting those months anticipating an investment that doesn't have any real meat on the bones?"

Lindsey's eyes wavered for a moment before he nodded. "Seeing how you're a friend of Brett's, I'll give you a hint as long as you promise not to repeat any of this. My partners would kill me if they knew."

"You've got my word."

"Okay, I'm trusting you with this." Lindsey waved Bogle closer, and with his voice lowering into a conspiratorial tone, he said, "We're working with this brilliant mathematician who has come up with a set of algorithms that picks the best player to use eighty-three percent of the time. We're trying to tweak his algorithms so we're better than ninety percent, but even if we're not successfully able to make those tweaks, we're going to revolutionize fantasy-sports betting."

"Wow. If that's true, this could be worth a lot of money."

"That's what we're counting on."

"What's the exit strategy?"

An apologetic smile. "We're too early in the game to be thinking about that."

"How many partners do you have?"

"I'm sorry, but that's confidential."

"You're going to be a tease and get me all excited about this, and then leave me hanging?" Bogle said. "How about if I sign an NDA? I'd really like to speak with your brilliant mathematician. And of course, also look over his data."

Lindsey offered another contrite smile. "That's just not possible at this time. I'm sure you understand."

"I might understand, but that doesn't mean I'm happy about it." Bogle showed an exaggerated frown, his lips forming a severe upside-down U. "I have ten million dollars sitting around, just waiting for the right investment. Too bad it can't be in your venture."

Lindsey's eyes, which had been unwavering until then, showed a slight flicker. "We're going to be looking for an initial seed funding of twenty million," he said.

"That can be arranged."

Lindsey nodded slowly as he thought this over. "I can't make any promises, but I'll talk with my partners. Maybe we'll speed things up. In any case, I'll call you within a week. Right now, my fiancée needs rescuing, but it was a pleasure meeting you."

Lindsey clapped Bogle on the shoulder as he brushed past him, and Bogle turned to see Mia Dickerson cornered by a middle-aged man who was standing way too close to her as he talked. He watched for a moment as Lindsey joined his fiancée, and he then pushed his way through the throng of guests until he spotted a waitress taking a break. He smiled inwardly, seeing the sullen look on her face as she sat smoking a cigarette.

"How'd you like to make a quick fifty dollars?" he asked her.

She gave him a disgusted look. "No thanks."

"Nah. It's nothing like that. This will only take a few seconds and you'll have fun doing it."

"What?" she asked suspiciously.

"See that guy over there?" He pointed out Lindsey. "I'd like you to *accidentally* trip and splash a glass of red wine on the front of his shirt."

She peered over at Lindsey and nodded slowly. "A hundred."

"Deal."

Bogle paid her, gave her a few additional instructions, and waved over Dickerson to join him. Several minutes later he signaled the waitress, and he watched as she appeared to lose her balance and send the single glass of red wine that she'd been balancing on her tray splashing onto the front of Lindsey's shirt.

"I'm so sorry," she offered profusely.

Dickerson moved her aside, telling her brusquely that accidents would happen. He signaled for a waiter to bring over one of the large cotton towels that were stacked near the pool for anyone wanting to go swimming, and he told Lindsey to take off his shirt.

"I need to give it to my housekeeper for laundering before the wine sets in."

Lindsey didn't seem to like the idea of doing this, but Mia also joined in asking that he take it off. "Come on, Kyle, honey, it's a pool party after all. Let's both take a dip."

She stripped down to the bikini she wore under her clothes. Reluctantly, Lindsey pulled off his shirt, and while he did this, Bogle used the opportunity to snap several photos.

Chapter 14

Griffin knew Los Angeles like the back of his hand, having spent eighteen months there not too long ago seducing wealthy married women and stealing their cars, which he would later sell to a chop shop. They probably all knew, or at least strongly suspected, that he was the one who took their cars, especially since he'd dump them right afterwards, but since none of them wanted their husbands to know that they were being unfaithful, none of them did anything about it other than file an insurance claim. Griffin was careful that way, only choosing women who had too much to lose to let their affairs become known. He also didn't kill anyone in the greater Los Angeles area, and instead went to San Diego three times and once to Santa Barbara to find his victims. He might've stayed longer in Los Angeles if things hadn't gotten messy with the last married woman he seduced after her husband caught them in bed. This was a violent guy with mob connections who chased Griffin naked out of the house with a butcher's knife, and the guy probably would've killed him if the police hadn't come to his rescue (an irony that still left him shaking his head whenever he thought about it). For obvious reasons, he didn't press charges, and as much as he enjoyed his time in Los Angeles, he realized it would be best to move on.

It was a quarter past eight that night when Griffin pulled up to the left-most garage bay door of the body shop on Telford Street in East Los Angeles and honked twice. The lights were off, and it had been three years since he had last sold a stolen car there. It was possible the business was now legitimate and no longer a chop shop, but it didn't matter if that was the case. He'd still find a shop somewhere in the neighborhood. Even though the place looked closed for the night, if it was still a chop shop someone would be coming out to see him.

He had left San Luis Obispo later than he had originally planned. As much as he had tried to keep the beast from taking over, the cute and slightly plump bride he had his rendezvous with died quicker than he had anticipated, only lasting a half hour. That was disappointing, and he wanted a chance to refine the technique he'd be using on Sheila Proops, so he waited for the husband. It seemed only fair for him to die also, since it was his fault that his bride suffered the horrific fate that she did. What kind of man leaves his newly married wife alone on their honeymoon so he can play a round of golf? When the husband returned to the room, Griffin surprised him by tapping him on the back of the skull with a champagne bottle. Not hard enough to kill him, or even knock him unconscious, but hard enough to crumple him and leave him stunned. Griffin then spent an intimate hour with him before the man succumbed. That was better, although Griffin was still going to have to make some changes to the routine he had devised because he wanted his time with Sheila Proops to last much longer than an hour. Afterwards, of course, he had to take a shower, and because of all this, he didn't leave San Luis Obispo until five.

Lights came on in the body shop and the garage bay door opened. A short, wiry man in his twenties signaled for Griffin to drive the BMW into the open bay, and then for Griffin to get out of the car. The man closed the garage bay door and gave Griffin a hard look.

"We're closed. What are you doing here?" he asked.

"It's been three years, but I used to do business here. Call Montez, tell him Pretty Boy's back."

The man's look turned skeptical, but he took Griffin's picture, warned him to wait where he was, and then disappeared into a back office. After several minutes, he emerged from the office and signaled for Griffin to join him.

Waiting inside the office wasn't Montez, but an older, heavyset man whom Griffin recognized from when he used to do business there.

"Where's Montez?" Griffin asked.

"He's not around anymore," the man grunted in a raspy voice. "A change of management."

This man's eyes remained half lidded as he stared at Griffin. Finally, he pointed a thick index finger at him and asked where he'd been the last few years.

"It makes me wonder if someone's working with the *chota* when they disappear like you did, and then come back as if nothing happened."

Griffin laughed at the thought of that. "I'm not working with police, FBI, or anyone else. I left LA suddenly due to health reasons."

"Such as?"

"A pissed-off husband who couldn't take a joke, and because of that he wanted to bury a butcher's knife into my chest. He might still want to, for all I know."

The heavyset man, who Griffin vaguely remembered was named Bruno (although he wasn't sure whether that was the man's first or last name), showed two gold teeth when he grinned. "How long have you been back?"

"Less than an hour. This is my first stop."

Bruno nodded as he made a decision. "Strip."

"Is that really necessary?"

"I'm afraid so."

Griffin shrugged and took off his clothes to show he wasn't wearing a wire. The short, wiry man carefully searched each item to make sure that there were no hidden listening devices. The clothes were handed back to Griffin and Bruno told him to get dressed. Bruno then got up from his desk and left the office while his assistant kept Griffin company. When he returned, he sat back behind his desk, and without saying a word, unlocked a drawer, counted out a stack of bills, and placed them in front of Griffin.

He picked the money up and thumbed through it.

"Fifteen hundred dollars," he said. "You're kidding?"

"That's the going rate now. You don't like it, don't take it."

Griffin knew the guy was trying to take advantage of him. The BMW chopped into parts would net at least fourteen grand, and three years ago he would've been paid 3500 for the car.

"How about making it two grand? You'd still be ripping me off."

"I can't do that. Economics of this business have changed since you were last here. But next time, maybe I'll be able to give you a better price."

Griffin rolled the bills up tightly and slipped them into his pocket. Given how tense the room had gotten, he knew if he didn't do this, he would've gotten shot in the back of the head when he tried leaving. But even if he didn't have to worry about being killed, he would've taken the money. He certainly didn't want the police to find the car and discover that Bryan Tasker's killer had driven to Los Angeles. It was more important to him to see the BMW disappear from the face of the planet than any extra money he might've gotten from it.

Griffin told Bruno that he needed to get his duffel bag and back-pack from the BMW, and then he'd be on his way. "Can you make sure anything else left in the car disappears?"

"Sure."

Bruno stayed in the office. His underling accompanied Griffin as he collected his belongings.

Chapter 15

When Morris returned home, Parker scampered to the door wearing a small toga and a laurel wreath on his head, his tail wagging furiously.

"Et tu, Parker?" he asked.

The bull terrier let out one of his excited pig grunts.

Natalie also came to the door, grinning widely. "I just wanted to remind you we'll be in Rome in eight days," she said.

"I can see that." Morris gave Natalie a quick kiss, then dropped to one knee so he could greet Parker properly by vigorously rubbing the dog's muzzle. Parker responded by pushing his head hard into Morris's body, his rear end squirming wildly as his tail wagged even faster. "How'd you get him from pulling off this costume?"

"It wasn't easy. We've been at it for the last hour. You're home late."

Morris nodded. He unfastened the toga and removed the wreath from Parker's head, then stood up and grimaced as he straightened his back. "As part of my ongoing efforts to wrap up loose ends before our trip, I met with Annie Walsh after her shift."

"How's Annie?"

"Thirsty. I bought her several mojitos. Also as far as I can tell, she's still holding the homicide department together."

"Hmm. About your ongoing efforts. How's that coming?"

"Pretty good. Fred closed a burglary investigation. I lined up another movie-consulting job this afternoon, but that won't be starting until after we get back. Other than that, the only other investigation that requires my attention is the one Annie's helping out on. Everything else is grunt work. Background checks, stuff like that."

"No serial-killer cases?"

Natalie said that as a joke, but Morris had picked up an underlying note of worry in her tone. As if he might actually take on something like that before their trip.

"No, not a chance. And as far as I know, Los Angeles is serial killer–free right now."

"Good." She took hold of his hand. "You must be hungry."

"Starving, actually."

"I've got takeout from Seven Star warming in the oven."

"Kung pao chicken?"

"Yep. Also pork fried rice and Peking ravioli."

Morris twisted his neck so he could kiss his wife on the cheek. "Nat, one of the many reasons I wanted to marry you. You know what I want before I know it myself."

She laughed at that. "How many years now have we been going to Seven Star?"

"At least ten."

"At least fifteen. When we go there do you ever get anything other than what I picked up?"

Morris pursed his lips as he thought about it. "Maybe not, but still, takeout from Seven Star is exactly what I'm in the mood for."

"It's always what you're in the mood for after you meet Annie for drinks."

Morris raised an eyebrow at that, but didn't ask his wife how she knew he was meeting the homicide detective. They continued holding hands as they walked together to the kitchen, with Natalie's slender, petite body playfully brushing against Morris's. She sat at their small oak kitchen table while Morris went to retrieve the food from the oven. His cell phone rang. Charlie Bogle. Natalie indicated for him to take a seat while she got the food together for him.

"Did you have an interesting evening?" Morris asked.

"I'd say so. Our client knows how to throw a shindig. Good food, tasty cocktails, stimulating conversations, and of course interesting guests, including our target, who I'm guessing did some prison time."

"From something he said?"

"No, he's too smooth an operator for that. But after I paid a waitress to trip and dump a glass of red wine on him, I was able to see that his shirt was covering some amateurish-looking homemade ink. I took some photos, and I'm betting we identify them as prison tats."

"Okay, good. Any chance his business venture is real?"

"I don't think so. He said all the right things, but he didn't seem eager enough to take my money and I'm guessing that's because he's working a larger con. Something else happened also. As you know, your Hollywood buddy, Stonehedge, loaned me some accessories so I could come off as wealthy. A gold chain that's probably worth more than my car. A pair of sunglasses that I could use to pay my next month's mortgage. What he also did was make a deal with a Rodeo Drive jewelry store to let me borrow a ridiculously expensive watch, some brand called Audemars Piguet. You know me, usually nerves of steel, but I'll admit when I found out what the damn thing was worth, I felt uneasy wearing it out of the store without armed guards protecting me. Lindsey did a good job of hiding the fact, but he knew what the watch was worth the moment he saw it, and I caught a fleeting calculating look from him where he was trying to think of how he could take it away from me. Of course, I can't prove that last part, but I've been around enough cons and criminals on the job to know what I saw."

"Anything else?"

"He's not twenty-six. Not a chance. I'd peg him at thirty-two. That's about it for now, at least until we identify those tattoos."

Morris got off the phone. He nodded to Natalie and told her that things were looking good with his one last investigation. "I think we'll wrap it up tomorrow," he told her.

He then dug into his dinner and only fell for a few of Parker's mooching tricks.

Chapter 16

Adam Felger had a hard grin etched on his face when he entered Morris's office. Morris had brought Parker with him that morning, and the bull terrier lay by his feet as if he were snoozing. His ears perked up, but he otherwise showed no reaction to Felger.

MBI's computer and hacking specialist said, "The guy's name isn't Kyle Lindsey. It's Chuck Macon. You want to know how I found that out?"

"You matched one of his tattoos to one used by a prison gang."

"That's right. The WZB. A gang unique to New Mexico prisons."

"WZB?"

"The Warzone Boys, the warzone being a tough neighborhood in Albuquerque."

"Which is where Macon is from."

"Correct. The prison identified him from photos I sent over. Macon served six years there for grand larceny and was released ten months ago. I figured you'd want to know this right away, so I haven't dug any deeper yet, but I'll get the court to send over his trial transcript if you want."

"Do that." Morris's fingertips drummed lightly on the surface of his desk as he considered this development. "Also get a copy of his police record."

Felger nodded and left. Morris didn't bother to ask him whether he thought Macon had assumed the identity of a real Kyle Lindsey, or whether the Lindsey identity had been manufactured and the credit reports and high school record that Felger had found were fake. FBI agent Julie Crasmore out of the New York office owed him a favor, and she would be able to answer that, and Morris planned on giving her a call. He picked up the phone, but instead of Crasmore he called Annie Walsh.

"You must be psychic," Walsh told him. "I was just about to call you. Do you remember Marty Wright? He used to work robbery, but he's now working organized crime, and he was able to identify the boss man from your photos. Pavlo Lebed. A Ukrainian mobster who's beginning to make a name for himself. Murder, bank robbery, prostitution, extortion, blackmail, shakedowns, to name just a few of his budding criminal enterprises. According to Marty, a really bad dude, so you should be careful. Marty says you can call him and he'll give you more."

She gave him Marty Wright's number. Morris thanked her, told her he owed her one.

"You bet you do."

"Anytime you want a job at MBI, you know you've got one here."

"That's what you keep telling me."

"I mean it."

"Yeah, but you also told me you've sworn off murder investigations. The job would be too boring."

"You'd still get to tangle occasionally with characters like Pavlo Lebed."

"Still too boring for me."

Parker opened his eyes and lifted his head as if he were curious as to how Morris would respond to that.

"Sometimes boring can be good," he said.

The bull terrier grunted as if in agreement, and lay back down.

Chapter 17

Perlmutter sat back in his chair, bleary-eyed, wondering what he had gotten himself into. He had been at the library since nine thirty that morning bent over a microfilm reader, and this was the first break he had taken. He didn't know much about the Skull Cracker Killer (SCK) when he had tossed out the idea to Lawrence Getzler about making a movie focusing on SCK's wife, but after spending four hours reading every newspaper article he could find about the killings that took place in New York, the subsequent killings that happened in Los Angeles, and the investigations that had gone on since then, it seemed obvious to him that Sheila Proops was the original SCK, and that she had gotten her sad sack of a husband to continue the killings in Los Angeles.

Wow. That was what he mouthed to himself several times as he tried to make sense of what he had read. It was inconceivable that Proops was not in prison, although to be fair, she didn't fully escape justice. One of her New York killings had left her partially paralyzed and in pretty rotten health. A chill ran down his spine as he thought about approaching this woman—who had to be a twisted and deranged serial killer—for her life story. If he hadn't all but gotten Getzler's blessing, he would've walked away from this, because this wasn't the kind of movie he had imagined making. That one would've been about an innocent and naïve woman married to a monster; someone completely unaware of her husband's horrific crimes. But this would be something very different. As he thought about what the true Sheila Proops movie would be, he was stunned to find himself excited by the idea. In his mind, he began seeing scenes of the movie playing out, and he started shaking as he realized just how big of a block-buster he potentially had on his hands. That if he made this, he'd be exploding on the scene just as his idol Orson Welles once did with *Citizen Kane*.

He had brought a pen and pad with him, and as fast and furiously as he could write he scribbled down the ideas as they popped into his head.

An hour later he had filled the pad of paper and he sat back, exhausted.

Griffin treated himself to a night at the Hotel Bel-Air. It was damn expensive. Six hundred and forty-five dollars, but he decided he had earned this luxury after driving all the way from Seattle. Besides, the decision to shell out the money for a night's stay was already paying dividends. One of their guests, a paper-thin blonde in her late forties who'd had enough Botox injections to leave her face a hard plastic shell, had slipped him her room number while he was having breakfast at one of the hotel restaurants. Maybe he'd make her one of his victims, or maybe he'd only steal her car. He'd decide which when the time was right.

He had lounged in bed until ten that morning and had lingered at breakfast over a plate of Belgian waffles and a pot of coffee. This had left him getting a late start, and he didn't leave the hotel until after checkout time. It wasn't until two o'clock that he finished the paperwork on a used Honda Accord. The car had 200,000 miles on it, bald tires, and spongy brakes, and it still cost him $1900, which he paid in cash. He was being ripped off, but he didn't bother haggling over the price. He needed transportation to Sheila Proops's home in Simi Valley, and he couldn't very well take a taxi or arrange for an Uber ride. Besides, the car was temporary, and the money he spent on it didn't matter. From what he had read, Proops was wealthy. He was sure he'd find a cache of hidden money somewhere in her home. If not, he would later be able to find plenty of wealthy women in Los Angeles who would have expensive cars for him to steal. Money had never been much of an issue for him. He always found ways of getting enough of it.

He made a mistake taking 405 North instead of US 101. Once he passed Vanowen Street traffic inched painfully until he reached the exit for 118 West. What should've been a fifty-minute drive to Sheila Proops's home on the outskirts of Simi Valley ended up taking two hours. Whenever he'd find himself growing tense, he'd calm himself by imaging the things he would soon be doing to Proops, and this would invariably leave him smiling. By the time he pulled into her driveway, he was feeling quite relaxed.

He wasn't being sloppy, parking the car at her home. There was an old, beat-up sedan parked in front of the house, and that was what would draw people's attention. But even if anyone later remembered seeing his Honda parked in the driveway, it wouldn't matter. The odds were good that if a neighbor saw it, he'd get the make or color wrong when he reported it to the police. Even if the neighbor got the description of the car right, and the salesman who sold him the Honda later connected it to Griffin, it still wouldn't matter since he had used one of his fake driver's licenses when he bought the car, so the police would be looking for Wade Hannifin from Leadville, Colorado. Any description the salesman might give of a lean, very good-looking man in his early thirties would end up fitting half the hopeful actors scrambling to gets jobs in Hollywood. So while he could've been anal-retentive about it and found a place to park where no one would remember seeing his used Honda, why bother? Besides, he planned on driving to a deserted strip mall in East LA later that night and setting the car on fire.

Griffin closed his eyes and imagined the beast rising until it filled his consciousness. Soon he could feel the beast's ferocity coursing through him like an electric current. He opened his eyes, his lips stretched into a harsh grin. Never had he been so on edge to kill as he was right then. He forced himself to take several deep breaths. He needed to control himself, otherwise he'd be ripping Sheila Proops to pieces within minutes of starting on her, and what he wanted instead was a slow dance that would last for hours. It wasn't going to be easy, though, given how enormous the beast had grown in his mind, and how the beast's demonic red eyes burned like fire into Griffin's very soul.

He took another deep breath and held it in until he could better compose himself. Then another one, this one even deeper. Once his facial muscles relaxed and his grin disappeared, he left the car, walked to the door, and rang the bell. A middle-aged black woman with a thick scowl answered.

"You here about the job?" she asked gruffly with a noticeable Haitian accent.

Griffin had no idea what she was talking about, but he nodded.

"About time someone came," she grumbled.

He followed her into the ranch-style house. After a couple of steps, she thought better of her decision to bring him to Proops, and told Griffin to wait where he was. "Better I talk to her first," she said, her expression the same as if she'd bitten into an especially sour lemon.

Griffin didn't mind waiting, and he watched as this woman disappeared into the house. She didn't go far, because only seconds later he heard her telling Proops that a man was there for the caregiver position. Sheila Proops's voice was too weak for him to make out her response, but he had no trouble hearing the Haitian woman subsequently yelling at her, her voice growing increasingly exasperated.

"Oh no, you're going to see this man, and you're not going to give me none of your nutty excuses why you ain't! I told you up front I'm only temporary 'til you get someone permanent, and I ain't staying here a minute longer than I have to! You don't see him, I'm leaving right now!"

He strained to hear what Proops said next, but he couldn't make it out. She must've capitulated, though, because the Haitian woman returned shortly afterwards. While she appeared at first to be mumbling to herself in a hot, agitated way, she told him that the lady would see him now, and he followed her from the hallway to a modest living room where Sheila Proops sat in a wheelchair.

Griffin had seen a photo of her in one of the newspaper stories, but it was still a shock seeing her in person. She wasn't exactly tiny, since she was probably five foot six, but she appeared shriveled, her flesh desiccated, and her body twisted in an unnatural way as if she were a gnarled carving done out of a large piece of driftwood.

Proops sat morosely, refusing to look at Griffin, and the Haitian woman's exasperation seemed to grow as she watched this. With her hands balled on her hips, she threatened, "You better behave yourself, or I'm right out the door. You better believe I am!"

The left side of Proops's mouth pinched into an angry, bitter circle, while the right side continued to droop unnaturally, but she consented to twist her neck and look at Griffin with cold, pale eyes. He smiled at her and was amused to see the left side of her mouth also twist upwards.

"I want to talk to him alone," she said in a painfully slow manner, as if it took a great deal of effort to push out each word.

"Fine with me," the Haitian woman said. "I'll go run errands. But you better behave yourself." She turned to Griffin. "Don't let her chase you out of here. You be here when I get back."

Proops made a soft wheezing that could've been laughter. "Oh, he'll be here, don't worry about that."

The woman gave Proops a look as if she were crazy, and then hurried out of the room as if she couldn't get out of the house fast enough. Sheila Proops waited until the front door slammed shut before telling Griffin that she had once been very pretty.

"Is that so?"

She nodded in a slow and deliberate manner. "Less than six years ago, but that doesn't matter." She paused for a moment as if she were gathering her strength, then, "I know why you're here."

He raised an eyebrow. "I'm not here about the job?"

"No, of course not," she said in her painstakingly slow cadence, as if it took everything she had to spit out each word. "The reason you think that you're here is because you want to kill me."

The woman was full of surprises. Griffin had to give her that.

He gave an exaggerated look of astonishment, and asked, "Why would you think that?"

"Please, don't treat me like an idiot. I recognized you immediately for what you are."

Griffin had had his fun, but his patience was quickly growing thin. It took Proops so damn long to spit out each word. Still, he reminded himself, there was no reason to be in a rush to get started, and he was curious about what she thought she'd recognized.

"What do you think I am?" Griffin asked.

"You're like me. Someone who has to kill."

She made that wheezing sound again that could've been laughter. "You look so incensed," she said. "Like I've insulted you."

"Of course I'm insulted," Griffin admitted, a hotness flushing his face. "I'm nothing like you. I don't need to draw attention to what I do. I'm more than happy staying in the shadows instead of being a publicity whore who kills only so the media makes me famous and gives me a cute name. It's disgusting what you did."

Her left eye sparkled while her right eye remained dead. "A true artist," she forced out. Even though only the left side of her mouth worked, she was still able to smile in a bitingly condescending way.

"Would it surprise you to know I killed hundreds before I began killing them the way I did in New York to earn me that name?"

That did surprise him. Quite a bit, actually. He took a seat on the armchair across from her, and began seeing her in a different light than he had earlier.

In her painstakingly slow method, she explained, "I became the Skull Cracker Killer not for fame, but because I discovered killing them that way was what I needed. That was the only way to release the pressure inside so I could breathe freely."

Griffin nodded to himself as he considered this. "It doesn't change anything. I'm still going to do what I came here for."

"Of course you are. But you didn't come here to kill me. Not really."

He smiled at her with a confidence that he was no longer feeling. Without saying another word to her, he got up from the chair and wandered over to the kitchen. He walked around the room opening drawers so he could take inventory of what she had. He picked up a solid oak rolling pin and felt its heft. That would work just fine on the Haitian woman when she returned. He would give her a little tap on the back of the skull; only hard enough to knock her to the floor, and then he would take his time doing things to her, and he would do all of this in front of Sheila Proops. He was beginning to feel an affinity to the woman who was once the Skull Cracker Killer, and he figured he'd let her enjoy one last killing. But no matter what kinship he was beginning to feel, he was still going to turn his attention to Proops after he finished with the Haitian woman.

Griffin moved back to the living room and sat in the armchair across from Proops, and slapped the rolling pin into his open palm as he waited. He wasn't going to say anything to her, but her last comment nagged at him, and when he saw the way the good half of her face had formed a cat-who-swallowed-the-canary kind of smile, he couldn't help himself.

"Why am I here if it isn't to kill you?" he asked.

The half of her face that was smiling grew more impish. "For guidance."

"That's ridiculous," he said.

"No, not at all. You came because you want the same infamy I stumbled into."

He shook his head. "You're wrong," he insisted.

"Once you stop lying to yourself you'll realize the truth. With my help and mentorship, I can make you the most infamous serial killer who ever lived. And that's what you really want."

Griffin tried to tell her she was wrong, but he found that he couldn't. He got up and went back to the kitchen so that he could put the rolling pin away. When he returned he sat quietly and listened to Sheila Proops's proposal.

Chapter 18

Morris had brought Parker along with him, and as he was directed, went around to the back of the Chinese restaurant on North Broadway and rang the bell by the delivery entrance. A man came to the door and stared at Morris in stony silence. When Morris had made the arrangement he told the person he talked with that he would be bringing his bull terrier, so the man must've known who Morris was, but he still waited for Morris to give the agreed-upon password before he stepped aside and let him into the restaurant's kitchen area. As the man led Morris past pans of frying pork and other sizzling meats, Parker let out a few angry grunts over the fact that he wasn't getting any of this food, but Morris held a tight leash and Parker behaved himself.

Morris was brought to a room off to the side of the kitchen. The man who had escorted him knocked once on the closed door, and then waited with his arms crossed over his chest for Morris to open the door and walk in. Sitting alone at a round table for six with a smorgasbord of noodles, beef, chicken, duck, and shrimp dishes was Mishka Stus. Earlier Morris had contacted Marty Wright from the organized-crime division, and Marty had helped him arrange a clandestine meeting with Stus, who worked inside of Pavlo Lebed's organization and was one of Wright's informants. Wright, though, had warned Morris to be careful with anything Stus said.

"Mishka's a lying prick," Marty had told him. "I think Lebed uses him to feed me misinformation, but every once in a blue moon I get something useful out of him."

Stus, a round man in his forties, was in the process of chewing and swallowing a mouthful of food. He took a quick swig of beer, then gave Morris a blank stare, his eyes half lidded.

"You have something for me," he said as a statement and not as a question.

Morris had carried a briefcase into the room with him. He took an envelope from it and tossed it onto the table. Inside was six hundred dollars, the amount that he had agreed to pay the informant. Stus thumbed through the envelope and, satisfied, he slipped it into his inside jacket pocket. Morris took a seat next to Stus while Parker stood at attention, his muzzle less than a foot from the Ukrainian's leg. Stus gave the dog a nervous look.

"Please move the animal," Stus said.

Morris ignored him and said, "I'm throwing that money away paying you."

Stus glanced again uneasily at Parker and squirmed in his seat to move further away from the dog, while Parker bulled his way forward another few inches to keep the distance between them the same. Stus must've realized that Morris had no intention of pulling the dog away because he didn't bother repeating his request, and instead wiped a handkerchief over his brow and asked Morris why he thought he was throwing his money away.

"Because I already know Kyle Lindsey is a fraud," Morris said. "An FBI agent confirmed earlier this afternoon that his real name is Chuck Macon, and that his Kyle Lindsey identity was manufactured four months ago. That was when his fake high school record and bogus credit reports were added. I already have enough to give my client so that he can send Macon back to prison." He pulled a thick manila folder from his briefcase and placed it on the table in front of him. "I'm giving that to my client this evening. Whatever Lebed was planning with Macon, it's over."

Stus blinked several times as he looked at the folder, then glanced down to give Parker another nervous look. He tried to inch further away, which caused the dog to bull his way closer by several more inches.

"Why are you here then?" he asked.

Morris shrugged. "Partly my own curiosity, partly so I can give my client as accurate a report as possible. Before coming to Los Angeles, Macon had spent six years in prison in New Mexico for stealing forty grand in jewelry from a wealthy woman he had formed a relationship with. The trial transcript is also in that folder. I'm guessing he found himself owing your boss a good deal of money, and he sold Lebed a scheme of getting a far bigger amount, and that his scheme involved Mia Dickerson. I'm also guessing that as part of their scheme your boss bought Macon his Kyle Lindsey identity. According to my FBI contact, something like that probably would've cost ten grand. How am I doing so far?"

Stus once more patted his forehead with his handkerchief. This time he also wiped his neck with it. "I must ask you again to move your dog. He is making me very nervous," the informant said.

"He should be."

Stus's eyes opened wide with surprise at that answer. "Why is that?"

"My dog has an uncanny ability to tell when someone is lying. If you lie to me, he'll let me know."

This was utter rubbish. Parker was acting the way he was because he was hoping to mooch some of the Chinese food, especially the twice-cooked pork, but Morris had said that convincingly enough that Stus appeared to believe him. A tremble could be heard in the Ukrainian's voice as he asked what the dog would do if someone lied.

"He'll rip into your leg the same as if it were a slab of bacon."

Hearing Morris say the word *bacon* caused Parker to let out one of his pig-like grunts, and hearing that grunt caused the round man to jump a bit in his seat and for his skin color to drop several shades.

"I'm very nervous right now because of that animal," Stus said. "Maybe he will mistake my being afraid for lying?"

"Usually he doesn't make that mistake. How'd Macon get mixed up with your boss?"

"You guessed it already," Stus said as he kept one eye fixed on the bull terrier. "He owed a lot of money from gambling debts. Maybe sixty thousand." He stopped for a moment to wipe more sweat from his brow. "I'm not sure the exact amount. Pavlo Lebed bought the debt from a bookmaker that Macon was foolish enough to use."

"Because nobody in their right mind would make bets directly with Lebed."

"True," Stus agreed. "There are some who do. But there will always be some foolish people in this world."

"What happened next?"

Stus shrugged as he kept a careful eye on Parker. "They came to an arrangement of sorts."

"To target Mia Dickerson?"

Stus shook his head. "Not then," he said. "At that time simply for him to find a rich girl."

"For what purpose? Kidnapping? Blackmail? Extortion?"

Stus made a face as if he were trying to figure out a way not to answer the question. Morris released several more inches of slack on Parker's leash, and the dog bulled his way closer to the Ukrainian. The dog was frustrated enough that he hadn't been able to mooch any food yet that he let out an irritated bark.

Hurriedly, Stus said, "Whatever their plans originally were, they changed once Macon thought he could talk that girl into marrying him."

"Why? Mia Dickerson doesn't have a trust fund for him to raid, nor does she have any money of her own."

Stus looked absolutely miserable. He said, "But the father is wealthy, and she is the only one who would inherit his wealth if something were to happen to him. As long as Macon could convince her to marry him without her insisting on a prenuptial agreement, he would end up with half of that wealth."

Or all of it if Mia was also later murdered. Morris had been warned about how ruthless Pavlo Lebed was, but this even caught him off guard.

"I've been more honest with you than I had planned," Stus admitted unhappily. "You now know everything I know about this matter. As you can see, your animal hasn't bitten me, so I haven't lied. I beg of you, can you please pull him away from me?"

"In a moment," Morris said. He pointed at the dish of twice-cooked pork. "Can I have that?"

Stus made a face as if he were confused by the question, but he nodded.

"He earned it, after all," Morris said. He took the pork dish and put it on the floor for Parker. The dog robustly attacked the plate of food. A gleam shone in Stus's eye as he watched this.

"That animal was never judging the truthfulness of what I was saying," he complained bitterly. "He only wanted my food."

"Exactly," Morris said.

Parker had licked the plate clean. He let out a couple of his excited pig grunts, and turned to the Ukrainian underling, his tail wagging.

* * *

Morris waited until he had left the restaurant before calling his client. "I'm done with your investigation," he said. "I'd like to meet with you right away. Tonight if possible."

"Is it as bad as I thought?" Dickerson asked.

"Worse."

Chapter 19

The long game or the short one.

Heads or tails.

Chuck Macon flipped an imaginary coin in his mind. The short game wasn't even a possibility until yesterday, and before then it hadn't occurred to him that he could attract a rich sap into investing millions into his bogus company idea. The only reason he came up with his fake fantasy-sports venture was to provide cover so that Mia and her pain-in-the-ass dad wouldn't have a clue as to what he was really up to, and it was a stroke of luck that he had settled on the idea he did.

He shook his head in awe as he thought about the pool party and how that Bill Hodges character seemed to be just dying to throw money at him. The more Macon thought about it, the more plausible the short game seemed. He could get someone to play a brilliant (and hard to understand) mathematician, as well as find a starving math PhD candidate from one of the local colleges to scribble out dozens of esoteric and mind-numbing formulas and algorithms that could pass as something legitimate. He'd also have no problem faking up to a year's worth of results that would look like the real thing as long as someone didn't study it too closely, and it also wouldn't be hard to find a couple of slick actors to pose as his business partners. If it worked, it would mean a twenty-million-dollar payoff. There would be expenses, and of course, that savage Pavlo Lebed would take a million off the top, and then 70 percent of what was left, but that would still leave him over five million.

His throat got so dry that he could barely swallow as he thought about what he could do with that kind of money. Macon took a long pull on a bottle of Bud, nearly draining it. *Five million dollars!* Jesus.

A much bigger payoff than the long game, which would've netted him about a million, maybe twice that much if Lebed was planning what he suspected. Still, even if it ended up being a million it wouldn't be bad, but nowhere near what five million would allow him to do. The short game, though, had bigger risks. When he met with Pavlo Lebed earlier that afternoon and told him about these new developments, the Ukrainian mobster's eyes dulled to the color of pewter as he listened. Macon was convinced that Lebed was only humoring him, and felt foolish as he continued explaining how they could pull off this short game. By the time he finished detailing it, he was sure Lebed was going to insist that they stick to their other plan, so it came as a shock when the Ukrainian told him that this new idea had merit.

"A nicer payoff," Lebed said. "You sure this man is stupid enough to take the bait?"

"I think so. He seemed to be salivating over the thought of it."

"Interesting," Lebed mused, his thick lips pursed. He gave the matter some additional thought, then said, "Contact him next week. String him along. See how easy it will be to reel him in. But if this Hodges discovers your company is a fake, it will ruin our other plans."

Macon nodded in agreement, because it was true. That was the risk. The Ukrainian mobster showed him an especially grim smile.

"If that were to happen," Lebed said, "I will be very unhappy, and I will still collect the debt you owe me. You understand what I will do to collect my money, correct?"

Macon nodded. He understood fully what the Ukrainian mobster would do to him. Lebed had demonstrated this early on, bringing Macon to a makeshift surgery room in the basement of one of Lebed's buildings so that he could watch as a man was strapped down to an operating table and his organs harvested. While this happened, Lebed explained to Macon how this man owed him a large debt, and disappointed him badly by failing to do what was asked of him.

Macon picked up the nearly empty Bud bottle and frowned at it. He pushed himself off the sofa so that he could get another beer from the fridge. Lebed had told him that he would leave the decision to Macon on whether to stick with their current plan or to try this potentially more lucrative scheme, and that he better choose wisely. He had a lot of serious thinking to do and he was glad Mia's annoying friend Courtney came by earlier to drag her away for some shopping.

Mia might look nice in a bikini, but she could be clingy and demanding as hell, and it would be near-impossible to think this through if she were in the apartment—and he needed to do some serious thinking. While the long game was safer, it still had its share of risks, especially if that Ukrainian mobster was planning what Macon suspected.

He brought the fresh Bud back to the sofa, twisted off the top, and took a long drink, emptying half the bottle. His thoughts drifted to how he had ended up in this situation. During his six years in prison he thought he had perfected his football-handicapping methods. The last two years of his incarceration, the bets he made on paper would've netted him two hundred and fifty grand if he could've placed them with a bookie. Of course, once he was out, he had to hit the mother of all cold streaks, and before he knew it he owed his bookie fifty-five grand, which was money he didn't have. He was expecting to get a beating, maybe even some broken bones, and he knew he'd have to work out a payment plan and find some wealthy ladies to rip off, but instead he got Pavlo Lebed and a couple of his goons knocking on his door, with Lebed explaining how he now owned him. Macon knew the instant he looked into the Ukrainian's eyes that was true. He didn't need the demonstration that Lebed later provided for him to fully understand the jeopardy he was in.

Lebed, though, offered him not only an out, but a way to pick up some money, possibly even a good deal of money. The long game. As long as he could find a gullible enough girl, it would work. And he found her when he found Mia. The original scheme changed, though, once he realized Mia wanted to marry him, and became something far more lucrative. Three weeks after he and Mia were officially engaged, he asked Lebed when he was going to arrange for Mia's dad to die. Because the new plan had her inheriting her dad's wealth, which was roughly nine million dollars, and Macon taking half of that when they divorced.

"Don't be in such a rush," Lebed said with a smile that never came close to reaching his eyes. The Ukrainian gave him what was supposed to be a playful tap on the jaw, but it was still hard enough to rattle Macon's teeth. "Let the man first enjoy seeing his daughter get married."

"I'd rather you do it sooner. I don't think he trusts me."

"That wouldn't be smart," Lebed said. "If she inherits his money before she marries you, a smart lawyer might insist she sign a prenup.

Better that we wait, and that you work harder to make the father trust you. You're clever enough. Figure out a way."

"I don't know. If Dickerson's alive, he'll probably push Mia into making me sign a prenup."

"I don't think so. This dumb girl, she wants to be a starving actress, yes? So her father knows she'll never make anything. You, on the other hand, could make millions with this brilliant company you keep telling him about. He won't want you to sign anything." Then a dark shadow fell over Lebed's eyes. "This discussion is becoming tiresome," he said.

Macon nodded. He understood perfectly well it was time for him to shut up. He also knew the Ukrainian wasn't all that concerned with whether Mia had him sign a prenup. If she did, Lebed would be killing her also. It would take longer that way, since he'd have to wait an appropriate amount of time to kill Mia so the situation wouldn't look too suspicious, but Lebed was going to collect his money. The Ukrainian was probably planning to kill Mia anyway even if there was no prenup, so he could collect the whole inheritance instead of only half of it. The knowledge that Mia was most likely also going to die if Macon chose the long game didn't bother him. The girl was an empty-headed ditz, and if he didn't take advantage of her for his own gain, somebody else would.

The doorbell rang, interrupting his thoughts. He got up and moved silently to the door so he could look out the peephole. Speaking of the devil, standing out in the hallway was Mia's dad. Macon thought about pretending nobody was home, but when he heard a key turning in the lock, he yelled out that he'd be right there, and swung the door open as he manufactured a friendly grin.

It wasn't just Dickerson out in the hallway, but a couple of thick-bodied hired hands. The type of guys with no necks and biceps thicker than Macon's thighs. He knew the moment he saw them that this wasn't good.

"Brett, this is a surprise. Mia's not home," he said.

Dickerson was smiling in an eerie sort of way. "Is that so?" he said as he walked past him and continued on into the condo's living room. "Let me guess: My daughter's out shopping with Courtney? How'd I do?"

Before Macon could answer him, the hired hands also entered the condo. One of them put his arm around Macon's shoulders as if they were best buddies and walked him back into the apartment, while the other closed the door shut and joined them.

"This really is a nice place," Dickerson said as he looked around the room, admiring it.

"Very nice," one of the hired hands agreed. "Top floor. Roomy. Must have cost a bundle."

"It wasn't cheap, that's for sure," Dickerson said. He turned his odd, eerie smile back on as he looked at Macon. "You and Mia enjoying living here?"

"Yes, of course. It's very nice of you letting us stay here."

"I'm not just letting them stay here," Dickerson told one of his hired hands. "I'm also paying their condo fees and other expenses."

"I'll be paying you back once I get this business going," Macon said defensively. "Thanks to you, the other day we might have found our seed money."

"I heard about that," Dickerson said. He turned to one of his hired hands. "Isn't that great?"

"Super," the man said.

Dickerson slapped the side of his head as if he was being absent-minded. He shook his head as he continued to smile at Macon in that odd, eerie way.

"Where have my manners been?" he said. "Let me introduce you to my two business associates. Roy, Zach, meet Charlie. Or is it Chuck?"

Before Macon could run, the hired hand named Roy drove a fist into his stomach. The blow dropped him to his knees. Zach grabbed him under his arms and lifted him to his feet, and Roy again drove his fist into his gut. Macon's body sagged.

"Chuck's looking kind of green," Dickerson said. "Let me find a sheet or something so he doesn't spew over the carpet."

"It's nice carpeting," Roy agreed. "Very plush. A wool fabric?"

"Yep. Top of the line," Dickerson said.

Dickerson left the room while Zach continued to hold up Macon and Roy wandered out onto the balcony. When Dickerson returned, he brought a sheet with him, which he laid out on the floor. Zach dragged Mason to the middle of the sheet. Roy came in from the balcony.

"Nice view from your balcony," Roy said. "I say we dump the creep from it. Let him make a nice big splat below."

Zach frowned at the suggestion. "Better that we mix him in with the foundation being poured for the West Sixth Street construction. Let him just disappear."

"Both have merits," Dickerson agreed.

Macon's stomach muscles were spasming so badly that it was a struggle for him to say anything, but he forced out in a breathless whisper that he hadn't done anything. "My name's not Chuck and I love Mia."

"Incredible," Zach said.

"The chutzpah of this creep," Roy said, shaking his head.

Dickerson balled his fist and struck Macon hard enough in the nose to leave it a bloody mess and bent to the left.

"Chuckie, I know all about your scheme with your Ukrainian gangster friend to kill me and Mia for my money," Dickerson said through clenched teeth, his breathing turning ragged. "So which is it going to be? Drop you seventeen floors onto concrete, or chop you up and throw you into the foundation we're pouring tomorrow?"

Macon had bit his tongue the second time he was punched. He spat out a mouthful of blood. "I'll disappear," he offered in a defeated tone. "Mia will never hear from me again."

"Where's the fun in letting you do that?" Roy complained.

Dickerson held up a finger to silence his associate. "You'll write her a farewell letter?"

Macon winced as he nodded. "Whatever you want me to write," he said.

Chapter 20

Wellesley, Massachusetts, 1997

Ever since he was a toddler, Griffin enjoyed sneaking about the family's large Tudor-style home and finding hiding spots where he could spy on his parents, and now that he was twelve it was no different. That night he had snuck into his mom's large walk-in closet and left the door open a crack so he could watch them. This was the safest place to hide. He could be as quiet as a mouse, and with all the rows of sweaters, blouses, and dresses that his mom had hanging in there, he could scurry behind them and hide if either of his parents came looking for him.

Griffin knew his parents weren't going to be having sex that night, but he wanted to watch them nonetheless. Since that afternoon when his mom found out about the Maguires' cat, she'd been giving him especially accusatory looks, even more than usual, and he wanted to hear what she might say to his dad.

His mom was already in bed, but she wasn't asleep. Instead, she was propped up by several pillows and had her night-table lamp on and was going through the motions of reading a book, but Griffin could tell from her brittle expression that she wasn't concentrating on it and was instead waiting for his dad to join her. Water was running in their master bathroom and Griffin heard his dad gargling and then spitting out mouthwash. A minute later the water turned off and his dad emerged from the bathroom wearing his silk pajamas. From the tense look on his mom's face, Griffin had a good idea what she was dying to talk to him about. Sure enough, she couldn't even wait until his dad had fully lowered himself onto the mattress before launching into it.

"I know Griffin's behind what happened to the Maguires' cat."

The night-table lamp lit up his mom's face, but his dad was mostly hidden in the shadows, so Griffin could only imagine the disgusted look his dad must've shown her when he muttered, "That's absolute rubbish."

"It's not!"

"Keep your voice low," his dad ordered harshly. "I don't want Griffin to have to hear your bizarre accusations. And I further don't want to talk about this at all. Damn it, Mary, just turn your light off already. I'm going to bed."

"We're going to talk about this," his mom insisted stubbornly, although she had consented to lower her voice.

"There's nothing to talk about."

"Our son butchered a cat!"

"You're talking nonsense. Griffin loved that cat. That damn creature was always coming over to our property and following him around."

His mom sat silently for a moment. There was just enough light to show that her mouth was moving as if she were chewing gum. Her voice sounded tired as she finally said, "Griffin's a clever boy. He spent months luring the cat over with food and gaining her trust so that he could do this."

His dad had been lying on his side, but he bolted upright then. Griffin imagined the damning look his dad must've given his mom, as if he couldn't believe what she was saying.

"Are you nuts?" he demanded, his voice a mix of anger and disbelief. "You're going to accuse Griffin of premeditating and carrying out an act like that?"

"That's what our son did. And he didn't just kill that poor thing. He nailed her paws to a tree, and then tortured her with a lighter and knife before finally slicing her open from her neck to her belly."

His dad's voice grew icy as he asked, "What makes you so sure Griffin did this?"

"Alice Connolly saw him in the woods near where Mandy was found."

"Mandy?"

"The name of the Maguires' cat."

His dad made a noise that was somewhere between clearing his throat and snorting, as if he were truly amazed at what she had just said. "It wouldn't surprise me if that crazy broad killed the cat herself."

"Be serious."

"I am serious," he said. "Besides, a lot of kids walk through those woods. So what if she saw Griffin? It doesn't mean a damn thing."

"She saw him less than two hours before that poor animal was found."

"That's why you're going to accuse our son of being a budding psychopath who tortures animals? Because he was probably one of a few dozen kids who walked through those woods that day?"

"He's the only one Alice saw."

"Again, so what?" He swore under his breath, then added, "That old crone seems off to me. I'd bet she has some form of dementia, and she's probably half blind also. Who knows who she actually saw, if she saw anyone. You have no right accusing Griffin of something like this over that kind of flimsy evidence."

"My husband, always the lawyer," she said with disgust.

"You bet I am! When did this happen? The day before Thanksgiving? Anyone could've been going through those woods that day. Not just kids, but transients, or maybe some deviant passing though. What in the world has gotten into you to believe such a horrible thing about our son?"

Griffin held his breath as he waited for his mom to answer. He'd known she'd been suspicious of him, and not just about the cat, but about other things, and he wanted to know why. He'd always been so careful around her. As far as he knew, she never caught him sneaking through the house so he could spy on them. And he had always made a point of being polite and well-mannered around her. So why was she so sure he had done this?

Whatever her reason, she decided not to divulge it and instead simply said, "It must just be my nerves. I'm sorry. Forget I said anything."

She put her book down and turned off the night-table lamp, leaving the room in darkness, as well as leaving Griffin both frustrated and dissatisfied. He knew he had his dad fooled completely. As far as his dad was concerned, Griffin was a good athlete and also a respectful and studious twelve-year-old. A chip off the old block, as his dad liked to say. Somehow, though, his mom had seen through his act, and he wanted to know how that happened. Was she just more perceptive than his dad, or was he making mistakes around her? He was going to have to figure out a way to win back her confidence, because he certainly wasn't going to stop with the Maguires' cat. His next victim was going to be a person. He already had an idea of who he was going to target, and he certainly didn't want his mom accusing him of that death also.

For now, he would wait in the closet until he heard the light snoring sounds his parents made when they slept, and only then would he creep out of his hiding place. He had brought a shish kebab skewer with him, as he almost always did. Usually his mom slept on her side, and what he liked to do was stand quietly in the dark and hold the sharp, pointy end as close as he possibly could to one of her closed eyes, and imagine driving the skewer through the eyelid and deep into her eye. If she was sleeping on her back instead, he'd hold it near her ear and imagine driving the skewer all the way into her brain. He would do this once or twice a week, and it would always help him feel more relaxed and at peace.

Of course, this was all for pretend. There was not a chance that he would actually hurt her with the skewer. He was too young to do something like that and get away with it. Someday, when he was much older and could live on his own, he planned to kill both of them. He frequently fantasized about making them suffer for hours before snuffing out their lives—his mom for being perceptive enough to see through his façade and know what he really was, and his dad for being so utterly clueless. Even if he loved them (whatever that meant), he would still have to kill them. He was their only heir, and he wanted the inheritance. He had no idea how much money they had, but he knew they were wealthy.

Griffin's eyes adjusted to the darkness of the room, and he could make out his dad's form from the glimmer of the clock radio as the older Bolling lay on his side. Within minutes he heard the slight sawing-wood sound of his dad's breathing as he slept. His mom seemed to be having a more fitful time of it as she tossed and turned. That was okay. He could be patient, as he had proved with the Maguires' cat. His mom had been wrong about how long it had taken him to win

Mandy's trust. It wasn't months. Instead it took a year and a half of feeding the cat bits of smoked fish before she would willingly climb into Griffin's lap. Eventually his mom would fall asleep, and if he needed to, he'd wait hours for that to happen.

Yes, he could be exceptionally patient when needed.

Chapter 21

Griffin watched as the McCulloch brothers pelted Craig Myers with snowballs. Myers was a thin and awkward-looking boy with thick glasses, big ears, and a mop of unruly brown hair that never looked properly combed. The first few snowballs hit him in the chest and stomach, and he reacted as if he were being punched by a professional boxer with the way he dropped his schoolbooks and staggered backwards. Jonas McCulloch's next snowball knocked off Myers's glasses while Owen McCulloch nailed him in the jaw at the same moment, and this sent Myers falling into the snow as if he'd been shot.

While Myers struggled to his knees so he could search for his glasses, both McCulloch boys continued to use him as target practice, both of them laughing like donkeys. This stopped when Griffin hit Owen McCulloch flush on the ear with a hard-packed snowball. Owen turned to him, enraged, with his hand clasped over his freshly swollen ear, while Jonas gaped at Griffin, clearly confused as to why he would come to this dorky kid's rescue.

"How about you leave Craig alone," Griffin said.

"How about you mind your business, Bolling," Jonas retorted back.

Owen had been in the middle of packing another snowball when Griffin surprised him. He continued to pack his snowball into something hard that could do damage.

"I should shove this down your throat," Owen said.

Both of the McCulloch brothers were beefy, rawboned boys who liked to get into scraps. Jonas was Griffin's age, while Owen was a year older. Griffin trudged through the snow until he was face-to-face with Owen, and he then slapped the snowball out of Owen's hand.

"You could try to do that," Griffin said, smiling. "But I could also take my dad's crossbow and wait outside your house one day. From fifty yards away I should be able to put an arrow into your knee. Or maybe your balls."

Owen had thirty pounds on Griffin, but as with most predators, he could sense when he was dealing with a more dangerous foe. The fierce stare he gave Griffin wavered and a flicker of doubt showed in his eyes. He took a step back.

"You better watch yourself, Bolling," he threatened somewhat halfheartedly.

Jonas, not being the most eloquent of boys, seemed stymied as to what to add, so he simply yelled out, "Yeah!"

Griffin watched as the McCulloch brothers strode away, and then joined Craig Myers in searching through the snow for the boy's glasses. Myers looked like he was on the verge of tears as he explained to Griffin that he couldn't see much of anything without them.

Griffin pulled the glasses out of the snow and used the sweater he had on under his ski jacket to dry off the lenses. He handed them to Myers, who fumbled with them for a moment before slipping them on.

"Thanks," Myers said. Somewhat sheepishly, he added, "You saved me."

"No problem." Griffin smiled good-naturedly. "The McCullochs are a couple of dumb gorillas, aren't they?"

Myers smiled at that. "Yeah, that's for sure."

Griffin helped this other boy to his feet, then helped him gather up the schoolbooks that he'd dropped. Griffin surveyed the area and said, with an exaggerated sigh, "It looks like because of those two apes we missed our bus. Oh, well. Among other things, I scored a new PlayStation and a sweet stack of videogames for Christmas. You want to come over? It's about a half-mile walk. We could play *Tomb Raider Two*."

"Sure." Myers hesitated for a moment, then, blushing in embarrassment, added, "I used to live in California. I'm sure you know we didn't move here until the beginning of the school year. It's different here, and not just because of the snow and how cold it gets. I've been having a tough time making new friends."

No kidding, Griffin thought. *Why else do you think I'm targeting a weak-ass loser like you?*

"Hey," Griffin said. "You got to meet the McCulloch brothers today."

Myers laughed. "Yeah, but apes like them I could do without. But hey, it's good to meet someone friendly."

Griffin bit hard enough on his tongue to draw blood so that he could keep from bursting out laughing. He had been so patient over the last two months as he waited for the perfect moment to befriend this awkward kid nobody knew or cared about. He should be sending those dumb McCulloch brothers thank you cards for making it so easy for him.

"Same here," he said.

Chapter 22

Wellesley, Massachusetts, 1998

"I don't understand what we're doing out here."

Griffin smiled devilishly and said, "I told you before: We're on a secret mission."

Craig Myers grumbled at that. "How can it be secret if you know what it is?"

"Because you don't."

Myers didn't seem to like that answer. "Come on, Griffin, it's cold and wet out here. Why don't we head back to my house? I've got a batch of new comic books. Or we could watch *Starship Troopers*."

For the last twenty minutes Griffin had been leading the way through the woods toward Morses Pond, and he certainly wasn't going to let them turn back. He'd been putting up with the whiny little bitch for three weeks, waiting for just this opportunity. Contrary to Myers's complaints, it had been an unseasonably warm several days, making it a perfect time to do what he'd been planning. Nobody had seen them heading to the woods, and this was one of the afternoons his mom volunteered at the cat-rescue shelter, which was something she'd started doing after the Maguires' cat was killed. Griffin figured it was some pathetic attempt on her part to assuage her guilt, over what he wasn't sure. Having Griffin as her son? How sick was that? Whatever her reason, it played right into his plans. Since she wasn't home, she wouldn't be able to dispute him when he later claimed that he'd been in his room since returning from school.

"Not until we complete our mission," he insisted.

Myers opened his mouth as if he were going to complain some

more, but instead he clamped his mouth shut. The kid could really be a whiny pain in the ass, and what Griffin wanted to do was nail him by his hands to a tree, and do the same things to him that he did to the Maguires' cat. His mom would be certain he was the one behind Myers's savage murder, and that would destroy her. Besides, it would be such a beautiful and poetic way to kill him. In the end, though, he decided it would be too risky. Old lady Connolly had told more people in the neighborhood than just his mom about seeing him in the woods the day the Maguires' cat went missing. And too many people had witnessed him and Myers acting as if they were best buds over the last few weeks for him to now torture and kill Myers in the same way he did to that cat without the police suspecting him. Unfortunately, Craig Myers's death was going to have to look like an accident. Still, though, it would be satisfying in its own way.

Griffin watched as Myers struggled through less than a foot of slushy snow, slipping and sliding as he fought to keep his balance. He looked like such a ridiculous little clown, and a thought struck Griffin then that was so profound it left him in awe. There were people in this world like Craig Myers who existed only so that he could enjoy killing them. That was their only purpose.

"What?" Myers asked.

Griffin's face reddened as he realized he'd been caught staring at the other boy. "I'm just thinking about what a surprise this secret mission is going to be for you," he said.

Myers nodded as if that made sense. "What do you have in that canvas bag?" he asked.

This was the fourth time Myers had asked him that, and each other time he had said the same thing. *That if he told him, their mission wouldn't be all that much of a secret.* Now, though, he simply told Myers that he'd be finding out soon enough, which was true because he could see the pond through the barren trees. Another five minutes and they'd be there.

"Whatever you got in there, it looks heavy," Craig Myers said.

Griffin shrugged, but otherwise didn't bother answering him. After all, it was a secret, right? As they continued their hike toward the edge of the pond, Griffin listened intently for any other voices. There weren't any, which made sense since there would be no reason for anyone else to be out there. Maybe if the weather hadn't gotten so warm recently, a few hardy souls might've been willing to make the trek out to the pond for skating, but they wouldn't be out there now with the ice so dangerously thin.

When they reached the pond's edge, they stood silently for a long moment; Myers so he could catch his breath (he'd been huffing and puffing the last ten minutes of their hike), and Griffin so he could savor the moment and imagine what was soon going to be happening.

"Okay, now what?" Craig Myers asked.

"Your mission, if you choose to accept it, is to walk across this pond."

Myers gawked at Griffin as if he were telling a joke he didn't get. "You dragged us out here for that?" he asked incredulously.

Griffin shrugged and pulled a hunting knife out of the canvas sack, the same one he had used on the Maguires' cat. It was a beauty: seven-inch stainless-steel blade and a hard wooden laminate handle that felt so perfect when he gripped it. Last summer he had ridden his bike to Newton, and from there took the subway into Boston so he could buy the knife at an Army surplus store on the lower part of Washington Street. He knew his mom had searched his room after the Maguires' cat was found, but their house had many good hiding spots, and in the basement alone he had discovered several that she would never find.

"Either you walk across the pond or I stab you in the eye."

Myers's mouth pinched into a tiny circle. He shook his head and said, "This isn't funny."

Griffin slapped Myers across the face, knocking his glasses off. Then he made a thrusting motion with his knife hand toward Myers's face, and the boy fell backwards onto the ice to avoid being stabbed.

"I swear I'm going to cut out your eye if you don't get moving."

In his panic Craig Myers crab-crawled onto the ice to get away from Griffin. "Why are you doing this?" he cried.

"It's your secret mission," Griffin said, smiling blandly. "Your initiation to prove you're not a pussy. Either you walk across the pond or I'll stab you in the eye. Maybe also I'll cut off your nose. And while I'm at it, your tongue."

"The ice is too thin! I'll fall through it!"

"Not if you're careful enough. You better get moving, or I'm coming out after you."

Myers was sobbing inconsolably as he gingerly got to his feet. His eyes had become red and puffy and his mouth hung open like a knife gash. It was a beautiful sight to Griffin. This was so much better than he could've imagined, even much more so than it had been with the Maguires' cat. There was something euphoric about it. He stood quietly for a moment, soaking in all of the boy's fear. Knowing that he was responsible for it made it all that much sweeter.

"Please don't make me do this," Myers begged, his face now something wretched.

Griffin pulled a stone out of the canvas bag. He had collected dozens of stones for this occasion.

"You better get moving or I'm throwing this at you," Griffin said. "And I've got a whole bag of them. Your only way out of this is to make it to the other side."

Griffin wound up and threw a fastball, hitting Myers in the chest. Last summer he had pitched for his little league team, and his coach had marveled at his accuracy. He would've liked to have hit Myers in the face, but he didn't want to leave any blood this close to the edge of the pond. The boy let out a cry of pain and scrambled several more steps out onto the ice.

"Why are you doing this?" Myers cried.

Griffin could've shared with the boy the revelation he'd had earlier, but he knew Myers wouldn't understand it. Besides, why should he share something like that with someone so meaningless?

"Because I can," he said. He took another stone from the bag and whipped it at the boy, intentionally missing his face by inches. Myers let out a shriek and took several more shaky steps out onto the ice. Griffin whipped another stone at him and hit him squarely in the back, causing Myers to cry and take more steps. Whenever Myers stopped, Griffin would throw another stone, and that would make Myers walk further out. Soon he was out of range of any stones Griffin might throw, and he had no choice but to continue on and try to make it across the pond. By this time he had made it past the halfway mark, and Griffin started worrying about whether he had miscalculated. He was sure the ice was thin enough that Myers would fall through it. The boy was such a skinny runt that maybe he'd actually be able to make it across to the other side. If that happened, Griffin was going to be in serious trouble.

Before he could worry too much about that, the ice broke under Craig Myers, and the boy disappeared into the water. Griffin stood and watched for several minutes. Once he was sure Myers was gone, he turned and headed back home.

Chapter 23

That night while the family was eating dinner at the kitchen table, Craig Myers's mom called. Mary Bolling answered the phone, and her face seemed to age a decade as she listened to whatever Mrs. Myers had to say. It was a quick conversation, and then she called Griffin over to her. Her voice had an odd heaviness to it as she asked whether he had seen Craig Myers after school that day. Griffin had been expecting the call. He shook his head as if he didn't have a clue that anything was wrong.

"Are you sure?"

"Yes, ma'am. I asked Craig if he wanted to come over, but he told me he had something he wanted to do. I tried asking him what, but he wouldn't tell me. It was some sort of big secret. Why, is anything wrong?"

"We don't know. He hasn't come home yet." She took a deep, heavy breath and added, "His parents are worried sick."

Mr. Bolling had been eavesdropping, and he piped in, "I'm sure the boy will turn up."

Mrs. Bolling nodded, although she didn't seem convinced. "I better call Janice back."

Later, at nine o'clock that night, Mary Bolling interrupted Griffin while he was working on his algebra homework to tell him that Craig Myers still hadn't returned home.

"Is there anything else you can tell me?"

As innocently as he could, Griffin asked, "Like what?"

She almost said what was really on her mind. Almost. Griffin could see her caving, though, and instead she asked whether Craig had recently made any new friends. Griffin squinted his eyes so he'd give the appearance of giving the matter the proper amount of serious thought. He nodded as if something had just occurred to him.

"A week ago Craig told me that he was going to be trading some comic books with an older kid. I think someone in high school."

Mary Bolling gripped her fingers as she studied her son's face. "Is there anything else you can tell me about this older boy?"

Griffin squinted even harder as if he were trying to pull a hidden speck of knowledge from the recesses of his brain. He shook his head. "That's all Craig told me about him."

His mom nodded, her face craggy and exhausted, and she left his room. Griffin, of course, had expected all this. During the next couple of weeks there will be a big uproar over Craig Myers's disappearance. That would happen if any kid went missing from a tony, privileged town like Wellesley. People would, of course, be sad for the Myerses, and Griffin would play his part as the best friend who only wished he knew more. Eventually they would find Myers's body at the bottom of Morses Pond, but that wouldn't be until the spring at the earliest, and then it would be a big mystery as to what he had been doing at the pond. People would obviously know that he had broken through the ice and drowned, but they would be torturing themselves trying to figure out why he was trying to walk across the ice, especially his parents. Griffin chuckled to himself as he thought about that.

At ten, he turned on the local news. The third story was about Craig Myers, and they showed a picture of him that must've been taken when he was in California. He had a big, goofy smile on his face and he looked happy. His parents were later interviewed, and his mom cried throughout while his dad (who also wore thick glasses and had big ears, and looked like he must've also been a skinny runt when he was a kid) tried to act brave. As Griffin watched them, he was especially glad he had chosen their son.

The next day, the principal of the school interrupted Griffin's social-studies class to ask Griffin to accompany him to his office. The look on Principal Hargrove's face was worrisome, but Griffin played along as if he didn't have a clue what this was about. All he could figure was that Myers's parents had come to the school and wanted a chance to talk to him, except that it was two thirty and it was strange that they would've waited so late in the day to see him. Griffin knew that wasn't what had happened when he saw the cop waiting for them in Hargrove's office. He wasn't wearing a uniform, but Griffin knew immediately the guy was a cop.

Hargrove cleared his throat and asked Griffin to take a seat. The cop, who was wearing a cheap gray suit and a narrow blue necktie, sat as impassively as stone, his eyes slits as he looked Griffin over. This wasn't right. Griffin knew that. This meant they suspected him of doing something to Craig Myers, but that didn't make any sense. Besides, he was only twelve. He had read about how cops were supposed to have the parents present when they questioned a minor. He realized they would later be claiming that they weren't there to question him, only to ask for his help in searching for the missing Myers boy. Fine, let them be sneaky like that. It didn't matter. His best move would be to play dumb. If he asked why his parents weren't there, that would only make this cop more suspicious.

Hargrove cleared his throat a second time and introduced the cop to Griffin. "This is Detective Stone. I'm sure you know that Craig Myers is missing. The detective would like to ask you a few questions that might help them find Craig."

Griffin nodded, wide-eyed. Even at twelve he had the natural instincts for this, and he bit his bottom lip as if he were trying to keep from crying over the fate of his missing friend. The police detective, though, sat unmoved. He looked at Griffin as if he were some kind of insect. Or maybe a reptile.

"You were with Craig Myers yesterday afternoon," the detective said.

"No, not yesterday."

The detective arched an eyebrow as he consulted a notepad, then looked back at Griffin and made a face at him as if he were full of it. Griffin knew for certain then that something very wrong had happened.

"You weren't walking with Craig by the woods near Weston Road?"

Those were the woods that they had hiked through to get to Morses Pond. Griffin shook his head.

"Craig was seen heading into those woods with another boy. If it wasn't you, who was it?"

Griffin's heart raced. He knew this wasn't good. He needed to remain calm. "I don't know." He looked away from the detective and stared dumbly at his hands, but wouldn't any kid his age do the same? "I went home right after school yesterday, and didn't see Craig."

The detective glanced down at the sneakers Griffin was wearing, as if he were studying them, and then shifted his slitted eyes back to Griffin's. In a voice that was more growl than anything else, he asked, "What type of winter jacket and hat do you wear?"

Griffin realized then that he was doomed. Whoever had seen Craig must've reported that the other boy he was with was wearing a blue ski jacket and a gray knit cap with a fuzzy red wool ball attached. Still, he scrunched up his face as if he was confused by the question, and asked, "Why are you asking me that?"

"Just answer the question."

"But I don't understand. How will it help you to find Craig by knowing that? I told you I went straight home after school yesterday."

Hargrove had been looking increasingly worried, probably realizing that this illegal interrogation of a minor whose dad was a high-profile lawyer could get him in trouble. He cleared his throat a third time and told the detective that was enough. "I believe any further questions you have for Griffin should be asked with his parents present," he said.

Detective Stone's lips twisted upward slightly, forming a brutal smile. "I have one last question for the boy. Is that okay?"

Hargrove didn't seem to like the idea of it, but nodded his consent.

The detective turned his brutal smile on Griffin, and told him that they were searching the woods now. "We have two dozen officers and another forty volunteers. What do you suppose we're going to find?"

"Hopefully Craig alive and well."

The detective looked at him as if he wanted to do nothing more than bash Griffin's head into pulp, but he got up and left the office, and Hargrove escorted Griffin back to class.

Chapter 24

Wellesley, Massachusetts, 1998

Griffin burst out crying during dinner that evening. Earlier, he wasn't sure he'd be able to put on a convincing act, but it turned out he was able to because it wasn't all completely an act. He had screwed up by wearing clothes yesterday that someone could identify him by. His blue ski jacket might be ubiquitous, but how many other boys in Wellesley wore a gray wool cap with a fuzzy red ball attached? He had been confused at first about why the detective seemed to be studying his sneakers, but later that afternoon he figured it out. It had gotten colder last night, and that must've helped preserve the tracks he and Myers made while they hiked to the pond. The police must've made a mold of sorts of his boot prints, and that detective was probably guessing his shoe size. Not only did they have a witness who had seen the jacket and cap he wore, but they'd be able to prove he was with Craig Myers by his boots. Even if his parents were willing to lie to the police about it, enough teachers and other kids that winter had seen him wearing that stuff, so if he tried hiding or getting rid of it, it would be as good as writing a confession to the cops that he had murdered Craig Myers. So he was desperate, and because of that what started off as an act soon became honest-to-goodness blubbering. His parents reacted to it as if they were stunned.

Griffin's eyes quickly became red-rimmed, and he wiped a hand under his nose, clearing away tears and snot. Through his sobbing, he admitted that he had lied earlier and that he had been with Craig yesterday.

His mom gasped, and she brought a hand to her mouth as if she were repulsed by him. A transformation came over his dad as he went into full-blown lawyer mode. He put a hand on Griffin's shoulder.

"Son, settle down and tell me what happened," he said in a cool, dispassionate voice.

Griffin nodded and his sobbing came to a stuttering halt. "Me and Craig hiked to Morses Pond," he said despondently. He wiped his hand again under his nose, and his expression crumbled, leaving him looking like he might start sobbing again. That time it was completely an act, but from the way his dad responded, a convincing one. He first made it look as if it were a struggle to regain control, and then said that Craig bet him that he could walk across the pond and that the boy broke through the ice while trying to win the bet.

"Slow down," Mr. Bolling ordered. "Here, use this napkin to wipe your nose. Why did you two go to the pond in the first place?"

Griffin sniffled several times, used the napkin, then explained how they were just goofing around that afternoon. "Craig was from California, and he'd never seen a frozen pond before. We collected a bag of stones and brought them there so we could throw them at the ice and see if any of them broke through."

His dad nodded as if it made sense for a couple of twelve-year-old boys to do something like that. Griffin peeked at his mom, and he could tell that she suspected he was lying, but was in too much shock to accuse him of it right then.

"Tell me about this bet," his dad said.

More sniffling, then, "After we threw all our rocks, Craig wanted to bet my new PlayStation against his comic-book collection that he could make it across the pond. I thought he was joking, so I said okay. After he took some steps onto the ice, I started getting worried that he'd get hurt, and I yelled at him to come back, but he just kept going. Right before he fell through the ice, he laughed at me, telling me I was only being a chicken about losing my PlayStation to him."

"What happened then?"

Griffin shrugged and looked as miserable as any twelve-year-old could possibly look. His dad was fully buying his act. He peeked again at his mom, and she was ashen and looking at him as if he were a monster.

"I tried going onto the ice so I could help him, but when I got close, the ice started cracking open. There wasn't anything I could do to save him."

His dad was grim-faced as he mulled this over. "To be clear, Craig was the one to offer the bet?" he asked.

Griffin nodded.

"Why didn't you call for help?"

"I knew Craig had drowned and nothing could be done to help him." Griffin squeezed his eyes tight and made a face that was the picture of abject misery. "I also know Mrs. Connolly has been telling people that I did those terrible things to Mandy. I was scared that if anyone knew I went to the pond with Craig, they would think that I somehow caused this to happen."

Mr. Bolling nodded to himself, accepting Griffin's explanation. Mary's complexion had turned an unhealthy gray. She looked as if she'd been punched in the stomach as she stared openmouthed at Griffin's dad.

"Frank, you don't seriously believe that story?" she asked.

He shot her a withering look. "What? Of course I believe Griffin," he snapped. "Why wouldn't I?"

Before she could answer, the doorbell rang. It turned out to be Detective Stone at the door. After the detective introduced himself, Mr. Bolling invited him into the house. "I was just about to call the police," he said.

Detective Stone nodded. "You saw on the news that we recovered Craig Myers's body," he said.

"What? Jesus. I didn't know that. What a terrible thing to have happened."

Stone's eyes dulled. He handed Mr. Bolling a folded piece of paper. "A search warrant," he said.

Mr. Bolling looked it over. The warrant was for Griffin's winter boots and two items of clothing: a blue ski jacket and a dark wool cap with a red wool ball attached. He told the detective that the warrant wasn't needed. "My son only minutes ago told me about the tragic events of yesterday. Let me take you to the living room, and Griffin can tell you what happened. Would you like some coffee? Tea? Anything else?"

"A glass of water would be fine."

Mr. Bolling left the detective in the living room, and when he returned, he had Griffin with him. He handed the detective a glass of water and asked Griffin to tell the detective the truth about what had happened yesterday. Griffin told the same story he had told his dad. As Detective Stone listened, his lips twisted into a hard smirk.

"That's quite a story," Detective Stone said.

"I agree," Mr. Bolling said, oblivious to the detective's sarcasm. "Just so tragic. A terrible accident."

"Your son's explanation of the events has been helpful. I'd like to bring him to the station to help us clear up a few loose ends."

"Griffin's not going anywhere without an arrest warrant," Mr. Bolling said. "He told you what happened and that should be enough for you. He's not answering any more questions."

Detective Stone put his water glass on the end table and stood up. "Your son lied to me earlier today," he said.

"It's perfectly understandable why my son would do so. Any twelve-year-old boy would do the same."

A film seemed to settle over the detective's eyes. "Don't you want to know what really happened?" he said.

"My son told me what happened."

The detective shook his head as if to say that he had to deal with all kinds in his job. "I want the items on the search warrant," he said.

"Certainly."

Griffin understood why the detective wanted those items: So that he could have them tested for any traces of Craig Myers's blood. Griffin shivered involuntarily as he realized how close he had come to stabbing Myers, and how disastrous it would've been if he hadn't fought his urges.

With Griffin's help, Mr. Bolling gathered the items on the search warrant and brought them to Detective Stone, who left the house without uttering another word.

That night Griffin hid in his mom's walk-in closet so he could eavesdrop on his parents. He expected to hear her saying terrible things about him. That she would try arguing that this wasn't an innocent accident like Griffin had claimed, but instead their son had somehow forced the Myers boy to walk out onto the ice knowing exactly what the result would be. But she didn't say a word. Instead, she turned off her night-table lamp as soon as Griffin's father came to bed.

Griffin sat in the dark, wondering why that was, and after a while he understood. His mom was too exhausted to argue anymore.

Chapter 25

On Thursdays, Natalie saw clients late into the evening, and so Morris thought he'd beat her home, but instead she was pulling into the driveway just ahead of him. He tapped his horn lightly to let out a short beep, and she lowered her window and waved. Parker began making excited pig-like grunts as he squirmed in his seat. Morris reached over and swung the passenger door open so that Parker could charge out and greet Natalie.

She dropped to both knees so she could wrestle Parker and half-heartedly fought off the dog's furious attempts to lick her face. When she could, she mentioned that Morris was home late. "It's already a quarter to nine."

He nodded. "I was working to close out my last big case before our trip. The guy we're investigating turned out to be quite a piece of work." He grimaced involuntarily as he thought about the scheme Chuck Macon and the Ukrainian gangster, Pavlo Lebed, had been involved in and added, "I'll tell you about it over the pizza I picked up for dinner, but MBI saved the lives of our client and his daughter."

"You're not exaggerating a bit, are you?"

"Nope."

"Wow."

Morris nodded and walked around to the trunk of his car so he could get the large pizza he'd brought home. If he had left it on the back seat instead, Parker would've gotten into it. As he came back around the car with the pizza, Natalie got back on her feet and gave Parker a couple of enthusiastic thumps on his side, which the dog loved.

"That's not from Lucca's," Natalie observed with a wry smile. She put her hands to her chest as if she might have a heart attack over the shock of Morris's break from tradition. He was a creature of habit, and in all the years they'd been together he always picked up pizzas from Lucca's.

"Neapolitan thin crust from a downtown joint Phil recommended," Morris said. "He claimed their margherita pizza's to die for."

"He's now Phil and no longer *Stonehedge*?" Natalie grinned at him. "And *to die for*, huh? You're going all Hollywood on me now?"

Morris shrugged. He caught up to his wife and gave her a kiss while Parker leaned against him and tried to stick his nose into the box.

"The guy knows good food," he said.

Natalie wrapped a thin arm around Morris's waist, and as they walked together to the front door, she told him how she had lunch with Rachel.

Morris unlocked the front door and held it open for Natalie. Since he was holding the pizza box, Parker was going to stick with him and not enter the house until he did, and as he went through the doorway Parker squeezed through alongside him. Morris asked how his daughter was doing.

"Good, I guess." Natalie sighed. "But she's working way too many hours. From what I can tell, eighty hours a week combining her internship at the district attorney's office and her paying job at that public relations company. I wish she'd let us help her. Or give up her apartment and stay with us so she could just focus on school."

"She's too independent for that."

"No, she's too stubborn, which she gets from you."

"Better that than my looks. Fortunately, Rachel took after you in that regard. We've got a beautiful daughter, Nat."

Natalie smiled at him as she took the pizza box from him so she could warm it up. Parker let out an angry grunt as the pizza box disappeared inside the oven.

"She's got your eyes," she said.

That was true. Rachel had his flinty gray eyes, which gave a hardness to her appearance that Nat didn't have. She was a tough girl and she was going to make a hard-nosed prosecutor when she finished law school. Still, though, like his wife, Rachel was a slender, dark-haired beauty who'd be breaking hearts if she wasn't so serious-minded and driven.

Morris asked his wife, "Wine or beer?"

"Red wine would be wonderful."

Natalie had picked up an assortment of Italian wines to get them in the mood for their trip. Morris didn't know one from the other, but he grabbed the first bottle of red wine he saw in the cabinet, a Montepulciano d'Abruzzo, whatever that was. As he yanked out the cork, Natalie commented how he must've fed Parker by now.

"The dog ate well. A fried pork dish from a Chinatown restaurant. It looked good."

She raised an eyebrow. "How'd that happen?"

"All part of a day's work. I'll tell you about it over a glass of wine while the pizza's warming." Morris glanced over at Parker and saw how intently the bull terrier was staring at the oven. "It probably wouldn't be a bad idea for me to give him half a can of his food. Otherwise, he might be mooching the whole pizza from us."

"Instead of only half of it."

"Exactly."

"I'll care take of it."

Natalie got Parker's food together, which the bull terrier attacked as if he hadn't eaten in days. After she brought a couple of wineglasses to the table, Morris filled them up, and they sat together at the table and sampled the wine.

"I like it," Morris said. "It's softer, more velvety, than the Chianti we had a couple of nights ago."

She grinned at him. "More *velvety*? Another expression you picked up from Mr. Hollywood? Morris, dear, I hardly know you these days."

"No doubt," Morris said, smiling in spite of himself. He took another sip of the wine, and told Natalie how Chuck Macon and his Ukrainian gangster partner were going to kill Brett Dickerson and probably Dickerson's daughter also for his money.

"That poor girl," Natalie said. "Are there any charges you can bring against these sociopaths?"

Morris shrugged. "I contacted Macon's parole officer in Albuquerque. The guy had disappeared on them and is in violation any number of twenty different ways, and now that they know what name he's using and where he is, they'll be picking him up. There's nothing that can be done to Pavlo Lebed unless Macon is willing to talk, and that's not going to happen."

"But the daughter's safe now?"

"Yeah. My client's making sure of it tonight." He took another sip of the wine, his eyes glazing a bit as he thought about how Brett Dickerson was going to handle Macon. As far as Morris was concerned, Macon was getting off lightly with just a beating, and at least the letter Macon would be writing would make things easier for the daughter. "Mia—that's the daughter—is going to UCLA also, some sort of MFA program in acting. A nice-looking kid. I'm glad I was able to help pry that leech off of her."

"Calling him a leech is being very generous."

"Agreed."

"That Ukrainian gangster isn't going to be happy losing millions."

"I'm sure he won't."

"Is he going to leave Mia alone?"

"I think so. He has nothing to gain by going after her. He's a vicious thug, but deep down he's also a businessman, and he'll chalk this up to a lost opportunity. The person who has to worry about him is Macon, but that's his problem. Still, I strongly tried to impress on my client that he should hire security for Mia for a few weeks just to be on the safe side."

The oven timer dinged. Morris got up to bring the pizza to the table. As they each dug into their first slice, Morris and Natalie agreed Stonehedge might've had a point about the pizza being to die for. Parker must've agreed with that sentiment also. After he mooched his first piece of it, his mooching went into overdrive.

Chapter 26

Griffin watched from the shadows as she left the building. He guessed that the woman was in her early forties. While the parking lot was mostly dark, the light from the building's vestibule had reflected off her face and had shown a haggardness, which made sense. It was after eleven, and she'd probably spent the last six hours cleaning offices and bathrooms, and no doubt wanted nothing more than to go home and go to bed. Even with how fatigued her face looked, Griffin still found her attractive. Not gorgeous, but certainly attractive. Small-chested, maybe, but with her dark hair and slim, compact body, she brought to mind an older, wearier version of the actress Mila Kunis. He waited until she was opening her car door (the only car in the parking lot) before sneaking up behind her and simultaneously putting her in a choke hold while pushing the point of a very sharp knife against her back. Up close, she smelled heavily of perspiration and disinfectant. She attempted to cry out, but he tightened his hold against her throat, choking her off.

"If you're a good girl, you're not going to get hurt tonight," he said, his voice slightly muffled by the Frankenstein-monster mask he had on. "As long as you behave yourself. Otherwise, I'll be doing terrible things to you. Do you understand me?"

She nodded. No crying or sobbing. Griffin was impressed, although she could've just been too terrified and exhausted to break out sobbing.

"I'm going to let go of you now. Don't even think about running away. You won't get far. Instead, you're going to do what I tell you to do so that later tonight you'll be going home as if nothing happened. Right?"

Again, she gave a terse nod. Griffin sensed a resignation take over in the way her body went slack. He let go of his choke hold and led her back to the office building. She fumbled for a moment with her keys before she was able to unlock the vestibule door. They then took the fire stairs and walked silently together to the fourth floor, with Griffin making sure to stay right alongside her as if they were attached at the hip. While she never looked directly at his face, she sensed that he was wearing a mask, and she must've taken that as a good sign. If someone was wearing a mask, that meant they didn't want you identifying them later, which further meant they were intending to let you live. Whether or not he wore a mask, he knew this woman (or whoever was cleaning this office building) would never have a chance to identify him, but having her think that was his intention would make her more pliable, and that was one of the reasons he wore a mask. But not his only reason.

When they got to the fourth floor, he had her give him her security key card for the office suite for Morris Brick Investigations, and the code for the keypad.

"If the security code you gave me is an emergency alarm for the police, you'll be dead before they get here."

"It's not," she said in a defeated tone. "It's what I use every night."

The card and the code unlocked the door for the office suite. Griffin had her lead the way into the suite. He next had her sit down in a chair while he took her pocketbook from her. A quick search and he found her driver's license.

"Elena Kotovksy," he said, reading her name from her license. "I now know where you live. You're not going to tell the police about this, right?"

She nodded as she bit down on her lip to keep from crying. Griffin said this only so that she'd continue to be compliant. Her life was over, but it wasn't a good time yet for her to understand that.

He had brought along his backpack and he dug inside of it for a bottle of orange soda that he had taken from Sheila's refrigerator. Earlier, he had crushed three of Sheila's Valiums into the bottle.

"Drink this," he told Elena as he held the bottle to her. "It will put you to sleep, and when you wake up I'll be gone and all of this will be over."

She made a face as if she were fighting hard to keep from crying, but she accepted the orange soda and drank it. Griffin then told her to get on the floor and lie on her stomach.

"But you had me drink that—"

"Didn't I tell you not to argue with me?"

She did as Griffin ordered, and he used the duct tape he'd brought to bind her wrists together behind her back. Next he bound her ankles. After that he rolled her onto her back. The Valium was beginning to take effect, and she put up no resistance as he gagged her with a rag that he'd brought and wrapped her mouth shut with duct tape.

He took her keys from her and began searching the office suite. While it would've been faster to break down each door, he was methodical about it instead, finding the right keys to unlock each door so he wouldn't leave any sign that he'd been there. Another reason for the mask was in case they had hidden surveillance cameras. If they did—well, that would be unfortunate, but Sheila's plan should still work, or at least a version of it.

Sheila Proops, bless her soul, had been right all along, even if he hadn't realized it until she spelled it out for him. The subconscious mind was a funny thing. He didn't search her out to kill her as he had convinced himself. It wasn't even because he was looking for a kindred spirit. What he really wanted was a mentor, and somehow he knew that she would be it. He had to admit her plan was a thing of beauty. It would bring him the notoriety that he secretly longed for even if he hadn't been aware of it until that day, and so they made an arrangement. He'd act as her caregiver; cooking her meals, cleaning and dressing her, doing any other errands she needed, and in exchange she'd continue to mentor him and give him the money that he needed. He had been right about her having a large stash of money hidden in her home, but she told him that he could take whatever he needed; that she had plenty more in the bank. There was one other thing he needed to do for her, and that was record his killings so that he could show them to her later. Not that this would be a hardship in any way. He rather liked the idea of it: Sharing this aspect of himself with Sheila.

He had to admit that he had begun finding Sheila increasingly attractive. Not physically. God no, although he could imagine that she was once beautiful, as she claimed. But it was her mind that he found so alluring. The two of them were just so spiritually aligned. After they had made their arrangement, they next brainstormed together to come up with a sufficiently cruel and devious method for him to use when he murdered his victims, so that the media would latch onto these killings and create a legend that would exist forever in Los Angeles lore.

When he bought the Frankenstein-monster mask at a Hollywood costume store, he didn't choose it randomly. Given what he'd later be doing, he expected the media to be calling him the Frankenstein Killer. Yeah, he had read Mary Shelley's novel and knew the scientist was the one named Frankenstein and not his monster, but if he was caught on video wearing this mask it would solidify the nickname that he wanted. Not that he wanted to be caught on video, but just in case he was.

The fourth office he broke into was Morris Brick's, and he found what he was looking for there. Most of the case files were for corporate accounts and wouldn't be any good for the plan Sheila had devised, but there were seven files that would work just fine. Griffin made photocopies of these files and returned the originals to Morris Brick's office. Before he left the office, a framed photo of a very attractive woman and a young girl who had to be her equally very attractive daughter caught his eye. They must've been Brick's wife and daughter. Before this was over he'd be including at least one of them in his plans.

Griffin went through the office suite, double-checking that he had left no clue behind that he'd been in there. Satisfied, he returned to Elena Kotovsky. She wasn't asleep yet, but she was out of it, her eyes unfocused. Griffin might only weigh a hundred and sixty-five pounds and appear as lean as a Calvin Klein underwear model, but he had always been athletic and was a lot stronger than he looked. Still, as he hefted Kotovsky onto his shoulder, he was glad she only weighed no more than a hundred and ten pounds, especially thinking about how he was going to be carrying her down four flights of stairs.

He was huffing somewhat by the time he got her out of the building and into the trunk of her car. He had parked his own car several miles away in a darkened alley. A few blocks from the alley was a public garage where he planned to dump her car after he moved her to the trunk of his used Honda. That was why he'd needed to get those Valiums into her. He was going to be leaving her alone in his car trunk for no more than twenty minutes, but he didn't want her awake and trying to make noise while he was gone. As far as her car went, it would probably take a week or longer before someone in the garage realized it had been abandoned there, which should be more than enough time, given his plans.

Or more precisely, Sheila's plans.

Chapter 27

Sheila Proops didn't own a car for obvious reasons, so when Griffin returned back to her Simi Valley home at one fifteen in the morning, he drove straight into her garage. Earlier, everything had gone smoothly when he transferred his captive, Elena Kotovsky, into the trunk of his car and shortly after that, when he abandoned her car.

Kotovsky was still out of it when he again hefted her onto his shoulder and brought her into Sheila's home. Sheila was, of course, where he'd left her, propped up in her wheelchair in front of the TV set, because where else was she going to be? He could smell that she had soiled herself, and that he was going to have to bathe her. If he'd had to do that for anyone else it would've infuriated him, but strangely, the thought of taking care of Sheila in that way didn't bother him. *It must be true love*, he thought, smiling mockingly. Not that he had any romantic interest in her. Instead, it was as if she were the big sister he never had. He felt a similar closeness to her that two siblings might feel when they grow up sharing a common history that no one else could ever understand.

With little fanfare, Griffin dumped Elena Kotovsky on the floor so that Sheila could get a better look at her. After forcing one of Kotovsky's eyelids open, he explained to Sheila why she appeared unresponsive, but that in a few hours she'd be waking up.

"We got lucky," Griffin said, which was true. They had no idea when he'd be able to snatch a cleaning person leaving the MBI offices. Sheila had thought he might need to spend a week or longer staking out the office building before he'd have his chance—but nope, everything fell quickly into place. He had arrived at the office building a little after nine, and when he saw only a single car in the parking lot, he knew this was the night. It was as if the universe was giving them a message. Their plan was meant to be.

Sheila absentmindedly licked her lips, her tongue moving lethargically. A brightness shone in her left eye, while her right eye remained dull as it sagged downward.

"We could change the plans," she said in her painfully slow and methodical speech, as if she barely had the energy to form each word. "There should be a drop cloth in the utility room." There was more sluggish, absentminded lip licking as she fought to slow down her ragged breathing, the excitement of the moment too much for her. Then, "Check my husband's tool chest, also in the utility room. I bet you find a screwdriver. You could use that as a chisel, and find something heavy to use as a hammer."

Saying all this exhausted her and left her slumped in her chair, but a hunger still shone brightly in her left eye. Griffin understood her hunger. It had been over six months since her husband had last killed for her, and the pressure building up inside must've been something terrible. She wanted this woman butchered in her old method so that she could breathe more easily.

Griffin slowly rubbed his chin as if he were thinking the matter over. "I could buy a chisel and hammer in the morning," he said.

Desperately, she forced out, "You don't have to wait."

"Maybe not, but I think it would be best if I did. A good craftsman always uses the right tools."

Disappointment crumpled the left side of her face while her paralyzed right side continued to sag, but she nodded. "You can wait until morning," she agreed, each word coming out slowly and painfully from her mouth as if they were tiny creatures being born.

"But I'd also have to find a place to dispose of her body," Griffin remarked, as if the idea had just come to him. "We can't afford to let anyone find her. If they do, and the police are able to identify her, it could ruin our plans." He shook his head as if another thought had just occurred to him. "If they find her with her skull cracked open, and I do the things you're just dying for me to do to her, they'll be tearing your home apart."

"You can bury her. Lots of land in Simi Valley for that."

Griffin scratched his jaw, giving the impression that he was sincerely considering the matter. "Too risky for that. Nah, better that we stick to the original plan."

He smiled inwardly seeing the way Sheila's left eye glazed. She had caught on then that he was only screwing with her. She might've been his mentor, his confidante, and his surrogate big sister, but like everyone else in the world, she was also someone for him to torment, even if the torments would only be in little ways. At least now she understood who was in charge.

"We should stick to the plan," she agreed, her painfully slow voice even duller than earlier.

"My thoughts exactly."

Griffin hefted the unconscious woman onto his shoulder again and carried her down into the basement. He might very well have to keep her alive for a week or longer, which meant he was going to have to periodically give her some water, but he'd wait until the morning for that.

He lowered himself, bending his knees so that he was sitting on his heels, and he pinched his captive's cheek and twisted her flesh. If the Valiums were wearing off that would've been painful enough to have woken her, but it had no effect. A shame. He would've liked to have been there the first moment she opened her eyes and realized what had happened. Oh, well. He was going to have to wait until morning.

Griffin headed back upstairs so he could bathe Sheila, and they could go to sleep. As jacked up as he was right then, he needed to get some rest. He was going to have a busy time of it in the morning.

Chapter 28

San Diego, the present

"Man, you got to chill," Freddy Silvia said. "Take a hit, bro." Chuck Macon accepted the joint being offered. He hadn't wanted to smoke any weed because he knew how dangerous his situation was, and he wanted to keep his wits about him. Now certainly wasn't a time to get stupid. But given how hard it was for him to sit still, Silvia had a point. Just look at the way his knees were bouncing up and down. He inhaled deeply on the joint, letting the smoke fill up his lungs. He held the smoke in for as long as he could before letting it out, and then handed the joint back to Silvia.

"You more chill now, bro?" Silvia asked.

The weed had almost no effect. Given that he had that ruthless savage Pavlo Lebed hunting for him, there was probably nothing he could do to calm himself down. But Macon didn't want to disappoint Silvia, so he nodded. The two of them had known each other since they were kids growing up in Albuquerque. They had lost track of each other when they were fifteen and Silvia was sent off to juvenile detention, but they were reunited years later in an Albuquerque prison. Silvia had confided in Macon then that he robbed banks for a living, although he was arrested because of an impulsive liquor-store robbery he did while high. In fact, Silvia, who finished his stretch eight months before Macon was given parole, had invited Macon to join him on future bank robberies when he got out. As Silvia had explained, when he planned the robberies, he got away with them. "With that liquor store, I was acting stupid. The guy behind the register pissed me off, and I was wasted enough to act stupid. But bro, when I plan them out, a bank robbery is like nothing. Walk in, grab ten grand, and walk out. That easy."

Macon at the time had no intention of taking Silvia up on his offer. Leading into his early twenties, he had committed his share of small-time armed heists, but he was done with those risks. Too great a chance of getting shot for too little a payoff. Besides, he was sure he'd make a fortune with his improved football-handicapping methods. If that didn't work out, he'd find a rich woman to sponge off. That had been his plan, but then he had to hit an ice-cold betting streak and get entangled with that Ukrainian gangster. Last night after getting worked over by Dickerson and his two friends, Macon was sent packing without any money—or anything else. Not only wouldn't Dickerson let him take any of his clothes, he wouldn't let him grab his passport or wallet. It wasn't possible to be more broke than he was right then, but that wasn't even the worst of it. When he was leaving the condo building, he spotted two of Lebed's hired men waiting for him. It was a miracle he escaped them, and with nowhere else to turn, he'd called Silvia collect and told him he wanted in on the bank robberies, and his old friend drove down from San Diego and picked him up. Macon needed money badly so he could buy a passport card and slip into Mexico, so whatever bank job Silvia was planning, he'd be part of it.

"When are you going to know about the job?" Macon asked.

Silvia smiled at him, shaking his head. "How many times you ask me that already? I told you, one of my hombres will be dropping by soon and we'll work out all the details. But it's going to be a nice score. Should be five grand each, easy."

Silvia handed him the joint again and Macon took another hit before handing it back.

"When do we do the job?"

Silvia made a face as if he were finding Macon's questions tiresome. "If everything works out we do it tomorrow. Just chill, okay? You're starting to drive me loco with all your nervousness."

Macon nodded. The weed was beginning to have an effect. At least his legs had stopped bouncing up and down like he was working a jackhammer. His mind, though, still raced like a rabbit on meth as he thought of all the things he needed to do before he'd be safe from Lebed.

"You'll be able to get me a fake passport that will be good enough to get me into Mexico?"

"Yeah, I told you that. The guy I know, it will cost a grand, and it will be as good as the real thing. Okay? So no more questions."

From the sound of it, a car pulled into the driveway. Macon involuntarily tensed, but Silvia leaned over the sofa and pushed the cheap floral-patterned curtains aside. The early-morning sunlight made Macon shield his eyes. Silvia let the curtain fall back in place, and turned to Macon, offering a grin that stretched from ear to ear.

"My hombre," he said. "See, I told you he'd be coming by first thing this morning."

Silvia handed Macon what was left of the joint while he got up to answer the door. There was a quick conversation between Silvia and his friend, except there was something funny and oddly familiar about his friend's accent. Macon sat puzzling about it for a brief moment before realizing what it was. The accent was oddly familiar because it was Ukrainian.

Macon jumped off the sofa and was racing toward the back of the house by the time Pavlo Lebed's hired man entered the room. He knocked over two chairs and a cheap card table, anything to slow down the hired muscle. He didn't dare turn around to look, but he heard a grunt as the man tripped over something, and it bought him enough time to reach the back door. When he swung it open, he stopped in his tracks, blinking wildly. Two of Lebed's men were waiting for him, and one of them was holding a long metal rod: a cattle prod. Before Macon could react, the man pushed it into Macon's chest, and the electric shock knocked him off his feet.

The two men grabbed him and dragged him into the house. The man who had tripped over a chair had gotten back up and gave him a hard, angry stare. Macon watched as this man handed Freddy Silvia a roll of bills. Silvia smirked at Macon and said, "Hey *pendejo*, easiest five grand I ever made."

Before Macon could respond, the man he had tripped moved quickly over to him and hit him with something hard and metal across the temple, and then there was only blackness.

Chapter 29

Los Angeles, the present

With Brett Dickerson's assignment wrapped up and nothing urgent demanding his attention at MBI, Morris decided to indulge himself with an extra forty-five minutes of sleep, and at eight that morning he was still sitting at the kitchen table dawdling over a second cup of coffee. Natalie, wrapped in a tan cloth robe and wearing fuzzy pink slippers, squinted against the sunlight as she entered the kitchen with Parker trailing close behind. While she didn't see clients on Fridays, she still usually spent half a day catching up on paperwork. She poured herself a mug of coffee from the pot Morris had brewed and left warming for her, and joined him at the table. Parker plopped down on the floor between the two of them and let out a soft grunt.

"You're getting a late start this morning," she said after having several sips of coffee, her normally soft voice huskier than usual from just waking up. Her long dark hair was also mussed up from getting out of bed only minutes earlier, and the skin around her eyes was somewhat puffy, but even still, she looked heartbreakingly beautiful to Morris.

Smiling thinly, he told her that he'd still be beating Polk to the office. "Probably Fred also."

"But not Charlie."

"Not much chance of that," he agreed. "So Charlie can have bragging rights for one day." Morris reached down so he could scratch Parker behind the ear. "Any plans for today?"

"I've got a few hours of paperwork to get done, and then I thought I'd take Parker over to Franklin Canyon Park and have him work off some of the pizza he mooched last night. Our little guy's getting a bit pudgy."

"Nah, it's all muscle."

"That's what he wants you to believe!"

If Parker took offense at this slight, he didn't show it. Instead, he rolled onto his side and stretched his legs. Morris looked deep in thought as he observed the dog.

"What?" Natalie asked.

"Hmm. I'm thinking we should figure out a way to take Parker with us to Italy."

"We're not taking the little guy with us. With all the restaurants we'll be going to and all the mooching he'd be doing there if he was given the chance, his stomach would explode."

This time Parker groaned in a way that sounded as if he were insulted.

Morris wasn't ready to give up. "Rachel's going to be too busy to take care of him," he argued.

"She's already scheduled to take those two weeks off from her internship, and her manager at the PR firm has given her blessing for Rachel to bring Parker into the office. He'll be fine. Our daughter will be fine."

Morris knew when he was beat. He tilted back his coffee mug to finish what was left, gave Parker another scratch behind the ear, and then got out of his chair so he could give Natalie a proper kiss.

"I'll be leaving by five tonight," he promised. "I'll pick up some steaks on my way home for a barbecue."

She nodded, smiling, but he picked up a hesitancy in her eyes, and they'd been married long enough for him to know what it was about. She was going to joke about him not taking any last-minute serial-killer cases, except it wasn't really a joke. Deep down inside she was afraid something like that might happen, and her worry wasn't just over how it might force them to cancel yet another vacation, but the toll those cases took on him.

"Don't worry about anything," he told her, and because they'd been together as long as they had she knew what he meant. And he did mean it. He'd had his fill of serial killers, and having this last investigation lead him to lowlifes like Chuck Macon and Pavlo Lebed was as close to that kind of evil as he ever wanted to get again. The only reason he took the Skull Cracker Killer case was because he was convinced the death count would end up higher if he didn't get involved, but as far as he was concerned he was done with serial killers. Besides, as abstract as the concept was of spending two weeks away from home and work, he found himself looking forward to this trip to Italy, maybe even more so than Nat.

Natalie nodded, letting him know she fully got the part of his message he'd left unspoken, but there was still a hesitant look in her eyes as if she didn't completely believe him.

Brett Dickerson sat on the patio of his Brentwood estate, eating a Brie and truffle omelet that his private chef prepared for him. Mia sat across from him with a bowl of fresh berries and a chocolate croissant in front of her, but so far hadn't taken a nibble of any of it. Not even a sip of her mocha cappuccino. Dickerson hated for his daughter to be this unhappy, and seeing how drawn and pale her face looked made him wish he *had* thrown Macon off the balcony, even though that had all been an act to scare the hell out of him. While he certainly didn't mind seeing Macon take a beating (although it wasn't nearly as severe as he would've liked it to be), the objective was to get him to write the letter Dickerson had dictated and to have his things cleared out of the condo before Mia returned home from her shopping outing with her friend Courtney.

Mia started sobbing again. Like the other night, it wasn't one of those explosive, outward displays, but more of an inward, quiet sobbing, as if she were struggling hard to control herself. It just broke Dickerson's heart to see it.

"Pumpkin, you're so much better off without that cheap con artist," he told her. "Forget him."

Mia nodded as she struggled to end her sobbing. Almost as if she were in a daze, she said, "He just never loved me. How could I have not known that?"

Dickerson clenched his jaw, hearing how she sounded like the same distraught ten-year-old girl he had comforted when the family cat died. The letter he had Macon write was mostly a version of the truth. It stated that he was an ex-con and a scam artist who had attached himself to Mia only so that he could steal her father's money, and that everything he had told her was a lie. The letter further had him explaining that he had skipped parole, and that he had to go on the run now because the authorities had tracked him down in Los Angeles. While Dickerson knew Macon had no conscience nor was he capable of caring about anyone but himself, he still had Macon add to the end of the letter that Mia was deserving of finding a decent man, and not to blame herself for falling for his act; that he had fooled plenty of women more experienced than her. Dickerson figured it would be better for Mia to get a letter like that than to have one where she might end up romanticizing that piece of scum, or worse, pining away for him.

"The guy's nothing more than a heartless shark," Dickerson said. "Guys like him know how to prey on bighearted girls who trust too easily." He paused for a moment, then suggested that she take the day off. "You can make it a spa day. Whatever you want, my treat."

She shook her head, her lips pressed tightly together, her expression resolute.

"You should pamper yourself," Dickerson argued stubbornly. "After what you've been through, you deserve it."

"Daddy, I'm not doing that. I'm not letting him have any sort of power over me where I don't go to work because of him!"

Dickerson nodded, but he wasn't ready to give up. Mia needed something to make up for what she'd been through. Because it really was mind-numbingly awful when he let himself think about what Macon and that Ukrainian gangster were planning.

"I've got a property I'm finishing on Malibu that's simply amazing," he said. "Private beach and every amenity you can think of. It makes my house look like a shack in comparison. Better yet, I have it furnished with everything top-of-the-line so we can sell it for a better price. Why don't you call Courtney and some of your other friends and stay there tomorrow? You haven't had a girls' night out like that in months."

"I don't know—"

"The property is a mile down the road from where your favorite actor lives."

"Philip Stonehedge?"

"Yep."

Mia smiled bleakly, which was the first smile of any kind she had shown since Dickerson picked her up last night and brought her to Brentwood.

"Can you show me pictures of it?" she asked.

"Sure thing, pumpkin."

Chapter 30

Perlmutter slowed down so he could read the address for the ranch-style home. When he realized the number matched the address he had gotten for Sheila Proops, he hit the brakes too hard and the coffee he'd bought at a doughnut shop ten minutes earlier spilled onto his lap. The coffee wasn't hot enough to burn his skin, but it left an embarrassing stain on his tan-colored pants. Not only that, he was quickly finding his wet pants uncomfortable as the material clung to his thighs.

Just effing great, he thought. He gritted his teeth, not believing his lousy luck. He had a decision to make: Whether or not to find a store to buy new pants. He decided not to bother. Proops was a cripple confined to a wheelchair, and a serial killer to boot. So what if his pants were soggy and stained?

Perlmutter parked in front of Proops's house, left his car, and headed to the front door with a determined pace and his chin thrust forward. Before he reached the door, though, his confidence wavered. Not only were his pants a mess, but this was a *serial killer* he was trying to see! Maybe the police weren't able to prove that fact, but still, she must've been the Skull Cracker Killer who had murdered twelve people in New York, and that wasn't even counting the people she convinced her husband to kill in Los Angeles. He almost turned around. *Almost.* But he couldn't do that, not with what amounted to a wink-and-a-nod deal with Lawrence Getzler. He also had a notebook filled with ideas. In his gut he also knew he had a great movie waiting to be made. A blockbuster. Something that would make him the new hot combination screenwriter and director on the scene. He sucked it in and rang the bell. Why in the world should he be scared of a half-paralyzed woman in a wheelchair?

He wasn't sure exactly who he was expecting to answer the door, but it certainly wasn't this Ryan Gosling look-alike. Or maybe the guy looked more like Philip Stonehedge—at least before the actor got his face carved up. Whoever the guy was, he completely took Perlmutter off his game, and the hopeful filmmaker found himself barely able to get the words out as he asked to see Sheila Proops.

The man glanced down at Perlmutter's crotch and smiled thinly. His gaze moved upward to meet Perlmutter's eyes, and he said in a smug tone, "I believe you've wet yourself."

"I spilled some coffee."

"Really? Because you smell like piss."

Perlmutter could feel his cheeks burning red. "It's coffee," he insisted.

The man shrugged as if he thought Perlmutter was lying. Nonchalantly, he said, "If you say so. What was it you were trying to ask when I answered the door? Whether you could come in here to poop?"

Perlmutter fully appreciated then that the man was playing with him. He snorted to demonstrate that he didn't find this man's comments at all funny.

"You know damn well what I said. That I'd like to talk to Sheila Proops about a business arrangement."

This Philip Stonehedge look-alike was in his early thirties, probably about the same age as the actor, but as much as he might've looked like an unscarred version of Stonehedge, there was something very different about him. Perlmutter realized what it was: a certain hardness, the kind you didn't get from doing Pilates or weight training. Given how lean he was, he brought to mind a knife blade. There was something dangerous about him, not to be taken for granted.

The man smiled innocuously and casually scratched his jaw, but the way his eyes deadened caused Perlmutter to shiver as if someone had dropped an ice cube down the back of his shirt.

"Why don't you tell me your proposal," the man offered. "I'll relay it to Sheila."

"It's confidential," Perlmutter insisted. "For her ears only. But it could be worth millions to her."

"Millions, huh? A pity Sheila will be missing out, since you just blew your opportunity."

Perlmutter blinked several times. He found himself becoming increasingly flustered by this person. "Listen, okay? I want to make a movie about her," he said, his words tumbling out in a rush. "I've already got a deal with Starlight Pictures, and I'm prepared to make Proops a partner in this film." He dug his wallet out of his back pants pocket, and fished out one of his business cards. The man arched an eyebrow and pursed his lips in an amused fashion as he looked the card over, and then ripped it into shreds.

"As I said, you're too late."

"You can't be serious!"

Whatever smile the man had been showing faded, and what Perlmutter saw then in the man's eyes scared the bejesus out of him. It was almost like there was a beast lurking behind them.

"I wasn't being fair, was I?" this Philip Stonehedge look-alike said. He stepped aside so that Perlmutter could pass by. "Maybe it would be best for you to come in."

Perlmutter found himself shaking his head. He stumbled back a couple of steps, and almost fell.

"Suit yourself."

The door was closed in a quiet way, but it still made Perlmutter wince as the door clicked shut. He wiped away the perspiration that was beading up on his forehead, and turned so he could head back to his car, his legs unsteady. He couldn't shake the thought that if he had gone into Proops's house with that guy, he wouldn't ever be leaving it. At least not in one piece.

Griffin rejoined Sheila in the kitchen where they'd been going over the MBI investigation files Griffin had stolen.

"Some clown who wanted to make a movie about you," Griffin said, explaining who had been at the door. "A total loser." He absently rubbed his thumb over his upper lip as he thought about the wannabe filmmaker and added, "I got the feeling that he was someone no one would miss, and I tried inviting him in, but..." He shrugged, "I must've scared him off. A shame. We could've had fun with him."

Sheila perked up at that, her left eye glistening. "Describe him."

Griffin sat back down at the kitchen table, and instead of doing as Sheila asked, took a bite of a chocolate cruller he'd picked up earlier that morning. He took his time chewing before finally telling Sheila that the guy looked like he ate too many chocolate crullers like this one. "He was just some balding, sloppy-looking fatso in his forties."

In her breathless, painstakingly slow cadence, she asked, "Can you try luring him back in here?"

Griffin's eyes opened wide as if he were taken aback by her request. Of course, it was an act. He knew the joker who'd come to the door perfectly fit the type Sheila was driven to kill. That was the reason he had decided to invite him into the house: so he could throw Sheila a bone, so to speak. The guy didn't bite the bait, but that didn't mean Griffin couldn't have a little fun at Sheila's expense.

"Damn. You're in quite a bloodthirsty mood this morning. First regarding our guest downstairs, and now this."

Earlier that morning Sheila had again begged him to take a chisel and hammer to the skull of the cleaning woman he had kidnapped. He almost weakened and went along with it. *Almost.* But he knew it would be an indulgence, and one that wasn't worth the risk. It would also be an unnecessary distraction.

"Please try again," Sheila pleaded. "You can tell him you discussed it with me and I want to do his movie. Tell him anything." She took several slow, ragged breaths before adding, "The pressure in my chest has gotten so bad. I need this to breathe better."

"Forget it, sweetie, I'm not wasting my time. The last I saw him, he was making a beeline for his car. But even if he had stopped to take a nap, it took you so long to spit that out, he'd be long gone by now."

"Please!"

Griffin rolled his eyes upward. Jesus, he hoped he never got like her. Mentor or not, she was nuts.

"Fine," he said.

He pushed himself out of the chair and strolled back to the living room, and after moving the curtain aside so he could take a look, rejoined Sheila in the kitchen. He waited until after he'd sat down and took several more slow bites of his cruller and drank half his coffee before telling her that the guy was long gone, just as he had expected him to be.

Disappointment wrecked the left side of Sheila's face, while the right side remained droopy and waxy. Griffin felt a tinge of regret seeing her like that. For a brief moment, he found himself empathizing with her, and empathizing with anyone was an utterly foreign experience for him. It left him startled in a way.

"Why get so worked up over this?" he asked. "If I didn't come here yesterday, you'd be in this exact same situation."

"But you did."

"Fair enough, but there will be other fish in the sea," he noted with a tenderness that surprised him. Somewhat gruffly, he added, "We should have one netted very soon, in fact."

She nodded, her movement slight and painful-looking.

He picked up the MBI investigation file that they'd been discussing before they were interrupted by the doorbell. "We're in agreement, right? This is who I'll be killing first?" he asked.

Sheila nodded again.

Griffin flipped through the file, stopping at key points that he had highlighted earlier. It really was an ingenious plan that Sheila had come up with. He had to give her credit for that, and he owed her more than he'd ever want to admit. Sometime during the last several years, simply killing his victims had stopped being enough for him, and she'd been able to look into his soul and understand that. Even more importantly, she was able to offer him what he truly needed: Notoriety. All the heinous murders he would soon be committing would leave Los Angeles stunned. Yeah, she would be getting her own kicks out of it, but still, because of Sheila he had found his true calling, and that explained the closeness he was feeling toward her right then.

"I better get busy," he told her.

Chapter 31

Perlmutter was troubled as he drove to Los Angeles. He wasn't necessarily worried about not seeing Sheila Proops—he'd have his chance once that scary dude, who in his mind he had named Mr. X, was out of the house, and Mr. X would have to leave sometime, even if it was just to run an errand. But the more Perlmutter thought about it, the more convinced he was that this person would've killed him if he had gone into the house. That was what his gut was telling him, and all great film directors—whether it was Welles, Hitchcock, or Wilder—were well known for trusting their gut.

Perlmutter kept playing over in his mind different horrific scenarios of what would've happened if he had stepped into the house, and he was still caught up in those thoughts when he entered the Star-Crossed Diner. He barely noticed Trudy at the hostess station, and he was too distracted to pay attention to her sighing and asking if he was going to continue to be a glutton for punishment and ask to be seated at one of Jane's booths. Instead, he just stared at her as if she were talking in a foreign language that he didn't understand.

"If you do, you'll have to wait," Trudy said.

"What?"

"I said, all of Jane's booths are occupied."

"I don't care where you put me. I just want to get some food."

"Really? Can pigs fly now?"

"What?"

"Never mind."

She brought him to a booth and left him with a menu, and he sat biting his thumbnail as he thought more about the way Mr. X had looked at him right before inviting him into Sheila Proops's home.

Something made Perlmutter look up and see Jane standing by his booth, peering at him through thinly slitted eyes.

"You again," she said, making little effort to hide her annoyance.

"Don't flatter yourself," Perlmutter snapped back. "I'm here only because I like the corned-beef hash. No other reason."

"Good," she said. A hint of a snide smile showed. "You sign your movie deal yet?"

"I have to finish the script first, but it's going to be amazing." He took a deep breath and let it out through his mouth. "Jane, I was being petty before. You've got talent; you deserve a break. When we cast, I'll make sure you get a part."

"I'll be waiting with bated breath."

"I'm not kidding. And I'm not saying that because I'm still hoping to win you over. That ship has sailed. I've got a new girlfriend. Really beautiful girl too. Gorgeous long legs, narrow waist, dark brown hair, eyes and lips that could melt butter."

Perlmutter had a crush on Emmy Rossum from the TV series *Shameless*, and that was who he was describing. Jane smirked at him, and asked whether his new girlfriend's name was Fiona, which was Emmy Rossum's character's name. Perlmutter had let it slip in the past how much he liked that show, so it wasn't a big surprise that she had guessed what she did, but still, he could've strangled her right then.

"What? No, her name is Peggy. Why'd you think it was Fiona?"

Still smirking, Jane said, "Forget it. Good luck with your movie."

Perlmutter watched her from behind as she walked away. Later, after Terrie, his waitress, had brought over the corned-beef hash with his usual three fried eggs over easy, he made a decision about Mr. X.

Chapter 32

Mia Dickerson had no intention of drinking that night. She had originally called Courtney only to arrange for their girls' night in Malibu, but after she told her friend about the letter that Kyle or Chuck (or whatever the jerk's real name was) had written her, Courtney had insisted they get together after work for drinks. And that was why she was sitting with her friend at the bar at Divine's, sipping on her second cucumber vodka and watermelon-juice cocktail.

Courtney signaled the bartender for another gin martini, and asked Mia whether it was going to be just them, Hallie, and Kaylee tomorrow night. Mia ignored the question and snatched Courtney's martini glass. She made a show of wrinkling her nose as she sniffed it.

"Why are you drinking martinis?" Mia asked.

"I'm in the mood for something sophisticated."

Mia made a face. "It smells like nail-polish remover."

"Girl, that's only because you haven't developed a refined palate yet." She giggled. "Only those of us with the most cultured tastes can appreciate a martini."

"Yeah, right. I bet it also *tastes* like nail-polish remover."

"How would you know? You haven't been drinking that, have you?"

Mia's eyes darkened. "I wouldn't be surprised if that creep was sneaking stuff like that into my food. Drano too." She quickly turned to her friend with an apologetic smile, her hand lightly touching Courtney's bare arm.

"I'm so sorry, Court, I'm being such a downer," she said.

"Girl, don't sweat it. You've got every right to be pissed. But how about you get it all out now so we can party tomorrow night in Malibu?"

"I'll try."

Mia put down the martini glass. Courtney took the little plastic spear holding three olives from it, and nibbled one of the olives.

"You conveniently didn't answer me before," she said. "About whether it's only going to be us girls tomorrow night."

"Just us girls," Mia said.

"We should invite some cute guys," Courtney said a little too eagerly. "Make it a really fun night."

Anger tightened Mia's mouth. "Absolutely not."

"Hey, if you fall off a horse, you have to get right back on. At least, that's what they say."

"I didn't fall off the horse. I was shot off of it. With an AK-47."

Courtney nibbled a second olive off the spear as she tried to think of a way to change Mia's mind, but then decided she didn't have to. She could make it a surprise. The yummy stud sitting on the barstool next to her was so unbelievably hot. Damn, he could almost be Ryan Gosling's better-looking twin, or that other actor, *whatshisname*, the one Mia liked so much. Several times she'd caught him glancing at her in a certain way to let her know he was interested. If it was any other night, she'd have already left with him, or at least introduced herself and exchanged numbers. But she couldn't ditch Mia tonight after what she'd just gone through, or even openly flirt with anyone if Mia was watching, even someone so insanely hot. But that was why she was drinking martinis. He was drinking manhattans, so she wanted to drink something equally classy as a kind of signal, and she did catch him smiling when she gave the bartender her order.

Courtney lifted her plastic spear, now holding the last olive, in a mock cheer. "Here's hoping Kyle, or whatever that jerk's name is, dies from inflamed hemorrhoids!"

Mia giggled at that. She lifted her cocktail glass. "That would be a truly fitting way for him to go. What a massive asshole he is. But then again, all men are."

The bartender, a thin woman with frizzy red hair, had stealthily dropped off a fresh martini for Courtney, and was at the moment sliding their dinner plates in front of them—a kale salad with avocado, quinoa, and figs for Mia, and a smoked bacon and fried-egg sandwich for Courtney.

"Amen, sister," the bartender said.

Mia looked up, surprised, not having seen the bartender approaching, nor realizing that she'd been talking loudly enough to be overheard. The bitter smile on the bartender's thin lips made her smile the same way.

"I'll bet mine was a bigger asshole," Mia said.

"You'll lose."

Mia tilted her cocktail glass back, finishing off what was left of the drink. Resentment tightened her face. "Every single thing he told me turned out to be a lie, even his name," she said. "He convinced me he wanted to marry me, but that was only so he could rip off my dad."

"Mine emptied out my apartment, took everything I owned. Even Mayer and Oscar, my two beloved dachshunds. As a parting gift, he maxed out my credit cards and left me over fifteen grand in debt."

If Mia had known what Chuck Macon's plan had actually been, she would've been able to beat the bartender's story and taken first prize, but since all she knew what was in the letter, she had to admit that the bartender's asshole ex topped hers.

Courtney used this whose-boyfriend-is-a-bigger-asshole competition to excuse herself, presumably to go to the ladies' room. What she was actually doing was chasing after the crazy hot stud who'd been sitting next to her. She caught up to him as he was heading out the back door.

"Hey, I've been wanting to talk to you!"

The stud turned and smiled at her as if he'd been expecting her to chase after him.

"What took you so long?" he asked. "I was sitting next to you for forty-five minutes waiting for you to say something."

"Well, my friend—"

The stud nodded. "Yeah, I know. I wasn't trying to eavesdrop, but I heard enough. When the which-guy-is-the-biggest-asshole contest started, I took that as a hint it was time for me to leave."

"Why? You're not an asshole, are you?"

He smiled in a way that showed only mischief. "The biggest yet. So don't say I didn't warn you."

She laughed and held out her hand. "Courtney."

He took her hand and she shivered slightly from how cool his touch was. "Biff," he said.

"Biff? Seriously?"

"Hey, don't blame me. Blame my parents."

As he held her hand, he gave her a slow, hungry look up and down that made her feel as if he were peeling her clothes from her body. If any other guy she'd just met had looked at her in the same way, she would've been offended or possibly creeped out. With him, she found it thrilling and goose bumps popped up on her flesh. He raised her hand and lightly pressed his lips against it, all the while his eyes piercing into hers. Time seemed to stop as he did this, and her heart pounded wildly in her chest.

"Shall we go someplace?" he asked.

Courtney hesitated for a moment before shaking her head. "I can't."

"Because of your friend?"

She nodded, making no effort to hide her disappointment. She could've been a ten-year-old who'd just been told she couldn't have the puppy she'd been begging for.

"How about tomorrow night?" he asked.

"That might work." She smiled impishly. "Do you have three hot guy friends you can bring to a party in Malibu?"

"If it means spending quality time with you, sure."

"Okay, give me your phone."

He smiled apologetically. "I seem to have misplaced it."

She dug a pen out of her clutch bag. "Your hand, then."

He held out his hand and she wrote the Malibu address on his palm.

"Be there tomorrow night at ten," she said.

He grinned at Courtney in such a sexually hungry way that it made her feel weak in the knees.

"I wouldn't miss it for the world," he promised her.

Chapter 33

After drinks with Courtney, Mia arranged for an Uber back to her dad's home in Brentwood. She wasn't sure when she'd feel comfortable going back to her West Hollywood condo, but she knew she was going to need more time. Venting that night had helped, especially with the bartender. A cool chick. If she wasn't ten years older than Mia and her friends, she would've invited her to Malibu.

As with the other night, she could only sleep in fitful starts and stops. No matter how much she tried to focus on other things, her thoughts drifted to Kyle (or Chuck or whatever he wanted to call himself) and how he had used her. Before this, she would've never thought herself capable of violence, but if she had the chance, she would slice his face open with one of the samurai swords her dad collected. The only time she felt herself at peace that night was when she imagined herself doing that.

She forced herself out of bed early Saturday morning, and even though she felt sluggish and exhausted, she went on a five-mile run through Brentwood. It didn't help her mood at all. When she returned, her dad was up and they had breakfast together. Seeing the worry in her dad's eyes made her feel better in a selfish sort of way. Not much, but a little.

Later, while he was having coffee and she was having a mocha cappuccino (her favorite), he told her the Malibu property would be ready by two.

"I have a crew there now getting the pool, Jacuzzi, sauna, tennis courts, and the rest of the property ready for you and your friends."

Later that afternoon, Mia arrived at the Malibu address with her three friends and she had to admit: The place was spectacular. She, Courtney, Hallie, and Kaylee had been besties since middle school, and hanging with them helped. For the first few hours they sat by the pool, which her dad had stocked with bottled water and soft drinks (Hello? They were all twenty-two. No booze?) and as they laid around tanning, they talked about only inconsequential stuff, mostly gossip about other friends from high school. That evening they had pizza delivered, and after that Courtney brought up how Philip Stonehedge lived a mile down the road (Mia, in a moment of weakness when they were drinking at Divine's, had divulged that information, and as an even bigger mistake, had given her Stonehedge's address!)

"We have to try to see him!" Kaylee insisted, her face flushing with excitement.

"How do we do that?" Hallie asked. "Just ring the bell?"

"For starters. We offer him a fivesome. That will get him answering the door!"

"That's disgusting," Mia said.

"Don't tell me you wouldn't be up for it!"

Mia blushed, because she'd had the biggest crush on Stonehedge ever since she was thirteen and saw him in his first film, *Little Crimes*. If there was anyone she'd be willing to have a fivesome with it would be him, but she'd die of embarrassment if any of her friends actually offered him that!

Even though Mia tried arguing that he probably wasn't home, she was outvoted three to one, and they drove over to his property. Kaylee buzzed the intercom by the gate, and when a voice that had to be Philip Stonehedge answered, all four of them broke out in nervous giggling.

"What can I do for you lovely ladies?"

That caused more giggling. "How do you know we're lovely?" Kaylee asked.

"Video surveillance."

"Well, that's not fair," Kaylee said, exaggerating her pout. "You seeing us while we can't see you."

"Very true. Let me rectify that."

The gate buzzed open, and Mia pulled the car onto the private drive and continued on for an eighth of a mile until she reached the house. Philip Stonehedge was waiting for them, but he wasn't alone. He had his arm around the waist of a stunning blonde who Mia quickly recognized was the actress Brie Evans.

Stonehedge winked at them, flashing them a brilliant smile. "How about some drinks on the veranda?" he asked.

Mia and her three friends were too startled to do any giggling or tittering, and they followed Stonehedge and Brie Evans to the veranda, where he served them freshly made strawberry mojitos and offered them the most delicious fish tacos Mia had ever tasted. It quickly became obvious that Stonehedge was simply a nice guy whose only motive for inviting them onto his property was to spend time hosting four of his fans who had the chutzpah to ring his buzzer. There certainly wasn't any chance of having a fivesome (or a sixsome, if Brie Evans were to join in,) and Mia found herself liking him even more. A charming, generous man, and just so decent. Brie was also very sweet.

For several hours, Stonehedge and Brie talked with them in such a down-to-earth manner and not as if they were big Hollywood stars, mostly asking Mia and her friends about their lives. At one point, Mia noticed Courtney began acting antsy, but when she asked her friend in a hushed whisper what was wrong, Courtney shook her head and simply murmured back, "nothing," which all but confirmed that something was wrong. This was further proven by the way Courtney kept checking her watch, and how she had gotten so sullen. Whatever it was, Mia couldn't figure it out.

Shortly after eleven, Stonehedge announced he was calling it a night. "You girls okay getting home, or should I call for a taxi?"

"We'll be okay," Mia said. "We're only a mile down the road."

Stonehedge nodded as he gave Mia a cautious look. She'd only had three mojitos over the two and a half hours she'd been there. Still, Stonehedge and Brie accompanied them to the car, probably to make sure she wasn't wobbling as she walked.

"That was unbelievable!" Kaylee exclaimed as they drove up Stonehedge's private drive. "Even if we didn't get our fivesome!"

"Those two were so nice," Hallie gushed.

"What's up with you, Court?" Mia asked.

"Absolutely nothing," Courtney said, making no attempt to hide her sullen mood.

Mia gave her a quick glance, but whatever was bothering Courtney, she had no clue. When they got back to the house, Mia noticed Courtney looking especially anxious, as if she were expecting someone. Whatever. Kaylee took a vaporizer out of her pocketbook and told the group she'd brought some exceptionally excellent weed. The vaporizer made it three times around the group before Kaylee jumped to her feet and started shedding her clothes.

"I don't know about you girls, but I'm taking a dip in the ocean!"

Hallie followed suit, then Courtney, whose mood seemed to have picked up, and finally Mia decided what the heck, and got out of her clothes too. Soon all four of them were racing naked out of the house, the full moon brightly overhead as they ran laughing down the steps that led to their private beach, and then into the ocean. The waves had a savageness to them that was both frightening and exhilarating. After several waves crashed over them, knocking them onto their bare asses, Hallie questioned whether there could be sharks in the water.

"Do you think they might come out more at night?" she asked.

That got them all out of the water and heading back to the house, but they were giggling and laughing as they did so. It was as if they were teenagers again instead of more jaded twenty-two-year-olds, who'd all had at least one major life disappointment so far. All four of them were near tears laughing when they made their way through the glass sliding doors that led into the house's massive great room. It was only after Hallie slid the door closed that they noticed the stranger wearing the Frankenstein-monster mask.

Kaylee opened her mouth wide to scream. The man raised a big, scary gun at her. Mia noticed then that he was wearing latex gloves.

"If you make any noise I'm going to shoot you in the mouth," he warned, his voice muffled by the mask. "Then I'll shoot each of your friends. But if you behave yourselves and do as I ask, nobody will get hurt. I'm here only to rob the house, nothing else." Addressing Kaylee, he asked, "Do you understand?"

Kaylee was at first too frightened to respond, but when he made like he was pulling back the trigger, she nodded furiously as tears leaked out of her eyes. The man in the Frankenstein-monster mask pointed his gun at each of them in turn, making them promise to be compliant, each of them struggling to keep from bursting out crying as they did so.

"You three," he said, waving the gun at Kaylee, Hallie, and Courtney, "lie facedown on the floor."

The three of them did as they were ordered. Mia had been in too much shock until then to remember that she was naked. She brought up her arm to cover her breasts and tried to shield her pubic area with her other hand.

The man shook his head at her. "Too late to be modest," he said in an icy voice his mask did little to filter. "Use these on their wrists. Make them tight."

He tossed a bunch of plastic ties in her direction. They landed on the floor by her feet. She picked up one of them and stared at it with bewilderment.

"Genius, you don't need to be a rocket scientist to figure out how to bind someone's wrists with that," he admonished. "I'll give you ten seconds to figure it out before I make this easy for myself and just shoot each of you."

Mia broke out sobbing, but she had Kaylee put her arms behind her back, securing her wrists with the plastic tie. After that she did the same to Hallie, then to Courtney, and during it all she kept telling herself that if he was going to kill them he wouldn't be wearing that mask. Maybe he planned to rape them, and maybe he'd do other horrible things to them, but as long as he wore that mask he was planning to let them live.

"Your turn now," he told Mia. "On your stomach."

She did as he ordered, and she cried out as he violently jerked her arms back, and then again as the plastic tie bit painfully into the flesh around her thin wrists. After that, he taped her ankles together and she heard each of her friends cry out in turn, probably as he did the same to them. He then dragged her by her feet across the floor before flipping her over so that she was lying on her back. He had moved her deeper into the great room so that her head rested a foot from a wall, and above her rose a thirty-six-foot cathedral ceiling. She tilted her head up as much as she could, and watched as he dragged over her friends, lining them up so they were in a row.

He disappeared for several minutes after that. When she could see him next, he had his back turned to them, but her blood chilled as she saw that he had taken off not only all of his black-as-night clothing, but his mask also. The only thing he didn't take off were his latex gloves. He left them again, and she saw that he'd been setting up a video recorder. She wanted to scream, but her throat had become too constricted by fear.

He returned carrying a large canvas bag, which he placed on the floor. He bent over the bag and dug inside of it, taking out a hammer, what Mia guessed was a box of nails, a soup spoon, and one of those sharp pen-shaped knives similar to what her dad used when he made detailed miniature models of the structures he built, all of which he lay carefully on the floor in front of the bag. The last thing he took out was a hunting knife, the blade of which looked razor sharp. Mia stared mesmerized as he ran his thumb along the edge of the blade, and then playfully shook his hand as if he had accidentally sliced his thumb open.

"Goddamn, that's sharp," he said.

He looked up then so that Mia and her friends could see not only his face, but that he was grinning. Even though her throat felt like it had closed up, she started screaming, the sound coming out of her not much different than what a strangled cat might make. She couldn't help herself after seeing what was in his eyes. Even with her lizard brain taking over completely, she found herself wondering why Courtney was yelling *no* over and over again.

The killer told them to scream as much as they wanted. That had to be what he was. A *killer*.

"This house is too well constructed and too far away from any neighbors. Nobody is going to hear you. But please do keep on screaming. It's my favorite kind of music. I like it even more than heavy metal. Even more than Metallica."

Mia twisted her head enough to see the killer kneel next to Courtney. He told her that he wasn't happy about being stood up.

"Think of how upsetting it was driving all the way to Malibu, arriving here precisely at ten as you asked, only to find the house empty," the killer said. "Because of your rudeness, you'll be first. Oh yeah, if you haven't figured it out yet, I lied before about not hurting any of you. There will be so much hurting."

Mia thought of how they'd left the veranda door unlocked when they made their naked run to the ocean. He must've been hiding in the shadows and used the opportunity to gain access to the house.

When she saw what he started to do to Courtney with the hunting knife, she squeezed her eyes shut.

Chapter 34

Perlmutter almost drifted off, and if the guy he thought of as Mr. X hadn't stopped to stand under the full moon as if he were soaking in the moonlight, Perlmutter might've missed him leaving the house. He woke up fully then, and watched Mr. X in silhouette as if he were a werewolf baying silently at the moon. Perlmutter sucked in his breath and pushed himself deeper into the bushes where he was hiding. It was a good thing he did, because Mr. X slung his bag over his shoulder and passed by so closely that Perlmutter could smell his muskiness. There was something almost bestial about the odor that came off of him. He watched as the man continued on toward the front gate, and no more than a minute later he heard what sounded like Mr. X climbing over it.

Earlier that day Perlmutter had gone to this odd little spy shop in downtown Los Angeles and overextended his credit cards, buying several items that he thought would be useful: binoculars, a lock pick, and a GPS tracking device. He would've also liked to have bought night goggles, but they were just too much money.

After his trip to the spy store, he made a quick stop at a doughnut shop before heading to Simi Valley. He'd originally thought he'd offer one of Sheila Proops's neighbors a percentage of his movie if they'd let him use their house to spy on her, but three of the houses surrounding hers had *For Sale* signs. When he investigated the house right across the street, he found it empty. It made sense. Who'd want to live that close to a serial killer? He walked around to the back of the house, and put the lock pick to work. He'd never used one before, but the guy at the spy store had demonstrated how to open a lock with it, and after several minutes and a lot of sweat, Perlmutter succeeded in unlocking the back door.

All of the furniture had been cleared out except for a card table and a folding chair, which he guessed a realtor had left for open houses. He had to hide his car so it wouldn't be sitting in the driveway for anyone to see. He moved fast, speed walking into the attached garage, pulling the garage door up, rushing outside so he could drive into the garage, then finally pulling the garage door down after him. He was close to hyperventilating as he stumbled out of his car and stood bent over with his hands resting on his knees. After several minutes he found he could breathe more normally. No sirens, no police banging on the front door, no sign that a neighbor had seen him do this. He reentered the house and stood to the side as he peered out the front window. It looked as if he was in the clear. In a whoosh, he let out his breath, not even realizing he'd been holding it.

He brought the chair up to the second level, and chose for his stakeout what must've recently been a little girl's room, given the unicorns and the little princess painted on the wall. He used his binoculars to watch Sheila Proops's house. If there was one thing Perlmutter had little trouble doing, it was sitting like a lump.

Much later, after it had gotten dusky out, Proops's garage door lifted open and Mr. X drove a dented-up Honda out of it. Perlmutter stumbled to his feet then, and in his rush to his own car, left behind the remaining three doughnuts from the dozen he'd bought earlier. Mr. X had a solid-minute head start over Perlmutter, but fortunately he drove the speed limit and stopped at all the stop signs (something Perlmutter didn't bother to do), and Perlmutter was able to catch up to him and follow him to Malibu.

By this time it had gotten dark out, and Perlmutter cut his lights and watched as Mr. X dumped his car in the driveway of a darkened house where the owners must've been gone for the night, and then carried a gym bag over his shoulder as he made his way on foot to the house where Perlmutter was now hiding. It was just ten o'clock when he had reached the gate. Perlmutter watched as Mr. X rang the intercom buzzer, and after several minutes of no one answering, threw the bag over the gate and climbed over it. Perlmutter then drove back to where Mr. X had dumped his car, and attached his GPS tracking device to the undercarriage of the Honda. He then drove around until he could pull the same trick that Mr. X did, parking his car in the dark-ened driveway of an owner who was gone for the night. After that, he jogged back to the property where Mr. X had rung the intercom buzzer. He was huffing and puffing badly by the time he got there. The gate was about four feet high. He waited until his breathing slowed down, and then somehow he was able to get over the gate without making too much noise.

Perlmutter quickly dropped to his hands and knees and moved carefully after that, staying where he'd be shielded from the moon-light. He didn't so much see Mr. X as sense his presence, and Perl-mutter then shrunk into the bushes and waited while the cool night air dried the perspiration covering his body. Forty minutes later the lights turned on in the house, then twenty minutes after that he heard what sounded like high school girls laughing as they raced to the ocean. It was only after the sounds of their laughter faded that Mr. X emerged from his own hiding space. Perlmutter could see him in the moonlight as he made his way to the back of the house.

Now that Mr. X was gone, Perlmutter crawled away from the bushes and clumsily got to his feet. His legs had fallen asleep, and he stamped his feet while trying to slap some feeling into his legs. Once the pins-and-needles feeling subsided, he cautiously made his way to the back of the house. He got onto the veranda, then moved silently toward the sliding glass doors, stopping only when his nose was an inch away from them. He strained to peer through the glass. The lights were set on dim in the great room, but something about the floor looked wrong. It was as if there was a puddle of something back there. Perlmutter tried the sliding door and found it unlocked. An uneasiness filled his chest as he walked into the house and con-tinued on to where he thought he saw a puddle. In the dimness of the room, he first saw the expanding purplish-black puddle, then his gaze lifted and he noticed the numbers scrawled on the wall: 43, 44, 45, and 46. Only then did he see the four naked girls lying under those scrawled numbers in what he guessed was a large pool of blood. They were dead. Perlmutter knew that right away. Anyone would've known that right away. But there was something very off about the way they looked. Their eyes were all open, but they seemed too large and mismatched. Their breasts also were mismatched. Perlmutter couldn't quite make sense of what he was seeing. He left to find the light switch. After he dialed the overhead lights to their maximum brightness, he returned to the dead girls.

Under the brightened lights, Perlmutter could see that the viscous liquid the girls were lying in was indeed blood, and that the numbers on the wall were also painted in blood. The girls looked so much paler in the brighter lights, and as Perlmutter studied them more intently, he realized why their eyes looked so wrong. Their eyelids had been cut off, and the eyes in their sockets weren't their own and weren't matched up. The killer (because now Perlmutter thought of Mr. X only as *the killer*) must've dug out their eyes and swapped them around. Perlmutter, while avoiding the pool of blood, moved closer, and he saw that their breasts had been nailed to their bodies. As with their eyes, the killer had cut off their breasts and had swapped them between the girls, leaving them mismatched.

He felt an intense coldness filling up his head. If this were a clichéd serial-killer movie, he'd be retching his stomach out, but this wasn't some clichéd movie. Perlmutter walked away from the dead girls and sat down heavily on a cream-colored leather sofa. He took out his cell phone and started to dial 911, but instead of hitting the *call* button, he turned his phone off.

If he called the police, they'd want to know why he was there, and if he told them about the killer, they'd want to know why he didn't call them earlier when he knew the man was hiding outside the house. Perlmutter knew there was something very wrong about him, and not just because the man was staying with Sheila Proops. But did he really believe the killer had come to this house to butcher these girls? He saw him ringing the buzzer earlier. Didn't that mean they were expecting him? The killer might've climbed over the gate, but wasn't it possible that his intention was simply to innocently surprise them when they returned?

Perlmutter sat numbly as he tried to figure all this out. He struggled to make sense of the thoughts he'd had when he was hiding in the bushes and heard those girls laughing as they ran to the beach. When Perlmutter saw that man leaving his hiding place and head toward the back of the house, he had imagined sickening things happening to those girls once they returned from the ocean, but at the time didn't he blame those thoughts on an overactive imagination? Spending his day following that man had seemed surreal. Dreamlike, almost as if he were watching a movie. Did he really believe that man was going to torture and kill those girls? But if not, why else was he drawn to the house to see what had happened?

As Perlmutter tried to sort through all of this and understand his role in the girls' deaths, he realized he didn't feel much of anything. He didn't even feel sorry for the horror those girls had gone through. Slowly, he accepted why that was. They didn't seem real anymore. The killer had left them looking like grotesque movie props. Even though he had only hours earlier heard them laughing with so much life and vitality, after what the killer had done to them it was impossible to think of them as ever being living, breathing people.

Perlmutter knew if he called the police he'd be publicly shamed for not doing anything to save these girls. He also knew he might find himself in serious legal trouble. That wasn't why he didn't call them. No, if that was all it was, he would've taken his lumps, even if it meant Jane thinking the absolute worst of him. But something else stopped him from completing the 911 call, and for a long time he couldn't figure out what it was. When the answer finally hit him, it was like a lightning bolt. He understood fully then what it was his subconscious had picked up on to keep him from calling the police, and he started trembling. Not out of fear, but excitement. Because he saw clear as day the new direction his movie had taken, and he understood the impossibly unique opportunity he'd been handed. A once-in-a-lifetime opportunity.

There was nothing he or anyone else could do for these girls. His movie was an entirely different matter.

Perlmutter found a towel in the bathroom that he used to wipe off any surface he might've touched, and he left the house.

Chapter 35

Griffin hadn't even taken two steps into the house when he heard Sheila calling for him in a voice that sounded like a sputtering, broken-down garbage disposal on the verge of conking out. Against her strenuous objections, he'd put her to bed before he had left for the night. He knew she'd be wide awake when he got back.

He had the impulse to ignore her, but he softened. After dropping his bag off by the TV in the living room, he continued on to her room. Even with the lights off he could make out her cadaverous, shrunken form under the blanket. An intensity burned in her left eye.

"Peaches, you called?" he asked.

Peaches was the nickname he had come up for her, since she reminded him of a peach that had been left out in the sun for weeks. The fruit might've been juicy and firm at one time, but now it was only a shriveled, dried-out thing without a single drop of juice remaining. That was Sheila, all right.

"Did you kill them?"

Griffin made a disgusted face, exaggerating it so that it looked almost comical.

"You couldn't wait until morning to ask me that?"

"Tell me!"

He sighed in a put-upon way. "What do you think?" he asked.

The left side of her face became rigid, while the paralyzed right side continued to sag. In her icy fury, she seemed to have even more difficulty than usual pushing out each word as she breathlessly demanded, "Let . . . me . . . see . . . the . . . recording!"

Griffin made a show of squinting at the clock radio on her night table.

"Peaches, it's four o'clock. You need your beauty sleep. Badly. I'll play you the recording in the morning."

"Now!"

"You really are a bloodthirsty little peach, aren't you?"

But Griffin lifted her out of bed and placed her in her wheelchair, and he rolled her out to the living room. He had only been teasing her earlier, as he had every intention of showing her the recording he had made of the murders. She wasn't just living vicariously through him. These murders were her idea, and while he might've been the one to wield the knife and other tools that he used, she owned these murders almost as much as he did. Besides, he was dying not only to see the recording, but to share it with Sheila. There was nobody else who would've been able to fully appreciate what he had done. The relaxed indifference he had been showing was an act. Inside he was so wired that he could imagine himself bouncing off the walls if he let himself go.

The first time he had ever murdered two people in the same afternoon was at that gaudy San Luis Obispo resort, and those murders weren't done at the same time. First the wife, then an hour wait, and then the husband. As thrilling as those killings had been, this was very different. This time he murdered those girls at almost the same moment, even timing it so they all bled out within a minute of each other. And these weren't just killings, but his legacy. The first of a set of murders that would make him one of Los Angeles's most notorious serial killers. The rush from it was indescribable. Even an hour and a half later he felt an intense buzz running through his body as if he were attached to a high-voltage wire.

Griffin connected the video recorder to the TV and started the recording. It lasted almost three hours, and he and Sheila sat in awed silence like they were in a special church that existed only for them.

When he was with those girls, he had imagined the beast coming out in all of its savagery. He knew logically the beast wasn't real, that it was only a trick of the mind, and that he didn't actually transform into a werewolf or any other supernatural creature. Even so, as he watched the video he swore that some sort of transformation did occur. Not that he grew fur or fangs or claws, but something subtle did happen.

The video ended and for several minutes Griffin and Sheila sat in silence as static played over the TV.

"Can you breathe better now?" Griffin asked.

Sheila had gone through a small transformation of her own. Her flesh looked less desiccated and her body slightly less twisted.

"Yes," she said. "Much better."

He got up and went to the kitchen to start a pot of coffee brewing. Once it finished, he poured his into a ceramic mug and Sheila's into a Styrofoam cup that would be able to fit into a cup holder attached to her wheelchair. He added sugar and cream to Sheila's so it would be the way she liked it, and he brought the coffees out to the living room.

They sat quietly for several minutes sipping their coffee, and then Griffin restarted the video, and as before the two of them watched with rapt attention.

Chapter 36

Like most Sunday mornings, Parker began grunting excitedly at seven o'clock when the doorbell rang. Morris rolled out of bed, slipped on a robe, and handed Parker off to Kat, their twenty-four-year-old dog walker, so that she could take him to Lake Hollywood Park. This was an indulgence for Morris and Natalie, and it allowed them to lounge in bed until ten thirty. When Kat returned with Parker at eleven, coffee was brewing and Natalie was chopping up a pineapple for a fruit salad while Morris fried up a favorite of theirs—French toast made with thick slices of challah and stuffed with Havarti cheese and Black Forest ham. Parker enthusiastically greeted both of them while keeping an eye on the French toast.

The French toast had already been flipped and both sides fried to a nice, golden brown. Morris was using a spatula to get the pieces out of the frying pan when his cell phone rang. Caller ID showed *Los Angeles Mayor's Office*. Morris frowned, thinking it might be Doug Gilman. Gilman was twenty-nine, ambitious, with a perfect head of hair, even more perfect teeth, and the type of bronze tan that you get from religiously using a tanning bed. Even though he had that hungry Hollywood look about him, he was not an actor, and was instead the mayor's deputy assistant. It was Gilman who had convinced Morris into taking on the Skull Cracker Killer investigation six months earlier.

"Morris Brick," Morris announced.

"This is Doug Gilman—"

"I'm not taking any more serial-killer investigations," Morris said, cutting him off.

"That's damn abrupt," Gilman said. "Damn succinct too. How'd you know that's why I'm calling?"

"Why else would you be?"

"Very true," Gilman said after thinking it over. "But Morris, this is a bad one, even worse than those SCK murders."

"That's what your homicide department is for."

"When you formed MBI, you took the department's best homicide detectives with you, including yourself."

"You've still got good people in the department."

"Yeah, I know, but four young women were butchered in the sickest ways imaginable. This happened last night in Malibu, and if you saw what was done to them, you'd understand why I need you and MBI on this. Jesus, Morris, if you came to the murder scene, I guarantee you'd want to take this on."

"Doug, that's why I'm not going to see it." Morris paused to let out a heavy sigh that came deep from his belly. "I'm sorry to disappoint you, but I'm passing on this."

"Okay, okay. Look, if you change your mind, call me. This maniac is going to be killing again, and no one else should die the way these four women did."

Morris put his cell phone away and got the last pieces of the stuffed French toast out of the frying pan before they burned. Natalie had stopped chopping up the pineapple, and he could feel her eyes on him. When he looked over at her, he could see concern lining her brow.

"There was a murder last night?" Natalie asked.

He nodded. "Four women murdered."

Natalie seemed to age a decade right then. "They think it's a serial killer?"

"Yeah. At least Doug Gilman thinks so."

"What do you think?"

"I have no idea. I don't know any of the details, and I don't want to know any of them."

Natalie shifted her gaze away from him, and her eyes glazed as if she were staring at something miles away. While she fell into her private thoughts, she bit lightly on her knuckle. Parker, who'd been sitting as still as a marble sculpture as he stared fixatedly at the plate of French toast, let out an impatient whine. That knocked Morris and Natalie out of the trances they'd fallen into, and Morris brought the plate of French toast to the kitchen table while Natalie brought over the large bowl of fruit salad. They ate quietly for several minutes, both lost in their own thoughts, both absently giving in to Parker's mooching and handing him bite-sized pieces of the French toast. Finally, Natalie broke the silence and asked Morris why it was so important for the city to get him and MBI investigating these murders.

"Annie Walsh is an excellent detective. And the department has other very good homicide detectives."

"True," Morris agreed. He put down his fork and his eyes softened as he showed a more philosophical look. "I'm afraid I'm a victim of my own success. When they hired me for the SCK killings, it was purely for cover. The NYPD and FBI had gotten nowhere in solving the killings that happened in New York five years earlier, and Doug was afraid the same would happen in LA. And so I was hired to show that the city was doing everything possible to catch SCK."

"So they wouldn't take as much heat when more killings happened."

"Yeah."

"And since you caught SCK, the city now believes they have to hire you, or they'll take heat for not doing everything possible to catch this psychopath if he kills again."

"Exactly."

Natalie nodded as she fell deep into more private thoughts. When Parker let out another impatient whine, she absently fed him the piece of French toast she was about to spear with her fork.

"How old were the women who were murdered?"

"I don't know. Doug said they were young."

"Rachel's age?"

Morris shrugged.

"I know you told me you weren't going to take on any more of these cases, but is this something you want to do?"

"No." Morris's face darkened. "I'm done with murders, and I'm especially done with serial killers."

Natalie nodded. She certainly didn't want him to take on any more of those investigations. The last serial-killer investigation he had worked before retiring from the force was the Hillside Cannibal murders, and that investigation almost killed him. Then the next one, the SCK investigation, ended up leading the killer to their doorstep. Even though Morris had turned Gilman down, the phone call had cast a pall over their brunch, and the two of them were mostly going through the motions as they ate their stuffed French toast and fruit salad. In fact, Natalie barely tasted any of it. Morris tried to break the mood they'd fallen into, remarking how Parker had been taking advantage of the situation.

"Nat, I think he's mooched half of our food."

"At least," Natalie agreed.

Morris's cell phone rang again. The way he frowned at the caller ID had Natalie asking whether it was Doug Gilman calling again.

"No, one of my clients. Brett Dickerson."

Morris answered the phone. Natalie felt an iciness run down her spine as she watched how grim Morris's expression became as he sat quietly and listened to what his client had to say. She could only guess what Dickerson was telling her husband, but still, tears welled up in her eyes. When Morris offered words of sympathy, she almost broke out crying. Finally, he got off the phone, his face ashen.

"Brett Dickerson is the client whose daughter you recently saved? The one who's going to UCLA and is Rachel's age?"

"Yeah."

"Was she one of the girls killed last night in Malibu?"

Morris gave her a bleak smile. "I have to look into this, Nat," he said.

She nodded.

He dug his cell phone out of his pocket and called Doug Gilman.

Chapter 37

Morris met a patrolman at the gate that he didn't know from his time on the force, and after identifying himself, was let in. A long line of cars and ambulances were already parked in the private drive leading up to the property, and Morris left his car at the back of the line. As he walked toward the house, he gave Doug Gilman a call to let him know he was making his way to the front door. The private drive was maybe an eighth of a mile long, and from a distance the house looked like the photos of the Tuscan villa that Philip Stonehedge's friend owned, except much bigger, newer, and grander. Morris had no idea what a property like this would be worth. Tens of millions at least, although having four girls killed inside would probably knock a few million off the value.

Gilman was waiting for Morris outside the house. The mayor's deputy assistant looked more gaunt in the face since Morris had last seen him, and his skin color had a greenish tinge to it. When they shook hands, Gilman's skin felt clammy, as if he were suffering from the flu. The mayor's deputy assistant attempted a queasy smile.

"What was done to those girls is something out of a bad nightmare," he confided to Morris. "I wish I had never seen it. To tell the truth, I'd pay a lot to be able to unsee it."

They sat on Adirondack chairs that had been arranged on the front porch, and Gilman explained how Brett Dickerson had developed the property, and how he had allowed his daughter and three of her friends to stay there for the night.

"He was going to surprise them by catering a brunch from Fineries here in Malibu. The caterers were given a key and a guest security code, and when they showed up this morning at seven A.M., they

stumbled onto the bodies. A sliding glass door in back was left unlocked. That seems to be how the killer got into the house."

Unless the killer was let in, or had been given a key and a guest
security code. Morris didn't waste time mentioning that, or asking
about the caterers. The police would check them out thoroughly, as
well as anyone else working at Fineries.

"Who's here now?" Morris asked.

Gilman wiped a hand across his eyes as if he were trying to wipe
away his queasiness. It didn't work.

"Crime-scene team. Commissioner Hadley. Roger Smichen. Detectives Walsh and Malevich. An FBI profiler out of the LA office
named Gloria Finston arrived here about a half ago. Uniformed cops
have been coming and going. A small army of them are now can-
vassing the neighborhood."

"I got a call from Brett Dickerson," Morris said. "He was here
earlier."

Gilman reacted with surprise that Morris knew that. "Yes, he was
here," he admitted. "Dickerson had gotten a call from the caterers
after they made their discovery, and he came straight here and forced
his way through the police and into the house. As you can guess, he
was distraught, and several uniformed officers escorted him back to
his home in Brentwood. He's already given the mayor an earful." He
lowered his voice as if he were gossiping information that he shouldn't,
and added, "Dickerson is a major donor to the mayor's campaign."

"Which is why you want to bring me and MBI into the investigation."

"One of several reasons," Gilman acknowledged. "Perhaps that's
the mayor's primary one. Mine is to catch this bastard before he kills
anyone else, and you being involved gives us the best chance of that."
He gave Morris a curious look. "Do you know Brett Dickerson?"

Morris nodded. "I'll explain how later."

Detectives Annie Walsh and Greg Malevich were huddled with
Commissioner Martin Hadley and a couple of Hadley's flunkies.
With his round, jowly face, thick, meaty lips, and white hair cropped
close enough to his scalp to look like fur, Hadley resembled a corpu-
lent English bulldog, and as he caught sight of Morris entering the
room, he showed the kind of cantankerous scowl you might see on a

bulldog. That was pretty much the reaction Morris had expected. The two of them didn't get along when Morris was on the force, and he knew Hadley had to hate the idea of throwing any business to Morris and MBI. But Hadley was first and foremost a political animal, and he knew that the politically astute move was to bring MBI into this both for the publicity value and for cover. Morris caught Annie Walsh's and Malevich's attention, and signaled that he'd talk with them soon. First he needed to see the four dead girls.

During his drive to Malibu, he had decided he would avoid examining the bodies. The odds were this investigation was going to be all about tracking down Chuck Macon, and if for some reason he needed any of the gory details, he'd be able to get them from the medical examiner's report, assuming he took on the investigation. Once he stepped inside the house, he had a change of heart and accepted that he needed to see the murder scene for two reasons. First, in case something caught his eye that others might've missed, and second, he owed it to the victims and especially to Mia Dickerson, the girl whose life he thought he had saved, to bear witness to what was done to them.

The pool of blood that had earlier surrounded the girls had been vacuumed up. Forensics would later sift through the blood for hair, fibers, and any other material that could help identify the killer. Morris noted that while the natural color of the hardwood floor was a deep red, it didn't hide the stain that the blood had left.

"Rosewood."

The medical examiner, Roger Smichen, had sidled up alongside Morris. A tall, cadaverous-looking man, with a completely bald head. Ever since Morris had known him, his face had always been as hairless as his scalp if you ignored his sparse light brown eyebrows, but Smichen now sported a carefully groomed goatee. Morris gave him a questioning look, and the medical examiner explained that the floor was rosewood. "I thought you retired from this kind of work," he said.

"I thought so too, but then this happened."

Smichen gave Morris an appraising look. A light clicked on in his eyes. "You knew one of the girls," he said.

Morris had been trying hard to maintain a stoic countenance. In this kind of work it was important to keep an emotional distance. If you let it get personal, you made mistakes. What was done to Mia and her friends was feeling very personal.

"In a way," Morris admitted. "Is it that obvious?"

"You look like how I feel. Like you want to rip someone's head off."

Morris realized then how clenched his jaw muscles had gotten. He breathed deeply to relax his facial features.

"Better?" he asked.

"Slightly. Now you only look like you want to rip someone's arm off."

"Progress, I guess."

Smichen nodded, his expression bleak. "These murders were every bit as horrific as they look," he said. "Ligature marks on their wrists indicates plastic ties were used to bind them. This victim—" he indicated Mia—"suffered a badly dislocated shoulder. None of the other victims did."

Softly, Morris said, "The killer had Mia secure her friends' wrists behind their backs, and afterwards the killer did Mia himself."

"Most likely. There's also adhesive residue on their ankles. I'll do tests later, but odds are it came from duct tape. I couldn't find fibers in their mouths, or any other physical evidence to suggest that he had gagged them."

"Because he didn't care if they screamed."

"No doubt he enjoyed listening to it. The mutilations were done while the victims were alive. I'm guessing those nails are long enough to have punctured those girls' lungs. I'll know for sure when I do the autopsies. One thing I can tell you definitively, death was caused by severing their femoral arteries, and from the way they bled their hearts must've been at a very weakened state."

Morris realized his jaw muscles were clenching tightly again. He concentrated once more to relax them. Still, his voice was strained as he said, "So this went on for hours."

A woman's voice to Morris's left said, "At least."

A slight, dark-haired woman in her forties had snuck up alongside him. With her narrow face, longish, thin nose and small, pale eyes, she made Morris think of a sparrow.

"Dr. Gloria Finston," she said, holding out an equally slight hand. "Special agent, FBI."

Morris took her hand. It was like holding a smooth piece of ivory. "Morris Brick," he said.

"I'm well aware." Her thin lips formed a small V. "Mr. Brick, or may I call you Morris?"

"Morris is fine."

"And please call me Gloria. Our killer seems to have enjoyed himself and he might've tortured these girls even longer, but he may have sensed that they were close to death, and that's when he cut their femoral arteries."

"That fits with the way they bled out," Smichen agreed. "Not much, if any, arterial spray."

"What do you make of the numbers he painted above the victims?" Finston asked Morris.

The obvious answer was that the numbers represented the killer's current score. If the murderer was Chuck Macon, as Morris suspected, then that meant Macon had killed forty-two people before entering this house. He found that hard to believe. From what he had read about Macon from his trial transcript and prison record, the guy was a chiseler, and most likely a sociopath, but there was little in his background to suggest he was a serial killer. He would've killed Mia out of anger and to get back at her dad. Painting those numbers in blood could've been done simply to make the police think they were chasing after a serial killer with a high body count as a way to throw them off scent.

"There's a very obvious reason," Morris said.

Another of Finston's small V smiles. "Which you don't think is likely."

"Has the FBI seen one other killing like this one before, let alone forty-two?"

"We haven't," she admitted. "What do you think the numbers are for, then?"

"Let me gather some people, and I'll tell you my theory."

Chapter 38

Morris took the seat at the head of the dining-room table while Gilman, Finston, Malevich, and Walsh sat around it. The room should've been far enough away from the murders so that he wouldn't have to smell the girls' blood lingering in the air any longer, but as he told them about Chuck Macon and Pavlo Lebed, it was as if his nostrils were clogged with the sweet coppery odor. He badly wanted coffee right then. Anything to get that odor out of his nose and the taste from his throat.

Walsh gave him an incredulous look when he finished filling them in.

"Why didn't you have LAPD pick him up? You could've had him held until an arrest warrant was issued for his parole violation," she demanded indignantly.

"I didn't have enough for a conspiracy-to-commit murder charge."

"I'm not sure about that," Greg Malevich interjected, throwing in his two cents.

Morris shook his head, heat prickling his cheeks. "If LAPD had picked him up, they'd have cut him loose right afterwards," he argued. "It was handled the way the client wanted it handled. Which was to get him out of the condo, and to keep Mia from knowing the full extent of what this guy was up to."

"You should've called me," Walsh insisted. "I would've found a way to keep him locked up. Now the guy's in the wind."

She was only Monday-morning quarterbacking. Both of the LAPD homicide detectives were. While Morris had discovered enough to know what Macon and Lebed had been planning, he never had any solid evidence. Lebed's inside man Mishka Stus might've confirmed their scheme, but he did so in such a way that Morris wouldn't be able to use his words in a criminal complaint. If Morris were still on the force, and a private investigator had come to him with the same bundle of guesswork and innuendo, he would've told the PI to get him something solid before he'd be able to arrest Macon, and he was sure Annie would've told him the same. What Morris had a difficult time reconciling was how convinced he was that Macon would run hard and fast to try to put as much distance between himself and the Ukrainian gangster once he realized their plan had fallen apart. He never would've expected Macon to hang around LA so he could enact this kind of grotesque revenge on Mia and her dad. If Macon really did do this, then Morris had badly misjudged him, and he'd have a hard time ever forgiving himself for that. Still, even though he knew Annie had said what she did out of anger and frustration, his defenses were up, and he was about to argue further when Finston interrupted their squabble.

"I don't think Chuck Macon is our killer." The FBI profiler met Morris's gaze and showed her tiny V smile again, and this time there was something apologetic about it. "These murders weren't done out of anger or passion. There was great care and deliberation involved. To our killer these murders were something glorious, and while I'm sure he enjoyed inflicting pain on these young women, he had a far more important purpose for what he did. I'm further convinced he didn't paint those numbers to confuse us, but instead because he has forty-two other victims. Except those murders were done more quietly. These were done to grab our attention in a spectacular fashion."

"Why the change?" Gilman asked.

Finston's smile turned up a notch. "Because of a recent event. Something transformative. The killer now craves notoriety, and he wants full credit for all of his killings."

"It's possible," Morris conceded. "It's also possible I misjudged Macon and he's far more than a sociopathic con man. Maybe he's even got forty-two other dead bodies to his credit. And maybe the transformative act you mentioned was having his latest scheme blow up on him."

Finston sat for a moment, caressing her very slight chin as she considered what Morris said.

"That's also possible," she agreed.

"When was that newlywed couple killed in that crazy place in

San Luis Obispo?" Malevich asked. "You know, that resort with those movie-themed rooms."

"I think that was Wednesday," Walsh said.

Malevich nodded, agreeing with Walsh's recollection. "We should check that out. See if the killer painted forty-one and forty-two in blood over those bodies."

Finston was interested. "Do you know any of the details of those murders?"

Malevich shook his head. "The SLOPD has kept a tight lid on it, but I heard from a buddy that the hotel room looked like a slaughter-house. Like they might have to rename it the Tobe Hooper room."

"The director of *The Texas Chainsaw Massacre*," Walsh explained to the FBI profiler.

"I'll get copies of the police reports, and see if these murders could be connected," Finston said.

"If they are, it doesn't preclude Macon from being our killer," Morris said.

Finston nodded. "Agreed."

Morris turned to Gilman. "I'll make this simple: If you want me and MBI involved, my condition is that I focus exclusively on Macon. Annie and Greg and the rest of the LAPD can look into the couple killed in San Luis Obispo and run down any other angles in the meantime."

"That makes sense," Gilman agreed. He paused for a moment, looking as if he were suffering a bad case of gas, and then asked, "You're that sure he's the killer?"

"No. Because if he is, I badly misread him. But I won't be able to sleep at night until I know for sure."

Chapter 39

Morris brought Parker with him to his hastily arranged meeting at Little Kiev. The sign on the door claimed that the Russian restaurant was closed and didn't open until five on Sundays, but that didn't stop two of Lebed's thick-necked men from letting Morris in after he knocked. Morris recognized one of the men from the photos Polk had taken at the Hollywood Hills Casino. That was the one who grunted at Morris, demanding to pat him down. When the thug took a step toward him, Parker began growling.

"I don't think he likes you," Morris said.

The Ukrainian stopped in his tracks as he gave Parker a cautious look. He asked Morris in a series of barely decipherable grunts if he was carrying.

"Nope."

The thug nodded toward the briefcase Morris was carrying, and Morris opened it to show there were no guns inside.

The Ukrainian looked at his partner, who shrugged in a way to say that looking inside the briefcase was enough, and it wasn't worth getting bitten in the ass in order to check Morris more carefully. The Ukrainian gave Morris a menacing scowl and lifted his cheap suit jacket enough to reveal a holstered Sig Sauer 9mm, and in more barely decipherable grunts warned him not to try anything stupid.

"I'll be on my best behavior," Morris promised.

With the warning delivered, they escorted Morris through the restaurant and brought him to a private dining room where Pavlo Lebed sat with several meat dishes and half a bottle of vodka sitting in front of him. Morris wondered if that was all these Ukrainian gangsters did during their downtime. Eat.

Lebed looked even more like a bull in real life than he did in

Polk's photos. He gave Parker a half-lidded stare before turning those nearly dead eyes toward Morris.

"You brought along muscle," Lebed said, his voice surprisingly a light tenor with very little accent. Given his thick, square body, Morris had been expecting a deeper bass than what he'd heard from his men.

"Nah, just taking him along for the exercise."

"Good, because he don't look so tough."

Morris was going to remark that the Ukrainian mob boss didn't *sound* so tough, but he bit his tongue, and took a seat on Lebed's right while holding a short leash on Parker so the dog couldn't bull his way over to Lebed.

"You haven't seen him in action," Morris said.

Lebed smiled thinly, although his eyes remained unchanged. He cut a piece of lamb from one of his plates and held it out to the bull terrier. The dog's tail wagged slowly, and Morris relented and let out more of the leash so that the bull terrier could grab the food. While Parker chewed on the piece of lamb, Lebed thumped the dog loudly several times on the side.

"Not so tough," Lebed said.

Morris shook his head at Parker. "Traitor," he said. The bull terrier sheepishly came back over to him and sat down.

The thin smile Lebed had showed faded, and his eyes took on a deadlier look.

"I don't like being threatened," he said.

In order to arrange this meeting, Morris had a message delivered to Lebed: *Meet me this afternoon, or MBI will be using all of our resources to put you in prison.*

"It wasn't an idle threat," Morris said. "Only what I expected to do. I want you to take me to Chuck Macon."

"Why?"

Morris took several crime-scene photos from his briefcase and tossed them in front of Lebed. The Ukrainian picked them up, and as he made sense of what he was looking at, a muscle twitched briefly along his jaw.

"You believe Macon could've done this?" he asked, his tenor voice a shade duller than earlier.

"Don't you recognize the dead girl on the left?"

Lebed shook his head.

"Mia Dickerson."

It took Lebed a moment to recognize the name. There was no faking his reaction, and it all but told Morris that if Macon committed these murders, he did it on his own and without the Ukrainian knowing about it.

Lebed handed the photos back to Morris. "When did this happen?" he asked.

"Last night."

Lebed nodded in an almost imperceptible way, as if confirming a thought he had. "Chuck Macon didn't do this," he said.

"Why is that?"

"By last night he was gone."

"What do you mean, *gone*? From LA?"

Lebed made a backhanded dismissive gesture like he was swatting lazily at a fly. "You got wax in your ears? *Gone* as in *gone*."

"Ashes to ashes, huh?"

"Your words, not mine." A shrewd look sparkled in Lebed's eyes. He winked at Morris. "This is what I heard from a reliable source, whose name right now eludes me."

"That's it? No proof you can give me?"

"That's it. He didn't do this. If he did, I'd have my men find him and bring him to you in pieces." A thought occurred to Lebed, and he waved a thick, sausage-like index finger at Morris. "And don't you think I had anything to do with this shit. I'm a businessman. I don't do nothing unless I can make a profit from it. What profit can I make from something like this?"

"None that I can think of," Morris admitted.

"That's right. So we're settled? You trust what I've told you and you won't make any more threats?"

Morris certainly didn't trust Lebed. What he *did* trust was his ability to read people and know when he was being lied to, even by a vicious, sociopathic Ukrainian mob boss. While an unmistakable undercurrent of violence had been present in Lebed's eyes, his expression had otherwise been inscrutable. Two cracks had shown through. The first had been a glimmer of surprise when he learned about Mia Dickerson being one of the four dead girls in the crime-scene photos. The other had been a brief glimpse of certainty regarding Macon already being dead when those girls were killed.

"You've convinced me," Morris admitted. "For now."

"Good." Lebed smiled then. He might've been a ruthless gangster, but from the looks of his smile he took exceptional care of his teeth, better than Morris did his own. He cut another piece of lamb and held it out to Parker, who wagged his tail more enthusiastically this time. Morris let go of enough of the leash to let Parker take the meat.

"Not so good for muscle," Lebed noted. "Too easily corrupted."

"You found his weak spot," Morris noted with a sigh.

"Very true," Lebed said, grinning. "My specialty." The mob boss barked out something in Russian or Ukrainian, Morris wasn't sure which. His two thugs who must've been waiting right outside, because they quickly they came into the room. Lebed gave them another order in whatever language they spoke, and his hired men escorted Morris and Parker out of the restaurant. Once he was outside and in the bright LA sunshine, he called Doug Gilman and told him that Chuck Macon wasn't their killer.

"That was fast," Gilman said. "Any chance you're wrong about that?"

"None."

"That's too bad," Gilman said, his disappointment evident. "You had me hoping we'd be able to clear this up quickly. So what now?"

"I'm not sure. Let's meet at MBI in two hours and figure it out."

Morris called Felger and Bogle, interrupting their Sunday afternoons, and they both agreed to meet up at the MBI office without any complaints. When he called Lemmon, his investigator thanked him.

"Corrine is about to pick my next task from her dreaded 'honey-do' list," Lemmon said. "I've got a sneaking suspicion it's going to be power-washing the deck. Yeah, I think I'd rather come in."

Polk, though, was another matter.

"I'm at the Dodgers game," he grumbled. "I was planning to have some cold ones and ribs afterwards with buddies."

Morris heard the ball game in the background. A large groan had just risen up from the crowd. Something bad had happened to the home team.

"You've got buddies?"

"Well, yeah, a few, but that's only because they don't know me well enough yet. What's so urgent?"

"We've got four dead girls who died badly last night in Malibu. LA is taking jurisdiction, and the mayor's office wants us to take the lead."

"Is there a way not to die badly?"

"Just about any other way would be better than what happened to these girls."

"I thought we weren't taking on any more murder investigations?"

"This one's different."

"Why?"

"Mia Dickerson was one of the victims. The other three were friends of hers."

"Jesus." The connection went mostly quiet for a long moment, with only some sporadic jeers from the crowd coming through. Morris figured things were not going well for the Dodgers. When Polk spoke next, his voice sounded as if his throat had tightened with emotion. "I was afraid you were going to say that."

"Yeah, I figured as much."

"That sonofabitch Macon killed them."

"That was my first thought, but he's not our guy. It's not Lebed, either. It looks like we've got a serial killer. A really nasty one. Maybe the same guy who killed the newlywed couple in San Luis Obispo last week."

"There hasn't been much in the news about that couple," Polk said.

"There hasn't," Morris agreed. "I'm going to call SLOPD when I get back to the office. The FBI profiler on these girls' murders is also going to be contacting them."

Polk chewed on that for a moment. "Awfully big coincidence that a serial killer would target Mia Dickerson a day after Macon is sent packing."

"It's a funny world sometimes."

"Yeah, but I'm not much in the mood for laughing right now. I'll be there as soon as I can."

"I can't ask for more than that," Morris said.

Chapter 40

Perlmutter might've had a small, cramped studio apartment, but there were still places for a cat to hide—even a fat, orange tabby—and shortly after 3:00 in the afternoon Orson emerged from behind the ratty brown sofa. He yawned as if he'd just woken up from a nap, and after stretching, he padded over to where Perlmutter was sitting at his computer desk, and meowed angrily.

As if he were in a daze, Perlmutter blindly reached down, picked up the overweight tabby, and plopped him on his lap. The tabby let out another angry meow and poked Perlmutter several times in the face. He didn't seem to notice. Instead, he stared at the computer screen with tears welling up in his eyes. Orson had to poke him several more times before he flinched and noticed his cat.

"Yeah, I know," Perlmutter muttered miserably. "You're still holding a grudge for not feeding you until three-thirty A.M. I'm sorry, okay? That was the earliest I could get home."

As if to further demonstrate his resentment, Orson turned and stretched up toward the computer, then started batting at the keyboard and adding random letters to the screenplay Perlmutter was working on.

"Go ahead," he said despairingly. "Whatever you type I'm sure will be better than the garbage I've been coming up with."

As yet a further act of protest, Orson leapt from Perlmutter's lap and onto the computer desk. After circling the monitor, he stretched out on the keyboard, lying on his side so that he faced Perlmutter, his olive-green eyes unblinking as he stared at his roommate.

"Fine. Lie there," Perlmutter said. "It doesn't matter. Jane was right. I'm no better than Sammy Bloom or any of those other hacks."

When Perlmutter returned back to his apartment in the early-morning hours, he first fed Orson his food and then went straight to work on his screenplay. It didn't come as easily as he had thought it would while he was driving home from Malibu. Instead. every moment was a struggle. Hour after hour he had worked on it, but everything he wrote turned out to be clichéd mediocrity. There was no nuance or subtlety. No cleverness. No underlying subtext. The characters were flat, no better than cardboard cutouts. He threw away his work and started over five times, and each time his writing only got more mediocre and scattered.

"Who am I kidding?" he told Orson. "I'm no screenwriter. All I am is a pathetic, delusional schmuck. Everything Jane thought about me is right."

His dream was dead. He was nothing but a fool who had thrown away a small inheritance and years chasing after a dream that was always going to be out of his reach. In many ways this was worse than death, and all he had left was to get his job back at the copy store. He knew if Griezersteen was still there, his old boss would make Perlmutter grovel. He had little doubt that Griezersteen would rub in Perlmutter's words when he quit—about how he wasn't going to waste his life working for a pinhead in some crap job, that bigger things were in store for him.

Perlmutter lowered his face into his hands and broke down sobbing. It seemed a long time before he was able to stop. He moved sluggishly as he got up and washed his face in the bathroom sink. As he stared at his bleary-eyed and blotchy reflection in the cracked mirror above the medicine cabinet, he made a decision. He was going to call the police and let them know about the killer, and how they could find him at Sheila Proops's house. He'd do this anonymously, though, which meant he wouldn't be able to use his cell phone. He thought he remembered seeing a pay phone on South Oxford Avenue near the basketball courts. A pay phone would work. That was a half mile away, but Perlmutter decided to walk it. He just felt so rotten inside, and he hoped walking would make him feel better.

He'd never be able to face Jane again. Or even Bloom, or any of those other wannabe hacks. How could he, knowing what an abject failure he turned out to be? He would instead disappear back into a meaningless job—whether it was at the copy store, or something even worse, and he'd accept that as his lot in life.

He was right about there being a pay phone on South Oxford, but it didn't take coins, only a credit card. If he used a credit card, the police would be able to match it up with his anonymous call. He was going to have to call them another way. Maybe buy one of the phones with prepaid minutes. What did gangbangers call them? A burner phone.

Perlmutter stood frowning at the pay phone while deep in thought about where he'd be able to buy a burner phone. In his peripheral vision he noticed a very pretty young blonde walking quickly toward him. Skipping, really. He turned to face her, and stared dumbly at her as she stopped less than a foot away from him. Up close he saw her dark roots and realized she wasn't naturally blond. Still, she was very pretty, and very young, probably no older than twenty. He was too startled to think of what to say, and he couldn't figure out why she had approached him. She was smiling, but it wasn't exactly a friendly smile.

"Yuck," she said.

She started laughing then, and she ran back across the street from where she came and joined a guy her age who was also good-looking, maybe even better-looking than her. The two of them got very chummy as they wrapped their arms around each other's waists and walked away, all the while laughing themselves to tears at their joke, occasionally looking back at Perlmutter.

At first Perlmutter was in shock as he watched them, wondering: *Did that really happen?* Slowly the shock wore off, and filling the void was an intense rage that he'd never quite experienced before. In his mind's eye, he imagined doing all the horrible things to those two that the killer had done to the four girls. Then, from somewhere inspiration struck, and it left his jaw dropping open. He nearly collapsed onto the pavement as he sat down, barely aware of where he was right then. With crystal clarity he saw how he could write the script that he had spent nearly the last twelve hours struggling over.

He had made things too complicated with his earlier attempts, trying to make it into some great psychological drama with all these confusing underlying themes. No wonder what he had written was so godawful. What he needed to do instead was keep it simple and make it all about his own story. A filmmaker who wants to make a film about a notorious serial killer, and instead stumbles onto the path of an even more noxious serial killer. The filmmaker would then follow this new killer around so he could observe him in action. Where the film would eventually lead, Perlmutter wasn't sure, but he knew when the ending came it would be something startling and explosive. Something amazing.

Perlmutter was trembling in excitement as he stood. He had cracked this nut wide open, and whatever crisis in confidence he had suffered earlier was over. All true artists suffer crippling insecurity at times, right? By the time he arrived back at his apartment he was drenched in perspiration, but he also had the first three pages of the script written in his head.

The Korean restaurant kitchen staff downstairs was making an exceptionally loud racket as they prepared for the Sunday-night dinner crowd. It sounded as if they were purposely banging pots and pans. Perlmutter didn't even notice. He was too busy typing fast and furiously as he tried to keep up with the thoughts racing through his mind. For the next hour he disappeared completely inside his script, and when he emerged he had the first fourteen pages written. He printed the pages out, and his hands shook as he sat on his ratty brown sofa and read them. Orson climbed onto his lap and Perlmutter didn't even notice. What he had written was gold. Brilliant, really. He was sure Getzler would agree. It was amazing that he had doubted himself earlier, actually letting himself think that he was no better than Bloom and those other hacks. Incredible, really.

His script was still going to need a lot of work. He needed to write at least seventy-six more pages so he could reach the industry standard of ninety pages. He didn't want Getzler to think he was some sort of amateur. This meant he was going to have to follow the killer a good while longer, at least until his script reached a natural conclusion. Perlmutter fiddled with the app he had installed on his smartphone when he bought the GPS tracking chip. The killer was still at Sheila Proops's house, or at least his car was.

Perlmutter figured the killer would be taking it easy today. After having a busy night last night, he probably needed his rest. Tomorrow would be different. Perlmutter had little doubt that tomorrow was going to be a hectic day for both of them.

Chapter 41

Almost a full house.

At five o'clock Morris had his full MBI team, Detective Annie Walsh, FBI profiler Gloria Finston, and Doug Gilman sitting around a table in MBI's only conference room. Parker was missing since Morris had dropped him off with Natalie before heading over to the office. Malevich also wasn't there. The LAPD homicide detective was on his way to San Luis Obispo so he could coordinate efforts with the detective in charge of the murder investigation for the honeymooning couple killed in their hotel room; also to show Chuck Macon's picture around the resort. The latter was to cover all bases, because the odds of Macon being the murderer were close to zero. That wasn't just because Morris believed he could read whether or not the Ukrainian mob boss had been lying to him, but from other developments.

The MBI crew and Walsh were drinking coffee, Finston tea, and Gilman a bottle of water. Morris had four pizzas delivered. Polk polished off three slices, but the rest were going to waste, as no one else in the room seemed in the mood to eat.

Morris gave a quick look around the table. Besides Gilman, who still appeared a little green around the gills, people's expressions ranged from inscrutable to bored. Still, he could sense an underlying tension growing in the room. He'd already briefed the MBI team on what happened in Malibu, and the last two hours since his meeting with Lebed had been a whirlwind. He nodded to himself. It was time to begin.

"Roger Smichen will be sending me autopsy reports as soon as they're ready," Morris said. "I talked to him a half hour ago, and he was able to tell me that the killer used four-inch nails when he nailed the severed breasts to the victims' bodies, and that all of them had punctured lungs. With everything else that was done to them, that was what was going to kill them within minutes if he hadn't severed their femoral arteries."

"Sick bastard," Walsh swore, her face grimmer than Morris had ever seen it, which surprised him. Before he left the force and started MBI, he and Annie had worked several gruesome homicides together.

"That's being kind," Morris said. He nodded toward Felger. "I asked Adam to dig around the Internet and look for unsolved murders that this killer might've done. He found a recent trail that started Tuesday in Seattle."

Morris took a sip of coffee. Not for dramatic effect, but because his throat was feeling froggy. Some sort of allergies. Normally, he would've had Felger give his report so he could take credit for his work, but when Felger showed up an hour and a half ago at MBI, his eyes had the unfocused, hazy look of someone who'd been spending the afternoon smoking weed. Morris and the other MBI investigators were all veterans of the LAPD, and were old-school regarding weed, with their drug of choice being alcohol, but Morris wasn't about to hold what his computer and hacking specialist did on his free time against him. Still, he thought it would be better to keep Felger out of the spotlight.

Morris took a second sip of coffee to better lubricate his throat, and told the room about Claire Bigelow being murdered Tuesday afternoon in her room at the Royal Mandarin Hotel in downtown Seattle.

"That's an upscale place," Lemmon remarked.

"When were you in Seattle?" Polk asked.

"Not that it's any of your business, but a couple of months ago Corrine and I were thinking of going and we checked out the hotels. That one was well out of our budget."

"We're getting off topic," Morris admonished. He waited a beat to see if Polk had a smart-ass comment waiting to be unleashed. He didn't. Morris continued: "I talked with the Seattle homicide detective in charge of this. Dick Haley. He's overnighting the autopsy report. What they got so far is Bigelow, thirty-two and from Chicago, was in Seattle for a business trip that had just concluded. Her coworkers took a boat trip to see Puget Sound, but she begged off, claiming she wasn't feeling well. At two eighteen room service delivered a steak dinner and a crab and shrimp salad to her room—"

"Was the salad an appetizer or entrée?" Bogle asked.

"Entrée."

"So she had company," Lemmon noted. "I'm guessing that was the last time anyone saw her alive, other than the killer."

"Apparently. Her coworkers were concerned when they returned from their boat trip and she didn't answer her door, but not enough to do anything about it. They were more alarmed the next morning when they still couldn't reach her. That was when hotel security opened the door and found Bigelow. She was left naked with her panties stuffed in her mouth, and her wrists and ankles tied to the four-poster bed. The killer had used the steak knife and fork to carve her up. The coroner, Dr. Maggie Wu, estimated that Bigelow had been tortured for over two hours before her throat was slit. Wu has a four-thirty to five-thirty window for time of death."

"Signs of the victim having intercourse?" Walsh asked.

"No."

"Was the steak dinner eaten?" Finston asked.

Morris glanced at his notes, and shook his head. "I don't know. Why?"

"It would show a certain degree of callousness and cruelty if he took the time to eat, assuming our killer is a *he* and not a *she*. The likely scenario is the killer arranged a rendezvous with Ms. Bigelow, probably at her hotel room since he wouldn't want to be seen in public with her. When he arrived, he had her order room service under the pretense that they would have food waiting for them after their tryst—"

"Tryst," Polk interrupted. "Is that a fancy word for a roll in the sack?"

"Ignore the ignoramus," Lemmon said. "I'll buy Polk a dictionary later."

"*Ignore the ignoramus*," Polk repeated. "Fred, I never knew you were a poet at heart."

"Maybe so, but I've known for years you're an ignoramus."

Polk smiled thinly, seeing he'd gotten to Lemmon. "Now that is a word I know."

"No doubt given how many times you've heard it."

Morris had let their squabble go on longer than he normally would've because he knew they needed to blow off steam. It was one thing to investigate murders of people you had no connection to. It was another to deal with the brutal torture and murder of a young woman whose life you thought you had just saved. He held both hands up, palms out, as if he were trying to stop a runaway car.

"Enough," he ordered. He smiled apologetically at Finston. "Sorry," he said.

"That's quite all right." Finston turned to Polk and showed him one of her small V smiles, although this one had more of an edge than the others Morris had seen. "To answer your question, it's not all that fancy a word. But yes, it has the same meaning, although Ms. Bigelow wouldn't have been expecting much rolling to have occurred, since the killer had convinced her to let him tie her wrists and ankles to the bedposts." She turned her gaze back to Morris, her smile gone. "It would be very telling to know if after he tied her up, he then spent time eating his steak dinner before beginning the physical part of the torture."

"Agreed," Morris said.

"We should also find out from Bigelow's coworkers and friends which way she swung," Bogle said. "It will help nail down whether the killer is a he or a she."

Morris nodded. Ninety-nine percent of these serial killers were men, but there were those rare women serial killers, like Sheila Proops, even though the NYPD and FBI were never able to nail her for those SCK killings in New York. You couldn't take anything for granted. He added that inquiry to the list he was keeping.

"Seattle police have anything?" Walsh asked.

"They have hairs, but they don't know if they're from the killer. Otherwise no witnesses, no usable fingerprints, no semen."

"What about the room-service guy or gal?"

"Guy."

"The police look into him?"

"Yeah. Haley told me the guy had acted squirrelly when they questioned him, but given the timing of when the torture and murder must've happened he couldn't have done it."

"He still could've seen the killer in the room," Walsh said.

Morris made a helpless gesture with his hands. "The guy claimed the only person he saw was Bigelow. Haley wasn't sure that was the truth, but whatever he saw, Haley couldn't shake it out of him."

Morris held up an index finger, because the question about the steak dinner had been bothering him. He took out his cell phone and called Haley. The Seattle homicide detective answered on the third ring.

"Was the steak dinner eaten?" Morris asked.

"What?"

"The steak dinner Claire Bigelow ordered from room service. Was it eaten?"

"Yep, the plate was licked clean."

"What about the other dish?"

"The shrimp salad? It wasn't touched."

"Thanks. As I mentioned earlier, I'll be sending over one of my investigators. First flight he can get."

Morris hung up and informed the others in the room what Haley had told him.

Finston nodded. "What I expected," she said.

To be difficult, Polk remarked that the steak could've been eaten after the torture and murder.

"The killer wouldn't have done that."

"Yeah? Because of what psychological reason?"

"The steak would've gotten cold if the killer had waited."

"Why did you guess the killer had ordered the steak and the victim the other entrée?" Gilman asked.

Until then the mayor's deputy assistant had been the forgotten man in the room. Finston blinked twice as she looked in his direction, almost as if she were trying to pick him out of the background. She showed him one of her smiles, a very slight one.

"The killer would want red meat, and if the hotel restaurant keeps records on it, we'll find out he ordered it rare."

"Maybe he has a seafood allergy," Gilman offered. "That could be why he didn't touch the salad."

"I think we've exhausted this subject," Morris said. "Let's move on. We have a good idea what went on in that room. Charlie, I want you to go to Seattle. Do what's necessary to put the fear of God in that room-service waiter and find out what he saw that he's not telling. Then do what you can to retrace Bigelow's last few days, see if you can figure out where she met this psycho. Fred, I'll need you in Chicago talking to her coworkers so you can help Charlie with that retracing."

Bogle and Lemmon both nodded. Polk looked put out. "What am I supposed to do?" he asked. "Sit around and twiddle my thumbs?"

"I'm getting to that," Morris said.

Chapter 42

Morris searched through his notepad until he found what he was looking for. "Polk, I need you to poke around Roseburg, Oregon."

Polk had heard that bad pun before. In fact, he'd heard it at least a dozen times from Morris over the many years they had worked together.

"What's a Roseburg, Oregon?" he asked.

"A place where a so-far unidentified body was found off of Interstate 5 Wednesday morning." Morris flipped the page of his notepad and read out the notes he had scribbled down.

"At roughly five-thirty A.M. on Wednesday morning, Patrolman Lannie McDowell from the Oregon State Police stopped on the interstate to investigate recently made skid marks on the southbound lane. He found dried blood and a pair of mangled eyeglasses at the scene, and soon after discovered a dead male in his thirties who'd been dragged about twenty feet into the brush."

Bogle asked, "Could he have crawled away into the brush?"

Morris flipped the notepad shut. "No, not a chance. He was dragged by someone. I talked with McDowell's commanding officer. The victim either jumped or was pushed out of a speeding car, and landed on his face. The damage done was brutal. His neck was broken, and at the very least he would've been paralyzed from the neck down. He had no wallet or cell phone, and the Oregon State Police have no idea who he was."

"When did this happen?" Polk asked.

"The ME narrowed down time of death between one and three A.M. Wednesday morning."

"Someone driving from Seattle to Los Angeles would be driving southbound on Interstate 5," Lemmon commented.

Finston nodded as she rubbed her narrow, meager chin. "If our killer did this, it would explain why he ended things abruptly with Ms. Bigelow by cutting her throat. He had made arrangements for a ride and needed to get going."

Walsh said, "He killed and tortured Bigelow as some sort of perverse going-away present to himself. Then he killed this poor guy for his car."

"If this is our killer," Morris said. "And if it is, it's possible this isn't the same person he got a ride with out of Seattle. He might've been dropped off before Roseburg, and the dead man could be some poor schmuck who had the bad luck of picking him up on the highway." He turned to Polk. "I'd bet money on it, though, that this is our killer's handiwork. I'd even give three-to-one odds on it."

Polk frowned. "Only a sucker would take that bet."

"Why aren't you taking it, then?" Lemmon asked innocently.

Morris paid no attention to Lemmon's crack, and surprisingly, neither did Polk.

"That's why I need you to go to Roseburg," Morris told Polk. "Work with the state-police investigators and figure out who this man was. While you're working it from your end, Adam will be searching through ride-share websites to get you names to look into. If this man drove our killer out of Seattle, we need to identify him."

Polk's frown turned more into a pained grimace. "I guess I'll be on my way tonight to Roseburg, Oregon, wherever that it is."

"It's somewhere in Oregon," Lemmon offered with a smart-alecky grin.

Polk gave Lemmon a sideways glance. "Make sure to chew thoroughly when you eat one of those Chicago bratwursts. I wouldn't want you choking on it."

"Same when you eat a bologna on white bread with mayonnaise sandwich in Roseburg, or whatever local epicurean specialties they might have."

"Snob," Polk said.

"A snob who'll be eating Chicago deep-dish pizza and grilled bratwurst soon."

"For all you know, I might get better food."

Lemmon laughed at that. "We can compare notes later."

This time Walsh interrupted their squabble. She didn't call them infants, but her tone implied as much as she suggested they focus on the task at hand. She asked Morris about the San Luis Obispo murders. "Given the timing of this man's death, could the same killer be responsible for the newlyweds?"

"Yes," Finston piped in eagerly. She gave Morris a questioning look, and asked, "May I?"

"Sure, go ahead."

"Morris, Greg, and myself had a brief teleconference call with Detective John Ogaz of the SLOPD, and he filled us in on what they have. The murdered couple were Paul Small, twenty-eight, and Molly Small, twenty-five, both from Elkhart, Indiana. Cause of death for both was heart failure. Either the pain or fear from the torture they endured became too much for them. Mrs. Small was killed first, her time of death being between two and three PM. Mr. Small had played golf that afternoon, and the course had him returning his cart at three-twenty, so he wouldn't have returned back to his hotel until three-thirty, at the earliest. The killer hung around the room waiting for Mr. Small after killing his wife—"

"My God," Doug Gilman whispered.

Finston offered him a sympathetic smile and continued. "The ME has his time of death between four and five. Both of them were tortured with a knife and cigarette lighter. The wife was raped vaginally with what appears to be a hunting knife; Mr. Small, anally."

Gilman lurched to his feet, muttering something about needing to make a call. As he rushed out of the room, his knees buckled and his skin took on a more greenish hue than earlier.

"I hope he doesn't mess up our carpeting out there," Polk complained.

Morris shrugged. *If he does, he does.*

Finston looked alarmed. "Should someone check on him?"

"He'll be fine. He just needs some air," Morris said.

Walsh looked deep in thought. She asked Finston why the killer so dramatically changed his method. "The man killed outside of Roseburg was out of expedience. He wanted the man's car and possibly his money. With Bigelow and the Smalls, he got off on torturing them, but there was still no deliberateness to the way he killed them. What happened in Malibu was very deliberate. Staged in a way. Why the big change?"

"Because he's now in LA," Polk said somewhat facetiously. "Everybody comes out here looking for stardom, right?"

"That's not too far off," Finston said. "At least with this killer. Ms. Bigelow and the Smalls were tortured and killed for his entertainment. I'm sure he very much enjoys what he does, and I have little doubt that he believes his victims exist only for his amusement. While I'm sure that part of him hasn't changed, he murdered those four girls in Malibu because he's now seeking notoriety."

"In his sick, twisted way, he wants to be a star," Morris said.

"Yes, exactly. Something happened to him recently that made him want to leave the shadows and make his killings very public."

Walsh didn't seem entirely convinced. She asked, "How sure are you the same killer is responsible for all these victims?"

"I can't definitively say he is, but if I were to bet on it, that's where I'd put my money, and I'm not a betting person." Finston showed another of her small smiles, but not a drop of amusement showed in her eyes. "In fact, I'd offer four-to-one odds."

Polk leaned back in his chair, his thick arms crossing his barrel chest. "Another sucker's bet," he grumbled.

Chapter 43

Griffin made macaroni and cheese so he wouldn't have to spend time chopping up Sheila's dinner into tiny, bite-sized pieces. At five minutes to six, they were both in the living room with the TV set on as they waited for the local news. Sheila sat in her wheelchair, a tray attached to the handles holding a bowl and a plastic cup of apple juice with a straw stuck in it. Griffin also brought a plate of macaroni and cheese for himself. As he watched Sheila slowly chewing her food, all he could think of was a badly diseased cow chewing its cud, and he found himself repulsed by her. There were times when he thought of the two of them as spiritual soul mates and he felt a closeness to her that he'd never thought possible with anyone, and there were other times like now where it was a struggle not to throw her out of her chair and do deliciously terrible things to her. His jaw muscles hardened so that they felt like stone as he watched her, and the impulse to hurt her became a quivering, unbearable thing. Fortunately, the news came on and diverted his attention.

The first story was about the four girls he'd slaughtered in that Malibu mansion. Except for when he had forced little Craig Myers to drown in the icy waters of Morses Pond, all of his murders up until that leggy blonde in Seattle were done quietly, and he made sure most of their bodies disappeared for good. The few that were found were people nobody cared about.

That blonde he'd carved up in the Seattle hotel room didn't make the national news, but he nonetheless enjoyed reading the stories he could find about it online in the Seattle papers. The couple he butchered inside that tacky San Luis Obispo hotel room also didn't get nearly as much coverage in the Los Angeles media as he would've expected, and the police so far hadn't released much about it, so the little he'd seen mostly focused on the human angle—about how tragic it was that a young honeymooning couple would meet such a senseless, violent demise. But still, the few stories he caught on the news about it left him exhilarated, especially when they would interview one of the couple's dumbfounded family members or friends back in Indiana.

With these four girls it was very different. As Griffin watched the muted reaction of the reporter as she talked about the horror that went on inside the mansion, he felt such a heightened sense of euphoria that pure opium instead of blood could've been coursing through his veins. He also realized he had grown rock-hard between his legs. Forget rock-hard—it was more like a throbbing rod of solid iron. Every fiber of his being felt alive. The reason for this was obvious. Those other murders were done for fun and the thrill of it, and because those sorry-ass victims existed only so he could take them as he pleased. These killings were so very different. They were part of his legacy. His immortality.

The reporter, a pixie-like blonde with hair so stiff that it looked shellacked, didn't give any specifics other than the girls were murdered sometime after midnight, and that their bodies had been mutilated in a sick, depraved fashion.

She had to know the real details, Griffin thought. *She had to!*

His euphoria dropped like a heavy stone when the reporter branded him the Malibu Butcher.

"What the hell's wrong with them?" he asked Sheila. His initial shock at hearing this nickname had given way to outrage. "Are they idiots? The Malibu Butcher? Not only is that so ridiculously lame, but it doesn't even make sense! It implies that I'm only going to be killing in Malibu, which we both know isn't true. Morons!"

It took Sheila half a minute before she could finish chewing and swallowing what she had in her mouth. "It doesn't matter," she finally said in her painfully slow way. "Let's see what they call you when they make sense of who you're killing."

Griffin was brooding now. "They won't change it," he said, choking back his despair. "Once they give you a nickname, it sticks forever."

"*Butcher* is not so bad."

He shook his head. There must've been dozens of other killers over the years who'd been tagged with some form of a *butcher* moniker. He wanted something original. Something that would separate him from all these other serial killers people had long since forgotten. *The Frankenstein Killer.* That had been what he was hoping for, and that should've been the name they gave him. Look at how he had left their bodies! It was as if he had pieced them together from spare parts. But instead he was now the Malibu Butcher. Unbelievable. What did he need to do so they'd see the obvious? Hammer bolts into those girls' necks?

"I should've left behind the Frankenstein-monster mask," he said somewhat childishly, because he knew he couldn't have done that.

Griffin had stolen the X-Acto knife and the box of four-inch nails he had used, and the police wouldn't be able to trace back anything else to him, but the Frankenstein-monster mask was too cumbersome to steal, and so he paid cash for it. The sales clerk, a very pale, doughy redhead, had tried flirting with him before he had made some unkind comments about her doughiness, and if the police started looking for anyone who'd recently bought that mask in Hollywood, she'd remember him.

"The name doesn't matter," Sheila said as she slowly formed and pushed each word out of her mouth. "They'll never forget you. Especially Morris Brick."

Griffin glumly nodded. He swallowed hard, taking his bitter resentment over that unoriginal and stupid name. Sheila was right. Once he was done, they would never forget him, Morris Brick included. He didn't know Brick and had nothing against the man, but after Sheila had told him about Brick, he spent hours reading about LA's celebrity serial-killer hunter, and he rather liked the idea that by the time he was done, his deeds were going to be haunting Brick until his dying breath. In a way, that would be adding a big, screaming exclamation mark to Griffin's legacy.

He gave the remaining macaroni and cheese on his plate a cold, indifferent look. The Malibu Butcher name might not matter, but it still caused him to lose his appetite.

"I'm going to feed and water our guest downstairs," he told Sheila.

He brought his food with him. He kept a jug of water in the basement so he wouldn't have to bother going to the kitchen for any. So far, he'd been diligent in feeding and watering their captive twice a day. He hadn't hurt her, either, not even a little. It was important that he keep her preserved, so when the time was right she'd look like all his other victims without having any additional injuries. His legacy was at stake, or—and he wrinkled his nose in disgust—the Malibu Butcher's reputation.

He opened the basement door and headed down the stairs.

Elena Kotovksy's time would be coming soon enough.

Chapter 44

At ten past seven, Perlmutter was at the Aero Theatre in Santa Monica buying a ticket for the 1958 classic film *Touch of Evil*. He'd been looking forward to this night ever since he'd spotted the movie on their schedule two months earlier, and after the day he'd had he deserved it! Before leaving for the theater he'd spent another two hours fine-tuning his script, polishing it so that it glistened like gold. He also added four pages of character backstory that he thought was some of the best writing he'd ever done. For now, that was all he'd be able to do until the killer gave him more material to work with.

While Perlmutter greatly respected *Citizen Kane*, Welles's *Touch of Evil* was the movie that he most deeply loved. He was thirteen when he first stumbled onto it on TV, and that film made him right then want to be a filmmaker. The three-minute-and-twenty-second uninterrupted opening sequence was a thing of exquisite beauty: A crane tracking shot followed a car with a hidden bomb as it kept pace with Charlton Heston and Janet Leigh as they walked on foot toward the US-Mexican border, with the car veering off at the last second and then exploding into a deadly fireball. As breathtaking as so many of the scenes were, it was the underlying theme of greatness corrupted into evil that left a thirteen-year-old Perlmutter shaking and in awe at the end.

Touch of Evil was the first movie Perlmutter bought on video, and he bought the DVD copy the day it became available, but this was going to be the first time he'd have a chance to see it on the big screen, and if any movie demanded to be seen on the big screen, this was it.

As he entered the lobby, he felt a sense of reverence, almost as if he were about to undergo a sacred pilgrimage.

I'm splurging for popcorn, he thought. *Why not? A month, two months tops, I'll be rolling in money.*

He turned toward the concession counter just as a vaguely familiar-looking twerp wearing cargo shorts, a NY Yankees jacket, and matching baseball cap turned away from it, carrying a soda and a bag of gummy bears. Sammy Bloom. Their eyes locked, and Bloom stopped where he was so he could wait for Perlmutter at the counter.

"Perlmutter," Bloom said with a nod.

"Bloom," Perlmutter acknowledged with an identical nod.

Bloom waited until Perlmutter ordered a large popcorn and a super-sized ginger ale before asking how his meeting with Larry Getzler went.

"Better than I could've dreamed. We have a handshake deal."

Bloom was smiling as if he were waiting for the punch line. When he realized Perlmutter wasn't joking, he said, "You're joking, right?"

"Nope."

Bloom's expression fell flat. "Just like that you got a deal?" he asked incredulously.

"We have an agreement. Not a deal yet. He loved the pitch I gave him. Now I've got to deliver a killer script, but I'm well on my way. I've already written eighteen pages of solid gold."

"What was the pitch?" Bloom asked, challenging Perlmutter.

While a baseball cap covered his thick, curly hair, with his close-set eyes, narrow head, and long, droopy nose, Bloom made Perlmutter think of an unfortunate-looking creature he'd seen a picture of once, something called a proboscis monkey.

Perlmutter said, "I can't tell you that. But once the deal's finalized, you'll be able to read about it in *Variety*. How'd your pitch to Faye Riverstone go?"

He asked this innocently, as if he hadn't heard about how Riverstone first politely asked Bloom to leave her alone, and when he continued his desperate pitch, her bodyguard physically picked Bloom up as if he were a sack of flour, carried him out the back door of the Pilates studio, and dumped him headfirst into a trash can. The story might've been an exaggeration, but their mutual acquaintance who told it to Perlmutter swore it was exactly what happened.

"We're negotiating right now," Bloom muttered, his expression looking like he'd eaten some bad fish.

The girl behind the concession counter brought over Perlmutter's popcorn and drink. Partly because Bloom was watching, and partly because he was feeling like a sport, he handed her a twenty dollar bill and told her to keep the change.

"Good luck with that, Bloom," Perlmutter said, a big grin breaking over his face. Yep, ever since he had his creative breakthrough, this day was just getting better and better.

Chapter 45

Parker kept his head lowered as he greeted Morris at the door, his thick, ropy tail wagging cautiously. Morris thought Parker looked guilty, as if he were still ashamed that he had cozied up with Pavlo Lebed for a piece of roast lamb. Or maybe Morris was only imagining it. He decided not to bring up the sore subject and simply rubbed the bull terrier's snout and got back a couple of relieved pig-like grunts in return.

He found Natalie at the kitchen table with an open bottle of prosecco in front of her. It looked like half the bottle was already gone.

"You're getting drunk without me?" he asked.

She gave him a wistful smile and filled a glass for him. "I saw on the news about those four girls who were murdered," she said. "They're calling the killer the Malibu Butcher."

Morris took the glass. "I didn't know they gave him a name already," he said, frowning. "We've been trying to keep the details hushed up."

"They didn't mention any specifics other than that the victims had been mutilated. They didn't say how. They also didn't mention that you or MBI were joining the investigation."

Morris picked up the glass Natalie had poured for him and took a long sip. He needed it after the day he'd had. It tasted good. Refreshing.

"The killer is a piece of work," he said. "He craves attention. Wants to think he's important, so we're going to keep a low profile."

Natalie nodded. She finished the bubbly wine in her glass and poured herself more. The bottle was emptying fast.

"I called up about our trip," she said. "If we cancel by midnight, we can still get half our money back."

"We're not cancelling. We're going to Italy."

She gave him a sad look, as if he were being hopelessly naïve. "How? Our flight is in four days."

"We're going to catch him before then," Morris said. He sat down next to her and took hold of her hand. It was slender like Gloria Finston's and almost as small, but it felt so different that his wife and the FBI profiler could've been different species. Instead of feeling like he was holding a smooth, cool piece of bone, Nat's hand was warm and fit perfectly inside of his own. "The guy's not nearly as smart as he thinks he is. He's already made plenty of mistakes and has left a trail from Seattle to LA for us to follow."

"You really think you can catch him by Thursday?" she asked, not convinced.

"I think so. If not, Charlie can take over. We're flying to Rome Thursday no matter what. You have my word. We've waited too long for our belated honeymoon."

He reached over and kissed her lips and when he tasted a saltiness, he realized that several tears had leaked from her eyes and had snaked down to her mouth. As he pulled back, he used his thumb to wipe away several more of her tears.

"I'm being ridiculous," she said. "And selfish. Whether or not we go on vacation is so insignificant compared to stopping this maniac. It's just that I'm worried—"

He hushed her. "Nat, we're going," he promised. "Why don't we start packing? It might make you feel better."

She laughed at that idea. "It's too early for that."

"I know you bought new luggage, and I know you've been hiding it in Rachel's closet." He opened his eyes wide in response to Natalie's mock surprise. "I actually am a somewhat competent detective—at least some people think so," he added. "I also know you've been buying new clothes for the trip, also hiding them in Rachel's room. So let's pack what we can."

They put their wineglasses down, and he led Natalie upstairs with Parker tagging along close behind.

Late that night Morris's cell phone woke him. His eyes couldn't focus right away, and it took a moment before he could make out from the caller ID that Philip Stonehedge was calling. He almost let it go to voicemail, but he remembered that the actor lived only a mile away from where the girls were killed.

"I was with them last night," Stonehedge said when Morris answered the call.

"What do you mean, you were with them?"

"Those four girls who were killed. I was with them."

Morris snapped fully awake. He bolted up in bed and became conscious of Natalie's soft breathing next to him. The call hadn't woken her. He took the phone with him as he left the bedroom, using the glow of the cell phone to help navigate the darkened room. At the last moment his toe felt Parker's form as the dog lay right outside the door, and Morris was able to step over him.

"Did you leave DNA in any of the girls?" Morris asked.

"Jesus, no, it wasn't anything like that. They were only kids. I didn't have an orgy with them. What kind of guy do you think I am?"

A somewhat spoiled actor living a privileged life. The girls were all twenty-two, not exactly kids. But Morris kept that thought to himself.

"What *was* it like?" Morris asked, his voice reflecting the cool informality of a man who'd been a homicide detective more than a third of his life.

"I was with Brie last night. We were having a quiet evening at home, barbecuing grouper and trying to replicate those fantastic fish tacos from my favorite Beverly Hills joint. Sometime around eight-thirty the buzzer rang from the gate, and it was these four giggling twentysomething girls. As a lark, I let them in. For a couple of hours I fed them fish tacos, made them a few drinks, and we talked about this and that. It was a nice evening. Very nice, actually. All four of them were just these goofy, sweet girls. I liked them. I didn't realize they were the ones murdered until I saw their photos on the news a couple of minutes ago. It was a shock, Morris."

"I can imagine. What time exactly did they leave your house?"

"Around eleven. Not much past then."

"Do you have video surveillance for your gate area?"

"Yeah. Jesus. Do you think the killer followed them from my place?"

The thought had crossed Morris's mind that the killer might've been planning to target the actor and had been watching Stonehedge's house, but decided on different victims when he saw the girls leave. If you were a serial killer seeking notoriety, there was not much more of a bigger splash you could make than killing two of Hollywood's biggest stars.

Morris said, "Possibly. I'll have someone come by soon to pick up your surveillance video. Maybe we'll get lucky."

"Okay, sure." There was a hesitation, then, "Something I missed that Brie picked up on was the blond girl named Courtney acted a little antsy. A few times, Brie caught her checking her watch, like maybe she had plans to meet someone. At least that was what Brie thought."

Morris felt an iciness in his temples. Courtney Williams could've been the one who drew the killer to the house and not Mia. Did she invite the killer to the Malibu property?

"Is Brie with you?" Morris asked.

"Yeah."

"Okay, both of you will need to give a full statement."

"That's what I was expecting. Why don't you come by instead of sending one of your lackeys?"

Morris thought about it. "Yeah, okay. Can you have Brie there tomorrow morning at seven?"

"It can be arranged. Bring the little guy. I'll make waffles, bacon, and scrambled eggs for all of us, and it will be the best bacon you've ever tasted. Maybe the best waffles too."

"Best bacon, huh? Do you get it from celebrity hogs?"

"Not exactly. I get it from a little butcher shop in Venice where they do their magic. Don't knock it 'til you try it."

"I'll reserve judgment. Parker's the connoisseur between us. We'll see what he has to say."

Morris found himself fighting a yawn. He felt bone tired right then. Seeing what was done to Mia Dickerson and her friends had taken more out of him than he would've guessed. No question that this had become personal. He told Stonehedge that he'd pick up the surveillance video when he came over the next morning so he wouldn't keep the actor waiting that night. After that, he ended the call. For now he needed to get some sleep.

Chapter 46

The next morning Morris brought Parker along with him to Stonehedge's Malibu address, and as promised the actor prepared an early breakfast of bacon, farm-fresh scrambled eggs, and waffles with strawberries that he grew himself and a sauce made out of Vermont maple syrup, melted butter, and Grand Marnier. Morris had to admit the bacon was damn good. Thicker cut, smokier, and tastier than he'd ever had. Parker concurred as he attacked with vigor the plate of scrambled eggs and bacon that Stonehedge put down for him, and didn't want to give up on it even after it appeared that he'd come close to licking the enamel off the plate. The waffles were also damn good. When Morris asked why that was, the actor winked and told him it was a recipe he'd gotten in Paris, and the chef had sworn him to secrecy. Morris didn't push it. They were good, but nothing he couldn't live without. He wondered how a guy who liked good food as much as Stonehedge kept so lean. A supercharged metabolism. If it was being chemically helped, Morris hadn't seen any evidence of it.

Brie Evans joined them, but she stuck to coffee. She seemed exceptionally brittle, as if those girls' deaths were weighing heavily on her. Even so, she was gorgeous. Maybe her melancholy made her even more so. Morris asked her about what she'd picked up from Courtney Williams, and he didn't get much more than what Stonehedge had already told him, only that she thought Courtney had started acting anxious that night shortly before ten o'clock.

"Any guesses why?"

Her soft brown eyes fixed on Morris's flinty gray ones. "She had plans to meet someone. I'm sure of it."

"You didn't ask her about it?"

She shook her head.

"Williams didn't drop any hints about her plans?"

The actress offered him a sad, subdued smile. "Nothing," she said.

So that was it. Very likely Courtney Williams had made plans to meet with the killer at ten, but maybe not. At least it gave Morris an investigative thread to pull on.

After breakfast Brie offered to drive Parker to the town beach while Stonehedge and Morris looked at the surveillance video. They spent an hour doing that, fast-forwarding at times, rewinding, looking at the edges of when the girls arrived and when they left. While the video showed some cars passing by the quiet, remote Malibu road, it didn't show anyone lurking in the bushes. Stonehedge moved the video to a flash drive for Morris, who, after nodding thanks, left to collect Parker. He found the dog sunning on the deck and looking pooped.

"He spent forty-five minutes attacking the waves," Brie explained. She looked to be in better spirits. An hour alone with Parker could do that to someone. "He's a tough little guy, but in the end the waves kept knocking him on his butt."

"He must've spotted a school of mackerel, and thought he'd do some fishing. Maybe he thought that's where Philip's world-class bacon came from."

Brie laughed, and Parker's ears perked up at the word *bacon*.

"It wouldn't surprise me," she said. "In any case, I hosed the saltwater and sand off of him and he should be dry now."

Morris thanked her for the dog-sitting and coaxed a reluctant Parker to his feet. He couldn't blame the dog. Given a choice of catching some rays in Malibu with a gorgeous actress or hunting a crazed serial killer, almost any sane person or dog would make the same choice.

Morris was a half hour away from MBI with Parker snoozing on the passenger seat when he stopped at a red light. He was going to use the opportunity to call Walsh, but she beat him to the punch.

"I was just going to call you," he said.

"And yet I was faster on the draw." She paused a beat, told him she was at MBI waiting for him, then added, "I heard this morning from Detective Wringer at Malibu PD. The alibis for everyone at Fineries check out."

"Not a big surprise," Morris said.

"Not much of one."

"Unless one of them was in Seattle last Tuesday."

"Only if you assume the same killer is responsible for all the murders," Walsh responded.

"Ah, you're a skeptic."

"And you're a true believer."

The light turned green and traffic started rolling again. The woman in the silver Mercedes next to Morris gave him a nasty look for being on his cell phone. He ignored her.

"It all fits, Annie," he said.

"I know that we can create a convincing narrative so it does. But Morris, it could also turn out to be a coincidence where we have two or more psychos at work. We've both seen stranger things during our time on the force." A heavy sigh rumbled out of her. "I'm not saying you're wrong. Odds are it's going to be one guy responsible. I'm just saying we should work these murders in Malibu independently of the others. If the murders in Seattle, Roseburg, or San Luis Obispo lead us to our killer, great, but I don't want anything slipping through the cracks."

"Nothing's going to slip past us. We're catching him. Sooner than later."

"I hope so. Why were you going to call me?"

Morris told her about the girls spending the evening at Stonehedge's, and Brie Evans's observation regarding Courtney Williams.

"You think she invited the killer to the property?"

"It's worth checking out. We need her recent credit-card charges and cell-phone records. Dickerson didn't offer the house to Mia until Friday morning, so we're talking a small window where Williams— or any of the other three—could've met the killer and invited him to join the party. If it was Williams, and we can trace her to a bar or restaurant or coffee shop during that window, we might find where she met the killer."

"We've got all of their cell phones. I talked with forensics this morning. There's nothing on the phones that's going to help us. They were a tight clique, and all of their calls and texts from Friday through Saturday were to each other."

"Credit-card records, then."

"I've already put in a request for all of their banking and credit-card records."

"Push Hadley harder. Let him earn his hefty paycheck for once. We're on a clock here, Annie. This psycho is going to be killing again soon."

"I know." She let out another heavy sigh. This one deeply felt. "I'll bug Hadley. I'm sure he'll love me for that."

"If nothing else, he should respect your initiative. I've got more surveillance video for us to give your video-forensics people. This is from outside Stonehedge's gate. I didn't see anything, but maybe they'll spot something."

The patrolmen, when they canvassed the area, collected surveillance video from all the nearby houses. In that neighborhood, everybody other than the property where the girls were killed seemed to have surveillance video. That property would've normally had video also, but Dickerson hadn't turned on security yet.

"You're thinking the killer was staking out Philip Stonehedge's home, and decided to go after those girls instead?"

"I'm thinking it's a possibility, but I'm also thinking the odds are better the killer went to Malibu that night to kill those girls. But as you said, we can't let anything slip through the cracks."

"Okay. I'm going to call Hadley now and pester him. I'll let you know when I get those records."

Walsh disconnected the call on her end. Morris soon found himself smiling. It wasn't much, but the image of Hadley's beefy, round face reddening with annoyance was at least something.

The nap had done Parker a world of good, and the bull terrier seemed his usual clownish self by the time Morris pulled into his reserved space at work.

Walsh was waiting for them when Morris and Parker walked into MBI's lobby. She showed her best poker face, but Morris knew she had something. He raised an eyebrow.

She said, "What do you think, Divine's on Vine a likely place for a twenty-two-year-old girl to give a guy on the make her phone number, maybe even invite him to crash a party in Malibu?"

Morris smiled thinly. "Hadley came through for once?"

"No. Let's not have any crazy talk. I got the credit-card reports from Felger. I didn't ask him how he got it."

"Smart. I never ask him, either. Some things we're just better off not knowing. To answer your earlier question, I'd have to think Divine's would be a perfect place for that."

"That's my thought also." Her green eyes glistened like emeralds right then, and a hard smirk twisted her lips. "Courtney Williams had a hundred-and-sixty-eight-dollar charge at Divine's that was put through Friday night at eight-fifty-seven."

"What time do they open?"

"Eleven."

Morris checked his watch. It was a quarter to ten, and Divine's was no more than a fifteen-minute ride.

"Let's head over," he said. "See if we can talk to them before they start letting in customers."

Chapter 47

Morris and Walsh sidled up to the bar, where a slender woman with frizzy red hair was slicing up limes. Parker was with them and he plopped onto the floor by Morris's feet, seemingly appreciative of the coolness offered by the terra-cotta tile.

"What can I do for you, officers?" the bartender asked without looking up once as she continued to slice and dice the limes.

"Are you Trina Zina?" Morris asked.

"That's right."

"Your manager told us you're the one we need to talk to. Do you remember this customer from Friday night?"

Morris pulled a photo of Courtney Williams from his briefcase and placed it on the bar. Trina stopped her slicing and dicing to look at it. She nodded after a few seconds of study.

"I remember her. She was here with one of her friends, sitting where your partner is right now." Her expression soured. "Ms. Tightwad worked up a decent bill. With food and drinks for her and her friend, it came out to just under a hundred and sixty. Left me a five-percent tip."

"Her friend a guy?" Walsh asked.

Trina shook her head. "No, a female friend. A nice kid. The one you showed me a picture of picked up the tab, but I had the feeling if her friend knew I was being stiffed she would've made up the difference."

Morris took three more photos out and placed them on the bar. "Any of these the friend?"

Trina, with little hesitation, picked out Mia's photo. "What's this about?" she asked.

"You haven't been watching the news?" Walsh asked.

The bartender gave her a confused look.

"These were the four killed in Malibu," Morris explained.

Trina looked at Morris as if she were expecting a punch line. When she realized one wasn't coming, the color in her face paled and her head jerked back as if she'd been slapped.

"I had no idea. Whenever stories about it have been on the news, I've been purposely looking away. I just didn't want to pay any attention. It's just so awful."

"Did you see them with any guys while they were here?" Morris asked.

She gazed off toward some distant place as she thought about it. Very quickly her thousand-yard stare faded, and her gaze moved back to Morris. She nodded, her jaw muscles hardening.

"Studley Do-Right bought them drinks. Afterwards he tried putting the move on this one." She nodded at Courtney's photo.

"He was Canadian?" Morris asked.

"I don't know, but he was here to do some mounting."

"Describe him," Walsh said.

"Early thirties, big, linebacker-type, with blond hair cut short to give him a flattop look. The type who was hot stuff back in high school, probably captain of the football team, and still thinks of himself that way. He was sitting over there."

She nodded to a spot across the horseshoe-shaped bar that was opposite to where Morris and Walsh were sitting.

"Did he get anywhere with Ms. Williams?" Walsh asked.

Trina shrugged. "I can't say. Like most Fridays, it was a busy night. He was chatting her up after buying the drinks, but that's all I had time to notice."

"You know his real name?" Morris asked.

"No, but Matt should be able to help you. He and the blond girl were the only ones I can remember ever buying martinis and firecrackers. It shouldn't be hard to match his bill to his credit-card receipt."

Matt was the name of the manager they'd already talked with.

"He used a credit card?" Morris asked.

"Yep."

That was a surprise. Morris would've guessed the killer would've paid with cash. Maybe he had stolen someone's card. Or used a fake one. If it was real, it would be a sloppy mistake—but then again, the killer seemed to be making a number of them.

Walsh was puzzling over something. "What's a firecracker?" she asked.

"Cucumber vodka, watermelon juice, and a twist of lime."

"Either girl talk to anyone else?" Morris asked.

"Not that I saw."

Morris, Parker, and Walsh left her to continue her bar preparations while they went off to get Studley Do-Right's real name.

Chapter 48

Studley Do-Right turned out to be Steven Hardaker, a manager for a local downtown gym. He seemed genuinely befuddled when Morris and Walsh showed up at his office to ask about his activities Friday night. Somewhat sheepishly, he admitted he'd bought several ladies drinks at Divine's and didn't have much luck with any of them. When Morris showed him a photo of Williams, Hardaker remembered right away that she was one of the girls he struck out with.

"A sophisticated babe. A martini drinker. She was with a friend. A brunette. Also quite a looker." He flashed Walsh a grin as if he actually had a chance with her. "Neither of them are in your class."

"What happened?" Morris asked so he could draw Hardaker's attention back to him before Walsh smacked the smarmy gym lothario in the face.

Reluctantly, Hardaker looked at Morris and shrugged. "I just wasn't on my game that night. Even the greats, like Adrián González, have their oh-for-four nights. What about the blond babe—she cause trouble or something later?"

Walsh, ignoring the question, asked what he had talked about with Williams.

"Nothing too heavy. I tried getting her number, but she was being coy about it. Told me that if I kept buying her and her friend drinks all night, maybe she'd give it to me later. I decided to move on. So what's this all about? Did something happen to her?"

Morris cut in again to speed things up. Not only did Hardaker seem legitimately perplexed, but Parker had begun demonstrating a supreme indifference toward him.

"Where were you last Tuesday?" he asked.

Hardaker's eyes squeezed into a squint and his forehead wrinkled to show his growing confusion. "Right here in the gym," he said. "From ten in the morning until seven, like I am every Tuesday. Why aren't you telling me what happened?"

"Can anyone verify you were here?"

"Probably half-a-dozen personal trainers and at least several dozen gym members." A glass wall separated his office from the gym. He nodded toward a very fit-looking brunette over by a matted area who was running a middle-aged woman through a set of complex exercises. "I'm sure Miranda over there remembers me being here."

"To answer your earlier question, the photos you were shown were Courtney Williams and Mia Dickerson, two of the young women who were murdered Friday night in Malibu."

Hardaker was showing a confused smile, but as he processed what Morris told him, he reacted almost as if he'd been punched in the gut.

"I didn't realize that," he murmured in a stunned voice.

As far as Morris was concerned, there wasn't a chance Hardaker was faking his reaction, or that this low-rent Casanova was a serial killer. Parker's continued lack of interest showed that he agreed. Even Walsh seemed mostly convinced. On their way out of the gym, they talked with Miranda and she backed Hardaker up, telling them that Mr. Legend in his Own Mind hit on her several times last Tuesday.

As they stepped out into the parking lot, Morris pointed out that with all the drinking the two girls did Friday night, they must've been tipsy, if not drunk.

"Very likely," Walsh agreed. "We've got their phones. We can see if either of them arranged for an Uber or some other ride-sharing service."

"The driver might've even been in Seattle Tuesday," Morris said. "The dead man in Roseburg could've been the one hitching a ride with the killer, instead of the other way around."

They were on their way back to MBI when Morris's cell phone rang: Polk. Morris put the phone on speaker so Walsh could listen in.

"Thanks to our computer nerd, I've got a bead on the dead guy here in Roseburg," Polk said.

"Adam's been busy," Morris said.

"For me, definitely. Felger got me a name of a guy who was supposed to drive Tuesday from Seattle to San Francisco, but never showed up. Bryan Tasker, another computer nerd. I talked to his sister, who also lives in San Fran, and she's worried. Tasker broke up with his girlfriend last month, and she's afraid he might've committed suicide. Roseburg's finest showed me the body and gave me a tour where it was found, and this was no suicide."

"The sister send you a photo?"

"Yeah. The photo isn't going to do much good in identifying the corpse, considering its face is gone. They're going to need DNA testing to know for sure, but size and weight are a good match. I have no doubt it's Tasker. He was driving a brand-new BMW 328i, painted Melbourne red, which I guess is simply red for us commoners. His pride and joy, according to his sister."

"License plate?"

"Felger can give you it, but I'm sure it's already been swapped out, just as I'm sure the car's already been dumped."

"I'll get an APB out for it," Walsh said. "And I'll get word out to our CIs we're looking for this car."

This was a good development. Morris could feel it in his bones. Parker must've also, given how he perked up from the backseat and grunted out one of his pig-like noises.

"How was breakfast this morning?" Morris asked Polk innocently enough.

"You're going to give me grief also? I grabbed a muffin and coffee. They were fine. And don't hold your breath for a lunch report. I'm done here in Roseburg. Right now I'm driving to North Bend to catch a flight. I should be back in LA this afternoon."

Even though it was Polk, Morris wished him safe travels. Once he disconnected the call, Walsh commented that this was big.

"He shouldn't have given us this trail," she said.

"Not very smart of him."

"Not at all. Odds are he dumped the car at a chop shop."

"That would be my bet."

"We'll find out which one."

Morris nodded, agreeing.

Walsh tugged lightly on her bottom lip as she thought about it. "You think it's still worth checking out whether Mia Dickerson or Courtney Williams arranged for a ride from Divine's?" she asked.

Morris nodded again, a resolve hardening his expression. "Leave no stone unturned," he said.

Chapter 49

Perlmutter was better prepared this time. Before leaving to Simi Valley, he practiced with the lock pick with his eyes closed until he could unlock his apartment door in less than thirty seconds. He brought along a cushion he'd be able to use with the folding chair, and packed two salami-on-rye with mustard sandwiches and a thermos of coffee. On the way, he picked up a gallon jug of water. When he arrived at the empty house across the street from Sheila Proops, he hustled quickly to the back door and had it unlocked almost without having to break stride. The folding table looked undisturbed from last time. If a realtor had come to this house since he'd been there, he or she must've left the folding chair upstairs.

Perlmutter went through the same steps he did the other time so he could move his car into the garage, but he felt calm and relaxed afterwards. He brought his supplies with him as he reentered the house and walked up the stairs to the second level. The folding chair was in front of the same window he had looked out last time, and the three doughnuts he'd left behind from his earlier visit had remained untouched.

By ten, the doughnuts were gone and he waited until noon to unwrap one of the salami sandwiches. Other than munching on food and guzzling coffee, he sat as motionless as a Buddha as he looked out the window and watched the Proops house. The binoculars weren't needed.

A little after one thirty Proops's garage door opened and the killer drove out in his dented-up Honda. Perlmutter worked his cell phone from his pocket, fiddled with the app he'd installed for the tracking device attached to the Honda's undercarriage, and checked to see its location was moving further away. The killer didn't know about the device. If he did, he would've gotten rid of it, maybe even attached it to another car's undercarriage. This meant Perlmutter didn't need to follow him. When the killer drove to wherever he was going, Perlmutter would use the app to get the address.

Perlmutter watched the app for several minutes to make sure the killer kept driving further away, and once he was convinced the killer wasn't going to be returning anytime soon, he used his vantage point to look out over the neighborhood. The street appeared desolate. There was no traffic, no kids playing outside, and no one strolling about, almost as if everyone wanted to give the Proops house as wide a berth as possible. It was so dead out there Perlmutter half-jokingly considered having a tumbleweed rolling down the street when he later wrote this scene.

Time to enter the lion's den. Or more fittingly, given that a crippled Sheila Proops lay inside the house, the spider's lair. He closed his eyes and played out in his mind what was soon going to be happening, and he was surprisingly calm as he did so. He might've been perspiring profusely, but that was only because of how hot the house was without air-conditioning. He smiled absently as he imagined using a crane shot to show his fictional filmmaker rushing from this house to Proops's when he filmed this for his movie.

It was almost as if he were watching himself from outside his body as he moved down the stairs, left the house, made a beeline to Proops's front door, and used the lock pick to gain entry into the ranch-style house. Even though he couldn't have been in the sunlight for more than twenty seconds, he had to blink several times to adjust to the darkened house.

A stale, unpleasant odor greeted him, causing him to wrinkle his nose. It reminded him of how his apartment smelled whenever he got too lax about cleaning out Orson's litter box, except this odor was more pungent. As he stood in the small entryway catching his breath and trying not to gag from the odor, he became aware of voices coming from deeper inside the house. A flash of panic sent his heart racing until he realized the voices were from a TV.

Perlmutter waited until his heart slowed down to a more normal rate, then started moving through the house. He was there for two reasons, both of which he considered important. First, he wanted to add a scene in his script showing his fictional filmmaker searching through Proops's house; and second, he hoped to find out more about the killer.

What struck him when he entered the living room was that there were no personal touches of any kind. No books or photos or knick-knacks or paintings. Only a TV set on a stand, and a cloth recliner and sofa. But what else should he have expected from a psychopathic serial killer confined to a wheelchair? He moved on to the kitchen, but again not a single personal touch. Just a circular oak table, two matching chairs, and the typical kitchen accessories. Perlmutter carefully pulled open drawers, but found nothing of interest in any of them.

Next, he crept down the hallway, at the end of which was the room where the TV noises came from. Wall-to-wall carpeting in the living room and hallway deadened his footsteps and allowed him to move silently through the house. The hallway led to three bedrooms and a utility room. The first bedroom Perlmutter looked in must've been the killer's. There was a duffel bag filled with grungy clothing, but nothing else: No grisly souvenirs from his victims. That was too bad. He'd been hoping to find something like that. What, exactly, he wasn't sure. Death-scene photos? Locks of hair? Jewelry? Perlmutter decided it didn't matter. He could still add something to his movie about the killer collecting keepsakes from his victims. What was the killer going to do for misrepresenting him? Sue?

He stuffed the clothes back into the duffel bag. Maybe the killer would realize someone had been in his room and had gone through his things. Perlmutter imagined how that scene might play out, and he rather liked it. Make the hunter feel like the hunted, or at least suffer a few pangs of paranoid worry. It would add a layer of underlying tension. Perlmutter considered making it more obvious he'd been there, but if he did, the killer might get paranoid enough to search his car carefully enough so that he found the tracking device. Eh, it didn't matter. He could always add the scene if he decided to.

Perlmutter left the room and moved quietly to the end of the hall so he could spy into the bedroom where the TV was playing. The door had been left open and he wanted to look at Sheila Proops. He held his breath as he crept ever closer. If she saw him, so what? She was a cripple confined to a wheelchair. What was she going to do?

Call the cops? He smiled at the absurdity of that, but still, as he moved toward the open doorway, a nervousness tightened his stomach.

He got close enough to the doorway so that he could see her. She was lying on the bed watching TV. Her body appeared withered and twisted in the sack-like nightgown that she wore, and there was something demented in her eyes. A chill caused him to shiver as he watched her. He had the sense that she knew he was there, but that she refused to look his way. He stood silently for another half minute before turning away. He had taken several steps before realizing he'd been holding his breath the whole time. No wonder he was feeling light-headed!

Perlmutter decided he'd had enough of this spider's lair, and the more he thought of how Sheila Proops looked as she lay on her bed, the more apt the description of a spider's lair seemed. In her ruined, wasted way, she sort of resembled a human-sized black widow spider—or at least that was what she brought to mind when he had looked at her. Another icy shiver ran through him as he thought again of the deranged craziness he had seen in her eyes.

He continued on toward the front of the house, but something made him stop outside the basement door. Maybe it was his nerves and he had only imagined it, but he could've sworn he heard a scuffling noise down there. He smiled grimly as he thought about what a perfect scene it would make if his fictional filmmaker found that Proops and her protégé serial killer were keeping a captive in their basement. Perlmutter slid his phone from his pocket and checked to make sure that the killer was still driving further away. He had more than enough time to satisfy his curiosity, and he turned the knob ever so softly so it made only a slight *click* as he opened the door, and then moved carefully down the wooden steps to keep them from creaking.

This was all a lark. An indulgence. He knew he'd find nothing in the basement but dust, dead insects, and the usual items people stored away, but he continued to navigate down the stairs, imagining the different ways he could write this scene.

When he got to the bottom of the stairs, he took only two steps before he spotted her: A small woman in her early forties with dark hair. She was lying on the floor, her head up against the wall. Perlmutter moved toward her until he could see that her ankles and wrists were bound and her mouth had been taped shut. Even though he could smell that she had soiled herself, he tried to convince himself she wasn't real. She had to be a mannequin or some other kind of life-sized doll. He was still trying to tell himself this when she turned her head to face him. It was her eyes that got to him. They were the puffy and red-rimmed eyes of someone who'd been crying for hours, maybe even days. She made muffled noises as she tried pleading for help, her tortured eyes beseeching him.

This wasn't like those dead girls. Perlmutter could at least tell himself there was nothing he could've done to save them, even if he didn't entirely believe that was true. This woman was still alive. He could save her life. He checked his pockets, but he didn't have anything that he could use to cut her free.

"I have to go upstairs and get a scissors or knife," he said, keeping his voice a whisper. He didn't have to whisper. Proops wasn't going to hear him as she lay in her bedroom with the TV on, but seeing this woman tied up and gagged scared the hell out of him. "I'll be right back. I promise."

He left her to go back upstairs. He couldn't find a scissors in the kitchen, so he grabbed a cutting knife. When he went back down into the basement, she was making more soft muffled noises, her eyes overflowing with tears. She was weeping. He was going to save her, so of course she'd be weeping.

He knelt down by her feet, ready to cut the tape binding her ankles together, but he froze. He just couldn't do it.

Perlmutter got back to his feet and took a step away from her. "Lady, I'm sorry," he said. "I'd like to help you, but I can't. The movie's too important and I don't have enough material yet to finish it. I'm really sorry, truly, and when I have the script finished, I'll come back. I promise. If you're still alive I'll save you."

He knew she couldn't possibly understand what he was saying, and must've thought he was a crazy man babbling out nonsense. He knew there was no point in explaining himself to her, but still, he felt he owed her that much, even though his words must've meant nothing to her. But he couldn't free her. Not yet, anyway. With the added scenes he was planning, he might be able to add another fifteen pages to his script, but he still had a long way to go.

He covered his ears as he turned and headed back up the stairs so he wouldn't have to hear any more of her tortured, muffled sounds.

Chapter 50

They drank too much coffee in Seattle. That was what Charlie Bogle thought as he entered his seventh coffeehouse in less than two hours. Earlier Fred Lemmon had called from Chicago to tell him the little he'd been able to find out from Claire Bigelow's coworkers. Bigelow had worked as head of new business opportunities for a small technology company that was trying to build a better (computer) mouse as opposed to a better mousetrap. Bigelow, her coworkers, and the company's CEO had flown into Seattle Sunday night, spent all of Monday in meetings with a Seattle computer giant concerning a licensing agreement for their advanced mouse, and had an additional Tuesday morning meeting that started at ten thirty and let up around one. According to Bigelow's coworkers, they got into Seattle late Sunday night, had a team get-together early Monday before their meeting with the computer giant, went out to dinner Monday night, and didn't get back to the hotel until midnight. Unless Bigelow's killer was another guest at the hotel, the only chance she would've had to meet her killer would've been Tuesday morning. One of Bigelow's coworkers remembered her saying she wanted to check out one of Seattle's famed coffeehouses while they were there, and that was why Bogle was on foot, walking to every coffeehouse within a one-mile radius of the hotel.

Bogle walked up to the counter and ordered a small regular coffee, no sugar, no cream. He did this at every coffeehouse he had visited. He'd sample two or three sips, even if the coffee was outstanding, and then throw away what was left. If he drank more than that, he'd be sloshing around by the end of the day. For all he knew he'd have another twenty coffeehouses to visit before he'd be done.

The woman who took his order was young. Very petite, her red hair pulled into a ponytail. Pretty in a wholesome, no-makeup sort of way. She regarded him politely and cautiously, as if she suspected he was a cop. Even though he knew the answer, he asked her if the heavyset guy with the buzz cut, face piercings, and neck tattoos who looked like he was taking inventory was the manager.

"Doug," she said, nodding.

Bogle waited until he got his coffee and had two sips before whistling the manager over. Doug gave him a dubious look before walking over to him.

"Sir, anything wrong with the coffee?" he asked.

Bogle shook his head. "I've been to seven coffeehouses in the last two hours, and this is the second-best coffee I've had."

"I would've liked to think we're the best," Doug said as if his feelings were hurt. He raised an eyebrow. "You're not writing an article for one of the local papers, are you?"

"No, sorry. How about you join me at a table and I'll tell you why I'm here."

Without waiting for an answer, Bogle brought his coffee over to the one empty table in the place and Doug joined him. From the expression on Doug's face, he did so grudgingly.

"What's this about?"

Bogle showed him a photo of Claire Bigelow on his cell phone. "Was she here last Tuesday morning?"

"She looks familiar," Doug murmured. "Who is she?"

"Claire Bigelow. The woman who was murdered in her hotel room last Tuesday."

Doug blinked several times as he looked away from the phone and gave Bogle a dumbfounded expression. "You think she was here?"

"That's what I want to find out. Can you check your credit-card receipts?"

"Sure, of course."

"Who else was working Tuesday morning who might've seen her?"

The manager nodded toward the petite redhead, who was standing behind the cash register. "Zoe," he said.

"Can you send her over here?"

He nodded and hustled away from the table as if he couldn't get away from Bogle fast enough. Bogle took two more sips of the coffee—because it was damn good—and he watched as the manager talked in an urgent, hushed whisper to Zoe. She gave Bogle a surprised look before leaving the counter area and coming warily over to his table and taking a seat.

"This is about the woman who was murdered?" she asked.

"Yeah." Bogle showed her the photo on his phone. Zoe studied it for a moment before a scared look showed on her face.

"She was here," she said. "I didn't realize it when I saw the stories on the news, but yes, she was here. I remember her now."

"Was she alone?"

"I think so. I remember her sitting at one of the tables absorbed in her laptop."

"Did she meet someone here?"

Zoe shook her head, but there was a fleeting look that passed over her eyes that made Bogle wonder whether Claire Bigelow might've hit on her. It was possible. When Fred talked to Bigelow's coworkers, the story he got was that Bigelow liked both gals and guys, so the killer could still be either a she or a he.

"Are you sure?"

She was more adamant this time as she told Bogle she didn't see Bigelow talking to anyone while she was in the coffeehouse.

"That's odd," Bogle said. "Because we think she met her killer here."

There was no mistaking the fear that wrecked her face right then. "How is that possible?" she asked in a tinny voice that showed a slight stutter. "You didn't know until just now that she had coffee here!"

He let out a weary sigh. "We think she met her killer wherever she had coffee Tuesday morning," he said, adjusting his earlier statement.

"Isn't it possible she met the psycho after she left here? Maybe on the street? I swear, I didn't see her talking to anyone while she was here."

Bogle had to admit to himself that was possible, but there was something this woman wasn't telling him. He could see it in how tense she'd become, almost like she was a trapped animal looking for an escape. As if she couldn't wait to bolt from the table.

"What aren't you telling me?" he asked.

She shook her head. "If I knew anything, I'd tell you," she promised. "Look, mister, I have to get back to work."

Bogle didn't say anything as she hurried away from the table. He sat and drank the rest of his coffee as he watched her. It was good coffee, after all, and he wasn't going to visit any more coffeehouses. He wondered what it was she was hiding from him. He'd bet almost anything she wasn't the killer. If she somehow was, he'd find out whether she had visited Bigelow's hotel, or had gone to San Luis Obispo on Wednesday, or Malibu on Saturday. But if that wasn't it, and if she knew who the killer was, why wasn't she telling him? Could it be a friend of hers? Bogle had no idea. All he knew was that she was keeping something from him.

He crushed his now-empty cardboard coffee cup. On his way to ask the manager for a list of their customers who had used a credit card Tuesday morning, he tried banking the cup into a garbage receptacle, but he front-rimmed the shot, and he had to take a quick detour to pick the cup off the floor and throw it away. The manager promised him he'd get the list together, and Bogle told him he'd be back for it in fifteen minutes. He waited until he was outside the coffeehouse and sitting alone on a bench so he could keep vigil on the place before calling Morris.

"I think I found where the killer met Claire Bigelow," he said. "A coffeehouse about a half mile from the hotel." He paused for a moment to rub his eyes. He'd had a long day so far, first getting up at five in the morning, spending four hours with the Seattle homicide detective in charge of the case, and then going off on other investigative avenues of his own. "A girl working there is acting kind of skittish. Like she knows something, but she's being stubborn about telling me what it is. I'm going to work on her in a bit and shake it out of her."

"That's good," Morris said. "It sounds like it's been one mistake after the next with this maniac. We know what car he took in Roseburg. Odds are he drove it to LA and dumped it here. Maybe we'll catch him before he kills again."

"Let's hope."

Morris asked, "Room-service attendant definitely in the clear with Bigelow's murder?"

"Yeah. From the timeline the police constructed, he couldn't have done it. This morning I got him to tell me his big secret. When he delivered the food, Bigelow answered the door naked."

"I wonder how often that happens?"

"He told me this wasn't the first time. He also thought she was putting on a show for someone else."

"The killer must've been watching from the bathroom," Morris said.

"That would be my guess. I tried asking him about that, and he told me he just wanted to get in and out of there as fast as possible. He has a wife and a baby on the way, and he didn't want to get into any trouble. That was partly why he originally kept quiet about that, but mostly he was afraid the police would tag him for the murder if they found out."

"One secret shaken loose," Morris acknowledged.

"Yeah, one anyway. Still one more to shake loose before I head back to LA. But I'll be gentle."

Chapter 51

Tim and Regina Pence were sitting at an outdoor table at Renaldo's. As chief counsel for one of the film studios, Tim Pence normally would've been up to his eyeballs in contracts at this hour on a Monday afternoon, but he had taken the day off to spend with his wife of eighteen years. For over seven months he'd been doing whatever he could to repair the damage his seeing a high-priced hooker had caused their marriage, and things were finally getting better. Following his affair came a messy blackmail episode, and after that came to a merciful end, he realized that he truly loved Regina and was grateful for a second chance with her. He patted his suit-jacket pocket and felt the diamond necklace he'd be giving her later.

The waiter brought over their drinks. He had ordered a concoction made up of tequila, muddled orange, basil, and lime juice, while Regina had ordered a glass of Chardonnay. They held up their glasses and clinked them together in a toast. Regina was trying to smile cheerfully, but Tim detected an underlying sadness, and it tugged at his heart to know that he was responsible for it. Time would eventually fix things—at least he hoped so.

"We had our first date here," she said wistfully.

"When we were young and foolish," he said.

"Speak for yourself!"

"I am," Pence said with a wry smile. "It was actually quite devious of me to convince you to marry me, and foolish of you to provide your consent."

Regina laughed. "A valid point, counsellor." She peered longingly at his tequila concoction. "That drink looks scrumptious."

Pence took a sip. "It is. Would you like to try it?"

"I don't think it would mix well with my Chardonnay. But let me take a picture for a tweet."

Tim dutifully held up the drink to his face and smiled obediently. Regina and her tweets. All their friends, and thousands of strangers on Twitter, had been informed they were going to Renaldo's this afternoon, and now they were all going to be privy to a picture of him smiling like a dummy as he posed with his drink. Well, not complaining was the least he could do.

"You know," he said. "This wasn't Renaldo's when we had our first date here. Back then it was Samantha's."

Her eyes became distant as she searched through years of memories. "You're right," she said. "You have a good memory. If I remember right, even then it was a hot spot for Hollywood stars. Think we'll spot any today?"

"I think I just did," Pence said. "Isn't that Ryan Gosling to your right?"

Regina dropped her napkin so she could discreetly look to her right when she picked it up.

"He looks more like Philip Stonehedge," she said, tittering, her hand covering her mouth.

"Except he doesn't have a scar."

She smiled contemplatively as she realized it wasn't either of those stars. "A doppelgänger, of sorts. He really does looks like he should be an actor, but darling, I won't embarrass you and tweet a picture of him. I promise."

Chapter 52

Wellesley, Massachusetts, 2000

Griffin was furious with his mom, and when he arrived home, he slammed the front door hard enough behind him to rattle the decorative rain-glass panels embedded in the wood. For over two years since the Craig Myers incident, he'd been working especially hard at playing the dutiful son. More than dutiful: the perfect son. He starred on his school's football, baseball, and basketball teams. He excelled in his classes. He'd even stopped sneaking around the house and spying on his parents. While he had his dad fooled completely, not good old mom. The crazy part was he gave her no legitimate reason to be afraid of him. Absolutely none. And yet she acted skittish around him, like she was a lamb being forced to peacefully coexist with a wolf. In a way, he enjoyed her fearfulness, even though he wanted to hide his true nature from her. When he was ready, he'd reveal to her what he was and then he'd have his fun, but until then he knew it would be better for him if they were to maintain their uneasy truce. Right then, though, all he could think about was getting his hunting knife from where he kept it hidden in the basement and skinning her alive.

Of course, he wasn't going to do that. It wasn't time yet. But he wanted to do something to her, something more than simply fill her with irrational dread, and he damn well had his reason. Everything in his life the last two years had been an act: sports, schoolwork, the few "friends" he tolerated. His only true passion had to be kept bottled up. What choice did he have after seeing how close he came to being blamed for Craig Myers's death? He knew his time would come, but he also knew that wouldn't be until he was old enough to go out on his own, and until then living his lie every day was a slow, methodical torture. Then three months ago he discovered heavy-metal rock music and it was a godsend for him. Not that it made up for the other part of his life that he had to keep buried, but at least it was something. A small crack so he could breathe. This new interest made it at least seem possible for him to bide his time until he'd be free to unleash the beast that was restlessly lurking inside his skin.

One of his new favorite bands, Cannibal Corpse, was supposed to be at Tower Records in Cambridge that afternoon, and the only favor he had asked of his mom in over a year was if she could pick him up after school and drive him to Cambridge. That was it! In her pathetic way she'd acted hesitant about it, as if she couldn't fathom the idea of spending time alone in the car with him, but in the end she agreed to do it. And of course, after school he stood outside waiting for her like a dope and she never showed up. After wasting twenty minutes, and then spending another twenty-five minutes running the two miles from the school to his house, he was going to miss them, even if they left right then. As he thought about that he wanted to hurt her badly, even if it meant giving her a glimpse of his true self.

He raced through their small mansion looking for her, and he found her in her bedroom, lying facedown on the bed. Before he saw the empty prescription bottle and the open bottle of vodka on the floor, he knew something had happened. He had felt it even before he entered the room. It was as if he had picked up a scent of death in the air. As he moved closer to her, she stirred. She wasn't dead, only dying.

Griffin avoided the puddle of vodka soaking a widening circle into the carpeting, and sat down on the edge of the bed. He gently rolled his mother onto her side so that she'd be facing him, and he used his thumb to force her eyelid open. She moaned and her eye looked cloudy, unfocused.

"Are you dying, Mother?" he asked.

She struggled, waving feebly at his hand, and he let go of her eyelid. Both of her eyes opened to thin cracks. Her voice sounded heavy and unnatural as she told him that she had taken pills.

Griffin had a good idea which pills she had washed down with vodka. Ever since Craig Myers had died, his mom had been sedating herself with Valium. He picked up the empty bottle so he could read the label, and sure enough, that was what she had taken.

"Call an ambulance," she said in that same heavy voice that he never would've imagined his mother being able to make.

"But weren't you trying to kill yourself?" he asked with a forced, wide-eyed innocence.

She had drifted off, and he slapped her lightly on the face until her eyes cracked open. Her voice was even heavier and more slurred as she again pleaded with him to call for help.

He smiled at her, because he decided he was okay with her dying this way. He didn't need to torture her for hours the way he'd been imagining, as long as he could see the exact moment when life left her. But he was still going to make it worse for her.

"You've been right about me all along," he told her in a soft, singsong voice. "I tortured and killed the Maguire cat and I forced Craig Myers to walk across the pond. I knew the ice was too thin and he'd fall through. He had me sweating for a few minutes because he almost made it across, but it was so sweet when the ice cracked apart."

The look she gave him was odd. Almost smug, instead of the look of horror that he had expected.

"You're a monster," she whispered, the words slowly bubbling out of her.

"I am," he admitted. "I had such wicked plans for you after I turned eighteen, but watching you die now will be almost as good. It's even worth missing Cannibal Corpse for. You want to guess what my plans are for good old dad? How I'm going to kill him without anyone suspecting me so I can inherit his money?"

He didn't get any response from her. Instead, she just closed her eyes. He sat quietly and watched as her breathing grew increasingly more shallow. He could feel that death was imminent, and he forced both of her eyelids open. There was almost nothing there. After several minutes passed, her eyes became as lifeless as glass. He felt for a pulse and couldn't find one.

An exhilaration struck Griffin so intensely that he thought he might pass out. This giddiness left him at first unable to move, but after several minutes he was able to get up and call for an ambulance. He even managed to sound distraught.

Chapter 53

Wellesley, Massachusetts, 2000

For the three days following his mother's suicide, Griffin's dad walked around like a ghost, occasionally breaking down into uncontrollable weeping. If Griffin was within arm's reach, his dad would pull him in for an embrace during these weeping fits. This was awkward and uncomfortable for Griffin, but he tolerated it.

Later that third night his dad entered his room without bothering to knock. At the time Griffin was working to catch up on the algebra classes he had missed. He had heard his dad, but tried to act as if he hadn't. It was exhausting pretending for three days straight that he was mourning his mother's death. He needed a break!

"Get up," his dad ordered.

The tone of his voice caused Griffin to look up, and an icy pit sunk deep into his stomach when he saw the stony detachment in his dad's face. There was nothing ghost-like about him anymore. Instead, something was very wrong. He wasn't looking at Griffin as if he were his son, but the way he'd look at one of his scumbag clients.

Griffin couldn't figure out what had happened. Maybe nothing had. Maybe his dad had gone full-lawyer mode because he was going to be explaining his mom's will, or some other legal necessity. Griffin convinced himself that had to be it, and he wondered if he had inherited any money directly from his mom.

"Why?" he asked.

"You're going to join me in my study. Now."

This wasn't open for debate. Griffin got up from behind his desk and followed his dad out of the bedroom, down the stairs, and through the hallway that led to his dad's study. When they reached the room, the older Bolling had Griffin sit in front of a small portable TV, which seemed like an awfully peculiar thing to have him do. But he obeyed. The look on his dad's face gave him little choice. His dad hit the *play* button on a VCR and Griffin watched in stunned amazement as his mom's last moments played out. His dad had the videotape positioned at the moment when Griffin entered their bedroom. While Griffin had talked softly when he had confessed to his mom about killing the Maguires' cat and Craig Myers, and when he later teased her about how he was going to kill his father, he had still spoken loudly enough for the hidden camera to pick up his voice.

With a sickening clarity he understood the smug smile his mom had shown him. She had set him up. She had actually committed suicide so that she could trap him! Griffin could barely believe it, but it's what had happened.

His dad waited until the video showed Griffin getting up off the bed to call for an ambulance before he turned it off.

An intense pain made Griffin double over in his seat the same as if his internal organs had been turned into ice. He was incapable of movement right then. Incapable of speech. The silence building in the room became something unbearable. When his dad finally spoke, his voice sounded as if he were under water. Even if Griffin was capable of it, he wouldn't have dared look at him.

"Your mother had left me a letter that I found only earlier this evening," the older Bolling said. "The videotape was in a nanny cam that she had hidden in the bedroom. Do you have anything to say for yourself?"

Griffin couldn't even move to shake his head. Even if he had thought of something to say, speech wouldn't have been possible. His worst fears had been realized. He had been exposed. All he wanted to do right then was shrivel up and die. It might've only been seconds, but however long it took before his dad spoke again, it felt interminable.

"You've been disinherited," his dad said. "I will be disowning you the day you turn eighteen. Tomorrow I'll be sending you to North Hills Military Academy in Pennsylvania. You will be boarded there until you turn eighteen. If you get yourself expelled, I'll be sending you someplace worse. Do you understand what I'm saying?"

Griffin was still bent over, but somehow was able to move enough so he could nod his head.

"A copy of this videotape will be left with my lawyer. When I die, the tape will be turned over to the police. You better hope I live a long life. Now get out of my study. I never want to lay eyes on you again."

Even though he felt as if every bit of strength had been bled out of his body, Griffin somehow was able to straighten up and rise from the chair. Now he was the ghost as he made his way out of the study. As he headed toward his bedroom, he fully embraced the lesson that he had learned. He was never going to let himself be exposed like this again. The only ones who were ever going to know what he truly was were the ones that he was going to kill.

Chapter 54

Los Angeles, the present

When Bogle called, Morris told him the drawing emailed to him looked a lot like Philip Stonehedge.

"Except the man doesn't have a thick scar across his cheek. The coffeehouse employee, Zoe, was adamant about that when I pressed her."

Morris grunted loudly enough that Parker lifted his head from where he was lying on the floor by Morris's feet.

"You thought Stonehedge could be our serial killer?" Morris asked.

"I wanted to make sure he wasn't. After all, he was with the Malibu victims the same night they were butchered."

Morris made another displeased grunting noise. "We don't even know if this is our killer."

"True. Zoe never saw him talking to Claire Bigelow. She also claimed Bigelow left the coffeehouse at least fifteen minutes before he did."

"Tell me again why she thinks this is the guy who killed Bigelow?"

Bogle hesitated for a moment. "It's not what she thinks, but more of a feeling she has. That's why I had to work at it to shake it out of her. She didn't want to accuse him of murder based on only a feeling."

"And again, that feeling is because he stood her up?"

From the way Bogle exhaled loudly, like air rushing out of a ruptured tire, Morris imagined his investigator shrugging hopelessly, as if he suspected he wasn't going to convince Morris of this.

"That's not the way she explained it," Bogle said. "More like she had an epiphany that if the guy hadn't stood her up she would've been the one killed."

This time Morris sighed, although his was softer. "An epiphany," he repeated.

"That's what she said."

"Nobody at the hotel recognized him?"

"Not yet. Before I fly back to LA, I'll be spending more time there showing the drawing."

Morris checked his watch. It was almost 10:00 at night. So far they'd had no luck with any of the CIs connected with LAPD's robbery division regarding Tasker's missing BMW. This drawing of a guy who nobody saw talking with Claire Bigelow was all they had.

"I guess an epiphany is better than nothing," he said.

"At least it's worth showing the drawing around the San Luis Obispo resort."

"Yeah, it is," Morris agreed.

The way Parker snorted right then, he wasn't convinced.

Regina Pence let out a shriek.

Tim Pence broke out laughing. "You're such a scaredy-cat."

"Shush. This is scary!"

Pence smiled. He had his arm around Regina's shoulders as they sat together in their living room, watching an early release of the serial-killer movie *The Carver*. One of the advantages of working for the studio was he was able to see movies six months before they were released.

The movie showed the killer sneaking into his next victim's house, but the camera abandoned him to focus on a young woman reading a book, and then they played the cheap trick of having her look up and gasp as she saw a face in the window at the same moment heightened music blasted. Of course, the face was her own reflection, but the trick got Regina sucking in her breath and drawing her body closer to Pence's. His hand was hanging loosely over her shoulder, and his thumb flicked against the diamond necklace he'd given her while they were having dessert and coffee at Renaldo's. She had loved it—as well she should've, given that it had set him back twenty grand. But as far as he was concerned, it was money well spent. For the first time in many months he felt as if they'd turned the corner. He was actually believing that Regina would truly be able to forgive him, and that they'd be able to move forward.

As Pence watched the movie, he found himself absently thinking how fetching the blond actress was, and wondering whether he could get her name from the producer. He caught himself thinking this and forced the thought out of his mind. What the heck was wrong with him? To be thinking something like that after spending all these months winning back Regina's trust? Still, she did look awfully appealing. Especially the way she was dressed in only a tight T-shirt and very short shorts.

Jarring music blasted as the actress looked up again, and this time she was staring directly into the killer's face. Regina clutched Pence's arm tightly, and she squeezed her eyes shut so she wouldn't see the knife slashing the actress's face. Each time the actress screamed, Regina tightened her clutch on his arm. After ten seconds or so the screaming came to an abrupt end, and for several more seconds the sounds from the movie were of a knife slashing into flesh, coordinated with a blasting, screeching noise. After that ended, Regina asked if the killer was done.

"For now," Pence said.

She opened her eyes and moved even closer to him. Another loud screeching noise blasted as the killer caught his reflection in the window. Regina tilted her head to one side as if she were listening to something far away.

"Did you hear that?" she asked.

"Hear what?"

"I thought I heard something in the kitchen."

Pence also tilted his head as if he were straining to hear noises within the house.

"You're right," he said. All at once he dug his fingers into Regina's side, tickling her. "It's the mad carver," he announced, laughing.

"Stop it! Stop it! I'm serious!"

It took Pence half a minute before he could stop laughing. He wiped several tears from his eyes. With an exaggerated sigh, he said, "If you're going to be such a scaredy-cat, I'll go check the kitchen. Keep the movie running. I'll be right back."

Pence got up off the sofa. Regina bit her lip as she watched the Carver call the police to report his latest killing. She screamed as a pair of hands reached over the sofa and grabbed her by the shoulders. Her husband broke out laughing.

"Sorry," he said. "I just couldn't resist."

She was furious with him, but she also couldn't help laughing from the trick he'd played. "I ought to spank you later for that," she said sternly.

"Please do."

She twisted herself on the sofa so she could watch her husband leave the room. Only after that did she turn back to watch the movie.

After the Carver called the police, he took out a notepad that showed the name and address for his next victim. Even though Regina kept telling herself this was only a movie, albeit one based on an actual serial killer, she couldn't help feeling like she might scream at any moment. But she wasn't going to let her husband play the same trick on her, even when she heard him sneaking up on her a second time.

"Forget it, Tim," she said. "It's not going to work again."

A pair of hands reached over the sofa. This time, her sneak of a husband had put gloves on in his juvenile attempt to scare her, and he didn't grab her shoulders, but instead he lightly wrapped his hands around her throat. This wasn't funny anymore.

"Stop it," she ordered.

Tim didn't listen to her. Instead of letting go of her throat, he tightened his hold. Not enough to choke her, but enough to make her gasp for air. She tried struggling, but his grip only tightened.

What was wrong with him? This really wasn't funny in the least!

He had bent over the sofa so his mouth was right against her ear.

"Boo," he said.

A mask muffled his voice. Regina only then realized that it wasn't Tim.

Chapter 55

Morris pulled into the leftmost bay at the body shop on Telford Street. He didn't hit the horn to have them open the garage bay door. Instead, he cut the engine and put the car in *park*. As he stepped outside, he squinted against the early-morning sun. No haze, just a big, bright yellow ball, even at eight in the morning. He didn't have Parker with him since he'd earlier left the bull terrier with Natalie. Walsh got out from the passenger side and followed him through a side door and into the building. A short, wiry man in his late twenties who'd been standing near a Mercedes moved quickly to meet them. Or to stop them. He didn't look particularly friendly. Walsh flashed him her badge and he stopped in his tracks.

"We're here to see Bruno," she said.

The man gave her a dead-eyed stare. "He's busy," he said.

"Not good enough, unless you want me to call for a van and haul all of you away."

His stare deadened further, but he turned and led the way to the back of the building. Three other men were also standing around the Mercedes; the other two bays were empty. They all stopped what they were doing so they could stare at Morris and Walsh.

The short, wiry man brought them to an office. He rapped his knuckles against the office door, and an angry, raspy voice from inside bellowed out for whoever it was to get lost. Walsh ignored it, opened the door, and walked in. Morris followed her.

Bruno and a heavyset woman both had their pants down, with the woman bent over the desk and Bruno behind her.

"What the hell—" Bruno yelled out, red-faced. Then he saw Walsh's badge and he swallowed back whatever else he was going to say.

"Both of you pull your pants up," Walsh growled. She used her thumb to signal for the heavyset woman to beat it. "Get lost," she ordered. Morris chuckled softly to himself. Walsh could be quite the hard-ass when she wanted to be.

Both of them hastily did as Walsh had ordered. After the woman was gone and Bruno was seated behind his desk, his thick face folded into a frown and he took on an aggrieved tone.

"You had no right barging in here without a warrant," he complained.

"Zip it," Walsh snapped at him.

Bruno reluctantly shut his mouth, his heavy arms crossing his chest.

"You bought a stolen red BMW 328i last Wednesday night—" she started to say, but Bruno interrupted her with an outburst of denials.

"I told you to shut up," Walsh said. "I don't care two figs about the car. What I care about is who sold it to you. So this is how it's going to work: You're going to cooperate fully with me, or I'm going to have two uniformed officers doing sentry duty outside this so-called business from now until doomsday."

Bruno sat back in his chair, his eyes cagey. "Why is this so important?" he asked.

Morris dug into his briefcase and handed Walsh the crime-scene photos from all the murders. Mia Dickerson and her three friends in Malibu, Claire Bigelow in Seattle, Bryan Tasker outside of Roseburg, and the Smalls in San Luis Obispo. Walsh tossed the photos onto Bruno's desk. The chop-shop boss's eyes scrunched up as he stared at them as if he were trying to make sense of what he was seeing. Once he realized what he was looking at, he blanched and squirmed uneasily in his chair. Almost desperately, he flipped the photos over so he wouldn't risk catching another glimpse of them.

"He did this?" he asked. "This isn't some kind of trick?"

Walsh dug out of her inside jacket pocket a document offering immunity from prosecution for buying the stolen BMW. "I told you I couldn't give two figs about a possession-of-stolen property charge. What I care about are those seven depraved homicides. So today's your lucky day. As long as you cooperate, you get a free pass on the BMW."

Bruno squinted as he read the document. "Should I have my lawyer look at this?" he asked.

"Unless you want me to rip that up, you better not waste another second of my time," Walsh said.

"We can't futz around," Morris explained. "We're trying to catch this psycho before he kills again."

Bruno nodded as he scratched at his neck. "He was here. Wednesday night. He came in after eight."

"Describe him."

Bruno showed a bleak smile. "Good-looking. Like he could be a Hollywood star. We used to call him Pretty Boy three years ago when he used to come by."

Morris showed Bruno the drawing that Bogle had emailed him from Seattle.

"That's him," Bruno said with certainty.

"His name?"

Bruno pushed up his lower lip and shook his head. "We only knew him as Pretty Boy."

"But you did business with him three years ago?" Walsh asked.

"He used to come around then," Bruno said. "But then he disappeared until last Wednesday."

"Anything left behind in the BMW?"

"No. It was all burned. Nothing but ashes now."

There were more questions, but nothing Bruno could help them with. As they walked out of the body shop, Morris gave Walsh a quick look and saw the intensity burning on her face. A hunter closing in on her prey. It was only a matter of days now, if that long. He felt the same coolness running through his veins that he always felt when he knew it was close.

"We're going to get him," Walsh said under her breath.

"It feels that way," Morris agreed.

Chapter 56

"I need a third act," Perlmutter complained to Orson. The orange tabby blinked once, rose to his feet, stretched, and disappeared behind the sofa Perlmutter was sitting on, moving more gracefully than you'd expect from an overweight cat.

Perlmutter was too deep into his own thoughts to notice the snub. He now had sixty-two pages written. Thanks to the GPS tracking app, he'd tracked the killer last night to a Culver City address. Perlmutter knew the killer would be using the same trick that he had in Malibu—finding a darkened home to park near his victims, which meant that Perlmutter might not be able to discover where the killer had gone, but he got lucky. By the time he drove to Culver City, the killer's car hadn't moved. He found a darkened place where he could hide and still watch half the block, and forty minutes later he spotted a shadowy figure slipping out from behind a house. Less than five minutes after that, the GPS tracking app showed the killer's car was on the move. Perlmutter emerged from his hiding place and made his way to the back of the ranch-style home that the killer had left. He noticed a door leading to the kitchen had been jimmied open, probably with a crowbar. Perlmutter put on a pair of gloves he had brought along and entered the house.

He found the two victims in the dining room. A man and a woman, both in their late forties, with the number *47* scrawled in blood on the wall over the man, and *48* scrawled over the woman. Like the girls in Malibu, they were naked, lying on blood-saturated carpet, their eyelids cut off, with their eyes gouged out and swapped around to give their faces a disorienting, weird effect. The woman's breasts had been cut off and nailed to the man, and his genitals had been sliced off and likewise nailed to her. The killer had added another gruesome twist. Their legs and arms had been cut off and swapped around, with the limbs duct-taped onto the bodies. Perlmutter had smelled burned flesh when he had entered the house, and he understood then that the killer had used heated metal to cauterize the wounds from their severed limbs so the victims wouldn't immediately bleed out.

He stared, bleary-eyed, at the clock in the kitchen area. It was now past nine in the morning. Since returning to his apartment hours ago, he had worked feverishly on his screenplay before printing out the sixty-two pages and reading through what he had so far. By the time he was done, he was nearly breathless, his hands shaking. That was how good it was. But he needed that third and final act. All of this had to wrap up soon, and in a powerful and explosive way.

Perlmutter pushed himself to his feet. He needed coffee so he could think more clearly. Once this script was done he was going to reward himself by sleeping for twenty-four hours straight, but for now, no sleep for the weary.

He made his way out of the apartment, squeezed his thick body down the narrow staircase, and trudged over to the small grocery store at the corner. Along with the coffee, Perlmutter also picked up a copy of the *LA Times*. He wanted to see if the police had made any headway in finding the killer.

The clerk, a young twentysomething kid with a scraggly goatee, wrinkled his nose when Perlmutter paid for his purchases. No doubt Perlmutter needed a shower. Probably a change of clothing also. Fortunately, if that was what the kid was thinking, he kept it to himself.

There was a small park two blocks away. Perlmutter wandered over to it and sat on a bench as he drank his coffee, read through the newspaper, and tried to knock some of the fuzziness off his brain. He also tried to think of what his film's third act could possibly be, but he came up mostly empty. He did come up with one idea. A small one. He dug the burner phone he had bought earlier out of his pants pocket, and called the police.

Charlie Bogle was still in Seattle and Fred Lemmon was on a flight back from Chicago, which left Morris, Walsh, and Polk to sit in Morris's office and debate the pros and cons of releasing the drawing they had to the media. The pros were obvious—get the killer's face out there. The cons were also obvious. They'd be alerting the killer that they were onto him, which would give him a chance to slip away, or disguise himself so he could continue his killings. Although Polk was being difficult, they'd pretty much come to a consensus to release the drawing when Morris received a call from Doug Gilman.

"I just got off the phone with Roger Smichen. Our psycho killed again," Gilman said, his voice angry and dejected. "This time in Culver City. A middle-aged couple. He broke into their home late last night and butchered them."

Morris put his cell phone on speaker so Walsh and Polk could listen in, then asked, "The same way?"

"I haven't been there, but according to Smichen these killings are nearly identical, except this time he went further." There was silence where Morris imagined Gilman clenching his jaw and fighting to compose himself. When the mayor's deputy assistant spoke again, his voice sounded tight, almost strangled. "This bastard cut off their limbs and mixed them up. He heated up a frying pan and used that to cauterize the wounds."

"How are they held in place?" Polk asked.

"What?"

"The arms and legs. How'd he attach them to the bodies?"

"Duct tape."

"Yeah, makes sense," Polk said. "You can use duct tape for almost anything."

Walsh shot him a withering look while Polk returned her an innocent smile. Morris asked Gilman whether the killer scrawled numbers on the wall.

"He did. Forty-seven and forty-eight. And he used the victims' blood, just like he did last time."

"Tell us about the victims," Walsh asked.

"As I said, a married couple. They were killed in their home. Husband was chief counsel for one of the studios—"

Morris felt a coolness filling up his head. His voice sounded distant to his own ears as he interrupted Gilman and asked whether the victims were named Tim and Regina Pence.

"That's right. How'd you know that?"

Polk groaned and muttered, "Ah, jeez."

The coolness in Morris's head had intensified and was now almost an Arctic blast. "Tim Pence was a client," Morris said.

Chapter 57

Perlmutter knew it was risky driving back to the murder site. Even though he didn't get there until almost midnight last night, the moon had still been mostly full and there was a chance a neighbor might remember seeing his car. He didn't care. He wanted this scene for his movie: His fictional filmmaker first calling the police anonymously to let them know about the Malibu Butcher's latest murders (even though these happened in Culver City), and then driving to the scene so he could engage one of the cops in clever banter. In his mind, Perlmutter could picture the cop being too dense to pick up the fictional filmmaker's hints about knowing more than he was letting on. He giggled as he imagined the scene playing out in his head.

A barricade had been put up to block traffic from entering the street where the murders happened. Perlmutter slowed down as he approached the barricade, and he could see police cruisers, an ambulance, and what had to be half-a-dozen unmarked police cars filling up the street near the victims' house. He rolled down his window and tried asking the cop manning the barricade what had happened.

"Keep moving," the cop ordered brusquely.

"There are a lot of police cars down there," Perlmutter observed.

The cop's eyes were slitted as he stared at Perlmutter. "I asked you to keep moving."

"Sure. I will. But what if I needed to drive down this street?"

That got the cop's attention. "Let me see some identification."

Perlmutter blinked several times. "What for?"

The cop's hand inched toward his service revolver. "I'm not asking you again," he said.

"Okay, sure, I'll get it for you. It's in my wallet. I just don't understand why you're asking for it."

Perlmutter felt the sweat building up on the back of his neck as he dug his wallet out of his back pants pocket and fumbled around for his license. This wasn't going the way he'd pictured it. Not at all. He almost slammed his foot down on the gas pedal instead, but told himself it didn't matter if this cop knew his name. He hadn't done anything. He was a spectator, nothing else. He knew things the cops didn't, but that didn't mean he was guilty. If they searched his apartment, what would they find? Absolutely nothing. Unless they picked up his screenplay ...

He concentrated to keep his hand from shaking as he handed his license to the cop. A slight tremor showed, but that was all. Still, the cop spent way too long studying the license before handing it back.

"You live in K-town?" the cop asked.

Perlmutter nodded. At that moment he didn't trust himself to talk. He could feel his damp T-shirt clinging to his skin as sweat spread out along the shirt collar.

"What are you doing here?"

"I'm a screenwriter," Perlmutter said, relieved that his voice didn't crack. "I'm setting part of my film in Culver City, and I thought I'd drive around and get a feel for this area. When I saw this street blocked off, I thought I'd ask about it. As a writer, you're always looking for ideas."

The cop seemed somewhat mollified by his answer. Perlmutter had to bite down on his tongue to keep from grinning, but damn, it was fast thinking on his part and he was proud of his answer, especially with how he'd be able to work this scene into his film. It was almost inspiring how he realized the best answer he could give would be to tell the truth. You didn't look like you were lying when you were telling the truth, even when it wasn't the full truth.

"Where were you last night?" the cop asked.

"Home. I was working on my screenplay. A marathon session where I wrote over thirty pages. I hit a brick wall this morning, so I drove here for inspiration and stumbled onto this road being blocked off and what looks like a lot of police cars down there." Perlmutter was feeling bolder. He leaned his head further out the window and asked, "So what happened?"

The cop's eyes had glazed. "Move it," he ordered.

Perlmutter drove away. A half mile later he broke out giggling as he thought of how shocked that cop was going to be when he saw the movie and recognized himself in this scene. There'd be changes, of course, but it would still be close enough to keep that cop wondering.

Chapter 58

"He's targeting my clients," Morris told Gloria Finston. "Either he broke into MBI, or he's been spying on us. But we don't have any signs of a break-in, and if he's been spying on us he's been doing it for seven months, because that's when we did work for Tim Pence."

"There's no question he's targeting your clients," the FBI profiler agreed. "But the way he killed Claire Bigelow in Seattle was too impulsive for me to believe he could've been planning these murders in Malibu and Culver City for seven months. No. This is recent. I'm sure of it. A life-altering event happened last Tuesday, probably only hours before he murdered Ms. Bigelow, and that's what sent him to Los Angeles seeking notoriety." She paused for a moment as she rested a very thin index finger against even thinner lips. "Could he have hacked into your computer system?"

Morris shook his head. "I spent too many years as a cop. Even with my computer expert harping on it, I've kept MBI a paper shop. None of our cases are on our computers. If this guy got into our case files, it's because he broke into our office."

Morris's cell phone rang: Annie Walsh. She had gone to the murder scene by herself so that Morris could attempt to get a handle on how the killer had targeted his clients. He took the call and listened quietly for several minutes before thanking her. After he got off the phone, he told Finston that Walsh had filled him in on what they had, and that she was going to email him copies of the crime-scene photos.

"They don't have much," Morris said. "No witnesses, anyway. Nothing other than an anonymous call reporting the murders. What do you think—our killer getting anxious for his notoriety?"

Finston's narrow, bird-like face showed nothing as she shrugged. "Possibly," she said.

A *ding* notified Morris that the email with the crime-scene photos attached had arrived. He forwarded it to Felger to print them out. He didn't want to see them, but he knew it might be useful for Finston to look them over.

"Who has keys to your office?" Finston asked.

"Only my MBI staff and the cleaning firm we use. Polk is heading over there now with a copy of the drawing."

"That's the only way in here?"

"That's it. You need a security key card and a password, and each key has a different password assigned to it."

There was a knock on Morris's door, and Adam Felger walked in with the crime-scene photos. Morris indicated for him to hand them to the FBI profiler. She studied them for several minutes before placing them facedown on Morris's desk.

"Why did he add to his repertoire?" Morris asked.

Finston showed another of her tiny smiles, although this one was pure grimness.

"I'd like to hear your guess," she said.

Morris shrugged and threw out the first thought that came to his head.

"He didn't like the Malibu Butcher nickname he was tagged with, so he's trying to change it by making it more obvious that's he reassembling his victims' bodies. Make them look like he's building a Frankenstein monster. I'm guessing he wants to be called something like the Mad Scientist Killer. Or maybe the Frankenstein Killer."

"Very good. If you want to give me your résumé, I can submit it next time we have an opening for a profiler."

"Thanks, but no thanks," Morris said.

His cell phone rang again. This time it was Polk.

"I'm at the cleaning company now," Polk said. "No one here has ever seen anyone resembling your drawing, except when they go to a Mr. Hollywood movie."

Mr. Hollywood was Polk's nickname for Philip Stonehedge. Something about Polk's tone had Morris asking, "What do you have?"

"They lost track of their key card to our office."

There was still something about Polk's tone that got Morris's pulse beating a notch faster.

"What else?"

"The employee they sent to clean our office last Thursday hasn't shown up to work since then. A woman, forty-two, unmarried, name of Elena Kotovsky."

MBI had their office suite cleaned every Tuesday and Thursday nights. Morris had been running around last Thursday night dealing with Brett Dickerson's investigation (was it really only five days ago?), so he wasn't in the office when Elena Kotovsky came in to clean the place, but he could remember her from other times. The cleaning firm often assigned her, and she would usually arrive at seven in the evening. A quiet, unassuming woman. Gentle, also. That was probably the strongest impression he had of her. He called Felger and asked him what time Thursday night the security card assigned to the cleaning firm was used.

There was a minute of clicking and clacking noises as Felger typed away on his keyboard, then him saying, "Hmm. That's interesting. The key card was used twice that night. Seven-oh-five and eleven-twenty-one."

Morris had his phone on speaker so Finston could listen in. "The killer wants to make this personal with you," she said. "He's going to target clients you worked with directly."

Morris nodded. "Most of our clients are corporate."

"Those aren't the ones he'll be going after. It will be individuals who brought more intimate work to you."

Again Morris nodded, because that was obvious to him also. "I'll have to go through the files, but I think there are six clients we need to focus on."

"We can catch him now," Finston said. "But we certainly can't afford to give your drawing to the media."

"We're going to be using them as staked goats," Morris noted glumly.

"They'll be protected."

A heaviness filled Morris's chest as he thought about how Mia Dickerson and the Pences weren't protected.

"I'll call them and let them know the danger they're in," he said.

Chapter 59

Morris met Rachel at her internship so he could pick her up. She wasn't happy about it and demanded that he tell her what this was about.

"Something's come up," Morris said, his voice heavy. "Let me take you to your mom's office so I can explain it to both of you together."

Rachel not only had his flinty gray eyes, but also his stubbornness. "Dad, if you expect me to budge from here, then you better tell me about it now."

Morris took her face in his hands and kissed her lightly on the forehead. "Please, sweetheart, let me do this my way. I wouldn't be here if it wasn't serious."

Rachel was going to argue further, but she saw something in her dad that she'd never seen before. A crack in his granite-hard exterior, exposing a glimpse of vulnerability. Reluctantly, she nodded, and left him so she could explain to the assistant prosecutor she'd been assigned to that she had a family emergency she needed to deal with. After that, she and Morris left together. While Morris drove, Rachel was at first going to press him for more information, but then relented when she saw the intensity hardening his face.

When they arrived at Natalie's therapist office, Fred Lemmon, who had earlier returned from Chicago, was keeping Natalie company, along with Parker. The dog instantly went into his whirling-dervish mode as he attempted to greet Morris and Rachel at the same time before finally plopping down by Rachel's feet, grinning in the clownishly happy way that only a bull terrier can.

Natalie took Rachel's hand. "You have me worried," she said to Morris.

"I'm worried also," he confided.

"I'll give you some privacy," Fred Lemmon told them, and he left the office.

Morris tried to force a smile, but couldn't manage it. "The serial killer I've been hunting, the so-called Malibu Butcher, murdered two more people last night," he said. "A couple living in Culver City. MBI was hired by the husband seven months ago."

"You were hired by the father of one of the four girls who were killed in Malibu," Natalie said, her voice falling off as if she were in a trance.

Morris nodded bleakly.

"But you thought it was a coincidence. That he had been invited to the home by one of the other victims?"

"He was, but he was still targeting Mia the whole time. This psycho waited outside of MBI last Thursday night and ambushed the cleaning lady who does our offices so he could force her to let him back in. Then he went through our files picking out his victims."

"Did he murder her also?" Rachel asked.

"We don't know. She's been missing since last Thursday. But this guy is going out of his way to make it personal with me, and he's maybe the most dangerous serial killer I've yet dealt with for the simple reason that he's not nearly as clever and smart as he thinks he is. This is unraveling for him, and we're going to be catching him soon, but until we do, I need both of you someplace safe."

Morris caught how Natalie squeezed Rachel's hand just that much harder, and the steely glint in Rachel's eyes as she shook her head, challenging him.

"I'm not letting him chase me out of town," Rachel insisted.

"You have to leave for a few days," Morris said. "The FBI profiler working this case is convinced he's soon going to be upping the ante and making it more personal by targeting someone close to me. Which means either you or Nat. I won't be able to concentrate enough to catch him if I have to worry about you two, and I'll also have to dedicate all of my MBI investigators to protecting you instead of having them go after him. I need both of you away from LA if I'm going to catch him."

"Where would we go?" Natalie asked.

"I booked you a suite at the Venetian in Las Vegas. Fred will be joining you to make sure you're safe."

Morris winced as he saw the sadness pass over his wife's eyes. That this was going to be as close as she'd get to the beaches of Italy. Fortunately, she let the thought slide, since Morris wouldn't have had the heart to comment on it.

Rachel clearly didn't like the idea of being forced out of town by this madman, but she accepted the practicality of it.

"So I really don't have any choice in the matter," she said.

"I'm afraid not."

Her cheeks puffed up like a chipmunk's—the way they did whenever she had to give in on something.

"When do we leave?" she asked.

Morris checked his watch. "Your flight leaves LAX in three hours."

Chapter 60

That afternoon Griffin had traded in his Honda for a used van. He had other errands to run, and it was a few minutes after six before he was able to pull his new vehicle into Sheila Proops's garage and enter her house. Sheila was where he'd left her in the living room: propped up in her wheelchair in front of the TV. She watched him with her good left eye and mostly-dead right eye before asking, in her excruciatingly slow cadence, where he'd been that day.

"Planning for tomorrow," he said with a wink.

"What happens tomorrow?"

He smiled in a cat-who-ate-the-canary way. "My masterpiece."

"Tell me!"

He walked over to her and pinched her right cheek. He did this hard enough that if he were pinching her left cheek instead she would've cried out in pain.

"You're such a bloodthirsty little peach. But no, I want it to be a surprise. Don't fret, though. I'll be recording it, just like I did last night. You'll see every gory detail. I promise."

He stopped pinching her and instead playfully caressed her nearly paralyzed cheek.

"You need to tell me what you're planning," she said, each word slowly popping out of her lips.

"Uh-uh, not this time. This one is all mine, baby."

Her mouth squeezed into the angry circle that Griffin knew all too well, and he could see the thought flickering in her good eye that he couldn't be trusted to make any plans without her help. This infuriated him. Granted, since he'd arrived in Los Angeles he had allowed her to mentor him, but it wasn't as if he was some callow amateur.

He'd taken forty-two lives before ever meeting up with her. Yeah, these killings were different, and were meant for maximum media exposure and fame, but it was still galling that she'd look at him that way. If it wasn't for the fact that he believed she was his spiritual soul mate, he'd be altering his plans for tomorrow to include her. But she was his spiritual soul mate. And so he smiled with a manufactured calmness and acted as if she weren't insulting him as she slowly and deliberately formed her response.

"Wouldn't it be better for us to discuss these plans?" she said at last, trying to be diplomatic about it. "After all, two heads are better than one."

"I think what would be best is for me to give you a bath. For Chrissakes, I've been having to breathe in through my mouth because of how bad you smell."

Griffin slipped one arm under her knees, the other around her waist, and picked her up out of the wheelchair and carried her to the bathroom so he could undress her. Her husband had had the master bathroom retrofitted with a changing station—the kind you'd see in public bathrooms for infants, but this one was large enough for Sheila. He placed her on the board, then started the water running in the bathtub, making the water extra-hot this time. Not scalding, but hot enough so it would leave her in discomfort. After that, he removed her clothing and her soiled diaper, tested the temperature of the water, and lifted Sheila off the board so he could lower her into the bathtub.

He smiled inwardly, seeing her wince from the temperature of the water, but she was smart enough not to complain. The first time he bathed her, he found the act demeaning, but since then he had grown to enjoy the power it gave him over her. He took his time scrubbing every nook and cranny on her body, lingering in places where it left her fighting to keep from squirming. During it all, her frustration over him not sharing his plans was palpable, but she knew better than to ask him about it again. He had to admit her body seemed less twisted and her flesh less desiccated since he had started up with these recent killings.

After bathing her, he dried her off and dressed her in a nightgown. He then brought her to the kitchen, leaving her in the wheelchair while he heated up a prepared dinner of meat loaf, mashed potatoes, and gravy that he had bought earlier. Once the food was divvied up, Griffin loaded a fork with a heaping mix of meat loaf and potatoes and popped it into his mouth. He chewed it slowly.

"Just like good ol' Mom used to make," he remarked.

Sheila didn't bother to respond, and instead continued to nibble half-heartedly at her food.

"You better clean your plate," Griffin warned. "I'm going to leave later tonight with our guest downstairs. All part of my plans for tomorrow. Before I go, I'll be putting you to bed, and you won't see me for at least a day, so this is all you're going to have to eat until then."

Sheila didn't respond and continued picking bird-like at her food, her mouth pinched in the petulant way she had whenever she held a grudge. For several minutes he found it amusing, but he soon grew tired of her pettiness. Damn, she was lucky he wasn't making her part of his plans, especially with the way she was just begging him to do so.

"Good ol' Mom," he said, partially to get his mind off how Sheila's behavior was pissing him off. "Yep, she made a tasty meat loaf. Did I ever tell you how frightened she was of me?"

Sheila shook her head, her stare fixed on her plate as she was determined not to give an inch.

"Mom was terrified of me," Griffin acknowledged, his tone growing reflective. "Somehow she saw through me. I couldn't tell you why that was. Not my old man, though. I had him completely buffaloed until Mom showed him the light."

"It was different with my mom," Sheila grudgingly croaked out.

Griffin nodded as he chewed on a mouthful of food. The night after he'd broken into MBI and made copies of their client files, Sheila had confided in him about her upbringing. He knew things had been different with her. That she wasn't born a killer, but instead made into one. But as far as he was concerned, it didn't matter how you got to where you were going, as long as you got there.

"But in the end she was terrified," he said.

Something frightening showed in her good eye. Griffin knew she was reliving the final moment with her parents. Whatever resentment she'd been holding against him seemed to become ancient history. While she continued to eat slowly and methodically, it was now due to necessity as opposed to peevishness. He polished off his plate a good forty minutes before she did, but he sat patiently until she finished. Once again, he felt that warm bond that he knew they shared.

He pushed her in the wheelchair into her bedroom, and was downright tender when he lifted her and put her in bed. He even fluffed up the pillow to make sure she was comfortable. In many ways, she really was the big sister he never had.

"I'll leave a glass of water on your nightstand," he promised her. "Some snacks, also."

"Okay," she croaked out in a way that actually touched his heart. *So vulnerable*, he thought.

He left her and went to the utility room where she kept a cache of money hidden. Earlier that day he'd taken ten grand, and this time he took another eight. That would be enough. Before he left for good, he'd clean her out. Not just what she kept hidden in the house, but the millions she had in the bank. He chuckled to himself, thinking of how she'd feel knowing that he had left her penniless.

With the eight grand in his pocket, he packed up his duffel bag and moved it into the van, then went down into the basement for their guest.

Perlmutter had convinced himself the killer was in for the night. Still, he was determined to continue his silent vigil. After only a half hour he started yawning due to lack of sleep the last two nights, and wished he'd brought a thermos of coffee.

Less than two and a half hours later his eyelids were drooping closed at the exact moment Proops's garage door opened and a van pulled out of it. Perlmutter had fallen into that somewhat hallucinogenic state between consciousness and sleep, and he briefly thought he was only imagining what he was seeing. Almost as if someone had yelled *boo* into his ear, he woke up with a start and fell out of the folding chair, and then scrambled to his feet and nearly toppled over again as he raced out of the room. He couldn't afford to lose the killer now that the man was driving a vehicle Perlmutter could no longer track with his GPS app.

Earlier that day, after he had added another six pages of solid gold to his script, Perlmutter saw the killer's car had moved to a different location in Simi Valley and seemed stuck there. Perlmutter was able to identify the address as a used-car lot, and he realized that the killer had swapped cars. That got him in gear as he drove to the same car lot, pretended to be interested in a used Honda, and when the salesman showed him the car the killer had been driving, Perlmutter got down on the ground, ostensibly to check out the undercarriage, but really to swipe back his GPS tracking chip. After that he went back to the house across the street from Proops so he could watch for the killer.

In less than a minute Perlmutter was pulling his car out of the garage and searching for the killer. Most likely the killer would be heading back to Los Angeles, and would be driving cautiously so as not to attract any attention. As he drove east through several Simi Valley neighborhoods, Perlmutter's heart beat rapidly and a thin sheen of sweat covered his body. He knew this would all be coming to an end soon and he even had a vague idea of how to wrap up the movie, but it all depended on catching up to the killer.

No more than ten minutes later Perlmutter caught sight of the killer's van. As he had guessed, the killer was heading toward LA and was driving the speed limit. Perlmutter slowed down. Later, when he had a chance, he'd be attaching the GPS chip to the undercarriage of the van. As long as he could keep track of the killer, this was all going to work out. He made sure to stay at least five car lengths behind, and as he drove the ending of his movie crystalized in his mind.

"Oh my God," he murmured once he fully understood how the movie needed to end.

Chapter 61

Greg Malevich took over for Morris at midnight, as had been scheduled. MBI's team and LAPD homicide detectives were keeping watch over the eight potential targets that were identified. Morris had picked Philip Stonehedge for himself because his gut was telling him this was who the killer was going after next. If he could've kept a twenty-four-hour surveillance on Stonehedge he would've, but he accepted that twelve-hour shifts made more sense.

He had taken Parker with him and spent most of the time pacing Stonehedge's grounds, and was only inside with his actor friend for less than an hour. The movie star had fed him and Parker, and tried to engage him in conversation, but Morris made for lousy company. He had a hard time sitting still as he was overcome by worry and guilt, his mind racing over what he could've done differently so his clients were not put in jeopardy. MBI's security system had a panic code that the cleaning woman, Elena Kotovsky, could've entered to silently alert the police, but she must have been too frightened to use it. Whenever Morris caught himself obsessing about how he might've better safeguarded his clients' information, or when his thoughts drifted to worrying about Natalie and Rachel, he'd shake himself out of it. He had a job to do. But it all made for a difficult night.

He called Natalie during his drive from Malibu to West Hollywood, and of course she and Rachel were safe. Why wouldn't they be? The killer had no reason to suspect they were in Las Vegas and they also had Fred Lemmon guarding them. Still, Morris couldn't shake the thought that this madman would go after his family if he had the chance.

When he arrived back home, things didn't get any better. He let Parker into the bedroom, and after warning the bull terrier not to get on the bed, ten minutes later the dog had his head resting on the pillow and was snoozing away on Natalie's side. Every few minutes the dog would either start snoring or let out a groan, but that had nothing to do with why Morris couldn't sleep. His mind just kept racing, and nothing he tried helped to slow down his thoughts. After a while he noticed he had this one particular thought nagging at the edge of his consciousness: What was the life-altering event that sent this madman from Seattle to Los Angeles? And why was he so determined to entangle himself with Morris? If he were to believe Gloria Finston, whatever this event was, it happened last Tuesday. After a while this was all Morris could think about. A little after four in the morning he rolled out of bed, a hard grin etched onto his face, because he had an idea of what it might be.

It didn't take him long to find what he was looking for. Last Tuesday, Seattle's major newspaper ran a story about New York deciding to close their file on Sheila Proops. That they didn't have enough to prosecute her on the SCK killings that occurred in their city, and they didn't expect they ever would. None of that was a big surprise, since her idiot husband had steadfastly insisted that he had committed all of the murders without his wife's knowledge. Morris remembered seeing the same headline in the *Los Angeles Times*, but he'd been mentally avoiding all stories about Proops. As he read through the Seattle newspaper article, he understood why the killer drove to LA: So he could make Sheila Proops one of his victims. Maybe he did kill her. And maybe, while he was having his fun with her, she sold him on the idea of seeking fame and notoriety by becoming the Malibu Butcher and targeting Morris's clients. Or possibly the two of them were now working together.

That was what made the most sense to him. *The two of them were planning these murders together.*

The thought gave him chills. He checked the time. Four-eighteen. He'd be waking the FBI profiler up, but this was too important to wait. He called Finston's cell phone and it rang through to her voicemail. He tried again, and this time she picked up after the third ring. Her voice sounded groggy as she answered with a *hello*.

Morris told her about the Seattle newspaper story. "That's what brought him here from Seattle," he said.

"So he could torture and murder her," she said, her voice now crisp, as if she'd woken up completely.

"That must've been his original plan."

"But she convinced him instead to let her make him a star."

"Something like that," Morris agreed. "How likely do you think that's what happened?"

"Very likely. Enough so that I'd bet money on it."

"Except you're not a betting person."

"Exactly. But I'd still put money on it. I'd even offer odds."

"Okay. I need you to write up a report we can take to a judge for a search warrant. And make it convincing, because this is all we have."

"Gotcha. I'll start on it now and I should have it for you by eight. And it will be convincing."

After Morris got off the phone with the FBI profiler, he dragged Parker off the bed and brought him to Simi Valley. At that early hour, there was little traffic, and Morris was able to average eighty miles per hour. When he arrived at Sheila Proops's house, he parked in front and waited. The house directly across the street from Proops had a *For Sale* sign, and so did both of her neighbors. Other nearby houses also had *For Sale* signs. This was a family neighborhood and Morris understood why nobody would want to raise a family anywhere near her, but this was still unfortunate. If these houses were vacant, it meant there were less people who could've seen the killer entering or leaving her house.

Shortly after 6:00 A.M., a woman in her forties left a house three over from Proops for a run. She was heading in the opposite direction—after all, who'd want to even run past Proops's house? Morris caught up to her. When he rolled down the passenger window and waved her over she reacted nervously, as if she thought Morris might be a mugger or worse, but there was something about Parker that helped put most people at ease. After he identified himself, she came around to his side of the car and he showed her the drawing he had of the killer. Her brow wrinkled as she studied it.

"He looks like that actor," she said. Her brow wrinkled more as she tried to recall his name.

"Philip Stonehedge," Morris suggested.

"No, the other one." She smiled as the name came to her. "Ryan Gosling."

"I can guarantee you that's not who we're looking for."

"I wouldn't mind finding him," she said, her smiling turning naughty. "Ryan Gosling, that is."

"This man," Morris said, redirecting her attention to the drawing. "Have you seen him in the neighborhood?"

She shook her head. "If I saw him, I'd remember it."

"Any recent activity at Proops's house?"

Her mood darkened in response to the question. "I'm sorry, no. I try not to pay attention to that house." She glanced impatiently at her Fitbit, or whatever it was that she was wearing on her wrist. "If I'm going to get my run in before work, I need to go now."

Morris nodded and watched as she jogged out of sight. He stopped other neighbors on the street as they emerged from their homes, but he got the same response from all of them that he got from the woman jogger. All of them took special care to avoid whatever was happening at Sheila Proops's address.

It was a little after 11:00 when Annie Walsh arrived with a search warrant. She also brought a coffee for Morris and egg-and-sausage sandwiches for both him and Parker. Parker's was gone in seconds.

"Sorry I couldn't get here earlier, but I had to go to three different judges before I was able to find one willing to give me a warrant."

That didn't surprise Morris. No matter how convincing Gloria Finston might've been in her report, that was still all they had. No physical evidence and no witnesses; only a theory from an FBI profiler. As far as he was concerned, the warrant was a gift. Without it he might've broken into Proops's house anyway.

Walsh gazed around at the *For Sale* signs surrounding Proops's house. "Those houses look vacant," she noted.

"I think they are," Morris said. "The blinds are all drawn, so I couldn't look inside, but I rang their doorbells earlier, and nothing. Nobody's come in and out of them since I've been here."

"How long's that been?"

Parker let out an impatient grunt as he watched Morris slowly chewing on a bite of his sandwich. He absently broke off a piece and fed it to the dog.

"Since five," he said.

"No one's gone in or out?" she asked, nodding toward Proops's house.

"It's been quiet."

"But you think the killer might be holed up in there?"

"I think there's a chance of it."

"If he is, he has to know you're out here."

"Yeah, but he doesn't know we have a drawing of him. He might think we're here investigating Proops for her past sins."

"I guess there's no time like the present," Walsh said. Morris joined her and brought Parker with him as they made their way to the front door. Walsh rang the bell, waited a minute, and rang it again. After another minute of waiting, Morris offered to check the back of the house for a window or flimsier-looking door for them to go through.

"This door looks like it would give us shin splints if we kicked it open," he said. "Mind watching Parker?"

He handed over Parker's leash and she gave him the search warrant. The ranch-style home had a four-foot fence that ran around the back of the property, and Morris had to boost himself over it. The backyard was mostly weeds, overgrown rosebushes, and a scattering of neglected cypress trees and junipers. All in all, a depressing backyard.

A back door that led into the kitchen had glass panes Morris could punch through so he could unlock the dead bolt. He took off his suit jacket, wrapped it around his fist, and was about to do this when he spotted a window that had been cracked open. He shrugged his jacket back on and investigated the window, which turned out to be in Sheila Proops's bedroom. His stomach muscles tightened as he saw her lying in her bed, a blanket pulled up to her chest. She looked cadaverous and Morris had no idea whether she was dead or alive, at least not until he lifted the window and her head tilted toward his direction. The right side of her face seemed to sag while a glimmer of malevolence showed in her left eye.

Morris waited until he crawled through the window before holding out the search warrant and telling her what it was. She remained mute as she watched him.

"Do you know who I am?" he asked, keeping his voice little more than a whisper.

Her lips remained sealed. She didn't show any hint of recognizing him.

"You should know. Six months ago you sent your deranged husband to kill me and my family."

"That's . . . a . . . lie," she croaked out, as if it took every ounce of strength she had to push the words out.

"What's a lie? That Henry Pollard didn't kidnap my wife and daughter, and then wait in my home so he could kill me first because you need the man's skull cracked open first so that you can get off?"

"The . . . lie . . . is . . . that . . . I . . . had . . . anything . . . to . . . do . . . with . . . it."

"Of course. Because you were a victim also."

"Yes!"

"But you recognized me anyway."

The left side of her mouth pinched closed while the right side drooped. A coolness ran through Morris's veins. He placed the warrant next to her.

"Read that at your leisure," he said.

Before leaving her bedroom, he checked the closet and looked under the bed. The air in the house had a thick, unpleasant staleness that no number of opened windows would ever erase, but there was something else. A certain vibe. At first Morris thought he was only imagining it, but he sensed something unseen prickling at the back of his neck. He moved quickly to the front door to let Walsh and Parker in. The bull terrier was reluctant to enter the house.

"I came in through the bedroom window," Morris said, keeping his voice low.

"Just like Joe Cocker," Walsh said with a hard smile.

Morris caught the reference to the Beatles song Cocker had covered, except in the song it was a woman who had entered through the *bathroom* window. He didn't bother pointing out the discrepancies, and instead told Walsh that the warrant had been served.

"I thought she was a corpse at first, but no such luck. She seems to be alone in here unless our guy's hiding in the basement. I'll check it out."

Walsh volunteered to search the rest of the house while he did that.

Morris tried to take Parker with him, but the dog stubbornly refused to go any further into the house, and Morris had to take him back to the car. Walsh waited until he returned.

"That was odd," she said.

Morris nodded. If Parker had picked up the scent of anyone posing a threat, he would've bulled his way toward that person. The dog had picked up something else. Most likely the same vibe Morris had sensed.

He left Walsh so he could search the basement. The stench down there was awful and he soon discovered the reason: A dead mouse and a pile of dirty adult diapers. There was no dead body, though. No captive. Nothing to indicate the killer had been staying at Proops's house. Other than the diapers, just the typical junk that people kept in a basement—even, as it turned out, a serial killer. Morris headed back upstairs and found Walsh in Sheila Proops's bedroom.

"I asked her why she's alone, and she claims her caregiver is running errands and will be back later today," Walsh said.

Morris took the drawing from his inside jacket pocket and held it out for Proops. If she recognized the person, she didn't show it from her expression.

"Is this who's running errands for you now?" Morris asked with a hard smirk.

"My . . . caregiver . . . is . . . a . . . woman," she said.

Walsh signaled to Morris that it was time for them to leave. On the way out of the house, she told Morris she didn't find any evidence of anyone else staying there.

"You had a hunch," she said. "It didn't pan out."

Morris wasn't so sure. "We should have a patrolman watching this house," he said.

Walsh looked like she wanted to argue with him, but instead she simply shrugged. "I'll request it."

Morris glanced at his watch. He nodded wearily at Walsh as she headed to her car, then called Malevich so he could tell him he was going to be late relieving him. That he was just leaving Simi Valley.

"A hot lead?" Malevich asked.

"I thought so."

"Don't sweat it. Phil just got up and is offering to make his famous Belgian waffles. Take however long you need."

"Don't get too cozy. You've got a job to do."

"Don't worry, I'll be doing it." Malevich lowered his voice. "Brie Evans is here. What a doll."

Morris cut the call short after that and got into his car. Parker's tail wagged slowly as he showed an exceptionally guilty look over being spooked earlier. Morris scratched the dog behind his ear, and told him there was nothing to feel guilty about, that he was spooked also. The dog's tail thumped the passenger seat harder after that.

Morris was twenty minutes outside of Malibu when his cell phone rang. A quick glance showed only LAPD. It turned out to be Martin Hadley.

"Brick, you've got a hell of a lot of nerve asking for twenty-four-hour surveillance when you don't have as much as a thimble's worth of evidence that woman's involved," the LAPD commissioner barked out, his voice as grating as a rusty door. "It's bad enough you're having us pay you to catch a serial killer because you were careless enough to let him waltz into your office and take your client case files, but I'll be damned if I call SVPD and request they waste their resources because you're too stubborn to admit one of your goddamn, famous hunches isn't worth spit—"

Morris disconnected the call. When Hadley tried calling back, Morris turned off his phone.

Chapter 62

Griffin used the keys he got from the building's live-in maintenance man to enter Rachel Brick's apartment. As he closed the door behind him, he smiled to himself over his cleverness and called out in a soft singsong, "Hello, is there anybody in there? Anyone at all?"

The lights were off. He listened intently for an answer and got none. No sound of anyone moving inside the apartment or calling for the police. The girl wasn't home. If she was, even if she was hiding in her bedroom, Griffin would've known. At the very least, he would've sensed it.

He flipped the lights on. The room he had walked into was a combination living room, dining room, and study. It was small and cluttered but nicely put together in a homey sort of way. Overstuffed bookcases lined one wall, and stands covered with plants were scattered about the room. A small square butcher-block table and chairs were set up near the galley kitchen, and a cozy-looking sofa was positioned eight feet in front of a stand holding a TV and a small stereo system. Prints of famous paintings and family pictures, most of which had a bull terrier in them, were hung up on the walls.

Griffin took off his Frankenstein-monster mask and packed it away in the gym bag he had brought. He strolled casually around the room and studied several of the family pictures and got his first good look at Morris Brick. He lingered over one picture of Brick's daughter and wife together, noticing again how much they looked alike. Both dark-haired, both petite and slender and very pretty. The wife had a softer look about her, while Rachel Brick had this indescribable toughness. Griffin had hoped to grab both of them. He'd spent most of the day watching for Natalie Brick to show up at her office before learning that she'd been called out of town, so it was only going to be the daughter. Disappointing, but he'd make do. How does that old saying go? *If you're only given lemons, then kill the shit out of them.* He chuckled lightly over his sophomoric joke, and went over to one of the bookcases so he could see what his intended victim liked to read. Two of the shelves were filled with mystery novels; the other shelves had more esoteric literary-looking novels. Griffin picked up one of the books and thumbed through it before moving on to the bedroom.

With the large, fluffy comforter, frilly window treatments, and a stuffed teddy bear perched on the dresser, this room had a more girly feel. Griffin continued on to the bathroom to make sure it was empty before returning to the bedroom. After checking the closet, which looked emptier than it should've, he sat down on the edge of the bed. It would be a while before anyone found the maintenance man. When Griffin first started working on him with his knife, the man had been rather obstinate, insisting he wasn't going to tell Griffin squat, but within five minutes he was willing to tell him anything. All Griffin needed to know was where the keys to the apartments were kept, what time Rachel Brick usually returned home, and whether the maintenance man lived with anyone in his squalid basement apartment, and after ten more minutes of using his knife, he had the man begging to answer those questions. No, the maintenance man wasn't going to be a problem, but Griffin's other victim that night was soon going to be an issue, if he wasn't already.

Griffin got up and pushed the blinds apart so he could look out the window, which faced the front of the building. It was dusk, and he had to crane his neck, but from what he could see the other victim wasn't a problem yet. Still, he needed to hurry this up. Either that, or he needed to come back much later, maybe at three in the morning. That would be tricky after what he'd already done, but not impossible.

Her closet should've had more clothes in it. That thought whispered to him, and that was why he pulled open her top dresser drawer—the one that should've held socks and panties. When he saw the drawer had been mostly emptied out, with only a few undergarments and mismatched socks left behind, he understood it wasn't only Brick's wife who'd been called out of town. The daughter had hastily packed a suitcase also.

He'd seen a landline phone in the other room. This was an odd thing for a girl Rachel Brick's age to have, but it would be useful to

Griffin. Along with the apartment keys, he also got her contact information, which included her cell-phone number.

He went back to the other room and used the phone to call Rachel Brick's cell phone. After the fourth ring the call was picked up.

"Hello?"

Griffin made his voice more gravelly as he said, "Yeah, Ms. Brick? There's a problem in your apartment. Water's leaking from the ceiling. Your super let me in to fix it. I think it's a burst pipe, and I'm going to get into the ceiling now, but when I do it's going to start flooding in here. I'll wait until you can get back and box things up, otherwise you're going to lose your stereo equipment and a lot of your books."

A long enough silence followed that Griffin thought she might've hung up on him.

"Ms. Brick, are you there?"

"I'm here."

"Will you be able to get back here? I'd hate to see you lose all your things."

"I'll be there in fifteen minutes."

"Okay, I'll wait."

The connection went dead. Griffin stood silently with the phone's receiver pressed against his ear. While he'd been talking with her, he was smiling pleasantly as if he really was a plumber going out of his way to be helpful, but he could feel his smile straining. He had heard the lie in her voice. She had no intention of coming back to the apartment.

He'd been wearing latex gloves since entering Rachel Brick's apartment, so he didn't have to worry about wiping away fingerprints. Plan A was no longer an option, not even a truncated version of it where he only took the daughter. That was okay. There was still plan B, and while it wouldn't torture Brick as much as plan A, in some ways he preferred it.

He left the apartment. Griffin needed to get back to his van before the police arrived, which he knew would be happening very soon.

Chapter 63

Morris had Parker off his leash as they patrolled Philip Stonehedge's property, and the bull terrier scurried off and ran up to the edge of the cliff overlooking the ocean. Morris joined him. The drop had to be at least thirty-five feet. It would be a waste having a house like this and not have any access to the beach, but Morris understood that Stonehedge had to keep it this way for privacy reasons, even if it was possible to get permission to build stairs to the beach below. If the killer was planning to get into Stonehedge's house, he wasn't going to be coming up this way. Not even if he had a grappling hook.

Morris's cell phone rang. His heart turned into an icy sludge when he saw from the caller ID that it was Rachel. He took several steps away from the cliff.

"What's wrong?" he asked.

"The killer is in my apartment right now."

Over the crashing sound of the ocean waves, Morris heard his heart beating strongly in his temples as he stood silently gripping his cell phone. Even though he knew it was a stupid question, he couldn't help himself from asking how she knew this.

"He called me on my apartment phone, pretending to be a plumber, saying that I needed to get home right away. That otherwise a burst pipe was going to ruin everything I owned. It was all pretty transparent. Pathetic, also."

"He doesn't know where you are, right?"

"He doesn't have a clue. I told him I'd be home in fifteen minutes. Dad, you know this, since you were the one to put the locks on my door. They're good enough that he wouldn't have been able to pick them. The only way he could've gotten into my apartment was if he got the keys from my super."

Morris nodded to himself. This shouldn't have happened. They had an officer in an unmarked vehicle watching Rachel's apartment building, and the killer shouldn't have been able to get past him. Either Hadley pulled him off the assignment or something worse had happened.

"I'll take care of this," Morris promised. "I've got to get off the line so I can call LAPD now, but you stay safe and keep your mom safe also."

"Don't worry about us. Our biggest danger is getting sunburned at the pool. Please be careful, okay?"

Morris promised her he would, and next called Walsh. "He's in my daughter's apartment," he said.

"You're sure about this?" she said, sounding dubious about the possibility.

"Yeah, I'm sure."

"We've got someone in front who should've spotted him."

"He just called Rachel from her apartment phone. He's there."

"Okay. I'll send squad cars and I'll be heading over myself. Are you coming?"

"I'm still doing my twelve-hour shift at Stonehedge's."

"I'll call you when I know more."

Morris walked back to Stonehedge's patio and sat down. He whistled for Parker and the dog came running, grinning clownishly. Morris sat silently, rubbing the dog's muzzle as he waited. It was only seven minutes, but it seemed much longer before Walsh called him back.

"I'm still on my way over there, but the responding units found the patrolman who was watching Rachel's apartment building. He was in his car, dead, his throat cut. Mark Hout. Did you know him?"

"Yeah," Morris said. "I knew him. A solid cop. A good man."

"His body was pushed to the floor so you wouldn't see him if you drove or walked past his car." Her voice tightened as she added, "*Forty-nine* was written in blood on the inside of the roof."

"They didn't get him," Morris said.

"Not yet. Her apartment door's locked. They're trying to find keys."

"There's a live-in super. I think his apartment's in the basement, but he's probably dead also."

It took Walsh a brief moment to process the reason for that. The killer must've gotten the keys for Rachel's apartment from the super. "Okay, I'll call you back when I know more."

Parker lay down by Morris's feet, and they both sat silently until Walsh called back.

"I'm there now," Walsh told him. "You were right, the super's dead. He was tortured with a knife before having his throat cut. *Fifty* was painted in blood on the wall above his body. We're going to break into Rachel's apartment. I'll call you back afterwards."

Morris and Parker continued to sit silently until Walsh called back. "Rachel's apartment was empty," she said. "He'd left her underwear drawer open. He must've realized she'd packed for a trip."

Morris acknowledged her with a grunt. This was what he'd been expecting.

"We're going to be busy here tonight," Walsh said. "But I'll get someone to fix Rachel's door and I'll make sure we have someone standing watch until that happens."

"Okay, thanks."

That was all he could think of to say.

Chapter 64

O ne of the reasons Morris had brought Parker along was because the dog acted as an early alarm system. This started backfiring on him when night critters started coming out and Parker began chasing after them, making sure to slow down just enough so he wouldn't catch any of them. When one of these critters almost led Parker off the cliff, Morris decided that was enough, and he brought the dog inside Stonehedge's home. It was after eleven then. The actor was still up and he made prime-rib sandwiches for all of them, and brought over bottles of Czech beer for himself and Morris.

Stonehedge asked, "Given how busy your killer's been earlier this evening, you still think there's a chance he's coming here tonight?"

Morris took a long drink of his beer before answering. "He didn't do what he wanted to do. He's frustrated. Even though we kept the Pences out of the news, he must know we found their bodies and that we're onto him. The guy's not very bright, but he's still smart enough to know that's why my daughter left LA. Whatever he has planned, he's going to try to do it tonight while he still can."

"And you think that's to kill me?"

Morris shrugged. "I'm not sure who he's planning to target next, but whoever it is, it's to send me a message."

Stonehedge considered this as he chewed on a mouthful of his sandwich. "I hope you appreciate my letting you use me as bait," he said.

Morris smiled thinly. He would've much preferred Stonehedge to leave town until the killer was caught, but when he suggested that the actor flatly refused, claiming he wasn't going to let himself be chased out of his home by a lunatic. The real reason was that he wanted to be part of the action.

"Yep, and I also appreciate the sandwich and beer," Morris said. "This is damn good prime rib and damn good beer."

Stonehedge beamed. "I get the prime rib specially made for me by Fernad's, which makes the best in LA. I had that beer in Finland two years ago while shooting *Dangerous Alliances*. Ever since I've been having cases shipped to me."

Their conversation became muted after that as they both slipped into their private thoughts, and when they were done eating, Morris suggested Stonehedge turn in for the night.

"If he's waiting outside, he's not breaking in until after the house goes dark."

Stonehedge somewhat reluctantly agreed, and headed off to his bedroom suite. He would be locking himself up and he also had a .38 caliber pistol Morris had brought for him. If the killer was going to get to Stonehedge, he'd have to get through Morris and Parker first, and if he was somehow successful, he was going to be in for a surprise once he faced a loaded .38.

Morris cut the lights throughout the house and settled in for the night, taking a sofa in the great room, while Parker lay next to it. When he took over for Malevich, he had told the LAPD homicide detective that he would cover a double shift, which had been more than okay with Malevich.

It was maybe an hour later that Parker sat up abruptly, his ears straight up. Up until that point Morris hadn't heard anything, and he whispered for the dog to stay where he was. When he reached for Parker's collar, the bull terrier bolted away. Morris was off the sofa and pulling his service revolver out of its holster as he ran after the dog. He heard the fierce rumbling of Parker's growling, and then a yelp and what sounded like a door being slammed shut. After sitting with the lights out for an hour, Morris's eyes had adjusted to the dark of the house, and as he turned a corner he saw a glint of metal swinging at his head. He ducked the blow and drove his left fist into what had to be the killer's stomach. The killer let out a loud *oomph*, and that was followed by his body hitting the hardwood floor. Morris continued after him, but tripped over the crowbar the killer had thrown at his shins.

As Morris picked himself up, he heard Parker growling and barking furiously from a room somewhere behind him. He next heard the killer scrambling to his feet and his footsteps leading away as he fled deeper into the house. Morris followed after him and saw the killer's outline in the moonlight shining through one of the windows. He swung his revolver toward him.

"Get on your knees now," Morris growled, his voice hoarse.

Something round and hard hit him in the shoulder, screwing up his aim. The killer had led him into Stonehedge's game room, and had thrown a billiard ball at him. Something instinctual caused Morris to duck as another billiard ball whizzed over his head. The killer used the opportunity to charge him, swinging a pool cue at Morris's face. He dove at the killer's knees and upended him. There was another loud *oomph* as the killer crashed to the floor.

Morris felt a twinge in his left knee as he got back to his feet and turned around. The killer was already running away and Morris grunted as he started after him, the twinge turning more into a slicing pain. He heard the killer go through a side door, and Morris fought against the pain as he followed after him. Once he was outside he heard the killer's footsteps crunching on gravel before seeing him silhouetted in the moonlight. As Morris ran, he took aim and fired. The killer fell to the ground, but was quickly up and running again, although not as fast as before. Morris wasn't sure whether he had hit him, or whether the shot had simply scared him, but whichever it was, the killer was moving at a slower pace. It was now more of a fair race. Even with the slicing pain in Morris's knee, he was gaining ground. He slid his gun back into the holster. He didn't need it. He was going to catch the psycho bastard.

The killer was no more than thirty yards up ahead when he reached the gate and struggled to pull himself over it. Morris slowed down to a jog. He used a security code to open the gate.

Morris stepped onto the road and could see the killer laboring badly to get away. It wasn't going to happen. He took another step, and out of the corner of his eye saw a flash of something moving toward him, and then he was lifted up into the air and rolling over the hood of the car that had struck him. In a dizzying whirl, he bounced off the pavement and everything went black for a moment. His body ached everywhere as he struggled back to his feet.

He fell back to one knee. The car that had hit him was gone. So was the killer.

Chapter 65

The bullet had only grazed Griffin, cutting a quarter-inch groove from his right side just under his third rib. He certainly wasn't going to die from it. He wasn't even bleeding that badly from the wound, but still, it hurt like hell every time he sucked in air.

He still couldn't believe that he had gotten away. He had heard the thumping noise when the car hit Brick, and saw the car driving past him, but he was in too much of a panic right at that moment to put two and two together. By the time it occurred to him that Brick might be unconscious or otherwise helpless, he turned and saw Brick picking himself off the road. He knew then he had lost his chance, so he continued on. Now that he was safely back in his car and driving away, he concentrated to replay in his mind how things ended up as badly as they did.

He had researched Stonehedge on social media, and saw nothing about the actor having a dog, so he certainly didn't expect one to come flying at him like a heat-seeking missile. He was incredibly lucky with the dog. He nailed it good with the crowbar, sending it careening into an open doorway, and was able to slam the door before the dog could get back to its feet. With the darkness of the room, he never got a good look at the animal, but when he realized Brick had camped out in the house, he remembered the photos he had seen in Rachel Brick's apartment and knew the dog had to be Brick's. That was another thing he hadn't counted on; that Brick would be waiting for him there. It almost worked out to his benefit, though. He stood and waited silently, the crowbar cocked back so he could take Brick's head off with it, but somehow the guy ducked under it and drove his fist into Griffin's stomach. Not only did the punch knock out his breath, but it knocked him on his ass and had him seeing stars. Again, he got lucky when he scrambled away and found that billiard table. Because of that he was able to get out of the house.

He wondered briefly about the car that had hit Brick, but decided it was just one of those things. Still, even with the lucky breaks he had gotten, things had not gone the way he had planned. Not at all. The night wasn't over, but his masterpiece was, at best, going to be a lesser work.

A fit of rage seethed up within him. He brought his fist back to punch the steering wheel, but the searing pain from this sudden motion nearly immobilized him. His fingers on his right hand gingerly explored the groove in his side, and came away sticky. He needed to bandage himself up, but that would have to wait.

He gritted his teeth as he swung the steering wheel and pulled onto the 101 North.

Perlmutter still couldn't believe he hit Morris Brick with his car. He had planned for everything to come to an end tonight, and so he was busy with a certain errand and missed the killer heading to Malibu. Once he realized where the killer had gone, he took off after him and was within a half mile of the killer's van when he heard the gunshot. He kept driving after that, his foot heavy on the gas. If the killer had somehow been shot dead, it would've ruined his movie, so it was both a shock and a relief when he saw the killer falling over the gate and running onto the road. Something was wrong with him, given the labored way he was running. Perlmutter realized he must've been shot. This was all good. He would be able to work that into his screenplay, and it would lead up perfectly to the ending he had in mind. When he saw that other man open the gate and head after the killer, he knew this man had to be a cop, and that his movie would be ending with a whimper instead of a bang if the killer were to be caught like his. He couldn't allow that, and without any conscious thought, he slammed the gas pedal down to the floor and drove into the man. A second before hitting him, he realized it was Morris Brick, the same guy who'd thrown him out of his office: A delicious piece of irony that Perlmutter would use in his script. At the last possible moment, Brick had jumped so that he rolled over the hood, otherwise the car would've crushed him like a bug.

Perlmutter felt no guilt or anguish over running down Brick, just as he no longer felt any over not helping the captive he'd found in Sheila Proops's basement. He understood fully why that was. He was no longer simply observing the killer so he could make his movie; he was now shaping the events for the movie. In a way, he was already directing it. The movie was what mattered. It was *all* that mattered. When the world saw Perlmutter's film, people would understand.

He'd been tracking the GPS coordinates of the killer's van, and when Perlmutter realized the killer was on US 101 North, he knew where the killer was heading next, and he couldn't help smiling.

Morris couldn't find his cell phone. When he was hit by the car, it must've gone flying off his body. He needed to call the police, but it was too dark out for him to find where it had landed.

He straightened up. His body was one big hurt. Something was wrong with his left knee, and he knew he had blacked out for a few seconds, but he didn't think he had any broken bones. Still, because of his knee, he had to hobble as he made his way through the gate and back toward Stonehedge's house. Up ahead, he heard the scrambling noise of an animal running toward him, and soon after he was able to make out Parker in the glimmer that the moonlight provided. When the bull terrier reached him, Morris dropped to both knees and hugged Parker as the dog fought to lick Morris's face. Through it all, the dog whined in a way Morris had never heard before, as if he were inconsolable and was blaming himself for letting Morris get hurt.

"I'm just glad you're okay, buddy," he said as he let Parker work his way through his defenses and get to his face. Up ahead, he spotted Stonehedge running down the long drive toward him.

"Are you okay?" Stonehedge called out, his voice heavy with concern.

"Do you have your cell phone on you?" Morris asked.

"No. What happened to yours?"

"I lost it when I got hit by a car. I need to call the police before it's too late."

"Wait—what do you mean, you got hit by a car? The killer did that?"

"No. Someone else."

"The killer's working with someone?"

"I don't know. All I know is I need to make some phone calls."

Morris tried to stand, but dizziness made him drop back to the gravel surface of Stonehedge's private drive.

"You wait here and I'll go get my cell phone," Stonehedge said. "You can make your calls while I drive you to the hospital."

Chapter 66

Griffin didn't pull the van into Sheila's garage, but instead left it in the driveway and used his keys to get in through the front door.

From somewhere in the living room, he heard a voice croaking out, "What happened?"

He turned toward his right and made a face when he saw Sheila in her wheelchair. He didn't bother asking how she got there, and continued on to the bathroom. Standing in front of the mirror, he carefully pulled off his shirt and studied the wound the bullet had made. It was uglier than he had imagined it would be. He forced himself to look away, and he next searched through the medicine cabinet and vanity drawers. No prescription-pain medications, unfortunately, but he mostly found everything else he needed. As he cleaned the wound he screamed, more from his frustration and fury than from the pain.

Sheila didn't have the type of large bandage he needed, but he made do by using cotton balls and smaller bandages. All of his clothing had been packed away in his duffel bag, and that he had left in the van, so he slipped his torn and blood-encrusted T-shirt back on.

Plan A had been a complete failure, plan B even more so. But there was still plan C. It wouldn't necessarily leave Brick in a tortured state of mind, but at least it would make Griffin famous. He walked back to the living room and smiled wistfully at Sheila.

"Morris Brick shot me," he said.

In her slow, croaking voice, she commented that it didn't look serious.

"No, I suppose not. I guess you'd call it a grazing. It still hurts like hell."

He moved close enough to her so he could bend forward and take hold of her face in his hands. Very gently, he leaned over and kissed her forehead.

"I've grown to think of you as my big sister," he said. "So in a way I regret what I'm going to be doing to you later, but c'est la vie. It appears the police are on to me, so I need to finish things up tonight and slip out of town. Leaving you as the Frankenstein Killer's last victim—"

"You mean the Malibu Butcher."

This was said with a level of scorn that surprised Griffin.

"Now you're just being petty," he scolded. "They'll change the name for good when they find you and that cleaning woman with my Frankenstein-monster mask left behind. And you have to admit, when they do, it will make my legend something LA will never forget. You'll get to be part of it, and it will give us a few intimate last hours together."

He bent forward again, this time to kiss her lips. Something hard poked him in the chest. He looked down to see Sheila held a gun in her left hand and was pushing the barrel into him. She was certainly full of surprises this night.

"Back off," she ordered, her voice no longer in that painfully slow cadence.

Griffin did as she demanded, his lips pulled into a hard grin. It wasn't just her voice that had changed. Her body no longer looked twisted and the right side of her face wasn't sagging anymore. In fact, he swore he caught a glint in what had been a dead right eye.

"How'd you get that?" he asked.

"Never mind," she said, her voice at most a beat slower than a typical person's. "I suggest you leave my house keys on the mantel and get out now while you still can."

"Sure thing, boss."

Griffin was still trying to wrap his mind around how Sheila's voice had changed as he sidestepped to her right. His plan was to circle her, since if he could get behind her, her gun wouldn't do her a damn bit of good. Before he could take a second step, she was out of her wheelchair. While she looked a bit unsteady, she stayed on her feet as she moved so that she continued to face him.

"I'm going to count to ten, and if my keys aren't on the mantel and you're still in my house, I'll shoot you dead." She smirked and added, "Even though I've grown to think of you as the little brother I never had."

Griffin was too stunned at first to move, but by the time she reached *three* he got his ass in gear and was out the front door before she counted to eight. It had all been an act, or at least mostly an act. He had seen the strain in her face when she stood, and he knew it must've taken a great deal of effort on her part to do what she did. But still, it amazed him that she had fooled him as much as she had.

He got back in the van and headed to Los Angeles. Once the shock over seeing Sheila's transformation had worn off, he sat seething as he thought about how badly things had gone. Eventually, his seething gave way to acceptance. Plans A, B, and C might have been busts, but he still had plan D. Whether he liked it or not, he knew things were ending for him here. While plan D might not have been much, it was still something. Besides, he had most of the eight grand he had taken from Sheila. He also had a fake passport in his duffel bag that would allow him to get into Canada. Once he was done tonight, the Frankenstein Killer would be retired and he'd head north to Vancouver. He would continue his killings—that certainly wasn't going to end—but he'd go back to killing his victims in the shadows, and he'd leave his Los Angeles legacy to live on. And he'd be safe. Even if Morris Brick survived being struck by that car, Brick never got a good look at him. The only one who could describe Griffin to the police was Sheila, and there wasn't any chance she'd do that.

Yeah, in a couple of hours—three at the most, depending how much he enjoyed this last Frankenstein killing—he'd be slipping safely back into the shadows.

When Griffin arrived at the Wilshire Boulevard address where MBI had their office, he backed the van up to the main entrance. He winced from the pain of the bullet wound when got out of the driver's seat too quickly. Once the pain subsided, he made his way to the back of the van, opened the door, and smiled dully at Elena Kotovsky as she tried to plea for help, the sound badly muffled by her gag.

"Sadly, it's just going to be you tonight," he said.

He looped the gym bag over his left shoulder, then grabbed hold of the woman's ankles wrapped together by duct tape, and pulled her toward the van's open door. He lowered himself and was able to get her onto his right shoulder, and had to once again grit his teeth from the cutting pain this caused him.

If it hadn't been so dark out and he weren't so preoccupied, he might've noticed the blood dripping from her hands, and if he investigated further he would've seen that she had gotten hold of a piece of broken glass from the van's floor and that she'd been using it to cut the duct tape binding her wrists together. But he didn't notice the blood, and so he was unaware as he carried her that the duct tape had been cut almost three-quarters of the way through.

He once again avoided the elevators and the surveillance cameras they most likely had, and headed up the four flights of stairs so he could get to MBI's office suite. The woman had lost weight since he had taken her captive and now couldn't have weighed even a hundred pounds, but still, thanks to the bullet grazing his side, it was a struggle carrying her up the stairs, and he was soon breathing heavily. He was halfway up the third flight when he realized he could've put on his Frankenstein-monster mask and used one of the elevators. That was just plain dumb of him not to have done that, and he was chiding himself angrily over it by the time he reached the MBI office door.

He still had the security key card for the office. If Brick had realized that this cleaning woman had gone missing, the key card would've been deactivated and Griffin would've had to chop her up in the hallway, but when he entered the code the door clicked open.

Maybe if he still weren't breathing so heavily he would've noticed that it took longer for the door to click shut behind him than it should have. It was only after he dropped Elena Kotovsky to the floor that his head cocked to one side, as he realized something was wrong. Then a buzzing noise filled him up. His body stiffened, and the buzzing noise grew so loud that he felt it in his teeth. His legs gave out and he collapsed to the floor. Even then the buzzing noise didn't stop.

Chapter 67

Parker hung by Morris's side when the doctor poked and probed him and tested his knee.

"It looks like an MCL sprain," the doctor said. "We should do an MRI and make sure there's no tear."

"How long would that take?"

"Thirty minutes."

"I don't have thirty minutes. Not tonight."

The doctor didn't argue with him. He knew that Morris had been hit by a car while trying to catch the Malibu Butcher. "We should take X-rays," he said.

Things got trickier then as Parker insisted on standing guard next to Morris, and Morris had to trick him to get him safely away. Once the X-rays were taken and Parker was let out of the bathroom he'd been tricked into, he rushed again to Morris's side, and no amount of trickery was going to get him to budge this time.

"You've got a deep bone bruise in your hip, but no broken bones."

"So I'm good to go?"

The doctor frowned at that. "For now. Let me get you a knee brace. Tomorrow come back for an MRI."

The doctor got him a knee brace, and after Morris fitted it over his injured left knee, he dressed and met Stonehedge in the waiting room.

"You okay?" the actor asked.

"Other than feeling like I've been hit by a car."

"Which you were."

"Makes sense, then, that I feel that way."

"I got you a surprise."

Stonehedge dug into his jacket pocket and pulled out Morris's cell phone.

"While you were in there, I drove back home and had the bright idea of calling your cell phone. I found it in a ditch off the side of the road. Still seems to be working."

Morris took the phone and a coolness flooded his head as he saw the text message his phone had received twelve minutes ago. It was the message Adam Felger had arranged for MBI's security system to send out if the security key card taken from Elena Kotovsky was used again.

"That sonofabitch is back," he only half heard himself say, and then he called Annie Walsh.

Perlmutter had followed the killer into MBI's office suite, and after tasing him into submission, he continued to use the Taser as he pulled the killer's arms behind his back and slipped a plastic hand restraint over his wrists. Once that was done, he used a chair to prop open the door to the office suite, and then went back down the four flights of stairs to the parking lot so he could get Jane Wickford out of his car trunk. He had abducted her hours earlier when she left the diner following her shift. She didn't look so beautiful anymore, with her eyes red and puffy from crying and her nose a swollen blob. She had tried putting up a fight when he grabbed her and he might've punched her in the nose then, but he couldn't remember doing so. It was also possible she hurt her nose from banging around in the back of the trunk. Whichever it was, it didn't much matter.

He had stuffed an athletic sock in her mouth and wrapped tape around her head to seal her mouth shut, so all she could do was make a kind of *mmm* noise when he first lifted up the trunk. She was probably trying to promise him something trite, like she wouldn't call the police if he'd let her go, but whatever it was it didn't matter. It was too late. The movie was what mattered now, not her.

"I told you I'd give you a part in my film," he said to her. He didn't say this to be cruel, but only as an explanation. He figured he owed Jane that much.

She made more of her desperate *mmm* noise, but he ignored it and put her on his shoulder like he had seen the killer do with that other woman. Jane was a shapely girl and had to weigh at least a hundred and thirty pounds. Even though Perlmutter looked round and soft, he was thick-bodied and deceptively strong. When he had watched the killer carrying that woman up all those stairs, he didn't understand why the killer didn't use the elevator, but as he walked into the building with Jane on his shoulder, it occurred to him that they must have security cameras. So he followed suit and carried Jane up the stairs also, and while he was perspiring badly by the time he reached MBI's office suite, he otherwise felt perfectly fine. Exhilarated, if anything.

He lowered Jane onto the floor, positioning her so she'd be third. The killer, of course, would be first. He emptied the killer's gym bag and lined the tools up. He knew what everything was for. The video recorder, X-Acto knife, spoon, hammer, box of nails, bone saw, hunting knife, blue thick rubber strip, and the butane torch. Also in the bag was something odd: A Frankenstein-monster mask. Perlmutter picked up the torch and turned it on, and watched as a blue flame came out. The killer would've known there wouldn't be any kitchen pans to heat up at MBI, so this was how he was planning to cauterize the wounds.

Perlmutter thought more about the mask and decided to slip it on. It would add an additional creepiness to his film's ending. His fictional filmmaker who stumbled onto the serial killer would, in the end, not only kill the actual fiend using his same gruesome methods, but would become him. This would leave the audience feeling both conflicted and with a vague uneasiness. While they'd be rooting for the actual serial killer to get what was coming to him, there would still be those two innocent women also tortured and murdered. Additionally, the audience would be left wondering whether this fictional filmmaker was going to keep killing after the movie ended.

Perlmutter didn't bother gagging the killer. He wanted to hear everything the man was going to say so he could use it in his script. When he was pulling off the killer's pants and underwear, and then cutting off his shirt, the killer at first unleashed a tirade of bizarre threats and then broke down into craven begging. Perlmutter had set up the video recorder to record everything so he'd be able to later get the scene exactly right, and he was especially glad that he was capturing what the killer was saying because there were some damn good lines coming out of his mouth. Once Perlmutter started using the X-Acto knife to cut off the killer's eyelids, the man stopped his begging, and then there was only screaming.

While he didn't get physically sick when he saw up close what the killer had done to his victims, Perlmutter hadn't been sure he'd be able to do the same butchery himself without becoming squeamish. As he did the same things to the killer that had been done to Tim Pence, he found that it didn't bother him at all. He briefly wondered about that and soon understood the reason: He was, in a way, only working out the details for the scene. That was all he was really doing as he removed the killer's eyes and genitals. Before sawing off both the killer's arms below the elbow, he used the rubber strips as tourniquets so the man wouldn't bleed to death before he had a chance to use the butane torch to cauterize what was left. The same when he took off the killer's right leg below the knee. The smell of the burning flesh didn't bother Perlmutter, either. He was too caught up thinking about the camera angles and lighting and editing cuts he'd be using for this scene to let anything bother him. An intensity burned on Perlmutter's face as he sawed off the killer's last remaining limb and he was too deep into his private thoughts to notice that Elena Kotovsky had cut away enough of the duct tape so she could free her wrists. He also was completely unaware when she grabbed the Taser that he had left next to the killer's tools. It was only at the split-second before Elena pushed the Taser into his neck that a befuddled look came over his face. And then the jolt from the Taser knocked him over and the back of his head bounced off the floor.

Elena dropped the Taser and scrambled for the hunting knife. Since being taken captive, she had eaten almost nothing and hadn't been given any water in over a day. She was dehydrated and lightheaded, and her hands and arms were pins and needles, her legs stiff as wood. For days she had accepted she was going to die and had made peace with that, but the broken piece of glass had given her hope, and that hope had her now fighting for her life as she cut away at the duct tape binding her ankles. A muffled noise escaped from her as the tape separated and her feet were freed. She looked over at the round, fat man she had tasered. With him wearing that mask, she couldn't tell whether he was unconscious, but at least he wasn't moving. As she kicked her feet to try to regain some feeling in them, she ripped off the tape from her face and pulled the rag out of her mouth.

She was panting heavily as she breathed through her mouth for the first time in days. For a moment she thought she was going to pass out. She tried saying something to the woman lying next to her, but her tongue felt too thick and her mouth just wasn't working properly, and instead what came out of her was the kind of noise a wounded animal might make. She tried again, and this time in a hoarse, croaking voice she told the woman everything was going to be okay.

Once the woman realized what Elena was trying to do, she tried helping by rocking her body so that Elena could flip her over. With the woman lying on her belly, Elena was cutting off her restraints with the knife when a hand gripped her ankle. A blind panic took over as she realized the round man wearing the monster mask had woken up. She tried pulling her leg free, but his grip was too strong. He was in the process of pushing himself onto his knees so he could lunge at her when Elena twisted around and planted the knife into his arm.

Perlmutter howled in pain. He also let go of the woman's leg and watched in a kind of dull surprise as she scrambled to her feet. The audacity! He was the director here, and this wasn't what he had scripted. He reached out for the hammer and went after her, but he was still woozy from his head banging against the floor, and as he tried to chase her, he listed to his right as if he were running along a ship's deck during a storm. He swung the hammer at her and missed wildly and almost fell over. She began screaming and he continued after her as she ran out of the office. While Perlmutter was moving like a drunk, the woman wasn't moving all that well herself. As he followed her down the stairs, he was sure he was either going to catch up to her or that she would fall and break her neck. Neither of those happened, but as they reached the first floor and he followed her down the hallway, his legs were already steadier and his head less woozy. He nearly had her as she pushed her way out of the building's front door. It was only after Perlmutter stepped outside that he noticed all the flashing lights. He took two more steps before he saw the policemen pointing their guns at him. There seemed to be a lot of them.

The woman had collapsed onto the ground only a few feet away. She was sobbing uncontrollably and the police were yelling at him to drop the hammer. He couldn't help smiling as he visualized how perfect this new ending would be: His fictional filmmaker cut down by a hail of bullets. Shocking. Absolutely brilliant. The audience would be left breathless.

Perlmutter lifted his hammer and took a step toward the woman. He barely felt the first bullet as it tore into his shoulder. He was grinning insanely as eight more bullets slammed into his torso, and it was only after a bullet took out his left eye that he crumpled dead to the ground.

Chapter 68

Walsh filled Morris in after he arrived at MBI. When she showed him Perlmutter's body, he told her that wasn't the same man who had broken into Stonehedge's home.

"He was wearing a Frankenstein-monster mask," Walsh said. "He chased Ms. Kotovsky out of your office with a hammer, and was trying to kill her when the police opened fire."

"It's still not the same guy," Morris said. "Although I'd bet he's the one who hit me with a car." Morris frowned as he took a closer look at Perlmutter. "I know him. He came to my office a week ago about wanting my help in making a movie about Sheila Proops."

Elena Kotovsky was being attended to in a parked ambulance. They had already heavily sedated her, but when she heard Morris's voice she opened her eyes a crack.

"He's still there," she whispered, her voice craggy.

"Who is?"

"The other one."

They found Griffin unconscious but alive. While the stump that remained from his left leg hadn't been cauterized, the tourniquet kept him from bleeding to death. Jane Wickford, after she was freed, helped them to better understand Perlmutter's role in what happened.

"I guess you're done," Walsh told Morris.

"Not yet," he said.

The killer had been taken to Los Angeles Memorial and Morris followed along after him. While he waited for the man to regain consciousness, he had an MRI done on his injured knee, and it revealed that he only had a strain and not a tear. Shortly after nine thirty he was told that the Malibu Butcher was awake. Morris was brought into the room.

"I only have one question," Morris said. "Was Sheila Proops involved with your murders?"

The killer's lips curled into something ugly and self-pitying. "I'm the victim. I didn't hurt anyone."

Morris could've pointed out just some of the overwhelming evidence they had against him, which included Elena Kotovsky identifying him as her abductor, his bullet wound, and that they would soon be doing a DNA test on the blood scraped off of Stonehedge's drive, but he didn't want to spend a second longer with this guy than he had to, so he kept it simple.

"If you answer my question, I'll have the police start calling you the Frankenstein Killer, and I guarantee you the media will pick up the name after that."

The killer's tongue wetted his lips as he came to a quick decision. "Yeah, the bitch was involved."

"How?"

"Picking the victims from your client files. Planning the murders. Giving me money. It was her idea I take out their eyes and swap them around."

Morris nodded thanks, something the killer wouldn't be able to see. He used a hospital phone to call Walsh and tell her about Proops's involvement.

"I'll arrange for a warrant. You want to be there when we arrest her?" she asked.

"Nope. I'm done. I'm going home." He paused for a moment before adding, "I've got things to do."

It was two hours later when Walsh called Morris back to tell him that Sheila Proops was already gone when they went to arrest her.

"SVPD had been watching her house since you called me earlier."

Morris didn't bother saying the obvious. That Proops must've seen something on TV about the Malibu Butcher being caught, and arranged a hasty escape.

"She's paralyzed," Walsh said. "How far can she get?"

"I don't know," Morris said. He didn't want to think about it. Besides, he had more important things to do.

Natalie and Rachel's flight landed at LAX at two thirty, and Morris met them at the baggage carousel with Parker in tow. Natalie's eyes welled up with tears when she saw how Morris tried to act as if his body wasn't one big bruise.

"I'm okay, Nat," he promised her. "It's over."

They melted into a group hug with Parker bulling his way into the middle. Natalie cried while Rachel fought hard to keep the tears at bay. After they separated, Morris glanced at his watch and handed his daughter Parker's leash.

"Your mom and I have a flight to Italy to catch," he said.

"We need to pack our bags," Natalie said.

"Already done, with the bags checked in. If I missed packing anything, you'll just have to buy yourself some new clothes in Italy."

"I guess I can live with that," Natalie said with a muted smile.

Morris carefully lowered himself to one knee so he could properly say good-bye to Parker, which mostly involved wrestling the dog to keep him from licking his face wet. He tried not to grimace as he stood, and took forty dollars from his wallet to pay for Rachel's cab ride back to her apartment.

She tried to hand him back half of it. "An Uber ride will cost me twenty."

"Take a cab. And take good care of the little guy," he said.

"He'll be ten pounds fatter when you get back. Have a wonderful belated honeymoon!"

Morris and Natalie waved good bye to their daughter as they walked away. Morris wasn't sure, but he could've sworn he saw a tear snake down Rachel's cheek. His beautiful but hard-as-nails daughter wasn't as tough as she wanted everyone to believe she was. A lump formed in his throat.

He put his arm around Natalie's shoulders, and she wrapped hers around his waist as they walked together to their terminal.

Epilogue

The waitress brought over Larry Getzler's breakfast order. "Here you go, hon," she said. "Brioche French toast and a side of sausage made from free-range chicken. Just the way you like it. Anything else I can get you?"

"Nothing right now, Doris," Getzler said. He didn't have to look at her name tag. He'd been coming to this Beverly Hills restaurant every Tuesday for years, and he knew Doris longer than he knew his wife. "Looks great, as usual. Smells great, also."

"Enjoy, hon."

She laid a hand on his shoulder before leaving. Getzler took a sip of his coffee and picked up his knife and fork so he could enjoy his food when he caught a flash of movement out of the corner of his eye. He looked up to see that a nebbishy-looking man wearing a Yankees jacket and baseball cap had taken the seat across from him. The guy had a narrow face, eyes that were set too close together, and a very unfortunate long and droopy nose. Getzler was about to signal for the waitress to have this person removed from his table, but something about the way the man was smiling at him stopped him.

"My name's Sammy Bloom." The man slid a business card across the table. "I have a movie script about Allen Perlmutter to sell you. He's the guy who was shot dead by the police after chopping up the Malibu Butcher."

"I know who he is."

Getzler frowned as he picked up Bloom's card. Normally, he would've chased this putz away from his table by now, but he couldn't help wondering why this guy seemed so damn confident.

"You met him two weeks ago," Bloom said.

That surprised Getzler. "How'd you know that?"

"Perlmutter and I were friends. He told me you two had a handshake deal."

Getzler nodded as if this were true. He had written Perlmutter off as a nut the moment Perlmutter had left his table, and had forgotten all about him until Perlmutter's name and picture were splashed all over the news a week earlier. The media had put out only a small taste about what had happened at that West Hollywood office building, but the little that was out there was enticing enough that Getzler was dying to get a project going.

"So you knew Perlmutter. So what? I've got some of the biggest names in the business wanting to do a movie about him. Why should I talk to you?"

Bloom's thin smile turned cagey. "Because I know things that the police will never know." He leaned closer toward Getzler and lowered his voice. "I know the whole story, and it's a shocker. A guaranteed blockbuster."

"He told you?"

"Not exactly." Bloom looked right and left to make sure no one was eavesdropping before saying in a voice barely over a whisper, "Perlmutter had a cat, and I started worrying nobody was going to take care of it. I knew where Perlmutter kept his spare key hidden, so the night after all the fireworks happened, I got into his apartment to rescue Orson—that's his cat—and I found notes he was taking, I guess for a script. Bloodcurdling stuff. Like Perlmutter following the killer to Malibu, and walking into that house right after those four girls were murdered. So I used those notes and wrote up a script. It's pretty damn good, if I do say so myself."

Bloom swung a worn leather attaché case onto the table, and took from it a manila folder that had been thickened by a hundred or so loose-leaf pages.

"Do we have a handshake deal?" he asked, his confidence ebbing slightly.

There was not a chance in the world Getzler would use this schmuck's script. The guy was a zero. A nobody. But Getzler could have his assistant go through it and make notes, and he could give those notes to the guy who wrote that crime film that came out last year, the one with that *Game of Thrones* star. Yeah, that would work. If Bloom made too much noise afterwards, maybe he'd pay him off five grand, or maybe not. The guy didn't look like he had a pot to piss in. So what was he going to do? Sue? Good luck!

Getzler held out his hand.

"Deal," he said.

Don't miss the next adrenaline-charged Morris Brick thriller by
Jacob Stone

Malicious

Coming soon from Kensington Publishing Corp.

Keep reading to enjoy a sample excerpt . . .

Chapter 1

The killer sat naked in front of the mirror and put in the cosmetic contact lenses to change his eyes from brown to blue. Nine months ago he'd shaved his head, and since then used a razor each week to keep up his bald appearance. He now carefully attached a hairpiece to his scalp that made him look as if he had neatly trimmed sandy-brown hair. It was an expensive hairpiece, and the killer was pleased with the way it altered his appearance. After taking a moment to admire the hairpiece, he glued on a fake goatee the same color as the hairpiece. Earlier that morning he had shaved off his eyebrows, and he now glued on fake ones that were the same color as the hairpiece and goatee. He also had other fake eyebrows that matched his natural hair color. Later, when he removed his disguise, he would use those until his real eyebrows grew back.

He put his face through a series of exaggerated contortions. According to his reflection, his fake hair held in place and looked natural. His entire adult life the killer had dressed casually. Chinos, either a button-down plaid shirt with sleeves rolled up to his elbows or a polo shirt, and always running shoes. He couldn't remember the last time he wore a suit. But when he left later today he would complete his disguise with an elegant Versace pinstripe, button-down tan shirt, a muted yellow tie, and a pair of calfskin Italian loafers that also matched the color of his fake hair. Finally, he would slip on fake glasses and a fourteen-thousand-dollar Hublot watch that he had bought specifically for this occasion.

The killer got up and wandered over to the kitchen area, and used his Nespresso machine to brew a single serving of caramel-flavored coffee. Right now his target was in a Pilates class. He had plenty of time before he'd have to leave. As he sipped his coffee, he was amazed at how calm he felt. He had spent a year of planning and preparing—really two, when you considered that he was forced to throw away a year's worth of plans because of that meddlesome Morris Brick. Now his vision was so close to coming to fruition that he could taste it. He smiled as he thought of how it tasted even sweeter than his caramel-flavored coffee.

The killer's mind drifted to thoughts of everything he had done since finalizing his plans six months ago. It was remarkable when he added it all up. Of course, he wasn't finished yet. There was still so much more to do, but if things worked out later that afternoon, tomorrow his masterpiece would be unveiled. People wouldn't see it in its entirety at once, since it would take ten days to play out, but once completed it would be absolutely stunning. Breathtaking. The world would never forget it. Nor would the city of Los Angeles ever be the same.

Art of this magnitude didn't come cheap. You had to bleed for it, or in this case, have others bleed. So far the killer had to take four lives. He didn't enjoy killing these people, but it was necessary and he had murdered them quietly without anyone noticing. Soon thousands more lives were going to be taken, and those deaths weren't going to be so quiet. He stood spellbound as he thought about how all these people were going to die, and how Morris Brick was going to be thrust into the center of the carnage.

A sensation below his waist caused him to glance downward, and he realized that these thoughts had given him an erection.

Chapter 2

Parker spotted Natalie first as she waited alone at the outdoor table. The bull terrier let out several excited pig grunts and bulled his way forward, dragging Morris along. The dog scooted under the thick velvet rope that the restaurant used to mark off their outdoor café area, while Morris had to step over it and at the same time switch the leash to his other hand to keep from getting tangled up. Natalie watched with amusement. As always, she looked gorgeous. A petite, slender dark-haired beauty who still made Morris feel weak in the knees with a smile, even after twenty-four years of marriage.

"Parker caught me off guard," Morris explained.

"He's good at that," Natalie admitted.

Natalie readied herself for the bull terrier's onslaught, grabbing Parker by his thick neck while the dog's rear end wiggled like crazy, his tail wagging at 200 beats a minute, as he fought to lick Natalie's face. While this went on, Morris snuck in a kiss of his own and took a seat adjacent to his wife. After a minute Parker calmed down enough to sit, panting.

"He's happy to see you," Morris said.

"Nah, he's just trying to soften me up for some heavy-duty mooching."

Morris laughed at that. The dog could certainly mooch food with the best of them.

A waitress came over with menus. She was new here, otherwise she would've known better than to bring Morris a menu. He was a creature of habit. Ever since the actor Philip Stonehedge had turned him on to this Beverly Hills restaurant, he had ordered only their fish tacos, and he did so again. Natalie took a menu, gave it a quick look before asking for an arugula and tomato salad. Morris also asked the waitress to bring a roast beef and cheddar sandwich for Parker. "You can skip the bread, horseradish, lettuce, and tomato. Just put the meat and cheese on a paper plate."

The waitress gave Parker a cautious look before asking whether the dog was friendly.

"He's a sweetheart," Natalie volunteered.

Morris concurred. "A bit of a clown, but a gentle soul."

This was mostly true, even though over the last year Parker had attacked two serial killers and bitten the arm of a hardened criminal who had pointed a gun at Morris during a jewelry-store robbery. But as long as you weren't trying to kill Morris or others, the odds were good you wouldn't see that side of him.

The waitress patted the short, bristly fur that covered Parker's cement-hard head, and the dog's tail thumped against the terra-cotta–tiled patio. "I'll make sure to add some extra roast beef," she said with a wink. Morris waited until the waitress left before asking Natalie how her day was going.

"Busy." Natalie worked as a therapist and had her private office in downtown Los Angeles. "Before breaking for lunch I barely had time to catch my breath. But I have the luxury of not having to be back for another hour. Yourself? No new serial-killer cases, hon?"

She said this mostly as a joke since Morris had sworn off those types of cases for his investigative firm, MBI, but some worry still showed in her eyes. Deep down inside she was afraid Morris would take on another of those cases, and she had good reason for this concern. The last serial-killer case had left Morris battered and bruised, the one before that had brought a deranged killer to their door, and the very last one Morris had worked on while he was still a LAPD homicide detective almost killed him.

Her question also didn't come completely out of the blue. Natalie had serial killers on her mind because that night they were going to the Hollywood premiere of *The Carver*, a movie that was based loosely on the notorious serial killer, Heath Dodd. Since Dodd's killing ground had been Miami, Morris wasn't involved in the investigation, but he had still been hired by the movie producers to consult on the film. Even with Morris's involvement in the movie, they probably would've skipped the premiere if Philip Stonehedge hadn't invited them to a private dinner party afterwards.

"As far as I know, Los Angeles is still serial-killer free," Morris said. "If that changes, the LAPD will have to handle it without my help. Anyway, as you well know, MBI has gone almost a hundred-percent corporate."

This was true. After the Malibu Butcher business, Morris had made a concerted effort for his firm to take on only corporate cases, most of which were either company fraud or employee-background investigations, although they were currently knee-deep in a corporate-espionage case that they were hoping to break soon.

"*Almost* a hundred percent?" Natalie asked. Parker, who had plopped down on the ground and was now lying on his side by Natalie's feet, let out one of his pig grunts to show that he also found the matter suspicious.

"We took on an unusual missing-person investigation this morning," Morris said. "A guy up and vanished four months ago. No sign of him or his car since. His wife brought us the case. She's desperate."

"She needs closure."

"Nope. She needs the insurance money."

Natalie gave him a reproachful look. "Hon, dear, don't you think you're being a tad cynical?"

"Not at all. She's convinced her husband is dead, and she needs a death certificate before she can collect on his life-insurance policy." Morris grimaced. "I felt sorry for her. She really is in desperate straits, and genuinely seems to have been mourning him. We're not quite taking it on as pro bono work, but close. MBI will only bill her if we find him or his body, and we'll be capping the bill off at five thousand."

Natalie bit her thumbnail as she considered that. "Do you think she's right?"

"I don't know. She's convinced that they were happy enough together and he was content with his life. She's also adamant that if he were alive he'd be home with her now. Maybe that's true. Or maybe he decided to start over someplace else. We'll see."

The waitress appeared with their food. Parker got to his feet and stared at the tray she carried. The paper plate she had brought held what looked like twice as much roast beef as would normally be used for a sandwich. Parker let out a few excited pig grunts as he waited for it to be placed on the patio surface. As soon as Morris let up on the leash, Parker attacked the food as if he hadn't eaten in days, even though he'd had half a can of his food that morning.

"Our little guy is getting pudgy," Natalie said with a sigh.

"Nah, it's all muscle."

Natalie gave Morris a funny look, but didn't argue. As she ate her salad, she seemed to lose herself in her private thoughts. When she shivered, he asked her what was wrong.

Natalie looked at him as if she didn't understand what he was asking, then offered a wistful smile.

"I don't know. Just something in the air, I guess."

Morris glanced upward. Not a cloud in the sky. If a storm was coming, he couldn't see it.

[credit: Photo by Judy Zeltserman]

Jacob Stone is the byline chosen by Dave Zeltserman, an award-winning author of crime, mystery, and horror fiction, for his new thriller series featuring serial killer expert Morris Brick. His crime novels *Small Crimes* and *Pariah* were both named by the *Washington Post* as best books of the year, with *Small Crimes* also topping National Public Radio's list of best crime and mystery novels of 2008.

His horror novel, *The Caretaker of Lorne Field*, was shortlisted by the American Library Association for best horror novel of 2010, a Black Quill nominee for best dark-genre book, and a *Library Journal* horror gem.

His Frankenstein retelling, *Monster,* was named by *Booklist* as one of the ten best horror novels of the year, and by WBUR as one of the best novels of the year.

His mystery fiction is regularly published by *Ellery Queen Mystery Magazine*, has won Shamus and Derringer awards, and has twice won the Ellery Queen Readers Choice Award.

Dave's novels have been translated into German, French, Italian, Dutch, Lithuanian, and Thai. His novel *Small Crimes* has been made into a feature film starring Nikolaj Coster-Waldau, Molly Parker, Gary Cole, Robert Forster, and Jacki Weaver. His novels *Outsourced* and *The Caretaker of Lorne Field* have also been optioned for film and are currently in development.

UNDERGROUND

JACOB STONE

DERANGED

A MORRIS BRICK THRILLER